Robbie turned to the trees and strained his eyes to see what Hail was looking at. Sitting in front of the overgrown wild plants was the largest rat he had ever seen. It was at least two feet tall, and its dark brown fur was plastered down to its head. Small black eyes peered intently at Robbie. Sitting up on its beefy hind legs, it showed great interest in the two strange people peering down at it.

"It's an agouti," informed Hail. "They're rare, and sort of belong to the rat family. Cute, huh?"

"Cute" was not the first thing that came to Robbie's mind. Let's face it, a rat is a rat.

But before he could say anything, an oversized lizard bounded out of the bushes on its hind legs and attacked the agouti from behind. It stretched its long neck over the rodent's head and bit its face as the rat squirmed and shrieked like a flag on a pole flapping wildly in the wind.

The lizard was about five feet long from head to tail and as tall as the agouti. It flipped its meal over to devour it from the neck down in just a few large bites, tugging on the meat that stuck to the bones with its long, sharp teeth.

Hail grabbed Robbie's arm and pulled him along. "Let's go."

"That looked like a dinosaur," said Robbie.

"That was an eoraptor," said Hail, not slowing down. "There will be others around and they'll kill us if they can attack us as a group. They get bigger the deeper into the jungle we go."

"How big?" asked Robbie.

"Huge. Haven't you seen them before?"

"No," he answered. He couldn't help but wonder if he had somehow been taken back to the prehistoric era.

THE MAN IN THE BOX

by Andrew Toy

a BlackWyrm book
Louisville, Kentucky

THE MAN IN THE BOX

A BlackWyrm Book
BlackWyrm Publishing
10307 Chimney Ridge Ct, Louisville, KY 40299

Printed in the United States of America.

ISBN: 978-1-61318-137-9
LCCN: 2012952225

Cover Design by Kyle Richardson
Edited by Jodi Black

First edition: November 2012

Thank you Sarabeth, for encouraging me to write.
You were there every single time the sun came and went.
And so of course, without hesitation,
this book is dedicated to you.

ACKNOWLEDGEMENTS

They say it takes many people to write a book. Not so with this one. There were many lonely nights and early mornings poring over the words in this book in frustration and anguish. But I'd like to acknowledge the following people who opened the blinds to let the sunshine in.

First I'd like to thank my parents-in-law. Stephen has always been supportive of my writing, and whenever I didn't feel like doing it, he kept me at it. Sally was the first one ever to read this book from cover to cover, and raved about how great it was. Without her optimism, the next seven drafts probably wouldn't have been completed.

Terry Byers helped me a lot when I was struggling with the first part of this book. Terry asked several tough questions that led to a lot of replacement and restructuring.

Jodi Black, my editor, fixed too many mistakes to count and challenged me to either strengthen characters or get rid of them (I strengthened them).

Ken Stewart has been rooting for me all this time while following my blog. He loved the book and submitted more corrections for us to implement. Thank you for that last coat of polish to really help this book shine.

Kyle Richardson has been my best friend through high school and beyond. Now, kids, a few dogs, and 3,000 miles away, we still talk and joke like it was yesterday. He designed the book's great cover. (Readers, if you need a really reliable, talented design artist, check out his business, enrichdesign.us).

After three years of searching and receiving (literally) hundreds of rejections, I actually gave up showing this book to publishers. But then I hesitantly passed it off to one more guy – the president of BlackWyrm Publishing, Dave Mattingly. He was crazy and gracious enough to give this aspiring author a shot. I can't thank him enough.

Part I: Discovery

CHAPTER 1

Robbie Lake finished off his martini and dropped it on the server's tray. He checked his watch. Just twenty minutes until his massage. The itinerary suggested that he ask for a Veronica at the front desk. He watched a young couple nuzzling each other by the side of the pool. He lathered some more sunscreen on his arms, then his stomach then his face, careful not to get it in his eyes. He could almost feel a burn coming on. He basked in the tropical sun as he listened to the sea gulls caw in the distance above the foamy ocean spray on the other side of the fence behind him just outside the pool yard. It was nice having the option between the fresh water pool or the saltwater ocean just a few yards-length away.

He eyed a pretty young woman strolling by in a small bikini, swaying her hips like the pendulum balls sitting on his boss's desk thousands of miles away. The woman batted her eyes at him and her lip curved up into a smile. A satisfying wisp of her strawberry-mango lotion drifted into his nostrils as she brushed past. He closed his eyes when she was gone and lost himself in the heavenly "Ka Loke" playing on the loudspeakers that monitored the utopian pool yard.

A different server placed another martini on the glass table beside him and asked if he wanted anything else. "Yes. Bring me the hula dancers again. And a plate of pulled pork and chocolate-covered pineapples," said Robbie.

"Right away, Mr. Lake. By the way, the light's green."

"Huh?" asked Robbie, as a vacant intersection replaced the pool in front of him.

"The light's green," said Rosalynn, sitting next to him.

The infamous Seattle mist blanketed the late afternoon sun and his arms were pasty white again. He moved along in his Honda Accord, wife and son in tow.

"I'm hungry," whined Jeremy from the back seat.

"You should have cleaned your plate like I told you to," Rosalynn called back.

"You were rushing me. I can't eat that fast."

"I'm sorry, but we don't want to be late to Taylor's game."

Robbie continued to drive toward the school, but his mind was still on autopilot. *Just fifty-six more hours,* he thought. Tomorrow would be his eleventh anniversary at work and his gift to himself was laying in his nightstand at home: a plane ticket to Hawaii. Of course, it was paper-clipped to three other tickets for his family, but he made sure they all knew that this was *his* vacation. The price of the whole vacation was daunting in the present economy. But as Rosalynn pointed out to him, if they didn't go now they never would, and just like him, the kids would never have a chance to see Hawaii. It took her several months to sell him on the idea, but as he began to imagine it more and more, he eventually realized he longed for it. Hang the money, he told himself finally, there'll be more on its way. And now their bags were mostly packed and ready to be driven to the airport in just four days. It was Tuesday evening and their plane would depart at 5:05 Saturday morning. He planned on spending a lot of that week researching tourist sites. Not a bad way to celebrate eleven years, right?

"Taylor and I had another blowout on our way to school," said Rosalynn. "I don't know what to do with her."

Robbie just stared ahead at the road, reluctant to tear himself away from his pineapples and margaritas. Lately just the thought of his fifteen-year-old daughter drove his mind into spinning convulsions.

Taylor was going through the stage where she was embarrassed to be seen with her parents, *especially* her dad. She had stopped talking to him the moment she realized his jokes were outdated and he couldn't keep up with the latest music, movies, or fashion trends. But so far, there had been no evidence of drug use or sexual activity. This set his mind somewhat at ease, at least for the time being. The plan was to get her out of the woods as quickly as possible and get her on her way to earning a respectable degree. Sometimes he felt like Taylor was just an unreasonable kid who was incapable of being parented.

"On the bright side, I didn't get any calls from Jeremy's school today," said Rosalynn quietly. Robbie glanced in the rearview mirror and saw Jeremy locked on the iPad.

"That's good," muttered Robbie. "They probably didn't teach anything today. Maybe they had a party instead. We all know he'd never disengage from something like *that.*" Impromptu comments like that made him think it was a good thing his seven year old tuned out as often as he did. "Did you learn anything in school today?" Robbie asked Jeremy.

No response. Disengaged as usual.

"Look out your window, there's a dead lion."

Rosalynn smirked at Robbie. Jeremy kept glued to his games.

At lease Jeremy would be easier to manage when he turned fifteen. He wouldn't be the hormonal sex-starved teenager Taylor was. His problem would likely be what Robbie's was when he was that age: fitting in. While Robbie spent most of his adolescent years reading comics and writing stories that never found themselves in anyone else's hands but his, Jeremy would be a computer geek, repairing old machines or developing video games. He just hoped his son could make a living out of it someday.

The scoreboard hung in the middle of the gymnasium and read 19 and 17, Owl's leading. The first JV volleyball game of the season drew in a sizeable crowd. The spectators, almost divided evenly, gathered on pullout bleachers on both sides of the court. With just enough room to spread their elbows Robbie sat next to Rosalynn who was enthusiastically cheering their daughter on. Jeremy sat on the other side of Rosalynn, finishing off the nachos she had allowed him to purchase from the snack stand with his allowance.

Robbie and Rosalynn rarely missed any of Taylor's volleyball games as long as the games were in town. Truthfully Robbie enjoyed getting out of the house to cheer his kid on in a competitive environment packed with hysterically flustered parents.

The Owls won, which was convenient because the Lakes had already planned on going out for ice cream after the game, and now it could be a genuine victory celebration. Robbie pushed his way down to the court through the flood of proud friends and parents to congratulate his daughter while Rosalynn and Jeremy hung back in their seats to chat with an old neighbor.

Spotting Taylor through a pack of people, Robbie was about to stretch his arms out to offer an embrace when a shabby college boy, dressed all in black, unapologetically invaded Taylor's personal space by putting his arm around her waist and kissing her. Robbie would not have been any more furious than if the kid had kissed Rosalynn.

He eagerly pushed through the crowd and strode up to them. "Who's this?" Robbie asked invasively, interrupting what did *not* seem like Taylor's first kiss.

Taylor pulled away from the lip-lock and masked her embarrassment with a stoic expression and grumbled, "This is Dwayne. Dwayne, my dad." Her voice dropped down to a mutter at the last word.

Fighting the urge to be cold, Robbie stuck out his hand and said, "Good to meet you." Although what he really wanted to say was, "If I ever catch your mouth on my little girl again, I'll neuter you with a lawnmower."

Dwayne limply shook Robbie's hand and mumbled some informal teenage greeting.

Taylor asked, "Dad, can Dwayne get ice cream with us?"

Robbie was afraid she'd ask. He would have said yes if it were a friend of Taylor's already accepted into the family. Choosing his words carefully, he did his best to keep the situation casual. "We were just going to keep it a family affair. Sorry, hon. Maybe next time."

Taylor shot her dad the same look Rosalynn gave him whenever he said something inappropriate in public. But Robbie stood his ground. "Shower up and we'll meet you in the car." Then he bid farewell to what's-his-name in a way he just couldn't resist: "It was good to meet you, kiddo." No college boy ever wanted to be called "kiddo," especially in front of his girlfriend. Robbie considered it payback to all the jocks who dissed him in college.

As he nudged his way back through the crowd, he could barely hear Taylor apologizing to her boyfriend for her father's lame behavior.

At their favorite ice cream parlor the Lakes tried to enjoy a nice celebratory evening, but tension was quickly thickening between Taylor and Robbie.

Once they were all seated with their ice creams, Robbie said, "I'm sorry we couldn't invite Wayne to join us."

"It's Da-wayne, and you know it," Taylor snapped. Jeremy sniggered and Taylor warned him to shut up. Then, turning back to Robbie she spat, "Don't pretend like you don't know his name; that just makes you look *ignorant*." She shoved a spoonful of Rocky Road into her mouth.

Robbie was about to raise his voice with her when Rosalynn, the soothing voice of reason, interjected on his behalf. "Honey, your dad and I just wanted to spend this evening as a family. We rarely get time with just the four of us anymore. And I know you really wanted your friend to be with us, but if he really cares about you, he'll wait until he's invited over at a time when we're more prepared to get to know him." Then she turned to Robbie and added, "Stop biting your lip, everything's fine."

Robbie had a bad habit of biting the inside of his mouth when things weren't going his way, or when he was nervous or upset. Rosalynn had once shown him how ridiculous he looked by holding a mirror up to his face mid-act. Even seeing how distorted his mouth got as his teeth reached something on the inside of his cheek to chew on didn't dissuade him from dropping the habit.

"You weren't there, Mom. You didn't see Dad act like a total jerk to Dwayne."

Wait a minute now! Since when was Robbie placed on the same level as Jeremy - a target for tattling? Frustrated, Robbie jumped in and said, "I'm right here; you don't have to tell Mom on me. And I was *not* acting like a jerk. You're the one who talked bad about me behind my back, calling me lame or whatever."

"You deserved it," Taylor hissed.

"Careful, Taylor," warned Rosalynn in a lowered voice.

Robbie had to admit, that one hurt. What was he supposed to do? He couldn't discipline her like the five year old she was acting like. But then, as much as he wanted, he couldn't just play buddy/buddy with her either.

In the end Robbie just had to realize that Taylor was not some problem to figure out. No, she was a human being to be reckoned with in the most loving way possible. Even if that meant tough love, which it likely did.

Still, the night ended in a near-explosion between Robbie and Taylor, but she retreated into her shell and refused to speak to him any longer. Robbie had long ago decided that the only thing that would win his little daughter back was time. The confusing part however, was what exactly he was supposed to do with her for the time being. Maybe Hawaii would afford them some bonding time.

CHAPTER 2

Robbie Lake pulled into CipherMill Publishing House at 1606 8th Street. In just two days he'd be sitting in coach, strapping himself in and watching Seattle vanish beneath the clouds with a Bloody Mary in one hand and a bag of pretzels in the other. But not for two more days. There was still one more day of work left and one day devoted to packing. He nodded to the security guard behind the desk as he walked through the lobby. As soon as he summoned the elevator, Don Stentson swaggered up behind him and stood uncomfortably close, breathing hard. The jaunt from the car to the elevator was clearly too long of a walk for a three hundred pound man.

"They're talking again," said Don.

"Hmm?" Robbie asked, disinterested.

"I overheard Kurt talking on his cell phone yesterday. I shouldn't have been listening, but it sounds like they're going to be laying more people off today."

The prospect of layoffs weighed heavily upon the few faithful employees who had survived the first wave of terminations seven months ago, and Robbie was no exception. The menacing thought always reared its ugly head: Would this be his last year? Self-publishing and electronic books had become a huge sensation, and book editors, like Robbie, suffered greatly for it. Seven months ago, the company was cut almost in half. The only reason Robbie didn't get hacked then was because of his tenure. This time around he wouldn't have that protection; anyone still working had been there as long as he had.

"I wouldn't worry about it," said Robbie. "You probably just misunderstood." The elevator doors opened and they both stepped in. Robbie wished he had taken the stairs, or at least that Don had taken the stairs to burn a few calories for his own good.

"What part of 'I'll start calling people in tomorrow' would I not understand? I saw him holding a list of names," insisted Don.

"Was your name on it?"

“I don’t know. I couldn’t see.”

“Then how do you know it was a list of names?”

“He said, ‘I’ve got the list of names right here.’ I almost just put in my two week’s notice, but then I wouldn’t get any severance.”

“I’m sure you’ll be okay,” assured Robbie as the elevator doors opened. Truthfully, Robbie was a nervous wreck, but he was determined not to let it get to his head today. Not his last week before vacation. “No one’s getting fired today.” But as they stepped out, they saw Bill Donahue walking down the hallway carrying a box. Robbie’s heart sank. The first lay off.

Strangely he wasn’t as worried about losing his job as he was about losing his hard-earned vacation.

“Morning guys,” said Bill, as he walked past.

“You seem a bit chipper,” Don commented, half offended. “What, did you hate working here that much?”

Bill shrugged and said, “It’s fine here, I guess. I’ll be back. I’m just dropping this box off down at the warehouse.”

Robbie and Don looked at each other and broke into grins. Bill didn’t ask, and he just continued on his way. “Kurt brought donuts in, by the way,” he said over his shoulder.

“Pity food,” said Don, resuming his pessimism.

They continued forward.

“It’s probably for my anniversary,” Robbie suggested.

“Right. Kurt refuses to even get a wreath for Christmas.”

When they reached the suite they each headed to their own offices. Don, of course, grabbed a plate full of donuts on his way.

As he walked past the editor in chief’s office, Robbie stole a glance through the window. Darrin Mackey was seated across from Kurt, and his head was drooped.

Maybe Don was right. It was only nine o’ clock and Kurt always had his office door open in the mornings. Was he just getting this out of the way? That’s what he had done during the last set of lay-offs.

Robbie quickened the pace to his office, shut the door behind him, threw his briefcase on the chair in the corner, and flipped on his computer. He pulled up sales records of the previous four months and compared his name with other colleagues. He matched what books were represented by whom with which ones were pulling in the most revenue. Just as he feared, he fell right in the middle. It all depended on where Kurt drew the line.

Who would have had enough foresight eleven years ago to know that books would eventually go electronic? Facebook was still no more than a small community of networking nerds at that time. Still, he blamed himself for getting locked into a dead-end career.

There was a knock at the door and Robbie froze. Was he next? Why wouldn't Kurt just buzz him in? Before he could say anything, the door opened and Don barged in with his plate of donuts. Robbie swore it was a new batch. He shut the door behind him and flopped down on one of the chairs. Normally Robbie would have been irritated at this intrusive behavior, especially coming from somebody he didn't really know that well.

"Darrin's gone," said Don, sinking his teeth into a pink frosted donut, spilling sprinkles all over his tie. "Kurt just fired him. I didn't have the heart to see who was next. I told you this was it!"

Robbie knew who was next because he just saw the sales records. It was Don. He couldn't lie. He couldn't tell him everything was going to be all right. Instead, he said, "He might be calling some people in for different reasons." So why not lie indirectly?

Don shoved the last donut into his mouth and mumbled, "You think so?"

Before Robbie could correct himself, Don's cell phone buzzed. He looked at it and his drooping jowls fell even further. He cried, "It's Kurt. He must have tried calling my office." A peal of guttural sounds rumbled around in his fat stomach.

"Answer," Robbie prodded.

Don nodded and brought the phone to his ear with a shaky hand. "Hello? Yes, sir. I'll be right there." He hung up and looked at Robbie with watery eyes. "He wants to see me."

Robbie closed his eyes and nodded his head knowingly. Don just sat in his chair, stunned, looking off into space. Kurt was waiting for him, and Robbie was starting to feel uncomfortable. "You should probably just get it over with."

Don dully nodded, then stood up, and like a man of the theater playing the part of the noble martyr, thrust his hand out for Robbie to shake.

"Maybe he wants to give you a raise," suggested Robbie, jokingly as he shook Don's meaty hand.

"You think?" Don asked, lifting his head.

"No. I don't know why I said that, sorry. Go talk to Kurt."

Don nodded and disappeared behind the door.

Robbie needed a game plan. But he had nothing to fall back on if he was going to be fired. He'd taken his posh job for granted, even during the current economy. The unemployment rate meant nothing to him until today. Now it was just a little too personal. He'd have to update his resume and rehearse his interviewing skills again. These were things that did not fit into his life plan. And until a few minutes ago, his life plan was to take his family to Kona Village for a couple of weeks and escape the humdrum hell of everyday life.

It didn't take long. Robbie saw, from out the window that overlooked the suite, Don leaving Kurt's office. Don's head, like Darrin's before him, was down. Was he really crying? Robbie watched as his ex-colleague dragged himself over to his office and a few minutes later he emerged with a box packed with his stuff. He left the building in a hurry, not even stopping to look back.

If Kurt was firing half the office, he, Robbie, would be among them for sure. It was just a matter of hours before he would be cleaning out his own desk.

CHAPTER 3

Robbie spent the rest of the day drowned in a wave of anxiety. Two more people were asked to pack their things and hit the road. At first, Robbie avoided Kurt at all costs; he avoided the break room when he knew Kurt would be there and he took the long way 'round to the bathroom so he wouldn't pass Kurt's windows. But by one o' clock, he began to grow curious and even hopeful. He was becoming convinced that he wasn't going to be fired after all. But in order to have a true peace of mind he would have to find Kurt and feel him out. Would he be awkward? Would he be cool as usual? But Robbie learned from a colleague that Kurt had stepped out of the office to meet with someone for the next few hours. He sat at his desk and wallowed in his misery. And no, he didn't spend the day looking up top rated Hawaiian tours on the internet.

What if he did get fired? The economy would crush him. He feared going back to retail or some other dead-end job. Though he wasn't wealthy by American standards, he didn't want to have to sacrifice his comfortable lifestyle to make ends meet. He didn't want to have to put every dollar on trial, or the necessity of every bill. He had been through all that and had grown up. This was supposed to be *his* time to live the easy life!

He glanced at a picture of Rosalynn and him posing in front of the ocean in Ventura Beach in Southern California, which stood next to his phone. The picture was taken when they were dating. They had met at USC. Actually, they were both attending USC when they happened to meet at a beach party one weekend. She looked absolutely stunning in her floral summer dress, her auburn brown hair falling straight down over her shoulders. He was skinny and sporting a facial hair trying to become a beard, just like any properly-groomed beach bum.

His reminiscing came to an end when Kurt phoned him and asked him to step into his office.

Robbie's legs felt like jelly as he made his way through the suite toward his boss's office. He felt every eye on him, conveying pity, just as he had looked at the others who were called into Kurt's office that day. To distract himself, he pulled his phone out of his pocket and pretended to read text messages. He muted it when reached Kurt's door and proceeded to knock, feeling like he was back in school about to see the principal.

"Have a seat," said Kurt when Robbie walked in. He sat down slowly, and as he did, he couldn't help but notice the painting hanging directly behind Kurt. It was a large picture of a panther, crouching behind tall grass in a dark jungle. Robbie felt like it was piercing him with its yellow-eyed stare, waiting for the boss to wound him so he could finish the job off.

"First off, congratulations on your anniversary."

"Thanks," said Robbie, sitting up.

"How many years is it now? Ten?"

"Eleven." *Would twenty be better?*

"Unfortunately it falls on a bad day. I'm sure you know we're letting people go."

"Don't do this to me Kurt."

"I'm sorry, Robbie. I know this hurts, and you've got your family to look after. I did all I could to avoid this, but there wasn't anything I could do."

Robbie's stomach tightened, and he was chewing on the inside of his mouth like it was gum; Rosalynn would have been having a heyday. The panther gazed lustily at Robbie, looking as though it were ready to pounce on him. "This is all I know, Kurt. Where am I going to look?"

"Check the web, for starters. There're all sorts of companies looking to hire. I'm sorry, Robbie. We're only keeping a small handful of people, if it makes you feel better."

Oh yes, much.

"After that... who knows?"

"What about my vacation?" he felt petty for asking.

"Technically, I can't pull that from you since you've already earned it. But I would cancel your plans. Think of it as two weeks added to your severance."

How kind.

Robbie's head was spinning as he cleared out his desk. Had he really been fired? He'd never been fired from a job in his life, and now he knew what it felt like. He wanted to kill Kurt for not being a better manager and avoiding this catastrophe. He never realized how many personal items he had until he saw how full the box was. What was he going to tell Rosalynn? How would she react? He flirted with the idea of not telling her until they got back from vacation. But no, Hawaii would have to be canceled. They'll need that money when the severance is paid out.

The sweet smell of sunscreen was fading fast.

He somehow survived the walk of shame through the suite. He noticed no one made eye contact with him. It was as though he were a leper making his way through the village and no one wanted to be ostracized for acknowledging him. He began to plop his box of things down in the backseat of his car when his phone rang. He glanced at it and saw that it was an unknown caller. He answered and recognized Don's voice. "Meet me at Mad Betty's."

"How did you get my number?" Robbie asked.

"Just come over here now. Park in the back."

Robbie drove his car across the street to the local bar and pub. He pulled around back as instructed and parked next to Don's Malibu.

Inside he found his ex-colleague waving at him from a corner booth barely illuminated by a hanging green light. The lingering smoke made him long for a cigarette.

"What's up?" asked Robbie, taking a seat across from Don.

"I've got something big," he said. "I was cleaning out the hard drive on my computer. You won't believe what I found. But I probably shouldn't tell you this."

"You probably should since you called me over here. There are other places I could be right now."

"Where? Work?"

"Shut up."

Don held up a small, folded sheet of paper. "I found Kurt's passwords and sign-in names to our system. That's how I got your number; it was listed under his employee information."

"No. I'm sure that's illegal, throw it out."

Don slammed his fist on the table, jarring the salt shaker. "I knew it. I shouldn't have told you," he declared as though he had debated with himself over the issue for hours.

"How did you get it?"

"The best I can figure is Kurt was in my office a couple of weeks ago showing me a few things. He signed in with his user name, punched in his password, and the computer stored it in the system. If you leave your password in an HTML field, or the browser auto-completes it, the password and user name can be retrieved."

Robbie looked at him blankly. These words meant nothing to him.

"It's a long computer thing; you wouldn't get it. Anyway, I couldn't resist the temptation to take it after he fired me. It was lucky, but I got it."

"Why are you telling me this?"

"Don't you get it? We have access to his leads, his clients, anyone who's anyone in the publishing industry. We use these leads, we'll have jobs again in no time. Or, we could start our own company and take his clients. He won't need them anyway with so many of us gone."

"This is insane and I'm pretty certain it's illegal. Besides, when did you get to be so gutsy? You don't seem to strike me as that type of guy."

"I don't know. I just kind of snapped when I was packing up my things. This is the fifth job I've been fired from."

"Wow. You *are* going to need help."

"Thanks. The restaurant business wasn't good for me. I had no self-control in the kitchen. Will you help me? We'll split the leads down the middle."

Suddenly, the idea seemed tempting. Robbie didn't want to have to spend the next several months competing with the rest of America's younger, sharper, and higher-qualified job seekers. He certainly didn't want to have to settle for some job cleaning toilets at a 7-11 while he tried to make ends meet. The idea made him sick to his stomach.

"What do we have to do?" he finally asked.

"Our computers are the only ones that have our system. So we'll have to do it from the office."

"You realize we can probably get arrested for this," said Robbie.

"We've just been fired in a crappy economy. How can it get any worse?"

"By having a felony charge on our records."

"Just shut up and listen. We'll have to do it from the warehouse downstairs. I'm pretty sure they have the same system we do. Kurt never goes down there, and he's the only person we've got to watch out for, so the chances of success are in our favor."

"This is insane."

"All we have to do is keep our cars parked out of sight. Hang out in the bathroom for a while until the warehouse workers leave, sneak in, pull up the information, print it out, and leave."

Robbie contemplated the scheme, rolling it around in his head. The more he thought about it, the more foolproof it seemed.

"Half of the leads is like two hundred publishers. That's two hundred chances that they're looking for someone to hire. Not all businesses are failing."

An hour later Robbie walked toward the door to the warehouse at the end of the hallway and pushed against the metal bar, swinging it open. The lights were still on and all the workers had all gone home. The computer screen was at the far end of the room. He rushed toward it and entered Kurt's user name and password when prompted.

When he asked Don why he didn't just print this stuff out in his office, he responded that he had panicked and just wrote down the password on a piece of paper and left. Robbie could understand that. What he couldn't understand was how he let Don talk him into taking on the most dangerous part of this mission while he, Don, stood on guard, phone in hand, ready to alert Robbie of anyone coming into the warehouse.

Following the user name and password keys on the torn piece of paper Don had given him he signed in under his former boss's name with no trouble. Clicking the mouse furiously, he navigated through the menu options in search of the coveted client list. But the computer was agonizingly slow. He had been there long enough. He needed to just find *some*thing of value and print it out. Finally, he came across the list of clients and leads and their contact information. The list was several hundred long. It shined like gold.

Of course the printer was more than a decade old. It spat out each sheet like they were worms crawling on hot pavement. During the ninth page, Robbie heard the metal bar on the door from across the warehouse. He panicked. All he could think of was Kurt walking in on him fraudulently printing up his personal information. He could not be seen in that warehouse. Not only could he lose the leads for good, but he could get thrown into jail. The thought of Rosalynn and the kids visiting him in the slammer was unbearable. He jumped into a cardboard box that lay next to his feet and pulled the flaps down over his head. He had to scrunch, but it nearly fit him perfectly. He wouldn't be able to stay crouching like that for long because at some point his old bones would give under the pressure of his body doubling up on itself.

No one came in through the door. His ears must have been playing tricks on him. Before he crawled out of the box he sat upright on his rear and laid his back against it and rested while the printer did its thing. He realized he hadn't been inside a box since he was a kid.

As he exhaled, he closed his eyes.

Instantly Robbie felt a cool breeze that sent a shiver up his spine. His knees were pulled up to his chest and his hands were at his sides and they were wet. He lifted them, dripping droplets of cool water all over his suit.

When he opened his eyes he saw that he was crouching in a giant puddle of crystal-blue phosphorescent water. The water glowed brightly enough to reveal a vast cavern surrounding him. A ray of light shone through a hole several hundred feet above his head.

Robbie shivered as he stood up to observe his surroundings. It was chilly in the cave, especially with little gusts of wind whooshing past him. He had no idea where he was, or where he had come from. But somehow, he didn't really care. He was just simply ... there.

He could hear tiny waves lapping against the cavern's rugged walls. The only other sound came from the echoes of leaking water trickling off the walls. The only way had to be down one of the several surrounding corridors surrounding him.

CHAPTER 4

Before Robbie had a chance to collapse into a state of claustrophobia, he heard footsteps splashing in the water. Someone was running down one of the corridors. Robbie, feeling soiled in his wet clothes, ran after the sound of the footsteps, and called out, "Who's there?" He was desperately in need of answers.

He heard the pattering of footsteps in response to his query. With the intensity of a bloodhound he followed the sound down the corridor.

The light did not reach this far into the cave, so he paused to let his eyes adjust to the darkness. Finally, Robbie could just barely see the figure of a child about ten feet ahead. He walked slowly forward, not wanting to scare the kid off.

"My name is Robbie," he said cautiously. "I just need to know how to get out of here."

Although he couldn't be certain in the darkness, this young child, a girl, was glaring at him.

"Can you tell me where I am?" asked Robbie as he inched closer to the child. "I promise I'm not going to hurt you."

He took a few steps closer, reaching out his hand toward her as if trying to feed a frightened fawn. The girl remained motionless, her arms down at her sides and her bare feet spread slightly apart.

"What's your name?" asked Robbie.

Then without so much as a warning the girl broke her scowl and hissed at him, warning him to stay back. He pulled his hand back in surprise.

"I'm sorry," he said instinctively. Then he realized she probably didn't speak English. So he tried the only other way he knew to communicate. He gestured with his hands.

"I'm," Robbie said, pointing at his chest, "nice." He said *nice* while smiling really wide and pressing his fingers into his cheeks. "I'm a friend," he clarified.

Then he waved his arm around in a big circle followed by an exaggerated shrug: "Where are we?"

The girl took a step toward him. Against his instincts, he stood his ground. She took another step and another, and gradually closed the gap between them. He could see her more clearly now. She looked like she was about eight or nine. She had long dark hair that dropped down her back in straight greasy lines. She wore a plain dirty beige cloak that hung down to her knees.

Now just feet away from each other, she moved her arm behind her back to scratch. Robbie wondered briefly what kinds of lice she might be carrying. Then he felt uneasy, even nanoseconds before she pulled her hand back in front of her bearing a dagger, her eyes narrowed at him and she bared her teeth like an animal. Robbie turned and sprinted in the opposite direction, all pretense of 'friendly grown up' behavior tossed aside as soon as he saw the dagger in the girl's hand.

He heard her hissing and screaming from behind as he tried not to fall over anything in the darkness. He had to run with his arms stretched out in front of him in case he hit a wall. After a few uncertain feet, he saw light ahead. Robbie set his tracks on the faint beam that shined through the dark cavern.

He feared that the little girl was more an expert in running in the dark through ankle-deep water than he was. His wet shoes and socks were weighing him down. He tried not to imagine the little girl's knife stabbing him in the lower back. She was close enough now to do just that.

Somehow, he made it to the light. The sudden brightness blinded him temporarily and all went black.

Next thing he knew, the ground gave way under him. He was falling. It all happened so fast that he didn't even think to scream. All he could do was wait for the impact, as he twisted and twirled in the air, and pray that he wouldn't feel it.

Suddenly he was submerged under lukewarm water and his body spiraled out of control as he plunged into the depths. He choked on the water splashing down his throat. When at last the current stopped thrashing him about he opened his eyes to determine which way he needed to swim for air. They had finally adjusted to the light and he was able to see the surface of the water and he swam toward the sun.

Just as he thought the water would never stop rising against him his head broke through the surface and he gulped in a huge breath of air. This had to have been the greatest satisfaction his lungs had ever felt.

As he breathed in the delicious air he heard a loud shriek coming from above, followed by a splash close enough to spray him in the face. The girl had jumped into the water from where he had fallen. She grabbed his foot and, with surprising strength, pulled him back under.

He tried kicking his foot to shake her off, but she grabbed onto his other foot. He couldn't believe how strong she was. The situation was quickly escalating into a full-on fight for his life as the girl began clawing at Robbie's legs. She climbed all over him, pulling him further underwater. She then let go of a foot to grab his right hand, and she bit down where his thumb joined his palm. Robbie screamed in agonizing pain, sending the rest of his air up in bubbles. He tried to tear his hand away, but the girl would not release her bite.

Finally, in a final act of desperation he swung at the girl with his one free foot, kicking her square in the stomach. The sudden release of her bite let forth a torrent of pain coursing through his hand. Now freed, he quickly made his way up to the surface and again refilled his lungs with air, swirling blood around him that gushed from his hand. His head spun wildly from lack of oxygen and too much pain.

As he treaded in the warm water, he began to grow nervous that he may have actually killed the girl, which of course was not his intent. He waited and watched the water, but she never surfaced. The only movement came from his own feet as he worked to stay afloat.

Panic grew in his chest as he started to believe he was a murderer. *It was self-defense!* he assured his imaginary critics. If he hadn't kicked her, she would have drowned him for sure. He ducked his head back under the water, but couldn't see any sign of her. The lake was an empty abyss.

CHAPTER 5

Robbie would have rescued the girl, but she was nowhere in sight. As he worked to keep his head above water, the heavy truth weighed on him: He had just murdered a little girl. He tried to convince himself that he had done the right thing, but something in him just wouldn't buy it. However, if he hadn't killed her, she would have pulled him under to his own death. Is it really self-defense if it means killing a child? Robbie strongly doubted it.

He swam toward the shore, but never once found the bottom of the lake. Instead the shore was like a rim that he swam up to, like he was in a crater. The lake was a perfect circle about hundred feet in circumference. Surrounding the water were trees of all kinds, painting the landscape with a deep lush green. The air was warm and moist like the water that held him. The wind was nonexistent, as if the air were holding its breath. It was so muggy Robbie wondered if there was much more air outside the water as in. He pulled himself up out of the water onto the edge, careful not to apply weight to his wounded hand. He ripped a leaf from a nearby plant and pressed it up against his thumb to stop the bleeding. He feared bacteria getting inside his hand, but at least this way he wouldn't be smearing blood everywhere. Who knew what sort of wild animals he would attract? Behind him a wall of jungle trees rose up and blocked out the sun blazing in the clear sky. The heavy humidity stuck to him like glue and he wondered if he would ever dry off. He looked up at the mouth of the cave he had jumped from. It was a hole in the side of a sheer wall of rock about fifty feet up. He didn't know it was possible to survive such a fall. A smooth ribbon of water trailed down the cliff from the mouth that looked peaceful and serene and caused a quiet trickling sound as it glided into the water.

Sitting with his legs in the water, he couldn't shake free of the awful reality that he had just killed a little girl. A child! What kind of a man was he? The time had long passed for her to survive being submerged, so now any inkling of hope he had for her was stored away forever. He knew this would plague him for the rest of his life and right now the walls of his mouth were suffering greatly for his stress as his teeth gnawed at them.

As he looked out over the lake he saw bubbles rising to the surface, and out of the water, the little girl emerged. Robbie marveled that the girl was alive, but his joy was cut short when she turned to him with a scowl. She swam toward him in smooth elegant strides, clearly a seasoned swimmer.

She glared at him with murderous eyes. He quickly stood up, and stumbled backwards a few steps. He wondered how she could have survived so long underwater, but when she picked up her pace, he ditched his query and turned and ran into the jungle.

He tripped on nearly every branch, twig, and root in his path. The low hanging tree branches scratched mercilessly at his arms. They reached out at him, grabbing and clawing at his arms and legs. He could hear little footsteps closing in on him, and his only thought was of escaping the girl and her knife.

He searched desperately for a place to hide, but didn't know which way to turn. For all he knew he could be heading into greater danger. He tripped and fell face first on the jungle ground. Within seconds the girl was standing over him and Robbie instinctively raised his arms to protect his face. But she didn't attack him. Instead she said, in perfect English, "Your name is Robbie?"

He nodded. "Robbie Lake."

"They said you'd be wearing funny clothes. I couldn't see what you were wearing in the cave because it was dark. And it's hard to tell under water."

Robbie looked down at his suit and tie. He did feel out of place.

"Are you cold or something?" asked the girl. "Is that why you're wearing so many clothes?"

"I don't know why I'm wearing these," confessed Robbie. It was true. He couldn't figure out why he was dressed that way. He still had no idea where he had been prior to appearing in the cave.

The girl took a step toward him and lifted his tie from his chest, dangling it in front of her eyes. "This looks stupid. Do you use it to swat at flies?"

"What do you care?"

"Is it a noose for you to hang yourself with in case the ghosts catch you?"

"Why did you try to drown me back there?"

"I thought you were an impostor," the girl said as she stepped back from Robbie so he could stand up.

"What's your name?"

"Hail. And you're really Robbie?"

Even the birds in the trees seemed to stop their hollering in anticipation of his answer. He nodded.

"It would be a pretty big deal if you really are. I don't even know what to do with you now. I guess maybe I should take you to see Sarcadui."

"Who?"

"Your guide. Someone's got to take you to the ocean. No one's been closer to the ocean than Sarcadui."

"The ocean sounds good," said Robbie. "Will there be a boat to take me out of here?"

"I don't know. I've never been there. But come on, we need to get you to Sarcadui before it gets dark."

Hail walked deeper into the jungle, but Robbie just stood his ground. When Hail inquired about his position with upraised eyebrows, Robbie said, "You've tried to kill me twice in the last ten minutes. I'm not following you."

She just shrugged and said, "All right. I have no emotional attachment to you. Good luck getting to the ocean by yourself." With that she continued on her way through the trees.

Robbie wasn't sure he wanted to be left alone in this strange place. The girl seemed harmless enough now. Grunting at his own indecisiveness, he jogged to catch up with her.

"What made you think I was an impostor?" he asked.

"Are you kidding me? People always show up in the cave claiming to be you."

Robbie was stunned. "Why would people claim to be me?"

"They need help getting to your throne. If they can convince us that they're you, then we'll take them to your castle." Hail looked condescendingly at Robbie and added, "But now that I see you, I'm surprised *anyone* would want to be you. I always thought you'd be bigger and, I don't know, stronger. But it turns out that you're a bad swimmer *and* you run away from little girls."

"I can swim just fine. You didn't see *me* hanging onto anyone in the lake, did you? How did you stay under for so long anyway?"

Hail took a dark piece of bark out of her mouth and handed it to Robbie. "It's breathing bark. It comes from trees that are filled with air. With one of these in your mouth you can breathe for a long time."

"Weird. I'm sorry for kicking you so hard. I don't make it a habit to go around kicking little kids."

"It's fine. You're a survivor; that's good. That gives you a chance to make it to your throne alive."

"I don't want to disappoint you, but if there is a throne out there, it's not mine."

"Don't say that to too many people. That could start an uprising."

"Why?"

But Hail was holding a finger to her mouth and gesturing toward the jungle with her other hand.

Robbie turned to the trees and strained his eyes to see what Hail was looking at. Sitting in front of the overgrown wild plants was the largest rat he had ever seen. It was at least two feet tall, and its dark brown fur was plastered down to its head. Small black eyes peered intently at Robbie. Sitting up on its beefy hind legs, it showed great interest in the two strange people peering down at it.

"It's an agouti," informed Hail. "They're rare, and sort of belong to the rat family. Cute, huh?"

"Cute" was not the first thing that came to Robbie's mind. Let's face it, a rat is a rat.

But before he could say anything, an oversized lizard bounded out of the bushes on its hind legs and attacked the agouti from behind. It stretched its long neck over the rodent's head and bit its face as the rat squirmed and shrieked like a flag on a pole flapping wildly in the wind.

The lizard was about five feet long from head to tail and as tall as the agouti. It flipped its meal over to devour it from the neck down in just a few large bites, tugging on the meat that stuck to the bones with its long, sharp teeth.

Hail grabbed Robbie's arm and pulled him along. "Let's go."

"That looked like a dinosaur," said Robbie.

"That was an eoraptor," said Hail, not slowing down. "There will be others around and they'll kill us if they can attack us as a group. They get bigger the deeper into the jungle we go."

"How big?" asked Robbie.

"Huge. Haven't you seen them before?"

"No," he answered. He couldn't help but wonder if he had somehow been taken back to the prehistoric era. "Where are we?"

"Oh. I bet a lot's changed since you were last here," said Hail. Robbie had no idea what she was talking about. She was just a confused child. "We're in Reveloin. Right now we're in the Arura Jungle. We're heading east into Langly where Sarcadui is."

Robbie thought this Sarcadui had the ring of a tough warrior-type. He wondered if he owned this land, or if he was a high-ranking soldier in an army, or the chief of some Indian tribe… He wouldn't admit it, but he was nervous about meeting him.

After putting some distance between them and the dinosaur, Robbie was able to enjoy the vast beauty of his new surroundings.

The jungle was completely cut off from the sun by the canopy of leafy branches stitched together overhead. The many tree types varied between massive kapuk trees with their unearthed roots stretching along the ground to the dazzling gallitos showing off their red leaves as if displaying their diversity amongst all their green-leaved neighbors. Some were huge and bulky and others as small as the average fig tree. A majority of the trees were completely covered with winding vines and moss. The leaves and plants were the jungle's carpet that stretched out before its visitors, some leaves as big as Hail. The leaves and the busted branches crunched under their feet as they walked. All this together was like herbs mixed into a jungly soup that cast its musty aroma into Robbie's nostrils. It reminded him of something… but his memory sensors claimed nothing, a blank slate.

Screeching birds and chirping insects from all around made it hard to hear their own footsteps. Monkeys screamed from up above the trees where Robbie couldn't see them. Small shafts of light shone through the treetops illuminating a fog that seemed to be closing in, but was always ahead, as though forbidding them to come further. But Hail pressed on and Robbie did his best to keep up.

Robbie's heart nearly stopped when a large man landed on his feet just less than a yard ahead of them. A long messy beard covered his dark face, leaving only his bludgeon eyes visible. He was bare-chested proudly displaying his rippling muscles, and was dressed in nothing more than a loincloth that wrapped around his waist. In his left hand he carried a bow, as though it were his most prized possession. Several arrows poked up from a sheath slung over his back. Robbie instinctively bent to pick up a rock to throw at him, but Hail started talking.

"This is *him*, Remusathi."

The man looked at Robbie contemptuously and said in a deep monotonous voice, "Are you sure?"

"Pretty sure. We should at least let Sarcadui look at him, don't you think?"

"I suppose so," conceded Remusathi. Then the big man stepped closer to Robbie and stuck his face near Robbie's. "I'll let you pass, but I'm not bowing to you until you sit on your throne. You had better be who we think you are. And you better show more respect to Sarcadui than you have shown me," he said, glaring at the rock in Robbie's hand, which he immediately dropped as though the look were a command.

Robbie nodded slightly but said nothing. He didn't care to insult the man any more.

"Thanks," said Hail, a little too familiarly. "I'm sure someone will keep you posted."

Remusathi nodded respectfully and stepped aside for them to pass.

Robbie and Hail pressed forward. "What was that all about?" he asked.

"That was Remusathi. He's one of the lookouts. They're everywhere, because we're nearing Langly. They're in the trees right now watching us. You won't see them if you look; they're good hiders."

Robbie glanced upward, but could see no one peering down from the treetops. And on second thought, he was thankful, because if they were all just wearing a loincloth like Remusathi, he didn't care to see the others from bellow. "What are they on the lookout for?"

"Trenchers. They weren't around when you were here last. They're traitors and we hate them. We want them all to die." Robbie smirked at Hail's honest bluntness.

By this point, however, his head was spinning and he decided not to press for any more information. He had heard enough about his supposed past for one day.

Soon the jungle trees cleared away. The greenery subsided, the leaves became sparse, and the rolling ground became flat. Surrounding them now was nothing but a barren wasteland littered with stone hedges and holes in the ground.

Robbie was startled when he saw a young child scurrying away from them like a frightened animal. The boy, wearing an old tattered cloak like Hail, disappeared into the ground through one of the holes.

Robbie wondered why the boy was so afraid of them. Then he noticed people's heads popping up from several different holes. All around them people came crawling out of the ground like frightened meerkats.

Groups of people emerged from some holes, and from others only individuals dragged themselves out. They were all wearing roughly the same thing – robes and garments held up by thin ropes that wrapped around their waists. Their hair was ragged and tangled in messes and though no one was skeletal, there wasn't a single person who looked plump; it was easy to assume that their dietary habits were modest. As they came out from underground they stood around in small groups. They looked cautiously at Robbie and Hail who were making their way through. Once they walked past them, varying people lifted their heads toward the duo and he could almost detect tiny glimpses of happiness in their eyes. Their skin colors were diverse; some were white, others black, all dark from sun exposure.

"Where are we?" asked Robbie, just loud enough for Hail to hear.

"We're in Langly," she answered.

As soon as she said this, Robbie felt a pair of hands graze over his shoulders from behind. He defensively turned around, pulling away from the gesture. When he turned he saw a woman with strawberry blond hair. She had a knowing smile, which annoyed Robbie. Her face tilted down and her cheeks reddened as she shrugged her shoulders. "You're exactly as I imagined you to be," she said.

"Er, thanks," said Robbie, not sure how exactly to respond politely.

"We're so glad you're finally with us," the young woman continued. She opened her arms and asked, "May I?"

Robbie looked at Hail uncomfortably. She smiled and encouraged Robbie with a nod. "Robbie, meet Sarcadui. She will be your guide to your throne in the sea."

Robbie was stunned. This was not at all what he expected a *Sarcadui* to look like. She looked to be in her early twenties. His long hair fell lazily past her shoulders, and she was dressed in the same dirty-beige garment as everyone else around them. But now that Robbie knew she was of importance, he saw her differently from everyone else. Her bright blue eyes and alluring smile set her apart from her neighbors. Another difference was that she had a well-worn knife that hung from the rope that wrapped around her waist.

Robbie reluctantly walked toward her, and let her wrap her arms around him and hold him tight. His arms remained at his sides as she cheerfully said, "Welcome back home, Robbie Lake."

This strange familiarity caught Robbie off guard. "How do you—"

But Sarcadui beamed and cut him off. "I can't tell you how glad we are that you're finally here! We were beginning to wonder if this day would ever come." She released him and stood back to get a good look at him. Her smile seemed to be permanently etched onto her face, which didn't annoy Robbie anymore, and he had a fleeting thought that it was placed there by the gods. Her voice was soothing and strangely, he wanted to hear more of it.

Then her attention turned to Hail. "Hail, I'm proud of you. And you thought he'd never come."

Hail shook her head. "I didn't even think it was him until I saw his dumb-looking clothes. But I remembered all the stories saying that he wouldn't be dressed like us. I almost killed him, though. I thought he was an impostor," Hail laughed.

To Robbie's surprise Sarcadui, along with some others in the crowd laughed along with her, as if murdering him were some leisurely matter. He was more than a bit insulted.

"Well good work." Then she snapped her attention back to Robbie. "All these years we had people stationed up in the Walei Caves to await your arrival. This was Hail's first time up there, but once they're of age to be out alone, everyone is required to serve their time. The clothes tipped her off that it was you. That's why we all dress like this, as unflattering as it is. Since no one alive knows what you look like, we had to rely on the stories that insisted on you wearing funny clothes." Then, changing tunes, she said with a grin, "So it looks like we've got quite a long adventure ahead of us."

He nodded. If this woman really was to be his guide then he was more than happy to oblige. *And,* he thought, *the robes are flattering on you.* There was something refreshing about her, but he would not let on, at least not in front of all these people.

"Maybe you can tell me where we are," said Robbie. "I know it's weird, but I really don't even know how I got here, so if you could maybe humor me with a little geography lesson, that'd be alright by me."

Sarcadui laughed and said, "I know nothing outside of Reveloin so I can answer any question you might have. I used to love going to the Walei Caverns just to splash around in the water and laugh while I waited for you. The echoes made it sound like others were laughing with me but really I was alone, so I could act as foolish as I wanted." Robbie couldn't help but notice her loose garment swirling around her slender figure.

"But the Walei Caverns isn't my favorite place," she continued. "My favorite place is the mountain tops on Candy Ridge."

A man standing nearby stepped forward and handed Robbie a small rock, which he took out of obligation. "They say that long ago you could actually taste the rocks and trees and they'd be sweet," said the man. "Go on, taste it."

Robbie looked skeptically at him. "Give it a lick," the man urged.

To humor him, Robbie stuck his tongue out and dragged the rough rock against it, which dried his tongue out instantly. He grimaced at the dirty, gritty taste in his mouth. Everyone looked at him with eager anticipation.

"How does it taste?" asked Sarcadui.

"Disgusting," said Robbie, attempting to build saliva back up in his mouth with obnoxious tongue clicking.

Hail broke the disappointed silence with a gleeful bit of laughter. "He fell for it! He's just as weird as he looks!"

"Hail," snapped Sarcadui, "it wasn't supposed to be a joke. We thought things would go back to normal since he's here." Then a smile broke onto her face and she turned to Robbie and said, "Still, it was rather funny to see your reaction. But don't feel too badly. I've tried to eat some leaves from the mountains more than once."

"Why in the world would you do that?" asked Robbie, still failing to find the reason behind this madness.

"Don't you remember? When you were here, everything was edible. Of course, I wasn't born at the time, but still, I've heard all the stories. But there are other things I like to do other than try to find remains of the past world. Like swimming in the rivers that flow in and out of the jungles, and exploring the abandoned towns where the cowboys used to fight. And sometimes if I'm feeling brave I like to visit the swamplands, but never at night of course. I'm always well hidden every night, no matter where I am. You can never be too careful once the sun's gone down. And they say that before I was born fairies existed and flew around freely at night.

But they don't come out anymore because they're too afraid. It's always been my dream to see a real fairy. But listen to me, telling you about your own world as if you've never been here. Now that you're back, maybe *you* can show me things I've never seen before."

In spite of himself Robbie laughed along with his new friend. She just wasn't going to accept the truth that he had never been in this place. Still, her mirth was hopelessly contagious.

"Do you think it's him?" asked an older gentleman from the crowd.

Sarcadui looked intently at Robbie and after a moment declared, "Yes. It's him."

The people began to smile one by one, and some started crying, stretching their hands out toward him. "What do they want?" asked Robbie, trying not to seem rude.

Sarcadui laughed and said delightedly, "They want to welcome you here. They've been waiting for you for many years."

"You mean they've *all* been expecting me?"

The people continued to put their hands on him.

"We've been waiting for this day for a long time," repeated Sarcadui, as if to punctuate the point.

Robbie was too weary to face the absurdity of this situation, so he simply succumbed to playing the role of the welcomed guest and smiled politely, trying hard not to stiffen against the nauseating odor that came with all the hugs and pats on the back.

Sarcadui, noticing his uneasiness laughed and said, "Relax. You're their hero."

"What for?" Robbie managed through held breath. "I didn't do anything for them."

"But you're going to. We're expecting you to save us from our deaths. We should have a party in your honor. Though unfortunately it can't last too long since we need to be underground before dark."

The crowd immediately dispersed with shouts of excitement to prepare for the celebration. Sarcadui lead Robbie to a rock and told him to stay put while she joined the busy crowd.

He still had so many questions to ask. Where exactly was Reveloin? Who were these people? How was he expected to save them? But the question that haunted him the most was, who – or what – did they have to hide from every night?

CHAPTER 6

The party began with loud music from varying homemade instruments made out of windpipes and twigs and pieces of metal. The people were swiftly swept up into dancing and laughter and it wasn't long before Robbie himself joined in the celebration. He danced long and hard, having to throw his suit jacket off to the side and roll up his sleeves lest he get overheated. He would have stuck close to Sarcadui but all the ladies lined up to dance with him and he was somewhat flattered by this. He gave into the excitement and before he knew it, he was having the time of his life.

Still, he couldn't take his eyes off Sarcadui for fear of losing her. She had changed into a long light-blue dress that draped down to her ankles and she looked ravishing. It accentuated her features more than the cloak ever could. She had told him that now that he had returned she could wear anything she wanted because no one had to be on the lookout for a man not dressed in island garb. Other people changed clothes for the occasion as well, but they were all strictly ordered to change back into their cloaks after the party lest they be seen by outsiders and arouse suspicion of Robbie's return.

He even found himself laughed at his petty jealousy of all the men lined up to twirl her around or just hold her close bouncing to the beat of the music. He didn't know the dances, but he did his best to follow along with the flow of the music.

Robbie smiled when he saw that Hail was next in line to dance with him. When she stepped forward he bowed politely to her and she curtsied back. He extended his hand to her and she took it in hers.

"Your thumb looks nasty," said Hail, careful not to touch the wound.

"No thanks to you," commented Robbie. His hand still throbbed with pain where Hail had bitten him. Her teeth marks were well defined where the base of his thumb met with his palm. Brown blood was just now starting to seep up from the newly applied bandage the nurse was so kind to treat him with. "Do you know Sarcadui well?" asked Robbie. Though it was a fast-paced song, he had given up trying to master the complicated steps.

Hail twirled around before meeting back up with him and answering his question. "We're practically sisters, but she likes to think of herself as my mom."

"How so?" asked Robbie, bumping into another pair of dancers who laughed at his clumsiness.

"Both of our parents died. So she sort of adopted me."

Robbie chose not to ask about the cause of their deaths because he didn't want to spoil the party. Still, Hail had sense enough to know that he was curious. "They were all killed by ghosts. They were pretty brutal deaths from what I've heard."

Robbie was still silent, not knowing how to respond. Was she joking, or did she just naturally take everything this lightly?

"Don't feel too bad for me, though. Just about everybody here has lost someone. It's just a way of life. We'd rather have them be killed by the ghosts than become a ghost."

Just a way of life! This was no way to live. As he spun around he caught Sarcadui's eye. She was dancing with another, and he forced a smile. She in turn broke into a delicious sugary laughter, which was contagious to everyone around her, especially to Robbie.

The food was strange, to say the least. It wasn't awful, but the meat, from whatever animal it was from, was tough to chew and often got lodged in his throat. He had to follow each bite with a swig of what he believed was a very tart wine or mead. Next to the meat, his stone dish contained potato slices, unbuttered, and all sorts of varying fruits like watermelon and grapes and berries, which Robbie mostly stuck to. Hail sat down next to Robbie on a rock while they sipped their drinks from small stone cups. Some people sat around them, while others were scattered about on stone slabs throughout the little village. There wasn't even as much as a communal table for everyone to gather around. Still, the feelings of friendship and community were evident. Even if Robbie weren't the guest of honor, he still would have felt accepted by these people, so relaxed and casual was the atmosphere.

Dinner was over just as the sun was beginning to set. Robbie had completely lost track of time, but that was all right by him. He found himself sharing many laughs with Hail, and was quickly growing quite fond of her. And, he guessed, she was warming up to him.

At twilight the music stopped and the jubilee died quickly. Sarcadui strode over to Robbie and said, "The shadow is here. We need to go underground now."

No one needed an explanation. Soon, with the exception of a few others, Robbie, Hail, and Sarcadui were the only ones above ground.

When Robbie spotted his jacket he picked it up. He noticed that there were no longer holes across the ground. Now it was just a field of rocks jutting out of the earth. Sarcadui beckoned Robbie to follow her toward a hole and they both descended into it following after the quick-footed Hail.

Sarcadui led Robbie down a rickety, wooden staircase that descended eight steps down into the earth. The inside was dark and cramped. It was so small that he was afraid of claustrophobia's potential descent. The walls were formed out of the earth clay and were rugged and sharp. There was nothing inside the hole except for a wooden bench with a pile of rags at the foot of it. This was probably Sarcadui's bed. He felt terrible for his friend's humble lot in life. He didn't know if he should apologize for her situation or if he should compliment the way the rags brought out the color of the dirt ground.

Robbie noticed a piece of rock sitting at the top of the steps with its base half covering the opening. Tied around the base of the rock were several ropes, slack only on one end. Sarcadui grabbed the ropes and, with a grunt and a strong heave, pulled the rock across the opening.

The covering cast a thick, inky darkness inside the hole.

"Follow my voice," said Sarcadui, casually.

He followed her to the other side of the hole where he heard stones and rocks scraping against each other. Then a faint beam of light shone through a crack that opened where a wall had just been. Sarcadui had opened a hidden door in the wall that led down several more stairs into another room where a family of four was lighting several sconces. Now it felt more like a large cavern rather than a dank cell, with the ceiling several feet higher, and with so much more open space. As Sarcadui pulled the rock shut sealing the wall back up, other doors opened up from all along the walls and other people invited themselves in. The friendly intruders just strolled around, most of them lying down on the hard dirt floor or curling up on a scattered bed to sleep. This seemed to be the usual custom. Other than sconces that lined the walls, beds were the only furniture throughout the cavern, spread apart in no certain order. Any more furniture would not have provided enough room for everyone to mosey in comfortably.

Sarcadui leaned up against an undressed wall and patted the spot next to her, inviting Robbie to sit with her. Hail ran over to Sarcadui and curled up in her lap.

"Sarcadui," said Hail, "can you tell a story?" This was not the same girl Robbie had met back in the cave, hissing at him and chasing him with a dagger.

"Not right now, sweetie. It's time to go to sleep."

The mention of sleep was very inviting. Until just then Robbie hadn't realized how tired he was from his eventful, albeit confusing, day. He leaned his head back. But he couldn't help but notice the eerie silence that had settled into the room. Many eyes nervously looked upward toward the ceiling.

At first Robbie couldn't hear anything. Then he thought he heard a long moment of clapping wind. But it slowly turned into shrieks and shrills, then heavy stomping on the ground above, mixed with rustling feet. Most of the people watched the ground shake violently overhead as shards of dirt fell from the earth onto their heads and in their faces. The screams were high-pitched and unearthly. They seemed to be coming from miles around. Robbie kept waiting for the ceiling to split, so violent was the cacophony above. Even through all this, some people somehow managed to sleep through the trauma.

"They come out every night," said Sarcadui to Robbie, who probably noticed the anxiety written all over his face. "They ravage the entire island." He looked at her to explain more. "They are ghosts who ensure there is no one living in these lands. If they find someone from our town who is unable to endure their torture, it'll lead them to the rest of us. This is why we take curfew so seriously."

"Why are they looking for you?" Robbie asked.

"As long as there is life on the island, there will be daylight. But once everyone is dead then the light will be extinguished, then the ghosts will have the freedom to come out at all times. The darkness always permits them to come out. People from our town get caught all the time; but luckily only far away from here. Langly is searched almost every night, but they haven't discovered us underground yet."

The tumult grew louder, menacing and sadistic. Chills went down Robbie's spine at the thought of supernatural beings reaping havoc mere feet above his head. Robbie glanced at a small family huddled together waiting out the terror. The youngest child seemed to have never grown used to this nightly routine as the mother did her best to calm him down. Robbie wasn't sure if he was comfortable with her smothering the boy's face with a towel whenever he was about to cry out loud.

When the horrific noise reached its climax Hail crawled from Sarcadui's lap into Robbie's and squeezed his neck tightly. But she didn't do this out of fear; she wasn't trembling or whimpering. This was just another night underground to her. She crawled into his lap because she trusted and liked him. And to her, he was a savior. But sill, some parental instinct kicked in and convinced Robbie that she was scared. He felt the need to comfort her and protect her. He covered her up with his bundled jacket and said to Sarcadui, "Tell me more about the ocean."

This brought a smile to Sarcadui's face and she seemed to find comfort in speaking of something so lovely. "The ocean is the most beautiful place anyone has ever seen. The water is like a window into another world. You can actually see through it all the way down to the bottom. And oh! It's filled with such beauty like you've never imagined."

Hail melted into a sweet slumber in Robbie's arms.

"Tell me more," urged Robbie, now more in the interest of satisfying his own curiosity.

When Sarcadui spoke it was as if the barbarity up above no longer existed, even though the ghosts had not quieted. At several points the rocks that covered up the holes shook so violently that it seemed like the ghosts were hammering away at them trying to get inside.

Sarcadui drew his attention away from these horrific moments by speaking more about the ocean. "When the waves crash on the shore, it sounds like thousands of little crystals being poured out in abundance. And the scent that comes from the sea breeze is like a delicious salt that flavors the air with just the right amount of seasoning."

"What's beyond the ocean?" asked Robbie.

"Memories," said Sarcadui as she drifted off to sleep. "Someone's memories long lost and forgotten."

Robbie held Hail close as he waited for the screams to subside, but he fell asleep long before the ghosts left.

CHAPTER 7

"Hey!" yelled a high-pitched voice, waking Robbie from a deep sleep. "Are you goin' home or are you stayin' here for the night?"

Robbie shook his head and rubbed the crick out of his neck, to little avail. It took a few seconds for things to grow into focus and slowly he began to recognize the tables and packing boxes all around him. Gone were the walls of earth clay and huddled families scattered about. Here, there was no fear of ghosts breaking in to attack him.

Like a dripping faucet filling his brain with one memory at a time he recalled the terrible events that took place at work earlier that day. A more naïve Robbie had started the day off with excitement over it being his eleventh anniversary as an editor at CipherMill. And how was he congratulated? He was terminated for all of his hard work and dedication. He could have done without that memory. He preferred to take his chances with the sharp-toothed dinosaur back in the jungle.

When his eyes fully adjusted to his surroundings he looked in the direction where the voice had come from. He saw one of the security guards standing at the entrance to the warehouse where Robbie had come in.

"I'm not supposed to let you stay here, but if your wife dumped you I can hook you up with a place to stay," offered the security guard jovially. His echo bounced off the walls in the large warehouse.

Robbie shook his head and began to push himself out of the box, but an unexpected pain shot through his right hand as he pressed down on the rim of the box. He jolted and looked at his hand and saw that there was a gash in the shape of a bite mark on his thumb. Dry blood caked over the open wound where a chunk of flesh had been ripped off.

Seeing the wound caused him to let out an involuntary gasp. He remembered the pain Hail had inflicted on him while she was trying to drown him.

He stood up without adding pressure to his wound. He was woozy from being scrunched up for… "What time is it?" he asked.

"What?" asked the security guard from across the warehouse.

Robbie cleared his throat of phlegm and fought to speak up over the droning hum of the A/C. "What time is it?"

"It's nine thirty-four," replied the security guard.

Robbie had entered the warehouse at seven-thirty.

"I usually close up earlier than this though. But my partner Larry isn't here, so I've been covering all his closing duties."

Robbie had never been this late coming home from work in the eighteen years they'd been married. What was he going to tell Rosalynn? "Sorry I'm late, hon. After I was fired I decided to flirt with the law and hack into my boss' files."

Speaking of, why hadn't he heard from Don? He was supposed to call Robbie if he saw anyone coming in.

As Robbie walked toward the door he pulled his phone out of his left pocket to see if he had called. He had set his phone to silent so it wouldn't give away his position. What a lousy secret agent he would have made. His phone showed ten missed calls and five voice mail messages.

"You okay? Looks like you've had enough to drink," said the gangly security guard whose nametag read Steve. He was a cheery black man whose uniform hung on him like loose rags. Robbie almost felt bad for not recognizing him.

"That's not it," said Robbie dismissively.

"Okay," Steve guffawed. "But if they find cans and bottles around here, I'm not takin' the blame."

"My keys are in 202. Is it open?" Robbie needed to at least pretend he still worked there to avoid all suspicion.

"Yeah, it's still open. I lock all the doors just before I leave."

Robbie thanked him and walked through the hallway, which led through all the downstairs offices. Once free he retrieved his phone from his pocket and listened to his voice mail. The first two were from Don. "Hey, Robbie, you've been in there for a while. Are you coming out? The coast is clear. Over." The next one was similar. In it, Don said that he was heading home, and told Robbie to call him with the "you-know-what information."

Robbie stopped by the bathroom on his way out of the lobby. He washed the blood off his hand and splashed cold water on his face as he searched himself for any other abnormalities. There seemed to be no more cuts or bruises and his suit was perfectly dry and intact. He was surprised that he didn't reek something fierce. Everything had seemed so real to him. His feet were sore but he chalked that up to his being scrunched up in a box for two hours. He just needed to get the blood flowing again.

The next three messages, which he listed to on speakerphone while he washed himself up, were from Rosalynn. She asked if he was all right and if he was going to be home for dinner. She had a more panicked voice in the next two messages saying that she's got leftovers in the fridge for him and she hopes he's all right and for him to please call her as soon as he can.

Once he determined he was presentable he stole away to his car still parked across the street behind the bar. When he was on the freeway he called Rosalynn back saying that he'd be home soon. He was careful to dodge any questions or go into detail about anything. He hadn't yet made up his mind about what to tell her. He hadn't even figured out what to believe himself.

As his car cruised steadily along the freeway, he was having trouble differentiating between his nightmare at work and the wonderful hallucination he had had about... what was it called? Revelon? No, Reveloin, with an O-I.

His memories for the moment seemed to blend together. At one point he considered the possibility that he might be suffering a stroke, but he brushed that thought aside. When he finally was able to separate fantasy from reality he couldn't comprehend what had infused such a bizarre dream. Was it possible for someone to have a dream filled with such vivid detail that lasted for so long? He hadn't eaten lunch that day, and his stomach felt fine, so it wasn't indigestion.

Robbie had read online somewhere that dreams only last in very small segments of 10 to 15 seconds. There was no way in the world his brain could have projected that jarring amount of detail, accompanied with such realistic sounds and smells in just seconds. The probability of that happening had to have been beyond impossible. He thought hard about where – or how – his mind could have pulled such detailed information. Sure Robbie had had an overactive imagination as a child. In fact, he spent most of his childhood locked up in his room just dreaming things up. And most of his adventures did take place in the jungle... but could it have been Reveloin? The name hardly struck him as familiar. He didn't think about his childhood often.

Nonetheless, it couldn't have been a dream if he had Hail's bite mark on his hand to show for it. He certainly didn't receive the wound *before* going into the warehouse. Or maybe a rat bit him just as he dreamed Hail did it? He remembered when he was a kid he would have dreams that mirrored events happening in real life. He recalled feeling warm and snug in many dreams, but in reality, he was leaking warm urine all over his legs and bed sheets that masqueraded as Jacuzzi water, or a heating pad or warm quicksand, and all the while he was helpless to consciously cut off the flow. This had to be the same kind of situation.

Besides, if he *had* transmitted Hail's bite mark between worlds, surely other results from his travels would have been evident. For instance, he had taken his suit jacket off during the party in the dream. How was it that he still had it on him when he woke up? Besides that, his clothes would have been muddy and absolutely ruined after trekking for so long through the jungle. Plus, he would have smelled terrible after spending the night underground without a shower. But he didn't. He still smelled like the office with a tiny whiff of aftershave still just barely clinging to him.

This was all very confusing and Robbie concluded that he didn't know much of anything at the moment. But there was one thing he knew for sure: He loved that dream. He would give anything to return to it again and be amongst the people he had befriended. Especially – what was her name? Sardooky? And Hail, sweet Hail! *The little brat*, Robbie smiled.

When he got home, Jeremy, their seven-year-old, was in the living room in his *Cars* pajamas watching TV. Taylor was up in her room either doing her homework or talking on the phone. Rosalynn met him at the kitchen entry, evidently leaving her book, which was sitting open-faced on the kitchen table. She was already showered and dressed for bed. When she met Robbie, a relieved smile came to her face.

"Where have you been?" she asked, concernedly. "What happened?" But before giving him a chance to answer, she insisted, "Here, sit down and I'll heat up some leftovers. We ate without you because we didn't know how long you'd be. I hope that's okay. But we saved some pasta for you. Stuffed shells."

"Thanks," Robbie managed, sitting down at the table, reclaiming his appetite.

Rosalynn took a plate of prepared food out of the fridge and placed it in the microwave. She was genuinely concerned for

Robbie. She sat down in the chair next to him and rubbed his back. Then, noticing his hand for the first time she asked in shock, "What happened?"

"I don't know," Robbie answered honestly. He had tried coming up with a believable story on the way home, but he just wasn't comfortable lying to his wife. But he wasn't any more comfortable with telling the bizarre truth, either.

Rosalynn fetched the First Aid kit and wrapped his hand up in a bandage while she waited for his food to finish cooking. "You don't get a wound like this and not know how it happened. It looks like a bite mark," she scolded.

"It is," said Robbie. "But I honestly don't know how I got it. I fell asleep in the... office. And when I woke up, I was bleeding."

"That's the weirdest thing I've ever heard you say," said Rosalynn, not buying it.

"No, no. It's true," said Robbie defensively. "That's why I'm late coming home. Because I fell asleep. Hard, obviously. And I had the most bizarre... no, the most incredible dream ever! I was on this island and this little girl was chasing me through some caves and she tried to drown me. That's when she bit me. Then we saw a dinosaur – an actual real dinosaur, Rosalynn. Isn't that crazy?" He had used the word 'crazy' the same way one might use the word 'cool.' But Rosalynn took it for its literal meaning.

"Yes, it is. Honey, I think you need to relax for a little bit. What do you want to drink?"

"Milk, please. But I'm telling you, I know it sounds ridiculous, and that I'm probably just having a breakdown, but it almost seemed more real than sitting here talking to you."

"Why would you be having a breakdown?" asked Rosalynn as she fetched the milk. "We're about to leave for Hawaii in a couple of days and you don't have to be back at work for two weeks."

Robbie steeled his resolve. "It'll be longer than two weeks before I have to be back," he said. "I got fired."

"Wha...? What happened?" asked Rosalynn incredulously.

"More cut backs. Kurt said he's only keeping two people onboard this time. I'm sorry. We've got to cancel Hawaii."

"That's fine," said Rosalynn, sympathetically. "Are you all right? No, obviously you're not. You're losing it already, talking about dinosaurs and child cannibals."

"And ghosts. I didn't even tell you about the ghosts."

Keeping the conversation at an adult level, Rosalynn said, "If you were fired today, then how did you fall asleep at work? Or were you fired *because* you fell asleep? I know you were up late last night, and staying up late is getting harder for you..."

"No, I didn't fall asleep on the job. I don't know. It's kind of weird, actually. I had to... er, print up some papers..." that's when Robbie remembered he had forgotten the list. He panicked internally for a second, but shook it off. He'd get them tomorrow.

"You're not making any sense, Robbie."

"I know. This is all really weird to me too, but I'm telling the honest truth. This dream, it almost reminded me of some world I used to make up as a kid, but I know it wasn't. It was different somehow..." his voice trailed off.

"We should talk about this tomorrow after you get some sleep."

"You're right. I'm probably just freaking out."

"I'll make the flight and hotel cancellations in the morning." She said it casually, but the reality of it stung Robbie in the heart and he nearly winced.

"After eleven years, this is the thanks I get. What a great job I had. I work and work and work, bending over backwards for this company and this is the thanks they show me!"

"Don't yell. You'll scare the kids."

Robbie shook his head as Rosalynn retrieved his plate from the beeping microwave and placed it in front of him. She sat in the chair next to him.

As Robbie ate his reheated shells Jeremy came into the kitchen for a cup of water. As he filled his cup up in the sink Robbie asked him how his day was. Jeremy just shrugged and said it was okay.

"Did you learn anything in school today?" asked Robbie.

Jeremy shrugged again and said no.

"Good news, buddy. You don't have to pack your clothes. I know you hate packing."

"Why not?"

"Well, we're not going to Hawaii anymore. We're staying home, so maybe we can hang out this weekend. Maybe I can take you to the arcade," Robbie tried.

"Okay," mumbled Jeremy.

"Did you find your book, sweetie?" asked Rosalynn, pulling her son in for a side hug.

"Yeah, it was under the couch."

"Good. Go get it. You can read in bed for ten minutes then it's lights out."

"Okay."

"I'll be up there in a little while to tuck you in."

"Why does he talk to you and not me?" Robbie asked when Jeremy left the kitchen.

"Because I'm his mommy. You guys have nothing in common yet." Actually they both knew the truth was that Robbie had been too preoccupied with himself and work, but he could tell she didn't feel like having that conversation again. At least not now.

In the shower he examined his body once more. The steam from the water exposed red marks lashed across his arms and legs that stung under the pressure of the shower. He would have to wear long sleeves to bed to hide them from Rosalynn. He would just have to turn the fan on high so he didn't overheat.

In bed, Robbie's mind drifted off to the wonderful dream he had had in the warehouse. He thought about Sarcadui and the mysterious jungle and Hail whom he loved holding so close as though she were his own.

But the more Robbie thought about it, the more he was convinced that it was no dream at all. Something had happened to him on his way from the bar to the warehouse. Something gave him the ability to be somewhere else. He was sure he knew how to get back to Reveloin.

He expected – and hoped – that he would return to that mysterious jungle island once he was asleep.

CHAPTER 8

Robbie didn't have any dreams about Reveloin that night. Instead he slept fitfully because reality continually trumped fantasy. He woke up every hour tormented with the memory of getting fired. Leaving the papers in the printer added pain to his reflections.

When morning finally came and the alarm went off, Robbie dragged himself downstairs. He had no idea what he would do on the first day as an unemployed citizen.

"What are you going to do today?" asked Rosalynn. She was about to step outside with the kids, who were geared up for school.

"Probably start looking for jobs," said Robbie, wishing more than ever that he had grabbed the list from the printer. *Two hundred publishers*. That's a lot of time that could have been saved job searching.

After Rosalynn and the kids left for school, Robbie convinced himself that he just needed to get back to the warehouse and grab those papers. In all reality they were probably still sitting in the printer. The worst-case scenario was that someone tossed them aside and all he had to do was stroll in like an employee from upstairs, grab the list, and leave.

On his way to the place of his previous employment Robbie pondered the many reasons why he didn't go back to Reveloin in his sleep. But no viable answers came to mind. Even as he tried to think logically about it all, he couldn't keep his mind from gravitating back to Sarcadui – not Sardooki like he had thought. He missed her; he needed to see her again.

Flying on the freeway, he thought about all the things that could have beckoned him to Reveloin. He recalled going into the warehouse. It was empty; no one was around. Then he recalled the box he had crawled into in order to hide from whoever was entering the warehouse.

That's it! The box had to be some sort of portal that transported him to some other dimension!

He condemned himself for actually believing this ludicrous mess. It sounded like one of Jeremy's Japanese cartoons. Nonetheless, sleeping wasn't the answer to getting back, so it wouldn't hurt to try sitting in that box again. Now he would have to inconspicuously grab the list and find the box he sat in last night and walk out with both. A few sheets of paper, and a cardboard box. It's not like he was robbing a bank.

He parked a block away from CipherMill and walked toward the back of the building, reminding him of when all the employees had to park in the back three years ago while they did construction to the front of the building. The sliding garage door was open for trucks to back into. He casually walked in, hoping that he looked familiar enough not to be bothered. The warehouse was bustling with blue-collar workers shipping and receiving packages that rode in on a winding conveyer belt and performing business as usual.

He strode to the printer and his heart leapt when he saw a manila folder titled "Kurt, 202" followed by a question mark. Robbie swiped up the folder casually and nodded to a woman glancing toward him.

Task one, check. Now, for the box.

He looked around the warehouse but there were no empty boxes lying around. Robbie tried to recall how the box was marked, but that was the last thing he thought to take note of as he jumped in it last night to evade any unwanted eyes.

In a far corner he found a pile of folded-up boxes stacked on top of each other. He walked over to them, realizing he was expiring his time, and took the top one for himself. He asked someone for some packing tape and he was directed toward a table. He grabbed the tape, assembled the box and set it down before him. But just before he stepped inside, he suddenly felt self-conscious; he realized that those around him had stopped their work to stare at him.

Robbie demurely smiled and apologized. He needed to be somewhere away from all these people. He picked up the box and walked off to some place where he could be alone to conduct his experiment.

Knowing no other immediate place that would provide privacy, Robbie, with box in hand, rushed outside – trying in vain to walk casually – through the open garage door and around the rarely visited back side of the building. There, he found the parking lot vacant except for a few scattered cars.

Once seeing that the coast was clear, Robbie sat the box down before him and stepped inside. Shivering with anticipation he could almost feel the cool trickling water rush past his ankles even before he sat down. He pushed his feet up against the edge and squatted down just as he had done before. This box was a bit smaller compared to the other one. But that was no matter; he didn't expect to have the same box as before. If that box could serve as a portal, why couldn't this one?

Once situated, Robbie closed his eyes.

CHAPTER 9

A gentle breeze blew across his face and he smiled. A bird chirped happily not far away. *I'm back*, thought Robbie. But when he opened his eyes his heart failed him. He was nowhere near the Arura Jungle; he was still sitting outside CipherMill Publishing House. The contrast of his mundane surroundings compared to the lush jungle where he expected to be sorely disappointed him.

Why couldn't he find his way back to the one place he so desperately wanted to be?

After re-contemplating his predicament for a moment, it dawned on him that it stood to reason that it would have to be the exact box he had gotten into the night before; *that* was the key. That particular box, for some reason, was his only chance of reuniting with Sarcadui.

But how was he ever going to find that exact box? He couldn't even begin to know how to identify it. Surely it had already been packed and shipped off by now. Or at the very least it had been stored away in some back room amongst thousands of other boxes just like it.

Robbie was teetering on the border of despair. He just had to think through every possible way of finding that box. Perhaps the security guard from last night – Steve, was it? – moved it. Or he could track down whoever opened the warehouse earlier that morning. These ideas gave Robbie back his hope.

Before trekking back inside he dropped the list off in his car, leaving the box behind. Then he swung around to the front of the building, praying he wouldn't run into Kurt or anyone who might mention to his boss he was there. The security guard's office was located in the lobby just behind the desk where one of the guards usually sat. The desk was empty. He knocked on the door but no one answered. He knocked again, louder, and the unmistakable voice of Steve yelled, "It's open!"

Sure enough Steve was at his desk reading a car magazine as Bob Marley played from an old stereo. The small room was a complete mess; empty carry-out boxes littered the desk, mops and brooms leaned against the walls in no particular order, and it smelled like milk had been left out for a week. Robbie wouldn't have been surprised if he saw a rat scamper across the floor. His nose itched from breathing in so much dust.

"It's the alcoholic!" exclaimed Steve. "My partner Larry is out for another week. His baby was born 'bout the time I found you passed out in the warehouse last night. He doesn't like you snobby office boys much, but when I tell him about last night, he'll definitely like *you*! Heck, that would have been the most excitement he'd have seen 'round here. It's dumb that his baby had to be born. No matter, though. He died halfway outta the womb."

Robbie was struck dumb by the man's insensitivity. "That's awful," he said.

Steve waved his hand in a dismissive manner and explained how Larry didn't even want the baby to begin with. The mom wasn't even his wife.

As Steve rambled on, Robbie was studying a monitor that sat on a desk behind the emotionally-challenged security guard. It was playing a surveillance video and the more Robbie studied it, the more familiar the image became to him. It was a surveillance shot of the warehouse! Disregarding Steve's jabbering, Robbie pointed to the screen and asked, "Does that camera run all night?"

Steve turned to look at the monitor then back at Robbie with a smirk. "Oh, I see. You stumbled into the warehouse last night with a woman and you want to cover the tracks from your wife! Man, you *was* drunk! And stupid! You shouldn't ever cheat on your woman!"

Robbie, irritated, shook his head, and cut to the chase. "I need to know if you did anything to that box I was in last night."

Steve thought about it. How hard would that have been to remember, Robbie wondered.

"No, I didn't do anything to it, no," said Steve.

"Okay. Can I see this morning's footage?"

"Of course you can. But don't you mean last night's footage?"

Robbie was about to argue with him but realized that if he watched last night's tape, he could see himself disappear and stick a piece in the puzzle of this great mystery. "Yeah, go ahead and put in last night's footage," he agreed.

Steve turned around and replaced the current disc with one from a case. Somehow Robbie expected it to be recorded on a VHS tape because it had been so long since he had seen a surveillance recording. As he fumbled with the switches Steve spoke as though this were a shining moment for him.

"They didn't want a surveillance camera in the warehouse, but I insisted that one be put up because a lot of junk goes on in there, if you know what I mean." Robbie didn't. "So I says to them, if you're not goin' to put one up, then I'm adding that to a list of my projects, 'cause *I* don't want to get the rap if they find some drugs lying around or whatnot. What time did you stumble in last night?"

"Seven-thirty."

Steve continued talking as he flipped through the frames on the screen. "Man, that's why I accused you of drinkin' last night 'cause if they found the bottles on my time, they'd have me shipped outta here so fast K-Mart wouldn't even hire me. That's what I hear happen' to the last guy anyway. So that's why I installed this camera so I don't get busted for nothin' I didn't do."

When he was done playing with the switches on the monitor, Steve rolled his chair away from the screen and joked, "Should I get us some popcorn?" to which Robbie humored him with a smile. *No, just show me the stupid video so I can get out of here.*

The video showed a wide shot of the warehouse. Near the top of the screen was the box resting near the computer. In the video Robbie went straight to the computer and began typing on the keyboard. The printer started spilling out paper ever so slowly, and Robbie stood there tapping his foot. Then he looked toward the entrance and quickly dove into the box next to him, pulling the flaps down over his head.

When no one came in, Robbie sat up and rested his back against the box.

Leaning with his arms on the desk, Robbie braced himself for Steve's reaction for when he disappeared. He planned on blaming it on a technical glitch. As they watched, Robbie found himself inching closer and closer toward the monitor staring intently at the screen. But so far, nothing was happening in the video except that Robbie just looked like he had fallen into a deep sleep inside the box.

"Are you asleep in that thing?" asked Steve.

"Yeah."

"That's so weird."

"What's weird?"

"Your head just stays up like that when you sleep. If I were sleeping like that, my head would be rolling all over the place like a rag doll. It'd probably just snap right off."

It was true. Robbie's head was held up perfectly as though he were awake and had control of it. Robbie guessed that a part of him wasn't asleep after all. He was like a mannequin; he never moved once, not even to shift his position.

"So where's the girl?" asked Steve.

"What girl?"

"Man, I thought we was goin' to get to watch one of them dirty shows! You mean to tell me you didn't bring no girl down there with you?"

Robbie ignored him and asked him to speed through. He wished he could see what really caused the injury to his hand, but unfortunately his hands were inside the box. Still, he didn't see any rats scamper across the floor or any other possible causes to his injury.

He did manage to catch the print on the side of the box, which read, "This Side In" accompanied by an arrow pointing up toward the opening. Didn't most boxes read "This Side Up"?

"You are one sound sleeper," said Steve. "What exactly are we watchin' for anyways?"

Realizing that his body was not going to disappear, Robbie answered, "I need to see who moved the box."

"Well why didn't you say so?" said Steve. "I could've told you that a long time ago instead of sittin' here watchin' you waste your lazy life away in that thing."

"So are you going to answer me or give me a lecture?"

"I oughta lecture you, but you'd rather know where that box is so I'll tell you. They packed that sucker up and shipped it off to Des Moines firs' thing this mornin' far's I know." Geesh, a little sensitivity could have been in order.

"Thanks for your help, Steve," Robbie said, crestfallen. Then he excused himself from the room, relieved at least, for the fresh air.

Exiting the building, Robbie tried to convince himself that the box was a one-time thing; that now his turn was up. No seconds. Still, he couldn't help but resent that fact.

But just as he was about to round a corner of the building he heard Kurt's voice, along with footsteps approaching. Robbie turned as if spun around by some invisible force and ran toward the other end of the building, stolen documents in hand. He had no idea if Kurt had seen him or not. He paused, bent down, and breathed for a minute. He decided he would just walk around toward the back of the building to get back to his car in order to avoid any more close calls. He chuckled to himself at the thought of Kurt seeing a grown man wildly running away from him.

As he walked through the back alley, the dumpster full of boxes caught his eye. Many of the discarded boxes had company labels printed on them, but one in particular was blank except for the words "This Side." Another box lay on top of it censoring the final word.

Vowing to just look at that one, Robbie walked toward the dumpster. The box was lying on its side next to the full bin. A gust of wind must have knocked the top layer of boxes off onto the street. Trash from the non-recyclable bin was gently exploring the street.

Robbie removed the veiling box and sure enough there were the bold words, "This Side In" in red and a black arrow pointing up, just like in the video.

Robbie stashed the box in the back seat of his Honda.

Now that he had the answer to getting back to Sarcadui, he decided to test his luck and see if anyone was home.

An empty house would give him the freedom to try out the box. And the odds were in his favor: Rosalynn had said she'd be gone all day.

Part II: The Box

CHAPTER 10

Not believing his luck, Robbie pulled into an empty driveway. He couldn't suppress his growing excitement as he dragged the box into the house and hauled it upstairs to the bedroom. He then laid it on the floor next to his side of the bed and stepped inside it. Tremors of excitement exploded in his stomach as he readied himself to be transported back to the island with Sarcadui.

But just before he could squat down, he heard the front door open and close and Rosalynn called out, "Robbie? Are you home?"

Robbie was irritable at his wife for coming home so soon. Regardless, he responded from the bedroom, "Yeah, I'm up here!"

He quickly tried to find a place to hide the box so he wouldn't have to explain it, or lie about it. Rosalynn was heading upstairs, so in a last-ditch effort he tossed the box into the closet just as she walked into the bedroom. "Hey, what are you doing?" she asked, not accusingly.

"Just taking a quick break. How are you?" Robbie asked walking toward her, quickly taking the focus of the conversation off of himself.

"I'm okay. Look, I'm really sorry about what happened to you yesterday," said Rosalynn. "I know I probably didn't sound very sympathetic, but I just wanted to say that I really am sorry." She must have assumed he was mad at her.

"It's not your fault, and I promise I'll make everything right. I'll get a job real soon; you'll see," Robbie answered, thinking of the glowing list of publishers still sitting in the passenger seat of his car.

Rosalynn wrapped her arms around him and said, "Do you think you could find a job in California?"

"I'll try." Then they briefly kissed. "You still want to move back there after all these years?" Robbie asked.

"Of course I do. It's where we met. And I'd love for the kids to see it, plus my family's there. Don't pretend you're against the idea all of a sudden."

"I'm not," said Robbie. In truth Robbie *had* always wanted to move back down, and he really did like her family, but there just hadn't been a good opportunity to uproot the family again.

"I have something for you that I was going to show you tonight when you got home," said Rosalynn.

She led him over to the edge of the bed and told him to sit down then to close his eyes. He obeyed. She said jubilantly, "I'll be right back."

Robbie heard her run out of the room. Then, in less than a minute he heard her bare feet shuffle back into the room across the carpet toward him.

"Okay, open up," said Rosalynn.

He opened his eyes and dully noted, "It's our journal."

She was holding it out in front of her with a wide grin on her face. About four years ago they had agreed to start documenting pivotal moments of their marriage in this journal. The goal was to write back and forth to each other, taking turns. At first they exchanged notes about every other day, but it wasn't long before that turned into once a month and then every other. Soon life got in the way and they had forgotten about the journal and inevitably it was lost. He hadn't seen that multi-colored striped journal in two years.

"I was just going to write you an apology note," said Rosalynn. "But I remembered this and I wanted to find it last night before coming to bed. Of all places, I found it in the hallway closet underneath the wrapping paper. I didn't get to write it till this morning, but here you go."

Rosalynn handed him the journal and he flipped to the last used page. He found a very sympathetic note about yesterday's events. He could tell that Rosalynn really felt like she had not handled the situation well, which honestly never even crossed his mind. *Men are from Mars,* he thought.

Robbie, I know you took a hard fall yesterday. I can't imagine the pain and anger you must be feeling, not to mention the fears and worries you must be dealing with. But if it's any consolation, please know that you don't have to worry that you have disappointed me in any way. You haven't. You are still my husband and our children's father. Nothing in the world could make me prouder. You are dedicated to your family, and you do all you can to keep us together. I love you more than you'll ever be able to imagine. Oh yeah, I almost forgot. You're still hot!

When he was finished, he looked up at Rosalynn with a deep feeling of sentiment and for a moment he almost forgot about the box.

"Thank you, hon," he said.

"I love you," responded Rosalynn, sitting on his lap and kissing him.

"What time do the kids get picked up from school?" asked Robbie.

"Much later."

CHAPTER 11

The Lake household functioned rather routinely that night as the crickets chirped their melodious spring tune in the halcyon yard. The upstairs windows were all lit up as everyone was getting ready to turn in for the night. Jeremy was in his room reading manga and Taylor was on the phone in the bathroom blabbering away as she readied herself for bed. Robbie and Rosalynn were in their room down the hall from the kids.

"How was your first day back on the unemployment field?" asked Rosalynn as she pulled the sheets back from the head of the bed.

"Fantastic," Robbie responded demurely as he stepped into the shower. He observed that the scratch marks on his arms and legs were already beginning to heal, but his thumb still hurt something fierce.

Robbie loved that he could talk with his wife from the shower of their small bathroom while she was in bed. They had lived in the two-story track house for seven years. Washington State was not on their list of moving choices when they were struggling in L.A. where he had taken a dead-end job. But when CipherMill Publishing House of Seattle offered him a position to work for them eleven years ago, he knew he couldn't pass the opportunity up. So with a five-year-old in tow, the young family packed their bags and waved goodbye to their friends and family. Despite all the protests from cynical family members warning them about the constant Northwest rain, the truth turned out that Washington, at worst, was only misty most of the year. Rosalynn worked full time as a secretary for a pediatrician while Taylor spent her days in daycare. That would become their living situation for three years until Robbie was promoted to the editing position he currently held, and just in time for the arrival of their second child.

They continued to chitchat while Robbie showered, swapping ideas about where he should look for work.

After throwing on his sweats, Robbie crawled into bed next to his wife and switched off the light on his nightstand. "Why are you wearing sweats?" asked Rosalynn. "Are you cold?"

"Yeah," Robbie lied. He was already sweltering. But that was better than her finding his red scratch-marks. "I think I'm coming down with a cold or something," he added, adding a sniffle for effect.

They cuddled in the dark for a minute before Robbie popped the question that he had asked repeatedly for the last year and a half. "What am I going to do with that girl? It feels like every time I try to get close to her she only pushes me further away. Why doesn't she like me anymore?" They had had another fight at dinner, so Taylor was fresh on his mind.

"Because she's growing up," commented Rosalynn.

"But when will she grow *out* of growing up?" Robbie pouted.

"If she's anything like us, never." She kissed him and they both pulled the covers up to fall into sleeping positions.

A few minutes later Rosalynn woke Robbie up and said that he needed to talk to Taylor. Rosalynn was still in the habit of checking on the kids after they had gone to sleep. "What's wrong?" Robbie asked, groggily.

"She's in her room crying. She won't talk to me. Her heart is broken."

Yes! Robbie's heart swelled with happiness. Still, this was a day he had been dreading since Taylor was a little girl – her first real broken heart. When she was just six her best friend Rory moved away and she suffered a mild depression. Fortunately Daddy was able to come to the rescue with a stuffed animal from the thrift store and an evening at the miniature golf course. Somehow Robbie didn't think declaring family night would solve her problems this time. That obviously didn't work now. But now that the real thing had arrived, he couldn't be happier. It couldn't have come at a better time in their disbanding relationship.

Once Rosalynn reminded him that her boyfriend's name was Dwayne, not Wayne, Robbie forced himself out of bed and down the hallway to Taylor's room. This was the opportunity to connect with her that he was looking for. He was indebted to Rosalynn for bringing this to his attention and letting him take the reins on it.

He tapped on the door but there was no answer. He invited himself in and he saw Taylor sitting up on her bed leaning against the wall with her face buried in between her knees.

"Honey?" asked Robbie. "Are you okay?"

"Go away," pleaded Taylor, apparently exhausted from all the spilt tears. He wondered if this was all because of what happened after her game the night before. No, this was more serious than just not being allowed to invite her boyfriend to dessert. It just wasn't like her to cry like this.

"Look, I just want you to know that we're all here for you," said Robbie, inching closer to her bed, feeling like he was borrowing a worn out line from some after school special.

"I don't care," Taylor pouted. Apparently she saw the connection as well.

He sat down on the edge of her bed and placed a hand on her bare foot. He took it as an invitation to stay when she didn't pull away. But now the hard part was trying to come up with something to say that would make her jump into his arms for one of those long-lost father/daughter moments he felt he didn't get enough of when she was younger. While he sat on the edge of her bed he stared at her walls covered with posters and adolescent paraphernalia and for a moment he was lost in a world of teenage vampires and drama in the school hallways.

Unable to come up with anything wise to say, he tried to summon up something on the spot. "Is there anything you want to talk to me about?"

Taylor sat there silently, holding to a vow of silence. Still, Robbie was determined to stick this through until they both shared a sappy laugh together.

But with exhaustion weighing in he cut to the chase and asked, "What's wrong?"

"I'm not telling you what's wrong," resolved Taylor, "So you can just sit there all you want but I'm not telling you anything; it's none of your business."

Luckily Robbie already had the inside scoop. He recalled Rosalynn's comment about Taylor's broken heart.

"You know, I broke up with your mom for a couple of months while we were dating, but we still got married." Robbie cringed at his final word and shook his head disapprovingly at himself. *Marriage* was the last thing he wanted to put into this hopelessly romantic mind.

"That's you and Mom. You're way different than me and Dwayne."

You got that *right*, thought Robbie.

"Just leave me alone," Taylor implored.

"Maybe he just wasn't the right one for you," Robbie tried.

Taylor flung herself from her bed with a loud huff of frustration, stomped across the room and perched herself on her spinning chair. She buried her face in her arms atop her desk. "He didn't break up with me. We're still together!"

Disheartened that she was still together with that sleazebag, Robbie now found himself at a loss as to what might be bothering his daughter. So he tried to recount her situation and reaffirm her feelings.

"So you and Dwayne are still together, but you have a broken heart..." He said this as though trying to fit two pieces of a puzzle together.

"What do you care? It's not your life."

He moved in to hug her, albeit a little too prematurely, and Taylor pushed him away and told him again to leave her alone. Worn out, he finally conceded and left her room, closing the door behind him. He wasn't going to get anywhere with her tonight.

Maybe he should be taking notes about how *not* to father a daughter. Right, then he could make it into a book, have CipherMill publish it, become an instant star, get his job back and spend thousands of dollars on buying back Taylor's happiness. With all that money he could spend all the time he wanted in the box with Sarcadui and...

Sarcadui!

Standing in the dark hallway, his stomach grew tingly as he remembered the box.

Reenergized, he snuck into the master bedroom where Rosalynn was breathing rhythmically. Quietly and meticulously he retrieved the box from the closet where he had stashed it earlier that afternoon. He made sure all the bedroom doors were closed, then he snuck downstairs with the box and entered the living room. Walking in the dark he bumped his knee on the corner of the coffee table knocking his cell phone, which he had placed there earlier, against an empty drinking glass. He froze, hoping he didn't wake anyone up. When all was still, he swung around to the back of the couch and set the box down, where no one would see him if they happened into the living room. On the other side of him was the sliding back door that opened to the yard.

He stepped into the box and sat down and closed his eyes.

He woke up feeling stiff and sore all over, having slept on the hard dirt floor leaning against the sharp wall all night. He felt like he was missing something from his arms. What had he been holding when he drifted off to sleep?

Hail! She was gone.

CHAPTER 12

Where was Hail? And Sarcadui was nowhere to be seen. The entire underground house was empty! The room had also grown significantly smaller; all the corridors leading to the other rooms were closed. And his clothes – he was no longer wearing the same dress clothes he had been wearing when he fell asleep. No suit, no tie. Now he was in long baggy sweats. And socks, of all things. Good thing, though, because he was shivering from the damp underground.

Light shone through the opening he had come into the cavern from, and Robbie made his way to it. He climbed up the stairs, walked through Sarcadui's room, and climbed the next few steps which took him aboveground and was pleased to see that people were up and about. It looked to be about noontime and everyone was having lunch. It took a minute for his eyes to adjust to the sharp sunlight.

Many people sat scattered around breaking and eating bread that almost looked stale. They were all back to wearing the same dry cloaks that they had been wearing when he first arrived. Some of the children were huddled in small groups playing games, which required them to strategically move their sticks or stones across lines they had meticulously drawn in the dirt.

When one of the elderly men spotted Robbie, he grinned a wide toothless grin and hollered that Robbie was back. This grabbed everyone's attention and the town seemed to come alive at the news of his arrival. Robbie was glad to see them all, but his knees nearly buckled when he saw Sarcadui gallantly strolling through the crowd to greet him with Hail in tow.

"Robbie," Hail shrieked, running up to him. "You're back!" She jumped up into his arms and he gave her a big squeeze. Her heartfelt enthusiasm moved him beyond words. Sarcadui strode up to him and kissed him on the cheek, which caused him to gush. As glad as he was to see her, he couldn't figure out why she was so excited to see him after just one night.

"Where did you go?" asked Hail, deeply concerned. "I woke up the other morning and you weren't there."

"Now Hail, that's not our business," scolded Sarcadui.

"No, it's okay," said Robbie. "I..." then he realized that Hail had said the *other* morning, and he asked, "How long was I gone?"

"For four days," said an older man walking up to them. "And you have no idea where you went off to, right?" This almost sounded like an accusation.

Robbie admitted, "Yeah, I have no idea. One minute I was falling asleep underground and the next minute it's the middle of the day. It's not even like I just woke up; I just happened to arrive – in less clothing, as you can see – and you were all gone." He said this to a small group of people who were gathering around but he was mostly addressing Sarcadui and Hail in an attempt to explain his long absence.

"Well, you disappeared. And when you did, I fell and hit the ground because you were holding me," said Hail almost out of spite. "If you're holding something and you disappear, what happens to it?"

"Well, none the matter," interrupted Sarcadui. "At least you're back. And now we can start on our journey to the ocean."

"Let's get to it then," said Robbie, eager to get going.

The old man cleared his throat and Sarcadui introduced him to Robbie as Ames. There was a way about him that made Robbie feel like he could trust him. The lines on his face gently whispered traits of wisdom one could safely confide in.

When the two nodded at each other Ames said to Sarcadui, "So you're taking your new friend to the ocean? That's a dangerous trek."

"Wait," said Robbie. He needed to backtrack. "How do you know this much about what happened to me the other night? Can you tell me more?"

"I can try if Sarcadui doesn't run you off so soon," Ames responded, looking to her for approval.

She hesitated, and then gave him permission to proceed.

Ames led Robbie away from the small group of people and invited him to sit on a boulder, which was likely the door to an underground home. Robbie walked carefully so as not to hurt his socked feet on the stony dirt. He would have to borrow someone's sandals.

"So you've got questions about this place, huh?" inquired Ames.

"Plenty. No disrespect to Sarcadui, but I think she's too connected here to give me real answers. To tell the truth, I don't even know where to begin," said Robbie feeling like Ames might prove to be a worthy portal of information.

"Questions are like food. No matter which order you ask them, they'll all be digested the same way," said Ames with a smirk.

"Let's start with this whole disappearing thing," suggested Robbie. "Is it normal for people to just up and disappear from this island?"

"Not everyone can just disappear in a moment's notice. But now you're back, so we know—"

"I'm sorry," interrupted Robbie. "But everyone seems to think that I've returned, like I've been here before."

"But you *were* here just a few days ago," Ames replied. "You confessed that yourself. Besides, *I* even saw you the other day."

"I know I was. But even then, when I first arrived, everyone, especially Hail and Sarcadui, kept insisting that I'd *returned.* And I have no memory of ever being here before yester – four days ago."

Ames crossed his arms, and after a moment, said, "I don't know how to answer that. But at least we know that your disappearing isn't anything permanent at this point. All I can say is that something from some other world called you away from here. But you have no memory of any place else?"

Robbie affirmed him.

"Huh," said Ames, perplexed. He stoked the rough whiskers on his chin as he thought. "So the only other possibility is that you for some reason get erased from time and space completely."

"Will it happen again?" asked Robbie, not wanting to be taken from Sarcadui or Hail and fearing that he might disappear forever.

"I don't see why not. If you were called out by another world, then that world clearly has mastery over you. If it does happen again, you need to do everything you can to cut strings from that place if you ever want to come back here undisturbed. On the other hand, if it's the case where you're just vanishing entirely, then you need to figure out what you can do here to stop it from happening again." Robbie took a mental note of this while Ames eyed him carefully. He continued, "Just don't forget about us when you're gone. You say Sarcadui's taking you to the ocean, huh?"

"So she mentioned."

"That's good. Really good. How did she talk you into going?"

"She didn't have to do much convincing. I'm happy to go with her." As foolish as he felt, Robbie couldn't stop the smile from breaking onto his face.

"While I condone this expedition entirely, let me advise you not to take this trip lightly," warned Ames. "Reveloin is not as safe a place as it once was. There are dangers on this island that you could have never dreamed up even in your wildest nightmares. Sarcadui has a tendency to live in the past and pretend everything's safe and well here."

"Well I'm sure she was getting around to telling me," stated Robbie with caution, not wanting to betray Sarcadui completely.

Ames nodded his head then said, "People have had a strong interest in the ocean for a long time. Many have died pursuing it. Let me make myself perfectly clear: No one is living today that has seen the ocean." He then gazed intently at Robbie and said, "Or what lies beyond it for that matter."

"So why pursue it at all?" Robbie asked.

"Because," said Sarcadui, approaching the two, "There's something out there that can put an end to the ghosts. You have to understand that we don't choose to live this way, hiding underground every night. The ghosts are keeping us from living freely. In the past we tried and we tried as a town to set up a normal civilization, but whatever we build during the day, they tear apart by night. That's why hiding underground is our only means of refuge."

"They don't want to take the chance of letting anyone near the ocean, because the…" Ames shifted his gaze to Sarcadui and concluded, "…wrong person could slip out to sea and destroy them."

Robbie was silent for a moment. Then he turned to Sarcadui with an air of accusation saying, "If it's so dangerous to go, why would you want to take me to the ocean at all?"

"Because she thinks you're the one who can destroy the ghosts," said Ames.

Robbie looked at Sarcadui for confirmation.

"Robbie, please don't be upset with me," pleaded Sarcadui, her eyes almost moist.

"What in the world gave you the idea that *I* could get to the ocean, or even do anything about these ghosts you keep talking about? I've never been here in my life! Why can't anyone believe that?"

“She’s basing her belief off of a promise made many years ago that you would return here.”

“Who promised that?” asked Robbie.

“According to the books, you did,” started Ames. “According to everyone, you created this world many years ago, before it was flooded and Reveloin became an island. You used to dwell on these very grounds. But you had to depart for a while, and you promised that you would return. The last place you were seen was in the Walei Caverns, and so it stands to reason that that’s where you would show up if you returned. Since then people have been posted there on a rotating schedule to watch for you. Since Hail found you there, everyone thinks you’re the one who is going to shed light on our dark world.”

Robbie attempted to clear up a question that had been bothering him for the last several minutes. He turned to Sarcadui and said, “You told me you’ve been to the ocean.”

“I’ve heard stories about it. I only told you what I’ve heard... and what I’ve dreamt of,” said Sarcadui, apologetically.

“Don’t bother with trivial issues,” Ames said bringing the topic back. “Everyone dreams of going to the ocean. Everyone dreams about venturing into forbidden territory.”

Robbie asked Ames, “And what do *you* think? You know, about me being this prophesied one?”

“What *I* think is inconsequential. However, since you asked, I’ll admit that I have my doubts about you. It doesn’t make any sense to me why you wouldn’t remember anything if you’ve been here before, much less if you created this place. I don’t see how that’s possible if you don’t find yourself at home in your own created world. But then again, it *has* been many years since you were last seen. Maybe omission from life causes you to forget things. But what do I know? I’m just an old coot waiting to see better days just like everyone else.”

“Well if anyone wants *my* opinion,” started Robbie, glaring at Sarcadui, “no, my *guaranteed word*, then here it is. I don’t know where I came from or how I got here, but I’m not who you think I am.”

Sarcadui seemed desperate to make amends with Robbie. She pleaded with him, “I know how dangerous it can be here. But I thought you knew too. That’s why I didn’t tell you – I thought you knew what you came back here for. I promise I would have warned you if I thought you didn’t remember Reveloin.”

"Ames doesn't seem to think you would be capable of informing me of the truth," sneered Robbie, wanting instantly to take it back.

"But," said Ames sternly cutting in, "if you *are* the one we've been waiting for, then you must find a way to get to the ocean. It is your duty. You would be remiss in not going."

"Why's that?" asked Robbie, perplexed.

"Because if you are who Sarcadui thinks you are then you would be our only hope."

"And if I'm not who she thinks I am?"

"Then you'll die, eventually, like the rest of us. We'll all spend our days continuing to live in fear, all the while wondering if you could have saved us."

"So then I won't go. I'd rather stay here."

"Robbie," said Sarcadui, "if you don't go, then we'll never have a chance of being free again. We'll always be ruled by the ghosts. We'll never be able to go back to our lives the way they used to be."

"So why not just fight them?" asked Robbie. "Declare war."

Ames shook his head. "They don't live. So they can't be killed. Victory would be impossible." Then he added, "There's also the time constraint to consider. You see, the ghosts' objective is very clear and simple. They aim to kill every living person on this island. Once they do that, then there will be no mortal life left. When there's no life, then the sun has no reason to give light, so it will go out completely. And when the sun is gone that will leave the ghosts with unlimited freedom to reign in Reveloin. Everyone has been taught that you are the source of our life, Robbie. Everyone on this island believes that you are the reason the sun shines. And if you die, they believe it will stop shining."

"I don't believe a word of this," said Robbie.

"It doesn't matter whether you believe it or not," Ames retorted. "Your beliefs don't dictate the truth any more than mine do. If what we've been taught is correct, then you're being hunted with more vengeance than the rest of us. You're a threat to the ghosts' way of life. They want to eliminate you from this world. They've been after the rest of us for many years; it would be easier for them to just kill *you*. If you die, then the light gets sucked out of Reveloin, then they'll be free to reign here without the hindrance of daylight."

"How does that work?" asked Robbie.

"If you're our creator, then you carry the light. So it stands to reason that your death would ensure total darkness forever," said

Ames. "That means the rest of us would have to live with complete darkness and we'd end up dying either by the ghosts or starvation."

Feeling indignant for his apathy, Robbie scanned the townspeople going about their sad, pathetic lives, hunched over and completely void of life and spirit. Then his eyes rested on Hail. She was playing a game of Tag with a little boy about her age. But even in their small moment of jubilee, Robbie could sense sadness beneath the surface of her face. Maybe not so much sadness as more of a resonating discomfort that seemed to always be with her.

His troubled mind must have shown because Sarcadui said, "Robbie, you don't have to go if you prefer not to. I'm sorry I got you mixed up in all this."

Robbie looked up at Sarcadui and then over at Hail who was still running around with the young boy. He knew that he had to at least try. If not for anything else, it would be for Hail and Sarcadui. They didn't deserve to live this way.

"It sounds like I was mixed up in all of this even before I got here. I'll go," said Robbie apprehensively. His anger against Sarcadui was beginning to mollify. "Only, if it's as dangerous as you say it is out there, why are you my guide?"

"Because she's just like her mother," said Ames. "She's the only one in this whole town crazy enough to venture away from here at all. She'll know the way better than anyone."

"No one else can come with us?" asked Robbie, resigning to Sarcadui's fate.

Ames shook his head. "I would go, but I'm an old man who can hardly hold my own. I'd only hold you back. Anyone else would just be wasted life. The more blood that's shed the closer to darkness we become."

"I'm going to go find some shoes for you," said Sarcadui, leaving Robbie and Ames alone.

"So what exactly do I do once I get to the ocean?" Robbie asked.

Ames stood up and cracked his back, bending it back and twisting at the hip. "If you get there, you're going to sail out to the sea for several miles until you get to a castle. Just continue to head northwest… you can't miss it. In the castle, find the throne and sit on it."

"That's it?" asked Robbie, somewhat disappointed by the simplicity.

"That's it. But if I were you, I'd worry about just making it through the island alive."

Robbie eyed him for a moment then said, "You really think I'm the one who's supposed to do this, don't you?"

Ames studied Robbie then took a step closer toward him and whispered, "I know you're the one we've been waiting for. But if you die, then the cat's out of the bag. Darkness will come and no one will have any reason to live. You really are our only hope, whether you think so or not."

Robbie contemplated this for a moment not knowing exactly what he thought. "You seem to think I'm not going to make it. Level with me; what am I heading into?"

Ames answered discreetly, "The amount of danger can only be measured by your willingness to confront it. I can't tell you if you'll succeed or not. I don't know your ability to survive in the jungle. But listen to what Sarcadui says; she knows how to survive out there. Stick with her and you should be fine."

Sarcadui returned with a pair of shoes in each hand and a wadded up cloak in another. She had changed into a long light blue dress that draped all the way down to her ankles. The dress, though plain, accentuated her beauty in a way the cloak couldn't. "Try these on," she said, handing them to Robbie.

They were hard leather sandals that buckled over the tops of his feet and around his ankles. With his socks on, they fitted perfectly.

"Don't we need to pack things to take with us?" Robbie asked.

"There's not much for us to take. We'll have to use what the island gives us," Sarcadui answered. "Besides, I've got this," she said, patting the knife on her waist. "And here, this one's yours," she said, handing him his own knife from underneath the cloak she still held in her hand.

He took it along with the cloak. The handle of the knife was made out of some sort of cast iron and the blade itself was formed from a sharp rock of some sort. Awkwardly, he said, "It's going to be too hot if I put this on over these sweats."

Getting the point, Sarcadui turned around, but not before blushing. He shed his sweat clothes and threw them in a pile on the ground and pulled the cloak on over his head, feeling more like a Reveloinian now that he looked like the others. While someone came and tied the knife to his waist with the belt that came already wrapped around his cloak, Robbie, not ungratefully, asked, "Why do I have to wear this?"

"So you fit in. We don't want the enemy seeing you dressed the way you are, because they'll automatically assume you're the prophesied one and kill you immediately," informed Sarcadui, nonchalantly.

"That's reassuring," Robbie mumbled.

They began to walk but Hail ran up behind them and stopped them. "You're leaving again?" she asked, more aggravated than heartbroken. "But you just got here."

Robbie, turning to give her a hug, said, "Don't worry. I'm sure I'll be right back." He turned to Sarcadui and said, "Right?"

"He won't be back for sure, Hail," said Sarcadui. "There's a chance that you might not see him again." So much for reassurance. "But think of it this way. How many times have I left town and not returned?"

"You always come back," said Hail, pathetically.

"Then that's just what we'll try to do, okay?"

"How long will you be gone?"

"For several days most likely. Maybe a couple of weeks."

Hail's face scrunched up into a pitiful expression of deep hurt and hugged Robbie's neck tightly. He was surprised that he had to swallow back a lump in his throat.

Other people gathered around and showed their remorse over Robbie and Sarcadui leaving, but they seemed hopeful that they would see them again. Many of them lined up to say goodbye.

"Remember to stay well hidden at night," said Ames. "But be just as careful during the day."

Robbie nodded his understanding, then after a few more goodbyes they were off, continuing in the direction they were headed before. Only this time Robbie had a vague idea of what sort of dangers they were heading into, and he was afraid.

CHAPTER 13

After several minutes of walking, Robbie's affinity toward Sarcadui had grown. In fact, he was more overcome than ever with the desire to know her better. "How old were you when things went bottom up?" Robbie asked as they crossed over a gentle river on a rickety bridge.

Sarcadui was reflective for a moment, as she strolled down the bank to the water. He followed her down and they both kneeled down to gather water in their hands to drink. The water seemed to sparkle with life as soon as she touched it. He couldn't help but stare at her as she reflected for a moment. He took a mental picture of her upturned nose that wriggled when she thought, and the slightest upward curve of the corners of her lips as she pursed them together.

"Five maybe. Younger than Hail. I always go back to that time in my sleep – the time before ghosts became an everyday part of our lives. I remember living in a home above the ground with a bed and enjoying the taste of food more than twice a day. I remember my dad taking me for walks at night. But I was born at the end of all good things, Robbie. So even then the ghosts had already begun to terrorize people." Sarcadui's voice trailed off as if she was deep in some reminiscent memory.

"Sarcadui, are you okay?"

"Yeah, I'm fine. They say the water used to taste like sugar. Sometimes I pretend I once drank water that tasted like that."

"Maybe you did," suggested Robbie. "...At least if you did, then I wouldn't be the only one with amnesia."

Sarcadui laughed, then as if snapping awake from a daze she exclaimed, "But there's so much else for you to see, I can hardly wait to show you!"

"So do fairies really exist?" asked Robbie.

Sarcadui shook her head. "If they exist, they all went into hiding. They won't come back out until the ghosts are all dead. That's why I want to see them so badly, because then that means we're free."

Robbie followed her back up the bank and they continued on their way. He had other questions, but Sarcadui had already exploded into a verbal menagerie about sights to see and adventures to experience in her sweet, milky voice. Not surprisingly Robbie complacently fell once more into a trance as if being cooed by some tender lullaby.

It wasn't long before they entered into an area where the birds suddenly stopped singing and all was quiet. The trees in these parts weren't laden with as many leaves and vines as through other parts of the jungle. It was as if Nature skipped over this area while adorning creation with her decorations. The alarming stillness was proving to be too eerie for Robbie's comfort, but Sarcadui was continuing her trek as though she was indifferent to the sudden change.

A few minutes into this dreadful stillness they came upon a young man's body hanging from a forked tree branch by his neck. Both legs and the left arm were broken in many places evidenced by the bones protruding from the skin. It looked like his foot had been gnawed off by a wild animal, as dried flesh hung loosely from the right leg like torn rags. The man's skin was pale and rotting. Flies swarmed noisily around the corpse, bumping into their larvae collecting fluids expelled from the flesh. Robbie gagged at the combination of sight and smell and threw his hand to his mouth to prevent himself from vomiting.

"The ghosts did this," said Sarcadui, standing before the body. "They caught him wandering out at night – maybe two nights ago by the looks of him."

"Can they *ever* come out during the day?" asked Robbie, suddenly afraid of this monstrous race that, for the first time, just became more than mere sounds to him.

"No," said Sarcadui. "They can only survive at night."

"So where do they go during the day?" he asked, still not convinced that one couldn't just jump out from behind a tree and maul him.

"Light temporarily kills them," said Sarcadui.

"What do you mean *temporarily* kills them?"

"They're already half dead," explained Sarcadui. "When the sun rises they return to a temporary death – some think they go into space, where it's eternally dark. But you'll never see them in Reveloin when the sun is out, even if clouds are covering its light. But at night, the moon can touch them and they won't die. They remain even in the most intense moonlight, simply because it's their time to live. But lights that we create can most certainly keep them away. That's really our only defense against them. Come on," she concluded, noticing Robbie was still feeling uneasy about the mangled body dangling before them. "It'll be okay for us as long as we keep moving."

They pressed forward and the more distance they put between themselves and the hanging corpse the more the jungle awoke from its deathly slumber.

They walked many more miles and the hours flew by like rose petals in the breeze. As Sarcadui spoke, Robbie noticed that once again, like when they had entered into the desolate town of Langly, the trees were thinning out and becoming more spread apart from each other. Then they saw a building – the first building Robbie had seen since arriving on the island. Sarcadui stopped talking as they continued moving on.

The building was a haunting two-story with windows perpendicular to each other on both levels. Boards were nailed diagonally to the windows causing the building to have a queer, slanted look about it as though it were frowning at them. The white paint was chipping off like bandages hanging off wet scabs. Sarcadui led him past it silently.

As they continued to walk, the buildings grew in number and in size. The jungle earth changed into a dirt road beneath their feet and soon, buildings stood on either side of the road and they found themselves in the middle of a town full of buildings that seemed to begrudge a lifetime of lonely nights filled with terror. The metal doors were dripping with rust and the windows were stained with dust and dirt. They were like dried tears that had never been wiped away. The haunting buildings grew taller the deeper into town they strode. And the taller the buildings grew, the more depressing and unkempt they appeared. The one thing they all had in common, aside from their desolate, mangled looks, was that each building had sconces on either side of the front doors and windows, all of which were unlit.

"Where are we now?" asked Robbie, not quite comfortable breaking the sacred silence.

"This is the town we came to every day to get our food and supplies. We also found entertainment here," said Sarcadui in a quiet voice. Then she added almost to herself, "There was so much life here. It's where the cowboys would meet with their posse and have duels in the street, and then gather for drinks and poker in the salons. But now it's just a ghost town, a faded memory of what once was."

The hour was growing late and the sun began to set behind the broken buildings causing a chill to glide through the air. Robbie clasped his arms around himself in order to stay warm.

"We need to go inside now," said Sarcadui.

She led him into a building, which was colder inside than it was out. She locked the door behind them with an iron latch that reached from one end of the oak door to the other. Shivering, he looked around and saw that he had been led into a massive library.

Inside was like a bright cavernous room that was filled from floor to ceiling with glowing books. Hundreds of thousands of books filled the walls like majestic curtains draping from the ceiling. There must have been fifty shelves of books lined one on top of the other wrapping themselves all along the walls. The books glowed radiantly in the thickening darkness. But many of them scattered throughout were not glowing and were just ordinary books.

On each side of the library, golden staircases wound their way to the top shelves. They had wheels, which enabled them to roll across the marble floor from one end to the other, so every book could be reached. The towering ceiling gave Robbie the urge to yell at the top of his lungs just so he could hear his voice reverberate. Their footsteps echoed on the floor as they made their way across the library. In the middle, stood a small wooden pedestal with a single glowing book resting on top of it.

"They're history," said Sarcadui about the books in general. She strolled over to a section of books and perused the shelves. "They tell about the early years that time forgot."

"All of them?" asked Robbie.

"There's a lot that has happened. And they're all personalized accounts," she said, pulling a glowing book out, fanning its pages. "This one's mine."

"You wrote that?"

"Sort of." Sarcadui crossed over to a pillar protruding from the wall. She leaned up against it with the book held across her chest. "When we're born, a book appears on a shelf here and our lives fill in the pages. So we don't actually write it ourselves, but we determine the story. Everyone has a book. You can imagine how many courtroom trials have been justly satisfied by just pulling out someone's book and looking through it for hard evidence."

Robbie was fascinated by this phenomenon. "So what's with the light coming from the books? Why are some glowing and some aren't?"

"The light tells us who's still alive in the world. Remember how Ames said life gives off light? Well, the glowing books are who's all still alive."

Robbie was astonished by the large amount of books – thousands, really – that were not lit. "That's a lot of dead people."

"Yes. There wouldn't be so many if it weren't for the ghosts. A lot of them *are* ghosts, in fact."

Shifting the focus, she sat down and she began to read the first few pages as Robbie sat next to her. The pages glowed luminously so that the words sank beneath the shafts of light that shot up from the book. The penmanship had a very neat and even otherworldly quality about it.

The book read like a journal of her everyday occurrences. It detailed every thought and action Sarcadui ever had and did from her point of view. She lingered more toward the front of the book instead of the latter pages as she searched for those days she was most fond of reminiscing. She didn't read anything solemn, though Robbie was certain she had seen a lot of tragedy in her life. He couldn't blame her for skipping over those many details.

Robbie was content just listening to Sarcadui reading from her book, as she laughed and recalled better days. He even grew jealous upon hearing the history of a childhood crush she had on some boy. It even seemed to blossom into a full-blown relationship as they grew older. But whatever was there, it was cut short and Sarcadui provided no reason for it. Robbie guessed the young gentleman had died at an early age, as he was not mentioned any later in her life. He was sure that if he found that young man's book it would not be lit.

The sun had completely set. But the books of those still living cast a strong enough light for the two of them to still see clearly.

"So what's that book on the pedestal?" asked Robbie when Sarcadui was done glancing through the early years of her life.

Sarcadui laid her book down then gently stood up, motioning for Robbie to stay put. She glided across the foyer to the wooden pedestal and picked up the book that rested on it. She blew the dust off its cover which exploded into a cloud of dry mist. She brought it back to Robbie and sat down once more.

She handed him the book and said, "This is what we hold to be the most accurate history of Reveloin."

Robbie flipped through the glowing pages and scoffed, saying, "This looks like it was written by a kid."

In stark contrast to Sarcadui's eloquently penned book, this one had eraser marks all over the pages and was filled with misspelled words and scribbling on the sides of the faint, blue-lined paper.

"Read it," said Sarcadui.

Robbie started at the beginning. The title was *My Adventures in Reveloin.*

I miss Reveloin a lot. I'm trying my hardest to stay focused on school and on things my dad says. Last week dad said I wasn't supposed to imagine things anymore. I guess I blank out when I do. But he didn't say I couldn't write about things. I promised Rico, Lahni, and Ewin that I would keep making adventures but I'm not there with them. So for now I'm just going to write about all the adventures I've already had. While they are still having lots of fun in Reveloin, I hope they think about me as much as I think about them.

"Who wrote this?" asked Robbie, looking up from the book to Sarcadui.

Sarcadui flipped ahead a few pages and pointed to a passage that made him laugh. In it, Lahni was calling the boy by name. "You did," she said.

He looked at her blankly, when he saw that she wasn't joking.

"If you're the Robbie they're speaking of, then this is your book. You wrote it."

Robbie shook his head sardonically then read on. Most of what was written focused mainly on the three people Rico, Lahni, and Ewin, being led by a young Robbie on all sorts of adventures. He felt that the writer, whether it was him or not, really knew these people intimately. He flipped to the last page.

"I can't come back here anymore," I told them. We were all standing in the Walei Caverns. "Dad says I can't come back."

Me, Rico, Lahni, and Ewin were going to go cliff diving. But we never ended up going that day. Instead we all stood in the big cavern where the water glowed.

"You're not coming back anymore?" asked Ewin. She was already crying. She asked what they would do without me.

I didn't have an answer for her. But I said that they could still explore and do all the stuff we normally do. Just without me.

Lahni asked who would show them new things. He reminded me that I was their leader and that I created everything. He was right. But I made him the official leader in my place.

Of course Rico had to bring up the fact that I've never listened to my dad before, so why start now? He always hated my dad.

He was right, but it was getting too hard going back and forth between both worlds. As much as I loved Reveloin and my friends, I knew this wasn't real life. I said that to them. Then I was like, "I'm sorry. But I have to go."

I remember Lahni just bowed his head and Ewin hugged me. She said, "We're going to miss you, Robbie." Then she thanked me for all the fun.

Then Rico, trying to act all tough (probably trying to impress Ewin, whom he'd always liked) said, "I'll make you a deal, Robbie-boy." He made me promise to come back and when I do there will be a castle built for a king waiting for me. He said it will be all mine. Then he was like, "After all, you made this world. Where would we be without you?"

I remember I said, "Okay, I'll come back. I promise."

"We'll hold you to it," Rico said. "We'll be expecting you. Don't forget about us."

"Good bye," I said. I was crying. We all were.

I miss them.

That was the last thing written in the book. Robbie closed it. Somehow the name Robbie-boy lingered with him as though he could almost recall it. But he kept that to himself, lest he get Sarcadui's hopes up.

"They kept their promise," she said. "They built that castle for you and that's where we're headed. When you sit on that throne…" her voice trailed off as she looked away from Robbie. Then, she looked up in alarm and said, "There's something wrong."

Robbie looked up from the book and asked, "What?"

"The books – their lights are going out."

Robbie looked at the rows of books on the walls. Sarcadui was right; many of the lights were going out of the books, some fading slowly, others switching off as quickly as an extinguished flame.

"They're people from home!" cried Sarcadui, pulling out books that had gone out and reading the names on the covers. "The ghosts got underground! They're in Langly!"

Robbie, thinking of Hail, jumped to his feet and courageously said, "Let's go save them! We can make it back, right?" He felt cheesy for saying it, but what else could he do?

But Sarcadui just stood there, deflated, her face devoid of any hope.

"Come on," Robbie pressed. "Let's go!"

Sarcadui instead shook her head and said, "It's too late. We can't go." She was crying now.

"Why not?" asked Robbie as the library grew significantly darker by the second.

"Because they're already here."

And just as she said this Robbie could hear the eerie cacophony starting up from a far way off, like coyotes howling beyond the hills at twilight.

The ghosts were coming.

CHAPTER 14

It was noticeably darker than it was just moments ago. Though she tried not to show it, it was clear Sarcadui was bereft over the loss of so many people she knew and loved. Robbie felt guilty for being at a loss for words.

Even though they sounded like they were a ways off, the eerie cries from outside made the hairs on the back of his neck stand up on end and his arms were covered with goose flesh.

Strangely, the familiar cries reminded Robbie of Hail because he got to hold her the last time he endured the noises. He was filled with a deep sadness over her fate. He hoped that if she was killed, that she at least died quickly. But then, maybe she wasn't dead...

Filled with hope, Robbie cast his book aside, stood up, and began searching through the other books. The strange names written on the spines of the books were in alphabetical order. He jogged to the other side of the library and climbed up one of the staircases. He narrowed his attention to a select group of books on a shelf twelve rows up where the H's were lined up. He scanned them going backwards: Hattey, Hallertin, Halesburry, Hailbrook, Hail.

He didn't need to, but he pulled her book off the shelf and found that Hail's book was still glowing as bright as any other book in the library.

"She got away," Sarcadui silently cheered as she came up behind Robbie and placed her hands on his back.

"She probably scared them more than they scared her," Robbie joked, thinking of when she had chased him in the cave with a dagger.

Sarcadui took the glowing book out of Robbie's hand and placed it back in its spot and they both descended the steps. She then walked Robbie's book back over to the pedestal. She placed it back on top and said, "We need to sleep if we're going to make any distance in tomorrow's sun." She invited Robbie to sit down with her.

The cries were growing nearer. "We'll be safe in here as long as there's still light from some of the books. Not everyone lives in Langly."

The books' lights continued to go out and caused the glow in the building to thin out significantly. Robbie kept a close eye on Hail's book and it never even flickered. Then a loud bang on the front door sent sharp shards of ice through Robbie's blood. The bang was followed by loud cries from outside the door and Robbie could see the door jolting from its violent assault by the ghosts.

"They know we're in here," Sarcadui said, matter-of-factly. Judging by the racket outside, the ghosts had their venomous aspirations set on breaking into that library. They screamed horrifically just outside the door, thundering mighty fists against it. The handle of the door looked as though it were about to shake loose.

"They're going to get in!" Robbie said, his voice sounding to him like a frightened child.

Sarcadui and Robbie both stood up in reaction to the noises pouring in from outside. It would be only a matter of time before the ghosts broke into the weakened building.

Together they looked up at the ceiling where they heard heavy clambering on the roof and more pounding. Shards of ceiling fell onto the marble from ghosts pelting away on the roof, desperate to get inside.

Robbie couldn't help but wonder what these ghosts looked like. Though they sounded more like monsters than like ghosts. Either way, he preferred not to find out.

It occurred to him that they were being hunted. He felt like the agouti, who became the dinosaur's lunch; only, his own death wouldn't be so instantaneous. Not if the corpse hanging from the tree was any indication of how the ghosts handled their victims.

"Robbie, listen to me," whispered Sarcadui. "The people you read about—" A thunderous pounding on the back door made both of them jump. Sarcadui continued. "Lahni and Ewin, they were my parents."

To Robbie, this didn't seem like the best time to talk about them. But he realized that she was making a noble attempt to distract him from the ghosts like she had underground in Langly. "What happened to them?" he asked.

A loud crash from the library delayed her response but eventually she said, "They were caught in the jungle when it was dark. They were searching for food to bring back to me. The ghosts found them and broke my father's neck. They beat my mother and left her to die."

Robbie could show no sympathy under the conditions, so in a way it was lucky for him when she stopped her narrative because it was apparent the front door wasn't going to hold much longer.

"We need to get out of here. Quick," she said, standing up, "We'll go out the back."

"But we can't go out there," said Robbie, thinking of how many ghosts would be waiting for them.

"We have no choice. I'm sorry I brought you here."

She led him to the back of the library where they passed through an open doorway that led through a small hallway. At the end of the hallway stood a door that would open to the outside. If they removed the iron latch that secured the door they would surely draw attention to themselves. It was still uncertain that the ghosts knew where they were in the building. Their anonymity was the only thing they had going for them.

To their terror they heard the front door of the library crash open and hellish shrills of victory resounded throughout the library.

"They're inside. We have to go," said Sarcadui with determination. Robbie nodded his consent. Suddenly the idea didn't sound so bad.

They unlocked the door with a loud clank that made Robbie recoil, and stumbled outside, back into the cool night where they found themselves in a back alley. On either side of the door were mounted sconces with a lit candle in each of them. For a brief instant, Robbie wondered who lit the candles – there was still plenty of wax to burn, so it had been done recently. Then he saw, with the help of the faint lights, silhouettes of zombie-like monsters dragging themselves toward them from both sides of the alley. If these were the ghosts, they were not at all what he had imagined them looking like. He thought they would be transparent and flying. You know, like ghosts.

Not knowing exactly why, Robbie snatched a candle off of one of the sconces. He grabbed Sarcadui's hand and dragged her back inside, throwing the latch back across the door. But when he turned back around to face Sarcadui, the small flame revealed, directly behind her, a large ghost – or monster – with no facial features but a wide mouth filled with sharp teeth, breathing heavily on her neck.

CHAPTER 15

Sarcadui stood stiff as a board, not willing to move, looking as though the wheels in her brain were spinning out of control. Even she was out of options.

The ghost certainly did not look like a traditional ghost because of its lack of transparency. In contrast it was quite physical complete with muscle and bone structure; it had blotchy skin like bruises on vegetables. Its long worm-like fingers wrapped around Sarcadui's trembling arms as it held her close to its heaving chest. Apparently one small flame didn't affect it as it snarled with a wide menacing mouth and strings of saliva dripped down its meaty lips.

Robbie impulsively grabbed his knife and thrust it forward toward the ghost, but it simply just grabbed the blade with a tight fist, spilling blood, and yanked it out of Robbie's hand with a jerk, and tossed it aside. It showed no pain.

Robbie's next, and most desperate move, was to shove the candle into the monster's face where its nose would have been, careful not to hit Sarcadui. This worked because its face turned out to be like a flammable gelatin. The candlestick impaled the creature and the flame instantly spread from the monster's head to its neck to its torso, exploding like a ball of fire.

The monster, its toothy mouth growing almost as large as its wanting face, shrieked so loudly that Robbie had to clap his hands over his ears, leaving the candlestick in the monster, lest his eardrums bleed. Robbie knew this was the most horrifying sound he would ever hear.

When the flames grew bigger the small hallway lit up to reveal at least three other ghosts approaching them from the main room. They all shielded their faces as if they had eyes and joined in with their comrade with horrific screams against the bright fire.

Sarcadui released herself from the monster's grip, turned, and pushed the inflamed creature out of the hallway using it as a walking torch to guide them back out into the ravaged library.

"We need to make as much fire as possible to send the ghosts away!" shouted Sarcadui. The inflamed monster kept all other would-be assailants at bay. She pulled her hands away when it became too hot to touch. Books lay scattered everywhere, the marble floor was cracked and punctured in many places, and the golden staircases had been toppled over by force and many of the shelves were broken.

The inflamed monster was convulsing on the library floor. Its body rolled around on the books lying on the ground, setting them ablaze so that a trail of fire snaked its way across the floor and set the walls aflame. The fire replaced the light that the books gave by a tenfold amount. A slithering trail of flames reached the pedestal that Robbie's book sat on.

"No!" cried Sarcadui.

But it was too late; the flames shot up the table and engulfed the book.

But that was not Robbie's concern at the moment. With the building engulfed in flames they were at least safe from other monsters. But remaining inside a burning building couldn't be any less dangerous than venturing outside in the dark where many more creatures were waiting to kill them; he could hear them howling outside above the screaming fire.

The original creature wriggled and writhed from what had to have been unimaginable anguish. Robbie wished it would just die already.

Staying inside the library wasn't possible without being burned alive or suffocating. Sarcadui looked like she had no idea what to do. With smoke billowing and the tiny flecks of embers shooting across the building, the air was quickly becoming insufferable. On a wing and a prayer Robbie dragged Sarcadui out of the library while it was still possible. As they sucked in as much air into their lungs as they could, they could hear the monsters screaming and hollering from all around them.

Desperate to keep the monsters away, Robbie grabbed a long wooden stick with a flame eating up its end and jogged through the town, Sarcadui in tow. He could hear the screams closing the gap between them from behind. But Robbie kept leading Sarcadui in a fast-paced jog. He knew with the size of his torch the monsters could only threaten them with lingering moans.

"I thought we were being hunted by ghosts," said Robbie. "They look more like monsters with nylon masks."

"No, they're ghosts," protested Sarcadui.

"Well they were once people, right?" asked Robbie.

"Yes. And then they became ghosts when they sat on the throne – *your* throne."

The two of them walked at a fast pace even as their predators followed closely, lingering just outside the ring of light.

"You mean they're not spirits? Like dead people coming back to haunt us?"

"No. They're just ghosts. Dead people don't come back. Once someone dies, they're gone from this world for good. These ghosts have always been here threatening our lives ever since they decided to try to take your throne. Didn't Ames say anything about that to you?"

"No. But Hail mentioned something."

"Well, people got tired of waiting for you to return so they decided to do your job, by sitting on your throne. Instead of accomplishing anything good, they were cursed and became ghosts. That's when the floodwaters came and covered up most of the country. It was intended to keep the ghosts from reaching the rest of us, but they built a trench under the ocean where it's always dark and that's how they got here. They can't die; they live forever. Unless of course, you can take the throne."

"What do you mean they can't die?" asked Robbie, jumping at the sound of a ghost that sounded too close for his comfort. "You saw what happened to that one we set on fire."

"That fire is going to die long before *it* ever does."

Robbie shuddered at the thought of living forever with most of his skin burnt through to the bone. He pitied his adversary.

"It'll probably be taken to live in one of the Game Pits."

"What are those?" asked Robbie. She paused.

"Nothing. You've got enough to worry about now."

The two continued to walk with the torch as their shield. But as they reached the outskirts of town, Robbie began to grow very dizzy.

"What's wrong?" was the last thing Robbie remembered Sarcadui saying. Then a loud ringing seemed to explode right in his ear. It was a sound that was all too familiar, somehow. Yet he couldn't quite put his finger on it.

Robbie awoke and quickly took stock of his surroundings. He was in the box behind the couch in his living room and his cell phone was ringing.

CHAPTER 16

Robbie instinctively reached for his pocket to grab his phone but there were no pockets on his sweatpants. Still trying to regain his senses he stood up and looked toward the ringing and saw it lying on the coffee table on the other side of the couch. He clumsily stumbled out of the box and over the couch, grabbed the phone, and saw to his dismay, the name HARVEY digitally displayed across the front.

It was his dad.

The time read eleven o'clock. He flipped the phone open and forgetting to clear his throat of phlegm, said, "Hello?"

The voice on the other end was indeed the unmistakable voice of his father.

"Robbie, I'm sorry for calling you so late. There was a fire."

"What! Are you okay?" Robbie asked as Rosalynn flipped on a light and came into the room. She must have heard the phone ringing. He switched it to speaker mode.

For a moment Robbie was afraid that he was leaving dirt and soot all over the furniture and he began to come up with an excuse for it, but when he looked down at his arms and legs, he saw that he was perfectly suitable to be sitting on the couch. He wasn't even sweaty. Besides that, he was glad to back in his sweat clothes even though he had discarded them in Langly for the cloak. If he had been found wearing some cloak from another world, he would have had a lot of explaining to do.

His dad had to yell over the howling winds and the sirens blaring in the background. "I'm okay, but the house is gone. I'm watching it burn now, Robbie."

Robbie wondered if the fire in Reveloin had to do with his dad's house. He swallowed a lump as he pictured his childhood go up in flames. Wasn't it just moments ago he was in a whole other world both perplexed and tormented by completely unrelated circumstances? And what about Sarcadui? Sure his dad was in trouble, but he couldn't help but wonder about her safety. For all he knew the torch could have extinguished when he disappeared, leaving Sarcadui vulnerable for a clean kill in the utter darkness. What was it Hail had said about him dropping her the first time he disappeared? Oh, yeah. She was had been snide and asked, "If you're holding something and you disappear, what happens to it?" The flame would have gone out if he had dropped the torch, wouldn't it? How was he supposed to know? He wasn't an adventurer; he had never held a torch in his life. And if the flame died, that would leave Sarcadui completely defenseless, because he saw for himself that her knives would be no match for the ghosts. What would they do to her? Would they beat her like they did her mother? And about her parents – those names he read in that book – though Sarcadui and Hail and Ames were new to him, Rico, Lahni, Ewin... those were people he made up as a child and played with in his imaginary world. He really had written a sort of journal when he was younger documenting all of his make-believe adventures he had with them. He imagined duels between cowboys and Indians and astronauts racing against the clock to build their spaceships before the volcanoes exploded, but he certainly didn't remember anything about imagining up monster-like ghosts that came out at night to hunt and kill people. His monsters were more like what he watched on TV that was popular in the '70s: dinosaurs, giant insects, stuff like that. But the question still begged for his attention: had his imaginary world continued on in existence even while he forgot about it? That had to be the case, because he certainly never imagined Lahni and Ewin having a baby – that just wasn't the sort of thing a nine-year-old boy would sit around dreaming about. Another matter troubled him as well. Why couldn't he remember these things while he was in the box? Though he was plagued by these thoughts and emotions he forced himself to remain in the moment.

"The firemen arrived about six minutes ago," his dad was saying. "And they're doing the best they can. I'm sorry to have called you, Robbie. I just didn't know who else to talk to. I mean, it *was* your home after all."

"Don't apologize, Dad. We're here to help," Robbie said, half-truthfully. "Just tell us what you need." Rosalynn took Robbie's hand in hers.

If she had asked, Robbie wouldn't have been able to tell her what upset him more: his childhood home burning down or hearing the voice of his long-forgotten dad on the phone... or being separated from Sarcadui.

There was a shuffling noise through the receiver. Then, "Those Santa Anas finally got us after all these years."

"Yeah, Dad. We were always lucky," Robbie imputed.

The Santa Anas were a dry and blustery wind that blew out of the desert and had the potential to cause great damage. The rapid, hot winds dried up vegetation, creating the danger of wildfires. Once those fires started, the winds fanned the flames and quickened their growth and spread over the Southern California region. These fires could be counted on to spread their wrath nearly every summer. Whether they reached homes or not was all determined by luck and the speed and availability of the firefighters.

"I was just thinking how I could almost hear you going on about how big the flames were when Mom was alive," continued Harvey. "Remember every summer we would drive around the valley trying to get as close to the fires as we could to see the flames?"

"Yeah Dad, I remember," said Robbie trying to brace himself against the nostalgic pull.

"Dad," interjected Rosalynn, "do you have a place to stay for a while?"

"I think I do. Chief Wilson told me that the city will be putting me up in the community center until I get re-established. That'll be for me and the people in the three other houses next door, which also went up. The young people on the end just moved in last weekend. I don't think they had insurance yet."

Rosalynn looked at Robbie pleadingly and Robbie shook his head at her gesture. He knew what she was thinking. She wanted Robbie to invite his dad to come stay with them. Apparently sensing the marital tension from 1,200 miles away, Robbie's dad said, "Don't do me any favors. I just wanted to check in on you."

That was by far one of the most pathetic lies Robbie had ever heard. He was almost tempted to remind his dad that he was forty-two, a grown-up now, and can now spot a lie when he heard one. But he thought better of it.

Unable to avoid Rosalynn's pleading stare, Robbie, with clenched fists and through gritted teeth managed, "Do you want us to fly you out here? We can put you up until you're back on your feet."

"No, no," said his dad. "I'll be fine here."

"Then why did you call?" Robbie wanted to scream. But Rosalynn gracefully intercepted and said:

"Dad, just keep us updated and know that the offer stands for as long as you need it."

"Okay. I've got to go. Chief Wilson wants to talk to me."

The only "I love you" came after they hung up the phone and it came from Rosalynn. Robbie was too distressed to intercept it.

They sat on the couch for the next hour making plans for Harvey to come stay with them. Of course this wasn't without Robbie spending the first half of that hour complaining about his dad's behavior.

Out of the blue, Rosalynn abruptly asked, "What were you doing down here so late?"

"I couldn't sleep," answered Robbie. "There's a lot on my mind with finding a job and all."

Rosalynn seemed to buy into this by her own choosing, though he knew she wouldn't hesitate to bring it up again if she were provoked.

When they decided to retire to bed they caught Taylor in the hallway sneaking out of her room, dressed in jeans and a v-neck. Eyeliner shadowed her eyes.

As a father, Robbie had feared this night for so long; he knew it would come, but why tonight? Hadn't there been enough drama? He suddenly longed for Reveloin. "Where are you going?" he asked.

"Nowhere. I was just getting a drink," protested Taylor, looking like a deer caught in headlights.

"Then why is there a car full of kids parked in our driveway?" asked Rosalynn crossing her arms and narrowing her eyes.

"They're here already?" asked Taylor a little too loud.

"Give me the phone," said Rosalynn stretching out her hand, eying Taylor's cell. "Now get to bed and I'll go take care of your friends. We'll talk about this in the morning."

Taylor surrendered her phone and growled in anger as she stormed back into her room saying, "You guys don't ever let me do anything!"

Robbie stood amazed at his wife's craftsmanship. "I didn't see a car in our driveway."

"That's because there isn't one." she responded coolly. "Yet."

As if on cue a text appeared on Taylor's phone which read, "R U ready?"

Rosalynn responded via text, "No. Parents R up. Go home."

Robbie looked outside the bedroom window just as a car, parked two houses down, turned on its headlights, and drove past the house, revving the engine as it passed. But before Robbie could form just one of his many questions Rosalynn said with a sly smile, "Unlike some people we know," referring to Robbie, "the rest of us were actually *cool* growing up."

Under the conditions it was good to laugh. Robbie was exhausted and he and Rosalynn headed off to bed. She was concerned about Harvey and also about Taylor's recent attempt at rebellion, while Robbie was entertaining thoughts of his heroic acts on the island of Reveloin that his wife could never know about.

As he lay on his back on top of the covers, Robbie realized that the bite mark on his right hand was completely healed, which was strange since a couple hours ago, before he got in the box, it was still a fresh wound. He wondered if wounds healed faster in Reveloin because time moved faster there. He rolled his sleeves up to examine his arms and saw that the scratches were gone as well. Happily, he peeled off his sweats and threw them on the ground beside the bed, glad to be back in his boxers.

A few minutes passed and Robbie asked Rosalynn, "Are you still awake?"

"Yes."

"How are you doing? Are you nervous about tomorrow?"

Rosalynn nodded her head and said, "I'm sure everything's going to be fine."

He knew Rosalynn was plagued by thoughts of the next day's doctor appointment which he hadn't given thought to until just then. She had moved the appointment date back when she cancelled the plane tickets. Originally the appointment was set for the week after they returned from their trip.

Robbie's mind drifted back to Reveloin and the terrors he had just encountered. How many times had his life been in mortal danger? He considered something he hadn't yet before. What if the ghosts did capture him and kill him, or he got burned to death, or even suffocated? What if he was killed in Reveloin? Would that mean he would just wake up from the box and have to start over like losing in a video game or would he really die? The latter thought sent shivers up his spine. After all, if he came back from Reveloin with wounds and sore feet he received in the box, then who's to say his heart wouldn't stop beating if he died on the island? He drifted off to sleep concluding nothing.

CHAPTER 17

The next morning started off with Robbie and Rosalynn waiting for Taylor in the kitchen. Usually she headed downstairs for a cup of coffee and a slice of toast as soon as she woke up. But this morning they heard the upstairs shower running before she even came down. She was making it clear that she was going to avoid them until it was time to leave for school.

"I'll take her," said Robbie, promising he'd make it to the clinic on time. In the clearness of daylight he was determined to get to the bottom of last night's episode with Taylor. They agreed that Rosalynn would take Jeremy to school and then they'd meet at the clinic. It dawned on him at one point that morning that today was supposed to be packing day for them. Their plan was to let the kids sleep in while he took Rosalynn to the doctor, come home, pack, and go out to dinner before their five A.M. flight to Hawaii the next morning. For the hundredth time he fought hatred toward Kurt. He thought about pulling the kids out of school since they were going to be off anyway, but neither of them seemed to care to stay home if there wasn't going to be a vacation to pack for.

On the way to school Robbie gave Taylor a few minutes to offer an explanation about last night's near escape. But she chose instead to sit in the passenger seat with her eyes glued to a smudge on the window.

The radio announced softly that the forecast was looking to be like another week of sunshine. Such unusual May weather for the northwest.

Robbie turned off the radio. Now it was up to him to break the ice. He said, "We missed you at breakfast."

Taylor continued to stare at the window with her chin in her hand.

"That coffee's for you," he said, motioning toward the mug in the cup holder in front of them. "Just cream, no sugar."

"I like sugar now," mumbled Taylor.

Robbie nodded, taking note of one of the many changes about his little girl. "How's Darrin?" he asked, but bit his tongue as soon as the wrong name snuck out of his mouth.

"It's Dwayne. And fine."

"You never did tell me why you were crying last night. I figured you had broken up."

"Dwayne wants me to go to a party that I know you're not going to let me go to; it's no big deal, okay? There, you know all you need to know." She said this as she pulled a piece of notebook paper out of a side pocket from her backpack and shoved it in his direction.

Robbie didn't know what frustrated him more: the fact that this twerp was pressuring his daughter to go to a party or that she was still dating him.

Wanting to steer clear of the romance department he ignored the paper she was pushing toward him and decided to just jump in feet first and get to the bottom of the most recent incident. He asked, "What happened last night? Where were you going? Were you going to that party?"

"It's not for a while. Next month or something," was Taylor's muffled response.

"You know you're grounded, right?"

"Good. I love missing out on my social life," snapped Taylor, throwing the paper on the ground in a fit.

"Hey. Don't get smart with me," retorted Robbie, growing angry.

Taylor threw back, "*You're* the ones who think you're so smart! You don't even know what I was doing last night!"

"It doesn't take a genius to figure out that you were sneaking out, *Taylor*. So maybe we're not as smart as you think!" Robbie shook his head and vilified himself for his absent-minded comeback.

Taylor just rolled her eyes and turned her head away, refocusing her sight out the window.

After a moment, a calmer Robbie asked, "So what *were* you doing last night?"

"What do you care? You're too busy coming up with reasons to get me in trouble."

"Not *get* you in trouble. We're trying to keep you *from* trouble."

Taylor just mimicked Robbie, sticking her lower lip out in mock gesture. He about blew a fuse. He prayed her own children would be just like her for the sole purpose of making her pay for all of his headaches.

"Here's a newsflash Taylor," started Robbie. "If you would just talk to us, then maybe we wouldn't be so suspicious of whatever you're doing. What is it Taylor? I care; talk to me. Is it drugs?"

"Dad."

"You're not into that voodoo Wicca stuff are you?"

"No."

"Is it sex?"

"*Dad!*"

"Oh please don't let it be sex. You already have a kid, don't you?"

"Yes Dad, I managed to hide my fat stomach from the entire family for nine months."

"You see! I don't know if you're telling me the truth right now or just being sarcastic with me which, as you know, would be *lying*," yelled Robbie. "I don't know how to read you."

"Why do you even have to read me at *all*? Why can't you just leave me alone?"

Robbie stopped behind a line of cars at the stoplight. "Because you're my daughter, and that's not what parents do, Taylor. Apparently you'll find that out in about fifteen years when little Wayne is sitting in your spot and you're driving *him* to school."

Taylor sighed in utter frustration saying, "I don't have a baby, Dad!"

"Is there a chance that you *could* be having one?" Robbie shyly asked, unable to suppress his curiosity.

As the light had yet to turn green, Taylor brushed the party invitation to the floorboard and before Robbie could react, she flew open the door and jumped out of the car yelling over her shoulder, "I'm walking to school!" Then she slammed the door.

Robbie, in a moment of utter shock had his eyes only on Taylor when he gassed the car to follow after her. He flew right into the car in front of him, throwing him forward, fortunately being caught by the seatbelt and pelted by the airbags. The sound of crunching metal sent him into a panic as he saw dollar signs float away on wings all around him. The coffee spilled all over his right leg sending him into a world of pain, and as he slammed on the brake after the initial crash he tried pulling his pant leg apart from his skin to ease the burn.

Pushing the airbags aside he looked at Taylor who was just a few feet away, expecting her to come back to the car. But she just gave him those eyes that told him he was just plain embarrassing and continued to walk off.

Through the smoke emanating from the hood of his car, Robbie could see the woman of the car he hit spring out of her Lexus. She was a middle-aged woman with short bleached hair who was dressed to succeed. She hurled herself frantically toward the back of her vehicle and observed the damage. She was yelling into her earpiece complaining about the idiot who ran into her.

Great, thought Robbie, *I had to hit the devil in Prada.*

The woman stormed up to his window, hurling all sorts of insults and profanities at him. Actually, at first Robbie didn't know if she was yelling at him or at someone on her Bluetooth. "Are you blind, you idiot? What in this God-forsaken world made you run into me when I've been sitting in front of you for the last three minutes! You better have insurance. Of course you don't. Eunuchs like you don't carry insurance for this *exact* reason!"

Robbie, feeling very pliant and vulnerable, struggled to push past the deflated airbag to pull out the proper identifications while she continued to rant. By the time he handed them to her through his window she was already on the phone with the police giving them their current location and Robbie's license plate number.

"Ma'am, I'm so sorry," said Robbie, getting out of the car after she had hung up. He did his best to shake his leg dry from the spilt coffee. The burn would last for a few days.

"You *should* be," she scolded. "I'm going to be late to my court hearing, and now because of you I'll have to reschedule."

A divorce hearing I'm sure, thought Robbie, cynically.

He surveyed the damage and saw that this was going to hike up his insurance significantly.

He wanted to chase after Taylor (mostly just to abandon the scene) but she was already out of sight. He couldn't blame her.

CHAPTER 18

The ordeal had ended with the woman, Clarisse, being snappy with the police and to Robbie, and cursing out all the people driving by who slowed to stare at the wreck. After determining that the car was still in driving condition he decided he would have it repaired at a more convenient time. He made it to the clinic with plenty of time to spare. He found Rosalynn sitting in the waiting room and he filled the vacant seat next to her. He bared the bad news about the car and she ranted the expected questions about any injuries and inquired about the car and reminded them both that at least no one got hurt, etc.

After the initial shock had worn off, Robbie glanced at his watch: 11:36. He and Rosalynn had been sitting in the doctor's office for half an hour. This was to be their eighth biannual visit. It had been four years since the doctors made that awful discovery. For four years Robbie and his family had been plagued with endless doctor visits, medications, and hospital bills.

Rosalynn had been complaining of severe chest pains and after a month of Robbie urging her to go to the doctor, she finally gave in. The doctors had found a tumor in her small intestine. Of course the first concern was whether it was malignant, to which the answer was that it was, at the time, between the two classifications, cancerous and non-cancerous. That being the case there was a good chance that Rosalynn could live the span of an average life. These types of tumors were usually referred to as "cancers in slow motion." But for the next five years, the doctors wanted to check up on her every six months to monitor its growth. After that, if the speed of growth did not increase, they could extend their visits to just once a year.

Robbie and Rosalynn made idle chitchat as they sat in the waiting area. The topics mostly centered around his fight with Taylor and his plans for finding a job. No problem there.

The nurse called them in at 11:50. The doctor came into the room a few minutes later and began to ask the standard questions:

Chest pains?

Yes.

Trouble breathing?

Sometimes.

When?

At night.

Do you have shortness of breath during your routine activities?

No, just a bit of nausea once in a while.

May I check your heartbeat? How are the kids?

The routine tests were endured: a chest X-ray, an MRI, and a CAT scan along with some minor physical exercises to monitor pulse and heart rate activity. The doctor said they would receive a call sometime next week with the results and they were free to go at ten past two.

CHAPTER 19

Robbie was euphoric when he was finally able to put his stolen list to use. He spent the afternoon calling and emailing editors and publishers. Unlike eleven years ago, he might find a position where he could work from home and send his work electronically. His phone rang in his pocket and he answered it without looking at the screen. "Hello?"

"Did you get it?" It was Don.

Robbie sighed. Truthfully he hadn't really forgotten about him. He had just decided that if Don wanted part of that list, he was going to have to make the initial contact since he skipped out on Robbie.

"Yeah, I got it," answered Robbie, feeling like they were discussing a drug deal. "Where were you the other night? What happened?" He had seen that Don had called him a few times while he was in the box, but he had decided to play dumb anyway.

"What do you mean? You disappeared on *me*. I called like eight times and you never answered." Robbie correctly recalled that he had missed two calls from Don. Two.

"Forget it. Yeah, I have the list. What's your email? I'll send you your half."

"Are you crazy? That's solid evidence against us. Give it to me in person."

Robbie rolled his eyes. "If that's the case, we shouldn't even be talking about this over the phone."

"I'll be at Mad Betty's in thirty minutes," he said, and then hung up, apparently taking Robbie seriously.

Robbie begrudgingly made a copy and hopped into his car and drove to the bar. At least this was the only way to get Don off his back.

He pulled into the back of the bar, not that fearful that he would run into anyone from work this time. What could happen? He waited in the car for Don to pull in so he could hand the list to him through the window and take off. He didn't want to talk.

As he waited he closed his eyes for a moment. It had been a long night and his body was winding down early. He heard footsteps outside his door. When he opened his eyes he saw it wasn't Don, but Steve, the security guard from work. This was fine because Robbie had a few words to share with the liar.

He rolled the window down and was about to say something curt when Steve said, "I saw you pull in here from the lobby. Lucky I saw you."

"Yeah, real lucky," said Robbie, blandly.

"You found that box, didn't you?"

Without conviction Robbie answered, "Yeah, I did. You told me it was shipped off somewhere. Thanks for your help." He punched the last sentence with as much sarcasm as he could.

"I *tried* to help you," said Steve. "But you just got yourself into a whole mess of trouble that you ain't ever gonna get out of."

"I don't know what you're talking about," said Robbie, finding this conversation getting weird. "Good bye, Steve," he said as he began to roll up the window. He was not about to admit to anyone, much less to Steve, how he had discovered a magical world – it was hard enough convincing himself.

"Oh come on man! You can't keep it a secret from me. I know you get in that box and find yourself someplace else."

Robbie left the window open a crack and looked Steve in the face. He studied him for a moment, and then considered this whole conversation to be completely bizarre. "You're insane, Steve," he said, sealing the window and closing his eyes. "I don't know what you're talking about." When he opened his eyes Steve was gone.

A few minutes later Don showed up with his fat grubby fingers and giddily took the list from Robbie. He was glad to be rid of Don, though thankful for his having included him on the scam.

With his fight with Taylor and the car accident and being dismissed from work and the absurd conversation with Steve, plus his anxiety over Rosalynn's test results, the camel's back was being loaded by bricks rather than straw, and it was rapidly breaking.

He merged onto the freeway as he wondered how his day was going to get any worse. As if on cue his phone rang. It was Rosalynn.

"Hey, what's up?"

"Your dad called," said Rosalynn. "He decided he wants to stay with us for a while."

CHAPTER 20

Rosalynn had already booked a flight for Harvey to fly out at noon the next day. He would arrive sometime in the afternoon. Probably the same time Robbie's plane, now four seats empty, would be landing in Hawaii. So, no, the irony was not lost on him.

Rosalynn relayed the conversation she had with Harvey who said that the city had put all the victims of the fire up in the community center and they had cots to sleep on and that it reminded him too much of Korea. Apparently there were several other neighborhoods around the valley that had been affected, so the center was quite full. Harvey told Rosalynn that it was a hard decision to come to, but he felt in the end it would be the right one. At least, said Harvey, this would give him an excuse to see the grandkids.

Robbie could have named off about a hundred other reasons for his dad to see the kids if he really wanted to, but he let that slide. He'd been throwing a big enough tantrum in front of Rosalynn anyway.

That evening Robbie helped Rosalynn tidy up the house and turn the guest room into a welcoming suite. Robbie joked that if they put up a cot his dad would take one look at it and would fly back to California. "Quick, where can we get a cot?" he jibed.

Unfortunately Rosalynn was way too optimistic about the whole situation for his liking. She vowed that this would be a great way for the two of them to reconcile their past differences and have a fresh start at becoming a real family now.

Robbie was exhausted. He and Rosalynn went to bed at ten and they both fell right to sleep.

Sleep came easily to Robbie after the day he had had, plus being up so late the night before dealing with Taylor and the box.

The sound came at three o' clock. It was loud enough to wake him, but not loud enough to wake Rosalynn. It sounded like it came from downstairs. He listened intently for a moment before moving then he heard it again. Something had dropped onto the kitchen floor. A pot or something. He looked over at Rosalynn and saw that she was still sound asleep.

He quietly crawled out of bed in order to go investigate. It was probably just one of the kids. But both of the bedroom doors were closed. This gave him more urgency to see what the noise had been downstairs. He quickened his step as he descended the staircase.

Out of nowhere he was overcome by a wave of anxiety over his dad coming later that day. This was more than just a visit; he was going to be *living* with them. There was no end in sight!

It had been years since he had even talked to his father. He figured that at some point a phone call or a letter from either party was inevitable, but for his father to come *live* with them after years of negligence on both ends? That was just too much to expect. He almost preferred that he meet a hostile culprit in the kitchen rather than see his dad.

When he made it to the kitchen it was concerning to see the toaster lying on the floor, crumbs scattered everywhere. He cautiously placed it back up on the counter where it belonged, looking about him, scanning the kitchen and living room for any sign of movement. There was none. Strange, but he was almost certain that a few days ago he would have been too terrified to come downstairs, but now... well, he had fought his way through and escaped dozens of monsters that were trying to kill him. This little thing in the kitchen was nothing.

But what was strange was that the box lay on the coffee table in the living room, as if trying to seduce Robbie, calling him to crawl inside. It didn't matter to him that he had last left the box behind the couch and now it just suddenly appeared on top of the coffee table for all to see.

Disregarding any concerns for this world, Robbie wondered where Sarcadui was, and what was happening in Reveloin. He had a sense that he was needed, and saw it his duty then, to return to Reveloin and save Sarcadui.

He resolved to only spend three hours in the box. He figured that was all the time he needed to find Sarcadui and complete his task. Anything above three hours might arouse suspicion.

He concluded that he got "woken up" when something was loud enough to shake him awake. First it was Steve the security guard who hollered at him in the warehouse. Then the ringing cell phone by his ear in the living room roused him – both noises that would have woken him up from a regular sleep. Accordingly, he set the alarm on his phone, which was next to the box on the coffee table where he had left it, for 5:50 A.M. He didn't need to be up that early for anything since it was a Saturday, but he knew Jeremy would be in the living room at around six and he wanted to be in bed before Rosalynn woke up. He brought the box behind the couch like he had the last time. He then placed his phone on the floor next to the box, aware that he was placing his full trust in it waking him up before anyone came downstairs.

He situated himself in the box and closed his eyes.

His heart was beating rapidly, and his hand was outstretched before him holding... nothing. Where was the torch? And how was it daylight all of a sudden? He was on the outskirts of town and Sarcadui was no longer by his side. There was no more howling or groaning from the ghosts. In fact, they weren't anywhere to be seen.

He could still smell the smoke from where the library used to stand about four blocks behind him. Ash fluttered in the breeze as he thought about what might've happened in just a flashing second, between running from the ghosts in the darkness and now, standing here alone in broad daylight. One minute he was walking with Sarcadui with the lit torch in his hand keeping the ghosts at bay and now all of that was gone, except that he was still in the exact same location where he was a moment ago. It was as if some divine hand reached down into his world and replaced the dark and hellish setting with this grotesquely mundane backdrop. The odd thing was, however, Robbie preferred the horrific setting because at least Sarcadui was with him. He did notice that he had on different shorts than he had a moment ago. But he also noticed a red bruise on his right leg that resembled a burn. He must have gotten that when he and Sarcadui were making their way through the burning library. Also, his left sandal was lying next to his foot, upside down. He bent down to strap it back over his sock. And his cloak, it lay next to him folded up in a neat pile. *Sarcadui had time to fold my cloak up,* he thought. *Or else someone else came by and folded it, but why?* Nonetheless, remembering how important it was not to stand out, he pulled it over his head and tied the belt around his waist.

As he did this, he couldn't help but worry about Sarcadui's whereabouts. Would it be safe to call out her name? Were other dangers looming about? He wondered what he was to do without Sarcadui. How was he supposed to know where to go? He had to find her. He wasn't comfortable with the idea of venturing out into this world alone for the first time. But then a terrible thought crossed his mind. What if the ghosts killed her when he disappeared? After all, he was the one holding the torch. What if it went out when it dropped to the ground, leaving Sarcadui completely vulnerable and defenseless? On the bright side, he didn't see an extinguished torch lying around anywhere. So then maybe she took the torch before it went out and, confused over his disappearance, decided to continue the journey to the ocean supposing he would catch up. He walked for a few minutes and soon enough found himself back in the canopied jungle and realized he was growing very hungry. His energy was running low now and he wondered how long he could make it without food. He didn't want to find out.

He observed the treetops for fruit, but to no avail. *Does fruit even grow in this jungle?* he wondered. While he was gazing upwards he heard the rustling of leaves and brush amongst tiny footsteps at his feet. He looked down and saw the ground rolling underneath him. Upon closer examination he saw that the ground was completely infested with hundreds of centipedes scampering over one another, crawling uniformly in the same direction.

They were all spilling out of a trench in the ground a couple yards ahead that stretched out of sight in both directions. Robbie walked up toward the trench on as light a foot as he could, crunching multiple bugs with each step. While he did this, he tried his best to ignore the churning in his stomach caused by both hunger and queasiness.

When he reached the trench he peered into it and saw a log nuzzled between the two slopes at the bottom. The trench was only about four feet deep. The centipedes continued their discharge from underneath the log and Robbie's curiosity was piqued. What were they all running toward? Or from? Was there some underground home like in Langly, only the door to this one was a log instead of a rock? If this were the case, then there would likely be food or someone inside who could give him directions. Possessed by the possibility he tiptoed down the slope and bent down to lift the log so he could see for himself what was causing the haste amongst all the insects.

He felt the tingling sensation of the centipedes slithering past his fingertips as he dug his fingers underneath the log. It was hunger that forced him to endure. But try as he might, he couldn't lift the log even an inch off the ground. So how were these centipedes able to squeeze out from underneath? Robbie reasoned that the soil was soft enough for them to dig their way out, but there was no way for him to tell because the ground beneath his feet was completely covered with long, slithery insects. Before he knew it, his arms were covered with centipedes. He jerked his hands away to brush them off his skin. At least three survivors made it up his cloak sleeves and into his shirt up by his shoulders. Many were crawling up his legs, and into his shorts. The tingly sensation sent him into a wild dance to shake the insects off of him.

When he had released the log it began to look as though it were about to roll away. It jostled as if unearthing itself. Then yellowish roots began to rise out of the ground, to the right of him and to the left of him and directly underneath him. Robbie jumped away from the dead tree, which was clearly coming to life before his very eyes. The roots then planted themselves on the ground and collectively lifted the log up.

It became apparent that this was no log at all, but a massive centipede that was waking up from a deep sleep. What Robbie thought to be tree roots were in fact, the centipede's legs lifting its body up. Robbie then realized that this centipede took up the entire length of the trench as dirt rolled off its back from both directions.

While backing up on the slope, Robbie nearly turned his foot on a stone, and he fell, which sent him falling on his rear to the sound of crunching bugs beneath him. He stood up quickly, feeling disgusted by the wriggly movement on his butt. He turned to run in the direction the river of centipedes was headed. It dawned on Robbie that the giant centipede must have just given birth to all the others.

As Robbie crunched through all the centipedes he heard a desperate voice from up in the trees call out, "No!"

Robbie looked up at the tree tops about sixty yards away and saw two young men with terror written all over their faces. One man was clinging tightly to the tree branches on all fours and the other had just slipped off a weak branch and fallen to the earth. Almost as soon as he landed, another giant centipede reared its ugly head up from a separate trench near the fallen man. It slithered toward the fallen body and crawled on top of him, straddling him so their faces met. The man was not quite dead but looked as though he were hanging on enough to elicit a moan as he struggled to turn his head from the centipede.

But before Robbie could watch anymore of this he turned and saw that his own centipede, the one he had awoken, was crawling out of its hole in the ground and was heading straight toward him. The sound of a hundred insect legs each too big to wrap two hands around was like a thousand pieces of paper being wadded up all at once from the rustling of the leaves and brush on the jungle floor.

Robbie pinned his back up against a tree, hoping the monster would just pass him by like the rest of the bugs. Instead it crawled right up to Robbie and sniffed his feet in a curious manner with its gargantuan feelers, as if examining what it was that had disturbed its slumber. Then it began to crawl up his legs and then his sternum and finally it was face to face with Robbie. Of course it was only the front part of it that pinned Robbie to the tree, but the groaning and cracking of the tree indicated that it weighed an excruciating amount. The rest of the bug's body trailed along the ground for about fifty feet.

The centipede somehow was able to look right at Robbie with huge black eyes, each the size of a person's head. Robbie scrunched his face up as the beast tickled his face with its hard, rubbery antennae, but he could still make out the distinct features of the centipede's monstrous face. Between its eyes a V-shaped birthmark met at a point where its nose would have been and right below that was a mouth loaded with hundreds of sharp teeth. On the sides of its face, connected at its cheekbones, were transparent yet hard pinchers that snapped their metallic ends together just inches from his nose.

Robbie could hardly tear his eyes away from the beast but he did so just in time to see the other man and whether he'd gotten up onto his feet. But Robbie looked just as that centipede ejaculated a spew of glob from its mouth onto the young man's face and suddenly he seemed to come alive with terror and screams of agony as he put his hands to his face trying to tear off the yellow gunk. But before he could pull it off, the centipede dropped its head a few inches and lurched forward with its pinchers and chewed out the man's stomach, spilling gore all around him.

That's when Robbie realized he was not pinned to the tree by some gentle giant. With the creature's legs on both sides of Robbie, he ducked down leaving the creature with nothing but the tree on which to spew its venomous glop, which apparently smothered its victims. But the centipede's legs pressed him like jail bars, trapping him underneath its segmented trunk. Unless the centipede lifted itself enough for Robbie to break away, the only way out was at the centipede's back end, fifty winding feet ahead.

At the base of the tree, Robbie squeezed himself into a position where he could army-crawl along the ground with the centipede's underside hovering over him. It wasn't until he did this that he noticed the small centipedes still blanketing the earth that he now laid on. Now it was a hopeless cause to keep the wriggly insects from crawling all over him and into his clothes. He just accepted the fact that if he was going to live through this, he would just have to welcome them all over his body.

The prostrate position Robbie took seemed to infuriate the monster because its legs began to trample all around him, kicking up dirt and brush and unfortunate centipedes that happened to be in the way. Robbie hadn't yet considered the possibility of being crushed until now. Who knew how much one of those legs weighed?

But by this point Robbie was already on his stomach and if he wanted to survive long enough to see the centipede rise up he'd have to tough it out while the monster trampled inconspicuously around. He knew that if he could get as far away from the head as possible he wouldn't have to roll around so much, avoiding the constant twists and turns of the centipede's thorax as it looked around for Robbie.

By now Robbie had resigned himself to the fact that he was going to die underneath this monster amongst all these bugs. At least they wouldn't have to travel far to find his corpse to feast on. He was about to give up hope and simply just accept death in the least painful way possible, when, out of his peripheral vision he saw the legs beside his waist rise up from the ground! It was now or never. He scurried backwards as quickly as he could and when he cleared the last grounded legs he rolled out from underneath the giant centipede and stood up, pulling a centipede out of his mouth and brushing dozens others off of him.

But when he took stock of his surroundings he saw that he was standing right between the centipede he had just escaped from and the other one who had killed the other man. The two monsters had risen up high off the ground and were face to face with each other with the intention to do heavy combat, and Robbie, the prize, was in the middle of it.

CHAPTER 21

If ever there were a good moment to skip forward in time like he had done twice before, now would be the opportune moment. But Robbie didn't stand around to wait for that to happen.

Up above him the monsters hissed at each other, pulling back for their initial attack, and then smashing into each other above his head with a violence that sent a flock of birds from the treetops. While they were dueling it out with one another, Robbie took advantage of the opportunity to sneak away from them before a winner declared itself.

After running for several yards, and being careful to dodge the maimed body lying on the ground, he heard a voice calling out to him from up above. He looked and saw the other man in the trees above him. He threw down a heavy vine and encouraged Robbie to climb up.

Robbie grabbed the thick green vine in his hands and began to heave himself up. He had struggled about twenty feet up the seventy foot vine when he saw that the centipedes had stopped ramming each other and realized their lunch had ran off. They both turned their scarred heads toward him and, declining to hesitate, scrambled across the earth in a desperate race toward Robbie. Their tremendous speed alone was enough to send him scurrying up the vine with greater haste, exhibiting a strength he never knew he had.

He climbed faster than he ever thought he could. Though this mattered little as the giant centipedes were still crawling at an alarming rate. The monsters decided that teamwork was the best way to guarantee lunch. When they reached the vine, one centipede stayed coiled underneath Robbie at the bottom so that if he fell, he would fall right in the middle of the centipede's deadly grasp and be devoured as easy prey. The other centipede decided to play offense by slithering up the trunk of the tree closest to Robbie, which was about twelve feet away. Robbie recognized that it was a very smart move on the tree-guy's part to drop the vine as far away from any trunk as possible. If he had been too close to a tree trunk the centipede could just crawl right up to him and pluck him from the vine.

But when the centipede on the tree looked as though it were about to lurch at Robbie, he nearly lost his grip and slid down the vine about six feet, rendering his hands useless. His palms screamed with pain as massive chunks of skin ripped off. He could almost see smoke emanating from his tight grip. Robbie looked up toward his rescuer for guidance, but he was no longer there. His heart failed him and there was no way to continue to climb – holding his body weight against the vine was torturous enough. He looked down at the other centipede and saw it snapping its pinchers in Robbie's direction, waiting for him to fall into its deadly trap.

Robbie looked up again and this time saw the man in the branches directly above him. "I can't go anymore," Robbie implored.

"Wrap your leg around the vine and let go," called the man.

"What?" asked Robbie, who would have laughed if his life wasn't just seconds away from ending.

"Do it. Secure your leg around the vine and let go," the young man repeated.

Robbie knew there would be no negotiating, especially since he had no ideas of his own to offer for consideration. He wrapped his right leg around the vine as tight as he could, using his foot to guide it around his ankle. But willing himself to let go was a whole other issue. Even without the monstrous centipede snapping its deadly pinchers at him, Robbie would still feel frightened letting go of the vine at such an alarming height.

"Don't think; just do it!" the young man commanded. But this only aggravated Robbie, so he resolved to hold on tighter, much as it hurt his hands to do so.

Then the centipede on the tree grew impatient and this time really did lunge for Robbie. Instinctively, Robbie let go of the vine, to the relief of his hands, and went sailing down to his death. Only, he wasn't falling down. He was actually being pulled *up*! He was being pulled up by the vine wrapped around his leg while the centipede was colliding with its rival at the bottom of the tree sending them both in a colossal uproar.

In the tree, the man met Robbie and helped him get situated on a fork of branches and untied the vine from his leg. The other end of the vine had been tied to one of the centipede's legs, which had caused a pulley effect that launched Robbie into the treetops when it sprang from the trunk. This explained where the tree guy had disappeared to, and Robbie was greatly impressed by this young man's agility and cunningness. For now it was pressing that they put as much distance as they could between them and the monsters.

"Just stay away from the trunks," said the young man who had an unusually high-pitched voice as though speaking through his nose. "The branches are sturdy enough to hold us, but not them."

As they crawled on the branches Robbie noticed the man stop and look longingly at the body of his fallen comrade whose face was enveloped in the yellow gunk, and whose guts lay splattered all about him.

"Was he your friend?" asked Robbie.

"My brother," said the young man, his eyes growing watery.

"I'm sorry."

But before any sentiment could follow, the branches behind them erupted into a million splinters and shredded leaves. One of the centipedes had reared its head through the branches and was now desperately clawing to get to Robbie and the tree-man.

"Come on," said the man, unfazed.

Robbie followed the young man across the tree branches for nearly half a mile, leaving the centipede behind. The young man had been right: The branches were sturdy, but not sturdy enough to support the weight of a beast that size.

Robbie's arms and legs were sore from having to support his body weight for so long while climbing across the branches. As for the burns on his hands, he was able to balance on his carpal ligaments just below his tender palms. With the exception of a few close calls by misplacing his hands or footing, he quickly got the hang of climbing along the branches.

Once the man felt they were far enough from the centipedes, he tied a vine to a branch and lowered Robbie down and then climbed down after him.

On the ground, Robbie thanked the tree-man for saving his life. He stuck out his hand for the man to take it, but to his surprise, the skinny man threw his arms around him.

After a brief uncomfortable silence, Robbie asked, "So, do you always sit in trees and rescue people from giant insects?" But to his discomfort, he realized that the man was crying, no – weeping – on his shoulder, staining his cloak with tears and snot. Then the young man looked up at Robbie and said weakly, "My brother died trying to save you."

"What was his name?" asked Robbie, feeling responsible.

"Flaux," said the man. "We were hunting the centipedes for meat. But my brother saw that you didn't know what you were doing with that centipod" (apparently the monster's official name). "He tried to get down the tree as quickly as he could to help you but in his excitement he slipped and fell. He had the weapons, which is why I couldn't do anything to save him from the blasted centipod. He always insisted on carrying them, that stubborn brute." Then he broke into another wave of tears.

When he was done crying for the moment, he unlocked his tight embrace and stepped back a couple of feet to face Robbie. "I'm Rhoe," he said, wiping his nose along his arm. He wore a torn white shirt and muddied brown shorts. His skin was badly sunburned and beads of sweat clung to his body. His peppery brown hair was disheveled, a testament to his wild tree-top excursions.

"I'm Robbie," said Robbie, half expecting his new acquaintance to burst out with excitement like everyone else had at the mention of his name.

Rhoe stood silently for a moment, then, to Robbie's surprise, he humbly bowed low and said, "I am honored to finally meet you. May I have a few minutes alone, my lord, so that I can be more able to stand in your presence?"

Robbie granted him time alone to grieve by excusing himself some yards away. He disappeared into some shrubbery where he tackled a berry bush which truthfully did nothing for his screaming stomach. As he munched on the fruit he couldn't help but feel around his right foot for something that was bothering him. He reached into his sock toward the heel and pulled out a flattened centipede.

After about a half hour, Rhoe found him and said unexpectedly: "Are you the expected one?"

"That's what I've been told," responded Robbie, leaning with his back against a tree. "What tipped you off?"

"Your name," responded Rhoe. "It's a weird name, but we've been expecting you to return to Reveloin and redeem us."

"That's what the stories say," said Robbie, unconvincingly. "What makes you think I'm not an impostor?"

"Why would you be? If you were it would be foolish of you to tell me that you're Robbie. If I were your enemy I would kill you."

"Well, I'm glad you haven't killed me," said Robbie. "But Rhoe, I really should tell you that I don't think..." but when he noticed Rhoe's hopeful countenance, he couldn't go on. He had just been the cause of his brother's death, why go and hurt him even more with speculations that he's not who Rhoe hoped he was?

"So you're on your way then, aren't you? To the ocean – where the castle is, I mean – to sit on your throne?" Rhoe's eyes were filling up with new tears, but hopeful ones this time.

"It sure seems that way. At least I promised I would try to find the castle. I had a guide with me, but we got separated a while back." Robbie wasn't sure how many hours or days had passed since he was last with Sarcadui. The first time he was in a time lapse, he had woken up underground in Langly thinking it was the next morning, but really several days had passed.

"I'm sure you'll find him," said Rhoe, reassuringly, referring to Robbie's lost guide. "I never would have expected my life's greatest tragedy and my life's greatest hope would be realized both on the same day. And I didn't have to suffer over my loss for long because you made yourself known to me and now I have hope that everything will be all right. Just think; soon you'll be sailing across the sea, then you'll find the castle, sit on your throne, and all the terrors of the island will disappear forever."

Rhoe went on. "I have just one request, if you don't mind, but please don't feel like you have to do it... I can't believe I'm even saying this to you."

"What is it?" asked Robbie, starting to feel quite important for the first time.

"Could you sit on the throne when it's dark? I want to be able to *see* them destroyed. The way I figure it, the only way to see them destroyed is if they're actually on the island. In fact, I'm going to find a spot right up in the trees and wait. You shouldn't be more than about four days from the ocean, I'm guessing?"

"I don't know," said Robbie. "I don't even know where the ocean is... it's just been so long since I've been here," he added impulsively, catching himself, ending each word with a period. "I was actually hoping you could take over for my guide."

"Oh no, I couldn't do that," protested Rhoe. "You don't need my help."

"Sure I do," Robbie tried. "Obviously I wouldn't be alive if it weren't for you, so it makes sense that you should accompany me. You wouldn't want me getting lost or killed, would you?"

"But I've never been to the ocean. I wouldn't know where to lead you."

"My instructions were northwest. I'm sure you can handle that. Come on, you know how dangerous it is out there; I'd never make it by myself. I need someone who knows the jungle like you do."

"I couldn't impose. I'm not worthy," stammered Rhoe, backing away.

Robbie was growing piqued. Finally he tried a different approach. He set his face into a cold grimace and spoke in the sternest voice he could muster. "You're right. You're not worthy to take me. I don't need you, but I'm still kind enough to ask for your help. Now you can choose to come with me, or else I will have to assume that you stand against me. If that's the case, then I'll have no pity on your soul when you burst into flames the night I take my throne. What will it be?"

Rhoe stood cautiously away from Robbie, caught off guard by his sudden change of countenance. When the command seemed to sink in, he slowly nodded his head and said quietly, "Northwest?"

Robbie nodded in return and Rhoe began to walk through the jungle. Robbie was quite taken aback by his acting skills and congratulated himself for pulling off such a stunt. "A wise decision," said Robbie, unable to drop the character just yet.

They walked on in silence for some time, neither of them feeling quite comfortable with their new relationship of lord and servant. Then Robbie stopped and pointed to a body lying sprawled near a tree. "Oh no," he said.

"What?" asked Rhoe who only meandered past it because he was in the habit of passing by the many bodies scattered throughout the island without looking at them.

Robbie ran up to the body and gently picked up her limp head in his arms. "She was my guide."

CHAPTER 22

Before Robbie could dissolve into tears, Sarcadui stretched her arms and when she opened her eyes to Robbie, she smiled. Robbie felt foolish for not even having felt for a pulse.

"Hi Robbie," Sarcadui said sleepily. "I knew I'd see you again."

"Of course you would. I won't ever leave you for good," said Robbie. Rhoe took a step back from the scene.

"I'm glad," Sarcadui said. "The next time you disappear I won't go anywhere if I can help it. I'll just wait for you to come back."

"And I'll always make sure your cloak is right where you left if so you can put it on," promised Sarcadui.

"Now, what if I appear somewhere else?"

"You've never done that, so I don't think we need to worry about that quite yet."

But just as she said this, a very strange and distinct sound was heard from somewhere in the back of his head. It somehow didn't seem to fit with his current surroundings.

"Do you hear that?" he asked. But the others were oblivious to the noise. It was growing louder. He turned to see what it was that was making the sound. When he looked, he saw his living room chair against the back wall. The sound was coming from his alarm clock on his phone lying on the floor next to the box.

It was time to wake up. He groggily turned off the alarm, then snuck the box out the back door and stashed it in the tool shed and locked it up. He did all of this with stiff joints and sore muscles, and his palms burned with great intensity. Also, his arms and legs, he noticed, were all cut up and scratched from all the tree branches he had climbed on. But his clothes were still intact and not a single rip had gone through them. Further proof that only his body was affected by Reveloin, not items on his person. Plus, his cloak did not come back with him just like before. He would have to be careful once again, to keep his hands from Rosalynn and dress in long sleeves and pants until the scratches healed.

After he changed into his sweat clothes again, he slipped into bed next to Rosalynn and she lazily drooped her arm over him and held him close.

"Where were you?" she asked drowsily.

"I was checking on a noise," Robbie said. "Everything's fine."

"Okay," yawned Rosalynn, going back to sleep. "I love you."

They slept in until eight o' clock, which Robbie was grateful for. Jeremy was already up and watching his Saturday morning cartoons as usual, and Taylor was lying on the couch behind him, still trying to wake up.

After they had breakfast together, Robbie declined going with them to Taylor's volleyball practice, because, he insisted, he had a lot of work to do with getting his resume out and all.

He spent most of the morning contacting the companies on his half of the list. He was quite proud of the resume he sent out to dozens of companies because he had compiled an impressive portfolio of popular books he had edited and articles he had written.

The second part of the list contained, to Robbie's delight, a group of CipherMill's top clients: Fifteen of them. Robbie wasted no time calling up Don Stentson, someone he never thought he would voluntarily connect with, and laid out his plans.

"We need to get these clients under our belt," said Robbie. "If we work together we have a better chance at snagging them."

"And what will we do with them exactly?"

"We'll play the middle man. We'll edit their work exclusively, they'll pay us generously as they had with CipherMill in the past, then we'll pass them along to a publisher, any publisher, primed and polished. What do you say?"

"It sounds sleazy."

"Tinkering around on Kurt's files was about as sleazy as you can get, Don. The only way you can go from there is up. Let's do this."

A long, fat sigh pushed its way through the receiver then, "Okay. I'm in."

Robbie delegated a handful of clients for Don to contact and told him to get back with him tomorrow. He hung up and got to work on his half of the list. For the first time on this side of Reveloin, Robbie was feeling great about himself.

CHAPTER 23

When Robbie finished his work – he received eight immediate responses to clients he had emailed and he threw some prices their way, seven of which replied back positively – he decided that a trip to the nearby bar was in order. You know, just an afternoon celebratory drink.

Pete's Dragon was just a few blocks from the house. He had a couple hours to kill before the kids came home from school. He chose to sit in a dark corner booth eavesdropping on the love-starved locals who were at home on their barstools and were on familiar terms with the bartender. Since his rehabilitation sixteen years ago he had often looked down his nose at these lowlifes. He wasn't one of them now. He wasn't sulking or wallowing his sorrows away by the bottle. He was celebrating a bright and optimistic future.

Splattered over the sticky glass-top table he couldn't help but reminisce how invincible he had been in Reveloin, battling those titanic centipedes. He thought long and hard whether he believed his new life was going to interfere with his old one. But the more he reveled in his excitement over his new mission the less he cared. So what if it interfered? What would he miss by visiting Reveloin once a night? A few hours of sleep? He had never been a hard sleeper to begin with.

When he got home a couple hours after Taylor's volleyball practice, he saw the trunk of Rosalynn's Volkswagen Jetta ajar. They must have forgotten to close it when they were carrying in his dad's things.

His dad. He had forgotten. The realization hit him hard in the gut.

He half expected to open the door to laughter and happy sounds but then remembered it was *his* family that had come to visit, not someone else's. In stark contrast to his illusion the house sounded more like a funeral home.

Robbie walked slowly toward the kitchen. It was surreal knowing his father was just steps away.

He entered the kitchen and there seated at the table were Rosalynn, Jeremy, and his gray-haired, overweight father who looked like he was due for a heart attack. He would probably get along with Don. The drastic advancement in his father's age nearly rendered Robbie speechless. He wanted desperately to just come out and say it: "What have you done to yourself?" But as always with his family, formalities trumped honesty and he blurted, "Dad, you look good. How are you?"

Harvey expended a huge amount of energy to stand up from his chair and make his way over to Robbie, with the aid of a cane, which Robbie had never known his father to have. When his father reached him, he clasped his hands on Robbie's arms and said, "I'm good son. How are you?"

Ignoring the question, Robbie asked, "What's the cane for?"

Rosalynn suddenly jumped in before Harvey could answer and said, "Why don't you ask him how his flight was?"

"How was it? Hopefully they didn't show *Backdraft*," joked Robbie. "You know, in light of what happened..."

"Actually, we did have a scary moment," said Harvey, always serious. "The plane hit an air pocket and we fell for about fifty feet." Robbie was sure "fifty feet" was an exaggeration, but Harvey concluded, "No one got hurt. Say, have you taken up smoking again? You smell like cigarettes."

"It's nothing, Dad," insisted Robbie. He couldn't figure out how his dad, even after all these years, possessed such a strong knack for making him feel sixteen again. And at sixteen his dad had made him feel like he was six.

"You smoked?" asked Jeremy, now perking up.

"Oh, *now* you want to talk to me? And no, I didn't. At least not today," stammered Robbie, angry with his dad for bringing it up in front of his son and defensive against Rosalynn's icy stare. "What's for dinner?" he asked in an attempt to step out from under the spotlight.

"Nicotine patches," shot Rosalynn as she pushed past him toward the oven. "Do you want some tonic with that?"

"Rosalynn's making us all a lasagna," said Harvey, now playing naïve to the topic at hand. He wasn't fooling Robbie.

A loud slap jolted Robbie. Rosalynn had just stomped her foot on the floor. "Disgusting!" she said.

"What is it?" asked Robbie. But his heart nearly stopped when she lifted her foot, and there under her shoe was a smashed centipede. They had never had centipedes in the house before.

"That's the second one I've found today," she said.

Robbie shook it off. It was just a freak coincidence.

"Is something burning?" asked Harvey, sticking his nose in the air.

"Oh no," cried Rosalynn opening up the oven as smoke spilled out of it. "The lasagna burned. I'm so sorry." She took the charred dish out of the oven and began flapping the smoke away with a towel. "Jeremy, fan the smoke detector would you? I've got to clean this mess up," she added, referring to the centipede.

Robbie rushed over to help his wife defuse the situation. He spotted his dad out of the corner of his eye standing anonymously near the kitchen counter offering vain attempts to help with the mess.

Robbie couldn't remember the last time she had burnt something. This meant that she was as stressed as he was. After several clumsy attempts to pitch in with the cleaning, Rosalynn said, "Robbie, order a pizza or something, okay?"

While they waited for the pizza Harvey dismissed himself to the living room to catch the news about the fires that were still raging out of control in Los Angeles. He was overly excited that his town was making national news.

While his dad was glued to the TV, Jeremy excused himself to his room, leaving Robbie and Rosalynn alone in the kitchen free to talk while they prepared the dishes for dinner.

"Where's Taylor?" asked Robbie, trying to keep Pandora's Box closed.

"Why do you smell like cigarettes?" came the sharp response.

"I asked you a question first," said Robbie playfully.

"She's at Lauren's house studying for a test they have tomorrow. I didn't want her to go because her grandpa is here, but she put up such a fuss in front of him that I ended up *making* her go. Now, answer my question. Why do you smell like cigarette smoke?"

"Are you sure it's not the burnt lasagna you're smelling?" This was Robbie's last feeble attempt to wiggle out of the question.

Rosalynn stopped dispensing the dishes, turned hard toward Robbie and said, "Were you smoking today?"

Finally an answer he could give! "No!"

"Then why do you smell like that?"

"I was at the bar and I had a few drinks, okay?" Robbie said. There. That wasn't so hard. No reason to get mad at that. Why was he so scared to tell her that?

"Why?" asked Rosalynn advancing on him. "Why were you at the bar? Who were you with?"

"Whoa," Robbie exclaimed. "What's with all the accusations? Calm down."

"Calm down? Then tell me why there was a message left on the answering machine from a woman looking for you! And then tell me you weren't meeting her for a few drinks. *Then* I'll calm down."

Robbie didn't know what to say. Who would be looking for him? Obviously someone calling him about a job. But he had his phone with him all day. Rosalynn had to have been talking about the landline they'd been meaning to get rid of.

"The call was from your phone, by the way. Don't bother checking the machine to listen to it; I erased it. You can find her yourself if you're that desperate." And with that Rosalynn left the kitchen to join his dad in the living room. That was the low point: Rosalynn choosing his *dad's* company over his.

CHAPTER 24

During dinner there was enough small talk that covered any grudges that might appear on the surface. Forget about what happened in the past; let's talk about the here and now because it's safer. No outbursts of any kind, just quiet, polite dinner table conversation, and we'll all keep our thoughts to ourselves. No sense digging up buried bones.

"Mostly everything burned up in the fire," said Harvey, "but I managed to save a few things: some heirlooms and necessities and whatnot. Jeremy, go through my suitcase and find a folder that has your dad's name on it, will you?"

Jeremy obediently got up from his seat. "It's in Grandpa's room," said Rosalynn, and Jeremy ran to the guest room. Robbie was intrigued. While they waited for Jeremy to return, Harvey asked the standard questions about Robbie's job. Not willing to tell his father that he had been fired, Robbie explained that he was still at the top of his game at CipherMill. Needless to say, Robbie avoided Rosalynn's accusing glare the rest of the night. When they were newlyweds and still on speaking terms with Harvey (at best) it was always a grievance to her that Robbie would sugarcoat everything just so he could imagine he was living up to his dad's expectations.

Jeremy came bursting into the dining room holding a thick manila folder up in the air. "Give that to your dad, Jer," instructed Harvey.

Robbie received the folder in his hands. His heart stopped when he opened it, pulled out a thick notebook and scrawled on the front was the title, *My Adventures in Reveloin*. As he eagerly flipped through the tattered pages, he asked his dad, "Where did you find this?"

"You spent so much time writing those silly stories that I never thought to get rid of it. It was stashed with all the other keepsakes that I managed to pack up."

It was just as he had remembered it from the library in Reveloin: worn out pages, sloppy handwriting, and eraser marks –

everything you would expect a nine-year-old's journal to look like. He pushed the folder aside so as not to seem too eager about it. He would give it more attention later.

The night ended with Jeremy disappearing back to his room and Rosalynn trying unsuccessfully to push a little bit of depth into the conversation. But Harvey wanted to flop down in front of the TV to rest and Robbie reluctantly joined his father. He would rather tune out next to his dad rather than argue more with Rosalynn. This is how the rest of the evening was spent.

Once his dad was situated in the guest room, Robbie and Rosalynn went upstairs to get ready for bed, which they did in a tension-filled, uncomfortable silence. In a way, it was good that they weren't on speaking terms at the moment because it made it easier for him to remain at a distance from her when he was changing out of his clothes so she wouldn't notice his scratched-up arms and legs. When he got out of the shower, convinced he was washing off dirt and centipede trails, Rosalynn was already in bed pretending to be asleep. He slipped on long sweats to cover up his body and thought about how fortunate it was that he hadn't received any bruises or scratches on his face.

In bed, Robbie's curiosity got the better of him, so after a painful silence he asked, "What did the message say?"

"Oh, like I'm just supposed to hand her message over to you on a silver platter!" sneered Rosalynn. "Why don't you just make it easier for the both of us – just tell me you're having an affair!"

"What?!" exclaimed Robbie, aghast. "What are you talking about?"

"It all adds up, Robbie," started Rosalynn, tears welling up now. "It all started when you came home at that ungodly hour the other night. You were up late the night after that with the phone in the living room... and you've been at the bar all day probably with the girl from the message machine."

Robbie, in an attempt to set the record straight, placed his hand on his wife's shoulder, trying not to cringe from his tender palm, and scooted closer to her, feeling his joints explode with pain. "Honey, I'm not having an affair. I promise."

"Then what's going on?" she demanded, keeping her face away from him.

Robbie's voice caught in his throat. He had no answer. What was he supposed to do, tell her more about the magical world he found inside the cardboard box, currently sitting out in the tool shed? He tried that once and she dismissed him as some nut job. As to the other mystery, he couldn't explain the message on the answering machine. Heck, he didn't even know the phone number to their landline, and doubted if anyone had even used it since they moved in.

"I don't care," cried Rosalynn after it was clear he wasn't going to answer. "Just leave me alone." She wiped her eyes and pulled away from him, clearly wanting to be alone.

Robbie gave up, too exhausted to prove himself otherwise. But not too exhausted to flip on the lamp and read through some of the stories in his folder. In search of some answers he flipped to the last page and did his best to make out the poor penmanship.

It was written like a compilation of short stories, one adventure after another. Robbie really had made up the characters Lahni, Ewin, and Rico. They were his best friends. He remembered they were as alive to him as a real flesh and blood person.

Of the three of them Lahni was the level-headed leader. Even though Robbie was the creator of their world, he would often look to Lahni for guidance in dangerous situations.

Robbie guessed that Ewin was the picture of his mother. She was sensitive toward Robbie, caring, and always went to great strides to comfort him in times of need.

Rico was the exact opposite. He had a mean spirit, always bullying the group into doing dangerous things. He felt he always had to maintain this tough-guy image. But his bullying is what challenged Robbie, pushed him to his limits to see what he was made of.

The world of Reveloin was exactly as Sarcadui had described it. As expected in a child's fantasy world, the leaves were edible and the water tasted like sugar. And of course his world was inspired by 1970's pop culture. There were cowboy fights in the ghost towns, dinosaurs roaming around volcanic wastelands and even a rocket ship waiting to blast off to the moon. It was everything a boy from the space age could hope for and more. Sarcadui had not been mincing words when she told him how wonderful and colorful Reveloin had been in the past.

So his childhood fantasy world had evolved in his absence. During all these years Ewin and Lahni apparently got married and had Sarcadui. A castle had been built for him awaiting his return, and over time the country had matured like he had. As he lost his flair for imagination, Reveloin gradually lost its innocent wonder that made it so unique and appealing to him as a child. Now it was just an island – very real and very hostile.

Robbie had nodded off to sleep but his head bounced back up, jolting him awake. He still held the pages in his hand. Seeing that Rosalynn was sound asleep, he slowly got out of bed and grabbed some clothes from the closet then quietly crept downstairs with his cell phone set to go off in six hours.

He dropped the clothes on the couch and headed out to the tool shed. When he opened the door to it and stepped inside, he gagged at the familiar crunching sound under his bare foot. A half dozen or so centipedes scurried out into the yard past his feet. They were very fast, even in this world.

"Hey, hey, hey!" Robbie yelled in a whisper. Something was chewing on one of the lids of the box. It was an eoraptor, the giant lizard Hail had shown him. So the centipede Rosalynn had killed was no coincidence at all... Robbie was more convinced than ever that he needed to complete his mission in Reveloin so nothing else could come through the box.

The small dinosaur looked at him and hissed. It sounded like a provoked Canadian goose. He grabbed a shovel leaning up next to him and swatted it as hard as he could, knocking it unconscious. He scooped it up, heavy as it was, its neck and tail hanging off the spade, and was about to walk it to the dumpster, but then he had a different idea. He tossed it in the box, and just as he suspected, it disappeared just as it hit the bottom. The only reason he himself didn't disappear was because he was part of this world. At least, that was the only thing he could come up with. It's possible that the dinosaur's body never left Reveloin when it came to this world.

He brought the box inside and placed it behind the couch just like before. He slipped out of his sweat pants and into the jeans and hiking shoes he had brought from upstairs. But before he stepped into the box he dashed toward the kitchen, careful not to walk loudly on the tile and dug around the drawers and found what he was looking for: a pocket knife and a packet of matches. He stuffed them into his pockets and jogged back to the box.

Ensuring that the alarm on his phone was set, he placed it next to him, then got in the box and closed his eyes.

The wind was howling, tossing brush and leaves along with its currents. It whistled through the tree branches and Robbie had to cross his arms together against his chest for warmth. It wasn't yet nightfall, but it was getting close. Apparently there had just been another time lapse. Just a second ago it had been midday without wind or clouds. And now instead of wearing shorts he had on pants and some better-fitted shoes for traveling, which were breaking the sandals he had had on a moment ago. He shook them loose and jammed his hands into empty pockets to keep them warm. Then he saw his cloak faithfully lying on the ground and put it on, insulating the wind from his body. Wherever he had just come from, he sure left better prepared for a long journey.

As if following his instructions to stay nearby when he disappeared, Sarcadui ran up to Robbie and wrapped her arms around him saying, "I'm so glad you're back."

"How long was I gone?" asked Robbie, hoping his face wasn't too red from blushing.

"Two days," she replied.

"Where's Rhoe?"

She seemed troubled at the mention of his name. "He's up ahead scouting the area. He's been checking in on me from time to time. He says the jungle gets worse up ahead because it's heavily guarded with trenchers."

"Trenchers?" asked Robbie. He vaguely remembered Hail mentioning something about them. "What are those?"

"Traitors. They're people who made alliances with the ghosts and patrol the island for them during the day while they're gone."

"Why are they called trenchers?" asked Robbie.

"There's a storm coming in," said Sarcadui. "We should probably get going if we want to cover ground. I can answer your questions on our way."

As they walked, Sarcadui obligingly recounted her knowledge of the trenchers.

"When the ghosts started coming to the island and killing people, many of them started forming alliances with the ghosts, selling their services to them."

"You mean, like… prostituting themselves?"

She shook her head, showing a slight smirk on her face. "The deal they made was that they would stand on guard for the ghosts during the day while they were gone, and they would kill as many people as they could. In exchange, the ghosts would not kill them, and they were then free to roam the island at all hours, day or night. They were marked by trench coats, which is how they got the name trenchers. But soon the trenchers figured out that they didn't have to kill anyone at all because they assumed the ghosts would still spare them as long as they were properly marked. Soon, the ghosts noticed that fewer and fewer people were dying, which was hindering their cause, so a new system was put into place."

"It's hard to imagine the ghosts can work under any sort of structure," commented Robbie.

"They were once people too," Sarcadui reminded him. "Anyway, this is how the system works now: if someone wants to spare his life and align himself with the ghosts then he is assigned a panther."

"Why a panther?"

"Because they can track anyone's blood from anywhere on the island. Once the panthers sniff the blood of a new traitor it can remember his scent and track it from anywhere.

"Why would it need to find the traitor? So he doesn't run away?"

"Pretty much. Every month the ghosts hold festivities around the island which every ghost and trencher is required to attend. There are four arenas spread out on the island called Game Pits."

"You mentioned those before," said Robbie. "What are they?"

"Game Pits," resumed Sarcadui, "are massive arenas where victims get thrown into and are killed by warped ghosts and any other kind of monster they can find to throw in there. They unleash these vicious creatures and the victims have to fend for themselves as thousands of people gather to watch. It's sick."

Sarcadui stopped for a moment then shook her head and continued, "Apparently there's something about part of your throne being scattered throughout them, but I don't see how anyone can know that since it's impossible to survive. Anyway, each month the trenchers are required to show up to their assigned arena with at least four victims to throw into the Game Pit to ensure that they're upholding their end of the bargain. If they don't meet their quota or they simply don't show up, then the ghosts send that trencher's panther after him and kill him. The panthers often drag their trencher all the way through the island to the ghosts and the ghosts kill him in their own twisted way, then let the panther eat the remains."

"How do you know so much about this?" asked Robbie.

"I know – or knew – someone who was thrown in," Sarcadui responded somberly.

"Who?"

Sarcadui just shook her head and declined to answer. Robbie respectfully withdrew his question. He concluded that it was the boy she had written about in her book at the library – her young romance. He recalled that she didn't linger anywhere near the end of his life nor comment on what had happened to him.

After walking a bit further, Robbie asked, "But what about killing every human being? In the end the trenchers are going to have to be killed too, right?"

"The trenchers don't think it will come to that. They think if they can find the prophesied one – you – and turn you in, then the ghosts would have no reason to kill them. Technically they're right, but who knows how long it would take the ghosts to turn on them when there's no one else to kill? It would just be a game to them."

"It sounds like it already is," commented Robbie, resentfully.

In the half hour since Robbie had arrived, the storm had found them and drops of water began to sprinkle onto their heads.

Soon they found Rhoe crouched down behind a tree steadying his gaze intently on something in the distance. When he heard them approaching he gave a slight jump, then he signaled for them to remain quiet but to join him.

"What is it?" whispered Sarcadui.

"There are trenchers ahead. And they're alert," said Rhoe matter-of-factly. Then, upon seeing Robbie, he whispered loudly, "My lord, hi!"

Robbie nodded, still not sure how he was supposed to respond to such admirations.

"Alert to what?" asked Sarcadui. "To us?"

Rhoe shook his head. "There's something else further up ahead that they've been following. I have no idea what it is."

Robbie peered around the side of a tree trunk to sneak a peek at the trenchers. At first he saw nothing, then after a minute, a shiny black panther crept through some shrubs. Robbie nearly whimpered at the size of it. Even from a hundred yards away it looked to be about nine to twelve feet long and about three hundred pounds. It was pulling tight on a chain that was wrapped around its neck, dragging a man. The panther crept low to the ground as though it was on the hunt for something. It pulled its chain tight, but its master obediently walked where he was led. The rain fell harder now.

"They suspect something is out there, but not us," said Rhoe almost to himself.

“How many are there?” asked Robbie.

“I’ve counted three so far, but only two trenchers. Talk quieter, my lord. They’ve been suspicious of something up ahead for the last hour or so. I know of an old cottage about two miles up. It’s where me and my brother would sleep if we ever got stuck out here at night. We have about twenty minutes before the sun goes down. But if we want to make it all the way there without them hearing us, we’ll have to be quiet. When the sun starts to set the trenchers should call it a day and head home to the east. That’ll give us a small window of opportunity to make it to the cottage as fast as we can before the ghosts come out for the night. But I’ve got to be honest. I’m nervous because there seems to be a lot more activity with the ghosts lately.”

“That might have been our doing,” admitted Sarcadui sheepishly. “We set fire to the library a few nights ago, so they think something’s up.” To Robbie the fire in the library was just a couple of hours ago.

Rhoe threw a hand to his mouth to stifle an exclamation. “How did you do that?”

“It was both terrifying and wonderful at the same time,” responded Sarcadui joyously as though about to go into a full narrative. “Robbie was so heroic – he actually set fire to one of the ghosts!”

As flattered as he was, Robbie was growing tenser the darker it became. He said, “Guys, can we talk later?”

“Yes, my lord,” said Rhoe dutifully.

Thunder rumbled in the distance as the three proceeded forward, trailing the trenchers and panthers through the jungle.

CHAPTER 25

The rain fell harder now, making it difficult to see ahead. Robbie whipped the icy-cold rain from his eyes as adrenaline surged through him like fuel. Rhoe kept a steady pace pushing through branches and shrubs.

Through an opening in the trees above, Robbie could see the clouds were dark brown which meant the sun was somewhere out there; its rays being too weak to penetrate. This explained the sepia-lit air which struck an eerie chord with Robbie's nerves.

As they continued to creep forward, Robbie occasionally heard twigs snapping under the footsteps just ahead. Rhoe would often hold the party back so as not to get too close to their rival's backs.

As it grew darker Robbie's pulse raced furiously. He strained his eyes to see through the thickets, trying to detect Rhoe's gradually disappearing body. He could no longer hear anyone's footsteps because by now the rain was coming down as hard as a waterfall, which made it nearly impossible to see. Had the trenchers gone home? Rhoe had said that they would depart just before sunset and it looked to Robbie like it was about that time. He couldn't help but feel like he was being watched from behind. Was Sarcadui still behind him? He didn't want to turn his head and risk taking his eyes off Rhoe lest he lose him.

Then, without warning, Rhoe stopped and summoned Robbie and Sarcadui to come near. In a voice just loud enough to be heard over the rain he said, "The trenchers are about to call it quits."

Robbie longed to walk all night with a torch as he and Sarcadui had done after their escape from the library, but that would be impossible since all the wood was soaked from the rain. Without a torch, Robbie felt utterly exposed to any dangers that might have been lurking behind the trees.

A couple minutes passed and the rain let up just enough to remain at a steadily flowing pace. Robbie could now just barely make out the familiar jungle noises. He listened for more footsteps up ahead, or even for some talking. But all he heard were Rhoe's,

Sarcadui's, and his own cautious footsteps through the thick mud. But because the mud was so thick and sticky and the rain had slowed down enough, they had to walk with greater prudence so as not to let their sloshing footsteps be heard.

But the thing that scared Robbie the most was the panther he had seen the trencher following. And Rhoe said there were at least two others. How long, Robbie wondered, would it be before the panthers detected them?

When the rain slowed down, so did Rhoe. Robbie figured it was because he was taking extra caution with their footsteps. But when he stopped completely, a bout of lightning revealed his intention.

It was dark enough now that they had to rely on the flashes of lightning through the treetops to illuminate their path. The lightning was so intense that it lit up the entire jungle like flashes of daylight and they could see for miles ahead. This, of course also meant that they too were just as exposed to uninvited eyes and could no longer stay sheltered behind a thick canopy of heavy rain.

When the lightning cracked, it revealed that all the landscape stretching before them was barren of people and panthers. However, that hungry gaze that pierced the back of Robbie's neck grew more intense as if the feeling itself were a muscle, pulsating and pumping icy-cold blood through his veins. He wished more than anything that he hadn't lost his knife in the fire.

Sarcadui whispered cautiously, "They're playing with us."

"Who?" asked Robbie. "The panthers?"

"Yes."

"What makes you think they're playing with us?"

But as soon as he asked, the lightning licked the earth, spitting shafts of light at their feet and Robbie looked where Sarcadui was pointing just ahead of them. On the ground, in the mud, were fresh paw tracks, but no footprints.

The panthers were loose.

CHAPTER 26

Robbie's heart nearly stopped beating and his spine erupted into icy-hot chills. He watched helplessly as Rhoe ripped a knife out from a belt that his shirt covered and said, "Take this, my lord. You need it more than I do."

Robbie conceded by taking the dagger. He wondered how efficient he would be with it if it came time to use it. In the thick darkness he could barely detect that Rhoe had picked up a stick large enough to carry with both hands, which he must have been planning to use as a bo in his defense.

They continued to walk carefully through the jungle, taking care to make as little noise as possible. By this time the rain had slowed down enough that only the water dripping down from the trees could be heard. If not for the imminent threats lurking just inches behind the veil of darkness, the dripping water would have been soothing.

He gazed around trying to see through the dark, but he couldn't see anything but small fireflies hovering in the trees above. They were so still. Could they have been fairies? No. Sarcadui would have noticed them.

After several more minutes of walking, Robbie began to entertain the idea that maybe the panthers had dispersed from the area finding the hunting opportunities sparse. But his thoughts only lasted for a second before they were interrupted by ghastly images of the ghosts he had seen seemingly just hours before.

It was nighttime now and they, the ghosts, would surely be out by now. This time there was no fire or light of any kind to chase them away and Sarcadui had said that fire was their only defense. It would be impossible to start a fire with any of this wet wood.

Robbie was succumbing to his paralyzing fears when he cannoned into Rhoe, who had suddenly stopped again. He was kneeling down. Sarcadui came up behind them. Lightning cracked through the trees and revealed what he was examining.

The paw tracks had come to an abrupt end.

No one needed to voice it; they were all thinking it. The panthers were in the trees.

It didn't take Robbie long to figure out that the fireflies above were actually the panthers' emerald eyes glaring down at them, their prey. The panthers *were* playing with them; testing them, teasing them. Once the panthers caught them, they would have even more fun feeding off of them.

One look from Rhoe in the darkness told him everything he needed to know if any of them were going to have a hair's breadth of surviving. They were to walk slowly, and not, under any circumstances, give the panthers any reason to believe they knew where they were.

In other words, don't look up or you'll die. Just keep walking as though you don't know they exist.

The panthers were up there, in the trees, waiting to jump at any moment they chose. He could almost feel the gaze of one piercing the back of his neck as he moved naively forward, struggling to walk the same way as he had before he knew they were above him.

They pressed on slowly. It became easier to see as beams of moonlight began to poke through the treetops.

Try as he might, Robbie could not push the terrifying images of his imminent death out of his mind. But what bothered him even more was that Sarcadui and Rhoe would face the same fate all because he showed up to their world and they decided to take a chance on him being someone he knew he was not. Their deaths would be in vain.

Robbie didn't have to see or hear the panthers leaping weightlessly from branch to branch to sense that they were keeping up with them. How soon, he wondered, before they were so overcome with hunger that they just had to pounce on his back and start clawing?

Finally, after a few more terrifying moments, Rhoe pulled back some thickets to reveal a clearing. In the middle of it stood a quaint little cottage home illuminated by the moonlight. It was undisturbed and a welcoming sight to Robbie and surely to his comrades. If they could just make it inside, one of two threats would be eliminated from their worries.

Since the cottage was set in a large glade they would have to run from the trees if they had any prayer of reaching it before the panthers pounced.

Rhoe said, "We'd better go all three at once." Then, looking at Robbie, added, "How are you doing, my lord?"

"Just get us inside and I'll be fine," said Robbie.

Time stood still as Rhoe counted down on his fingers from three.

Three.

Two.

One.

At the last moment Robbie slipped his knife into Sarcadui's hand, knowing she would be more protected with two knives instead of one. Then all three shot through the foliage and darted across the open glade. The whole time, Robbie felt his shoulder blades tighten up and tingle as if that was exactly where the panthers would bite into him.

Robbie was the first to reach the cottage door only because Sarcadui and Rhoe slowed down to defend him from any panthers that might attack from behind. Another thick cloud drifted across the moon blanketing the world once again in total darkness.

He jiggled the handle and found the door locked.

CHAPTER 27

Robbie turned from the door just in time to see a distant flash of lightning stretch its fingers across the dry sky. It pointed at two panthers eerily sneaking their way toward Rhoe and Sarcadui who were now looking at Robbie for results on the door. Robbie froze in his spot and tried to find the words to warn them of their imminent attack. But they didn't need Robbie's warning. "We know," came Rhoe's voice from the darkness. "We can hear them."

"Just don't move," said Robbie, aware that he was not an expert on the behavior of wild animals.

Another strike of lighting revealed one of the panthers lunging mid-air toward Rhoe and the other toward Sarcadui. The illumination from the lightning dispersed just before the panthers hit their targets. Robbie braced himself for the onslaught, wishing he had kept his knife. But in the darkness he only heard hissing and savage snarling from the monstrous cats as they struggled with their prey.

Through his eyelids Robbie saw that the sky was lit up again, so he dared to look. The lightning lingered long enough that he saw both panthers lying dead on the ground, one with Rhoe's stick wedged deeply into its side and the other lying just feet away from Sarcadui in a pool of its own blood. Both of Sarcadui's knives hung at her sides dripping with fresh gore. She said to Rhoe, "There'll be others as soon as they smell the blood."

"There's nothing more we can do about it. We've got to get inside," said Rhoe.

Rhoe and Sarcadui jogged toward Robbie. Rhoe pushed him away from the door saying, "Excuse me my lord," and kicked the door, but it did not budge. "It's *never* locked," he said aghast.

Robbie looked back into the jungle and saw the glowing eyes of the third panther perched up high on a tree branch waiting intently for its moment to strike.

Before Rhoe could kick the door again it flew open.

It was Ames, the old man Robbie had met in Langly. He pulled Robbie in by his cloak and Rhoe and Sarcadui followed.

"You three are sure doing a fine job calling the ghosts," said Ames with a grunt.

The cottage was plainly furnished. It took a moment for Robbie's eyes to adjust to the bitter darkness but eventually he was able to make out shapes in the small abode. In one corner was a wooden chair and in the other was a table with a blanket strewn atop it that must have served as a bed. True to Langly style. Above it was a window not quite large enough for a man to crawl through. The ceiling was low and was supported by thick beams, which made the cottage seem even smaller.

While Ames bolted the door shut he said, "You look exhausted. Take a seat." The three of them sat awkwardly cross-legged on the hardwood floor while Ames sat down in the chair in the far corner.

The moon was beginning to come back out and it cast an eerie glow through the window on Ames's hard face. "I'm sorry I don't have any food for you. If I had known you were going to come here, I would have been more prepared. How's your journey been treating you? Quite eventful I imagine."

"Ames, what are you doing here?" asked Sarcadui.

"I'm keeping ahead of you. I'm clearing the road of potential danger."

"Why didn't you just come with us then, instead of sneaking around behind our backs?" asked Robbie.

Ames leaned forward in his seat. "If you want to have any hope, at all, of making it to the ocean you need more than just a guide, you need a protector. It's best to know that protector isn't around so you're not worrying if he's going to show up to save you at the last minute."

"And how have you accomplished this?" asked Sarcadui. "I'm confused."

"Let me ask you this… other than the party you hosted at the library, have you had any other run-ins with the ghosts?" asked Ames in turn.

"No, that's been our only encounter. But we weren't protected from them. They found us and could have killed us if it weren't for Robbie taking a candle…" Sarcadui's voice trailed off as if making a connection.

"*You* lit those candles?" asked Robbie.

Ames nodded. "Guilty. I would have expected Sarcadui to exercise such tactfulness. But *you*, Robbie? *You* took the candle? Very impressive. Maybe you're starting to remember your old days in Reveloin after all."

"I was just trying to protect Sarcadui," said Robbie sheepishly.

Rhoe shifted uncomfortably in his spot.

"But that still doesn't explain how the ghosts found us," said Sarcadui. "It seems to me that you were neglecting your job as our protector."

"It does seem that way, yes," admitted Ames. "But how much trouble did you have *until* you reached the library?"

"None at all," answered Sarcadui. "But the sun was out. We wouldn't have had trouble anyway."

"We can spend all night tracking all the different ways I've kept harm out of your way but there are more pressing matters to attend to."

"Was that you the trenchers were tracking earlier?" asked Rhoe.

"Yes it was. I was trying to lead them *away* from you guys. Are you the one who chose to follow them?"

Rhoe said, "Yes. I knew this cottage was here. I didn't know the door would be barred."

Ames sneered. "Idiot."

"Hey," said Robbie in Rhoe's defense, "if you ask me, he's done quite well for a guide. We're all alive, aren't we? Besides, there was no other choice."

Rhoe beamed with pride at these words from his lord.

"By the way," continued Robbie, "if you knew we were out there, why *was* the door locked?"

"Even guardians have to protect themselves," insisted Ames.

Suddenly a loud shriek from just outside made everyone jump. "They're here," said Sarcadui. "They smelled the panthers' blood."

Heavy raindrops began pelting the roof.

Robbie shivered from a gust of wind that broke through a chink in the wall. He strained his ears to hear footsteps creeping toward the house. But he heard nothing. "Let's run for it," suggested Robbie.

"Hold on, genius. The front door is the only way our friends are going to get in. And that's the only way out," said Ames. "And right now they're all out there waiting for us like a pack of starved dogs."

They waited some more in the dark.

The silence itself seemed like a threat as if it were taunting them. Robbie was biting the inside of his mouth, feeling like time was suddenly their greatest enemy. The more time that passed, the more danger they were in.

"You know what they're doing, don't you?" asked Ames. The floorboards groaned under his feet as he stretched forward in his chair.

"You should keep your voice down," said Robbie in a whisper.

"Oh hush. They already know we're here. They've got the house surrounded. They'll start creeping up real slow like. They won't be slow because they're scared. No, they'll be slow because they want to intimidate you. Fear is their choice seasoning. They'll want you to know what exactly they're doing just before they kill you. They're generous like that. They'll want you to know how you're dying. Just like their lives were slowly sucked from them, they want you to suffer the same fate."

"Shut up," commanded Rhoe. "We're not going to die tonight. Besides, Lord Robbie told you to keep it down."

Robbie rolled his eyes. Being called Lord was getting on his nerves.

"You're not being yourself, Ames," said Sarcadui.

"I hope you don't find it off-putting," answered Ames. Then turning to Rhoe he asked, "You've got any other bright ideas?"

"Actually there are some loose boards on the ceiling that'll get us to the roof. The sun will hit the roof first. If we're going to be stuck here all night, there's no better place to be than up there."

"Let's get to it," Ames instructed.

"That's it?" asked Robbie. "We're just going to sit on the roof and hope they don't find us in the next seven hours?"

"At least it's safer than being in here," said Ames. "Unless you have any other ideas?"

Robbie searched his brain for something, but came out empty-handed. He shook his head.

With great agility Rhoe leapt up and grabbed hold of one of the beams and pulled himself up. He then proceeded to lift up two of the ceiling boards and moved them aside letting the rain fall in. He pushed aside the straw thatching to expose the cloudy sky above. Then he straddled the beam on his stomach and reached down with both arms to pull Sarcadui up, who hardly needed help at all. Together they helped Robbie and Ames up, then all worked their way outside.

With the clouds gathered back in front of the moon, they all laid against the wet straw covering on their backs. Robbie avoided looking down for fear of seeing the hideous ghosts again. But he couldn't avoid hearing them.

They managed to break the door down and began snooping around while making clicking sounds with their tongues against their teeth. Robbie smelled the stench of the panthers' decaying corpses and nearly gagged. Of course, some of the smell came from the ghosts themselves. He was growing sick.

Then it grew quiet. Too quiet. Sarcadui grabbed his hand and squeezed it tight. His scalded palm had healed. How he noticed this even as the panther jumped up onto the roof was beyond him.

It began crawling toward them, its teeth bared.

CHAPTER 28

It was that third panther Robbie had seen in the trees just before he entered the cottage. Ames instinctively kicked it hard with his foot. The only reason the gigantic cat fell to the roof's edge was because of the wet straw. It slid away, but not before it swiped at Ames's leg, causing him to yelp in pain. The ghosts shrieked in response and they began to climb up the beams, knocking the boards off the roof. Robbie and Rhoe raced to the top of the roof on hands and feet, careful not to slip.

Sarcadui was trying to drag Ames up by his robe. Knowing she wasn't going to give up, Robbie and Rhoe stumbled back down the roof to help her pull the wounded man up.

Just as they made it to the top of the roof, a slithering hand with elongated fingers grappled through the boards reaching whatever it could find. This almost drew attention away from the panther that was again making its way toward them. Robbie looked down the other side of the roof and saw ghosts gathering at the ground just like the centipede had done when he was climbing up the tree vine. Only, this time there was no place to go but down.

Then, from out of nowhere there came the faint sound of a blare being blown through what sounded like a conch horn. The ghosts and even the panther stopped and looked up in response. Silence amongst the ghosts loomed for a second as they ceased their jeering and hissing. Only some birds were heard cooing from inside the jungle, but even they were quiet about it. Ever so quietly Ames said, "Run."

Rhoe and Sarcadui needed no explanation. Sarcadui grabbed Robbie's arm and pulled him down the other side of the sloping roof and Rhoe dragged Ames down off the edge with him. They all landed amongst a crowd of ghosts with a thud. Robbie was back up on his feet immediately, but not before Sarcadui, who dragged him through the open glade toward the jungle trees before fear had a chance to set in.

Before reaching the tree line, Robbie managed to turn his head and steal a glance at the ghosts behind them and he perceived that they were fighting ruthlessly amongst themselves.

"What's that sound?" asked Robbie as the group stumbled along into the trees.

"It's Harvest Time," said Ames. "It's the end of the month. The trenchers are being called to the Pit to offer their provisions."

"What provisions?" Robbie asked.

"People," said Sarcadui. "Remember the Game Pits I told you about? The trenchers and ghosts are being called to attend. That's what that sound is. Many people are going to die tonight."

So many questions were filling Robbie's mind as the conch horn continued blowing somewhere in the distance behind them. But it was drowned out by another sound coming from far away. It was a sound that was alien, yet familiar to Robbie at the same time…

"…It seems to me like the fires are finally getting under control…"

Robbie jumped as if jerking awake from the deepest sleep.

Ever so slowly senses began to crawl back into Robbie's head and he was able to piece together his surroundings. Gradually his memory touched pieces of familiarity and his living room came into focus. But what was that constant noise?

"So far only two casualties have been reported."

Robbie slothfully stood up from the box and saw that the TV was turned on at an irregularly high volume. His dad was sitting up on the couch glued to the television. Robbie checked his phone for the time.

Eleven thirty-eight.

He examined himself for any new cuts or bruises. The bite mark from Hail had completely healed. His palms were no longer red and tender, his arms seemed to be healing nicely, and even his thigh was virtually painless when he pressed down on it where he had received the burn from the spilt coffee. But his back was sore from scratches and cuts he had accrued from sliding on the hay roof. And the pocketknife and matches were still in his pockets, but they hadn't been available to him in Reveloin.

So apparently, clothing could only be transported from home to Reveloin, but not from Reveloin to home; hence he again did not have his cloak. And any bodily injuries could be transported both ways. But items of his choice that would aid him in his travels remained behind. *Who made up these rules?* Robbie wondered.

He stepped out of the box slowly and carefully so as not to startle his old man. But because his legs were asleep and his head was spinning from standing up so fast, he tumbled onto the couch nearly into his father's lap sending him through the roof.

"What are you doing down here?" Harvey nearly yelled, trying to catch his breath.

"I was just checking on the noise," said Robbie. And, cutting his dad off from asking why he was behind the couch, he added, "Are you okay? Why are you up?"

"I can't sleep without a TV on, and there's no TV in my room."

"I'll look into that. I'm going back to bed," Robbie said dismissively. He felt like a prison warden taking down another pitiful request from an unhappy prisoner.

"What are you all dressed up for?" Harvey asked. "You look like you're going camping with the Waltons."

Robbie glanced down at his jeans that were tucked into his hiking boots and gave the only answer he thought fit to give. "You need TV. Sometimes a stroll in the backyard helps me to relax."

"Hey," exclaimed Harvey. "Sit down. I want to bring something to your attention."

Robbie, not quite sleepy, took a seat on the ottoman opposite the couch.

For the first time since Robbie could remember, his dad was beaming. When Robbie was settled, Harvey exclaimed, "Why don't you and I go into business together?"

Robbie froze. Drowning puppies would have been a better idea. But, just to humor him he asked, "What do you have in mind, Dad?"

"Well I've been lulling over this idea I've had in my head for quite some time now. It's a little mechanic shop I'd like to open."

"Like what you retired from?" asked Robbie dully.

"Not so much. This one will also be a '50s diner. People will pull their car into the shop and be served shakes and burgers while their car's being repaired. Yeah, we'll even have cute little skirts on roller skates serving customers at their car windows."

"That sounds unsanitary," said Robbie bluntly. He glanced at his dad's cane leaning up against the arm of the couch and almost asked him about it, but he didn't want to spark another late-night conversation. He was suddenly tired. "Tell you what. Why don't you work on that idea. Let me know once you've got it all figured out. I'm going to go to bed now."

“Alright. Put some notes together. Maybe later this week we can compare ideas.”

“Sure, Dad,” Robbie lied.

“By the way, your house is infested.”

“I know.”

“I’m finding centipedes everywhere. I must’ve killed three of them today. You might want to get that checked out. And you’ve got lots of lizards here. Big ones too.”

“What?” Robbie froze, instantly searching for an excuse for there being dinosaurs running around his backyard.

“Yeah, big ol’ suckers scurrying around on all fours up walls. I didn’t think you had them this far north.”

He breathed easier. “Yeah, there’s not many, but they’re out there. Especially this time of year.”

Robbie tossed the box outside the sliding glass door, lest any other creature come out of it and invade his home. Then he headed upstairs and changed into his usual nighttime attire, ditching the sweats, as his arms and legs had healed enough not to provoke any questions from Rosalynn. He crawled back into bed with her. She was sound asleep. He prayed nothing else would ever come out of the box. He didn’t need his family caught up in the mess he was in.

CHAPTER 29

The next morning Harvey had prepared eggs and coffee for everyone.

He had always been an early riser, and his advancement in years had not stopped that. After breakfast, Rosalynn took the kids to church with her, a habit she had never been able to break and one that Robbie had never gotten onboard with. He disappeared into his study where he found his golden list and began composing emails to potential clients. He had told Rosalynn that since he'd be at home for a while he could help out around the house and spend time with his father.

Of course, he had an ulterior motive.

But before he could go back to Reveloin he had to at least accomplish something. He had received a few more emails from people wanting to run their work by his editing desk. He smiled. He was in. He would charge just under CipherMill's price, and he'd still be making more than he did while working for them. Don should be calling at any time to compare notes.

He was responding to his third email when Harvey, also a church-avoider, tapped on the open door with his cane and asked if he wanted to grab a burger later. Robbie declined.

Don called eventually and they discussed business. Robbie learned quickly that unemployed people don't have the benefit of weekends. He wasn't having as much luck as Robbie, so to be helpful, he gave him some pointers on wooing people.

A half hour later Harvey burst into the study again with two full pages of scribbling and pulled a chair next to Robbie completely disregarding his work. Without giving Robbie a chance to dismiss him, he jumped right into the messy details of his business venture. It was all there: the hamburgers, the oil change with complimentary tire refills, milkshakes for half the price when you have your air filter changed, and of course the "babes on wheels."

Robbie's cell phone rang. It was Rosalynn asking him to start the laundry and clean the dishes in the sink. Church was out and she and the kids were going to lunch with some friends. This at least gave Robbie an excuse to leave his father alone to his own bizarre aspirations.

Finishing the chores, he realized he wouldn't be getting any work done with his dad being as disruptive as he was. Not that he really cared. He retrieved the box from the backyard and brought it upstairs to his side of the bed. Rosalynn wouldn't be home for another ninety minutes or so because that's how long lunch with her friends usually lasted. So without further adieu, Robbie set his alarm to go off in one hour and anxiously climbed back into the box with butterflies loose in his stomach, as always.

And thus the pattern was set for the next several days.

If he wasn't editing projects from committed clients, he was spending time in the box. He had to constantly be aware of Rosalynn's schedule. He mostly avoided his dad whenever he could, but he never really got around to seeing the kids since they were both usually locked up in their rooms: Jeremy, because he was absorbing his manga, and Taylor, because she was still grounded. When they needed to be dropped off or picked up from school or volleyball practice Harvey usually volunteered to drive them, leaving Robbie at home with his box, which he always took the opportunity to get inside of for another adventure.

Robbie awoke in bed one day to the early noon sun shining in his eyes through the window. As he slowly came to, he tried to come up with a reason why he'd slept in so late. He rarely slept in past nine, but this whole box thing was starting to throw his sleep schedule off kilter. He vaguely remembered Rosalynn trying to wake him up at least twice earlier.

What time did he get in the box last night, and for how long was he in it for? He and Rosalynn had gone to bed around ten. He stayed up reading his journal until around ten thirty when Rosalynn had fallen asleep. Of course as soon as she was asleep he dove into the box, his phone alarm woke him at five in the morning, and he slothfully dragged himself back to bed. And now it was noontime. That had been the longest night he had spent in the box.

Robbie had just spent an entire day and night in Reveloin. He had learned long ago that Reveloin's time did not match time in this world. And it didn't always tick at a consistent speed; it fluctuated however fast or slow it wanted. But Sarcadui and the others were always faithful to remain right where he had left them.

Robbie thought back to that day in Langly when Ames had told him that an outside world was going to continue to suck him out of Reveloin and that he had to do whatever he could to cut strings from it.

He wondered often if life in Reveloin with Sarcadui and Rhoe was his reality.

No, it couldn't be, he reasoned. This was reality, right here in his bedroom, lying on his bed on top of tangled sheets, trying to come up with an excuse as to why he was still there in the middle of the day. This was reality. This was life as he knew it.

But the other life was so much better. Surely, if he had a choice – and he did – which would he choose? More importantly, concerning Sarcadui and Rosalynn, *who* would he choose? His heart still pounded every time he thought about Sarcadui even on this side of the box. The more he got to know her, the more convinced he was that he was falling for her, as ridiculous as that sounded.

By this point, at half past twelve, Robbie thought it futile to do any work. There was always tomorrow to start catching up. Now, what to do...

Like always, the thought of getting back in the box sent a feeling of excitement pulsing through his veins. He went downstairs to see if the house was empty. Rosalynn was home washing the dining room windows. He'd have to wait to get inside the box until she left the house.

"Look who's finally up," said Rosalynn.

"Yeah, I just wasn't feeling too great," Robbie said.

Rosalynn tossed a damp paper towel into a plastic trash bag. She crossed over to Robbie and gave him a hug. "Do you want me to make you lunch?" she asked as she brushed his hair with her fingers. "A cheese sandwich or something?"

Robbie shook his head. "I think I'm just going to go back to bed," he said. He'd retrieve the box from behind the couch and bring it upstairs with him when she wasn't looking. He had stopped storing it outside because nothing else was coming through it. If anything, he just wanted the security of the box by his side. She told him to call her if he needed anything.

When Rosalynn went back to cleaning, Robbie went behind the couch to get his box. But it wasn't there. He went upstairs to check by his bed. Nothing. He looked in the bathroom, in the closet, but still no box. Robbie's heart was pounding. His box was gone!

Then it hit him. Rosalynn was cleaning the house. When she was in cleaning mode, nothing stood in her way that was of no use to her. If she happened upon something that she couldn't find use for or didn't think anyone needed…

Robbie ran to the window to confirm his fear. His box sat at the end of the driveway, folded up, next to the recycling barrel.

"What are you doing?" asked Robbie, jogging downstairs to confront his wife. "Why is my box out by the trash?"

Rosalynn, brushing a strand of hair out of her face, said, "It was either behind the couch or in the closet, and it was never being used…"

Robbie didn't let her finish before he slammed the front door and marched toward the recycling bin by the side of the road. He shook his head. Unbelievable.

He yanked the box from the side of the street and stormed back inside with it pressed against his side. "I hate it when you throw my stuff away without asking," he mumbled as he walked past her.

Before he reached the stairs he heard her say, "What's the big deal? What do you need it for anyway?"

Robbie stopped at the foot of the stairs and said, "This isn't about the box. You're always throwing my things out without my permission."

Rosalynn bit her tongue and nodded. He knew the last thing she wanted to do was fan a flame that was big enough already. She said, "I'm sorry you're sick. Why don't you go get some sleep?"

Deterred by her compassion Robbie nodded his head and said, "That's what I'm doing."

"Oh, and Robbie?"

Robbie faced her.

"Happy birthday."

He had forgotten.

With the unmade box next to him, Robbie laid on his bed with his hands folded across his chest staring at the ceiling. He thought about how he was going to buy more time to visit Reveloin. He sorted through a myriad of ideas, but nothing was coming to mind. If he took it to a park or an open area outside he'd likely get mugged being unconscious and all. He couldn't keep sneaking around the house every night because Rosalynn was on to him.

Forget it, Robbie thought.

He didn't care if Rosalynn walked in on him. He was tired of all the secrecy. He retrieved some packing tape from the hallway closet where the wrapping paper was kept and reassembled the box next to the bed. Without setting his phone alarm he crawled back in the box.

He continued his adventure with his three friends. When he asked how much further to the ocean, Ames reported that there was only about one more day left of traveling. *What will happen,* wondered Robbie, *when I sit on the throne? Will I still get to exist here?*

He woke up from the box to his phone ringing. He pulled the phone from his pocket and looked at it. It was Rosalynn.

He answered.

She said she was out doing errands and she was sorry for the argument they'd had. How long ago was it? Robbie wondered. The clock on the wall read somewhere between 1:15 and 1:20.

Then Rosalynn asked how he was feeling and if he needed her to pick up some medicine while she was out. He said he was fine but she should get some just to have on hand. She said she'd be home in an hour.

Robbie, freed from his wife, dressed himself appropriately for another adventure and dragged the box downstairs behind the couch because she would most likely check the bedroom first if he was looking for him before looking behind the couch. As far as he knew, she had never walked in on him while he was in the box. His secret was still safe.

He set the alarm. Might as well keep it that way.

CHAPTER 30

Even though the journey's progress was slow, Robbie was enjoying Sarcadui's company with a deeper and deeper affection. On a particular full moon night when Robbie was supposed to be keeping watch, Sarcadui stayed up with him. They were camped near a river which they had found earlier that day and decided it best to follow it to the ocean as long as it flowed northwest.

The trickle of the soft flowing water tickled their ears as they leaned up against a wide tree trunk, which draped willows over them underneath the starlit sky.

"Do you remember your parents much?" asked Robbie.

Sarcadui smiled at the mention of them and said, "I do. My father was timid of a lot of things. He was always afraid for my mother and wanted her to be kept safe. Mother though, she was the adventurous type, always looking for ways to get into trouble and push herself to the limit. She was so beautiful, and my father could never help but love her despite her recklessness. She often encouraged me to find adventures and explore the world."

"I can see that," said Robbie, looking into Sarcadui's stormy blue eyes. Those eyes did a lot more smiling than her mouth ever could. Not that he had complaints about her lips... "I sometimes feel like I remember them; like I actually knew them when I was younger. Even just walking through the jungle I sometimes feel like I recognize certain places. But I know that's not possible."

"Yes it is. And you did know my parents, Robbie. They talked about you all the time."

"They did?"

Sarcadui nodded. "You were their hero. You were the one that inspired the adventure in them, and encouraged them to seek out the hidden treasures of the world. You *created* their world, Robbie."

"But I left them."

"Yes. But you eventually kept your promise. I just wish they were here to see you now."

Sarcadui remained somber for a moment then scrunched her eyes in an inquisitive manner and asked, "Where do you go when you leave, Robbie? Can you remember anything at all?"

Robbie shook his head. "I really can't recall a thing. But sometimes I feel it in my gut that somehow this is all just a dream, and only when I leave here do I ever really wake up in some other reality."

Sarcadui moved closer to Robbie and put her hand on his. "Do you feel this?"

"Yes."

Then she put her hand on his chest and asked, "What do you feel here?"

His heartbeat was rapid at the touch of her soft hand, which felt like cotton on his chest, even though he had two layers of clothing on. "My heart."

She was looking deep into his eyes and he was growing increasingly lost in hers. He was hypnotized by her beauty. She closed her eyes and leaned in toward him and whispered, "Then this is your reality. Not a dream."

Robbie leaned in to meet her lips but stopped suddenly by a rush of guilt flowing through him. He pulled back quickly and said, "I can't do this. I'm sorry."

Sarcadui was hardly offended. She smiled and said, "Maybe Ames is right. That other world has a strong hold on you. Or maybe you have a hold on it, and you're not willing to let go yet."

"I don't know," was all Robbie could say. "It's this place... it's Reveloin. It does something to me, it changes me or something. But I don't know what it changes me *from*. I don't know who I am when I leave here; I don't even know who I am *here*. It's just all too confusing..."

"Well I have faith that you'll figure it out. After all, you figure out how to come back here every time, don't you?" Sarcadui said encouragingly.

Robbie smiled. "Yeah, I guess so."

He realized he had completely lost track of time when light started filling in from the sky. "Some watchman I am," he said scrambling around the tree. "I haven't even—"

He stopped talking when he saw Rhoe and Ames were missing from the campsite. "Where did they go?" he asked as Sarcadui rounded the other side.

"Surely they would have told us if they were going anywhere."

Robbie had a sick feeling in his stomach. "Wait here," he ordered.

"Hurry back," said Sarcadui. "I'm coming after you if you aren't back. Five minutes."

Robbie hustled through the bushes and scurried through the jungle's misty morning terrain.

He heard something up ahead. It was Rhoe's voice:

"Just stay back," he was saying. *"Don't move a muscle."*

Robbie took a few more steps forward and through the trees saw Rhoe positioned between Ames and a black panther that was crouching down, ready to pounce. Rhoe had two knives in his hands and Ames was unarmed, staring helplessly at the savage predator.

Robbie stood in helpless anticipation as he watched the drama unfold. Was it the same panther that had confronted them on the rooftop?

Then without warning the panther lunged in the air, pouncing over Rhoe and headed straight for Ames. But Rhoe stuck his weapons in the air and sliced the cat's stomach open as it sailed over him. "Run, Ames!" yelled Rhoe.

Ames didn't need to be told twice. He turned and ran in the opposite direction and the monstrous cat landed right where Ames had been, but before it could bound off toward him it staggered and limped as blood poured freely out of it, and then slowed to a crawl, gasping and heaving strenuously.

Robbie grimaced at the gruesome scene. Sarcadui emerged from some bushes and when she saw the lifeless panther sprawled on the ground, she asked, "What's going on?"

Rhoe, clearly not wanting to linger on the subject said, "Nothing. Let's keep going."

Ames came back and patted Rhoe on the back and thanked him for saving his life. The four continued to walk forward with Ames leading the way.

"I'm sorry we weren't at the camp my lord," said Rhoe, while they lingered behind the other two.

"Why was that panther after Ames?" asked Robbie.

Rhoe shrugged.

"Oh, and could you do me a favor?" said Robbie.

"Anything, my lord."

"Stop calling me your lord."

Rhoe was silent for a moment. Then Robbie said, "I'm glad to have you with us. I know I'm in good hands as long as you're around."

Rhoe beamed. His smile conveyed his gratitude.

"How close do you think we are to the ocean?" Robbie asked.

"We should be there by tonight," said Rhoe. "As long as you don't disappear on us anymore."

Robbie heard his name being called from behind. He turned to Sarcadui and said, "What?"

She looked at him quizzically. "I didn't say anything."

Someone was calling his name from somewhere else. He knew what was happening. "No," he pleaded. "We're almost there..."

"Robbie."

"No."

"Robbie?"

Who is that? I know that voice.

Robbie woke with a start. Rosalynn was calling his name from somewhere in the house.

He was downstairs behind the couch. She had gone out to do some errands and had come home earlier than expected. His alarm was set to go off in two minutes. He quickly stood up, bracing himself against the back of the couch and stepping out of the box just as Rosalynn entered the living room.

"Hey, what are you doing up?" she asked.

Robbie, still dizzy, just shrugged giving her an inquisitive look. "Were you looking for me?" He didn't know if they were still fighting from earlier that day or if they had just agreed to move on. Reality was still trying to peel itself away from fantasy, so Robbie may have seemed a little disoriented.

"Yeah. How do you feel?"

"Better," said Robbie, casually walking around the couch.

"Good. I thought you might. Can you come to the store with me? I need you to help me pick out a rug for the living room."

"Since when were we getting a rug?"

"Just... will you come with me? Please?"

Robbie sighed and said, "Sure. Just give me a minute." Inside, he was fuming. He was so close to the ocean.

"I'll be in the car."

He went to the bathroom to wash up. Rosalynn was already in the driver's seat of the Volkswagen when Robbie reached the driveway. This was odd because Rosalynn hardly ever drove unless asked. He got in and she pulled out of the driveway.

Instead of feeling tension from their recent dispute, Rosalynn seemed to be her chipper self again.

What is she thinking? Robbie wondered. Was she wondering about the box that he so desperately wanted to hold on to? Was she putting it all together?

She spoke cheerily about insignificant things like the new department store opening up in the mall and that she made an appointment to get her hair cut on the fifteenth. Robbie smiled and nodded cordially and offered any bits of "that's nice," and "you don't say," that fit.

But all the while he couldn't shake his mind from what had almost happened between him and Sarcadui back in Reveloin. He had had no idea where that feeling of guilt came from that interrupted what would have been a passionate kiss.

Now, outside the box, he knew the source of the guilt. He was a married man; he couldn't do that to Rosalynn! And here he was falling for some other woman – a woman that existed only in his mind – but still, another woman. Or was she really just in his mind?

It angered Robbie that his life was getting in the way of his fantasies. He hated that he was tied down to the responsibilities of reality. He hated being called out of Reveloin, because there, bills nor work nor mundane family issues ever plagued his thoughts or demanded his time. He would much rather face a swarm of ghosts than have to deal with such nonsensical issues of everyday life, which included his failures, his shortcomings, and his wretched limited mortality. He would never be able to outrun a panther in this world.

They pulled into the parking lot of Robbie's favorite Italian restaurant, Fabilo's. "Is this my birthday dinner?" he asked.

"Yes," Rosalynn grinned. "I hope you're not too sick to go out."

"Thank you. I feel great. We haven't been here in months."

When they walked in, Rosalynn told the hostess that they were here with the Lake party.

The hostess led them back to the private dining room and there, at the table was Harvey and the kids. On the far end of the table was piled a modest stack of presents and balloons.

Everyone yelled "Happy Birthday!" mixed with "Surprise!" when they walked in. Robbie smiled politely. He wondered if this is what his birthday would have been like in Hawaii. No, there would have been hula dancers and flame throwers and suckling pig roasting on a stake. This may have been his favorite Italian restaurant, but somehow a little bistro five minutes from home didn't compare to a tropical luau five feet from the ocean watching the tide foam on the beach beneath the moon.

As Robbie and Rosalynn took their seats, a waiter came in and introduced himself as Tom. As he handed everyone their menus and quoted the evening's specials, a server came in with two baskets of steamy hot rolls wrapped in warm cloth napkins. They were laid on the table on either side of a butter dish filled with chilled butterballs. Tom left to give everyone time to decide on their dishes.

It was unusual to see everyone at the table at once. Rosalynn wasn't driving Taylor to or from volleyball practice and Jeremy was actually out of his room and his face wasn't stuck to a comic book or a video game.

"It's good to see you," said Harvey. "I was afraid you wouldn't be up to leaving the house especially since you didn't know food would be involved."

"I'm glad I'm here," said Robbie. Honestly, he would have preferred to be back in Reveloin, lighting ghosts on fire, but he decided to make the best of this evening.

"Aaand," said Rosalynn in a sing-song voice, "I made you an ice cream cake. It's at home so we'll eat it tonight when we get back." That's when Robbie almost felt guilty for wanting this night to be over. He hoped his face didn't betray him.

Everyone studied their menus. Robbie was eyeing the meaty lasagna layered with four different kinds of cheeses.

After Tom collected their orders, Jeremy suggested Robbie start opening his gifts. Robbie didn't know if he was just seeing things, but he thought his dad looked unusually giddy. He looked like he was on the verge of exploding with a secret he had been containing with much difficulty.

Robbie opened the gifts, which weren't anything to get excited about. He felt like he was in a Father's Day commercial pulling out typical gifts from the wrapping paper and being forced to fabricate a smile. He got a coffee cup, some new pants, a reading light, and a wristwatch.

He didn't get anything from his dad, which was no surprise.

"Thank you, guys," said Robbie.

"Wait," said Harvey leaning across the table toward Robbie, looking as though he were finally freed to share his secret. "I got my idea patented and my loan approved. You know, for the 50's diner mechanic shop. I want to offer you the position of co-owner. We can run it together as a father and son team. What do you say? We'll call it Harv's and Rob's."

Robbie was silent for a moment. Who was idiotic enough to approve such a stupid idea? Or was his dad being taken for a sap? His family looked on him expectantly, awaiting his response. What was he supposed to say? Without thinking, he opened his mouth and the words came falling out spontaneously:

"Dad, I've got to say, I really don't think going into business with you is a great idea."

"Why not?" Harvey asked, looking more offended than hurt.

"Well, we don't have the greatest relationship, so there's nothing that can convince me that we'd have a good business relationship. Besides, I'm doing well, doing what I like. And I've got to be honest, I don't even think your idea is sanitary. I think it's a bit over the top, and I'm not going to jump on board with you. I'm sorry."

Harvey sat back in his chair with a very pained expression. No one said a word. Even Robbie was speechless at what he had just said. Was he really the only one who saw the fallacy in his dad's idea? What a tool he must've looked like!

Tom and two other servers came in with hot plates to go around. "Who got the shrimp scampi?" he asked.

"Look, Dad…I'm sorry."

Harvey held up a hand and said, "No, don't be. At least you were honest with me. Let's just eat. I'll see if I can get you a real present this week."

"It's not about that," said Robbie, rolling his eyes.

Rosalynn and the kids sat in silence as if they just witnessed a crime.

"Shrimp scampi anyone? The plate's hot," said Tom.

CHAPTER 31

"What was with you tonight?" asked Rosalynn, throwing the covers back on the bed.

They were finally alone in their room. It had been an arduous ride home with tension filling the car as thick as paste. The kids in the back seat never even bothered to say anything. Even Taylor, with her smart mouth, understood her boundaries enough to stay out of it. No one even remembered the birthday cake in the freezer.

"I don't know what came over me," confessed Robbie changing out of his clothes. "There's just a lot going on and I snapped."

"So you took it out on your dad? That's real mature. Robbie, what's going on with you lately? I mean, I know you're busy with your new editing projects, but you said you'd help out around the house and spend time with your dad, but all week you haven't done any of that."

"What do you think I've been doing, then?" He was testing her for information.

"Oh come on Robbie. It's no secret that you're avoiding your dad as much as you can. You're always saying how you're too busy to do anything with the kids, so your dad helps out all the time. You promised Jeremy that you'd take him out last weekend and you never did. Plus, it's like every time I wake up in the night you're not there, so I don't know what you've been doing all week."

Uh-oh.

He could have said "Sorry." He could have beckoned her into his open arms and promised her he would be more attentive to the family. But what was the point? He knew that would just be a lie. He didn't intend to spend more time with the family. No, he'd much rather be back on the island with Sarcadui and Rhoe and Ames. He'd rather be anywhere than this dull, grey world of feeble importance.

"So what if I do spend time for myself? It's not like it's been a lifelong habit. So it's a bit stressful that my dad's here. And doing freelance editing isn't exactly the best form of job security. Are you really going to blame me for that?"

"Oh, boohoo!" mocked Rosalynn. "Your self esteem is hurt, I'm so sorry. Here's a piece of advice for you that'll help boost your *ego*: Get a real job!" It was rare for Rosalynn to have an edge to her voice.

"That's the plan, but in case you haven't realized it jobs are a bit scarce these days! Plus, we both know that if *your* parents were here, you'd be acting the same way."

"I so would *not*!" Rosalynn yelled in defense.

Okay, that was a stretch and he knew it; his argument had no merit whatsoever. He was just grasping at straws. The only reason Rosalynn would ever show discomfort around her family would be because Robbie would act tense or nervous around them for very insignificant reasons.

"Unlike you, I can actually tolerate my parents. In fact, I even *like* them. No, in fact, I'd much rather be living with them than with *you* the way you've been acting."

"So go ahead!" Robbie wasn't about to stop her. "Get online and get your ticket. No one's stopping you."

"Why do you want me gone?" Rosalynn yelled desperately. "What did I do to make you so upset?"

Dejected, Robbie answered, "You're *always* here!"

Silence dropped on them as a result of Robbie's rash bluntness. Rosalynn's countenance reflected the pain of a crushed spirit. Had what Robbie just said really come from his heart? Was that actually the truth?

"Well forgive me for trying to do things for you, like keep the house clean and take care of the kids and entertain your dad, and make your life the best that it can be."

"I don't want to talk about this anymore," Robbie retorted.

"Fine. Go to bed. Let's just drop the subject completely since that's what we always do anyway. We just keep sweeping things under the rug whenever you're too tired or apathetic to deal with anything. There's a huge lump of trash piled up under that rug that we've never dealt with and one day it's going to catch up to us. And while we're waiting for that day to come, I'll keep on cleaning the house and cooking your dinners and raising your kids. Then, when that day comes, when we're forced to clean under the rug, do you know what we'll find? All sorts of things that you've yet to account for, like you going to the bar the other night, and who knows how many other times, and spending time alone in the living room every night, and the phone messages and... Where's your wedding ring?"

Robbie glanced at his left hand lying on top of the covers. His ring was gone. He had no recollection of ever taking it off.

"I don't know where it is. I'll find it. But you need to drop this. I'm tired, it's late, and neither of us is in the right mind to discuss any of this right now."

Rosalynn sighed in utter frustration. She fitfully resigned herself under the bed covers and said, "You're just so caught up in your own world that you don't care about anyone but yourself. You expect the world to bow down to you just because you think you've accomplished so much."

"No, that's not..."

"Then what is it Robbie? Why do you treat us like we're nothing but burdens to you?"

He didn't see it coming. But just then, the wellsprings of his wicked heart overflowed and he bared his ugly soul to his wife. "Well, maybe it's because you *are* burdens to me! All you and my sorry-excuse of a father do is pull me down from what I'm *really* capable of! I live in a world where nothing I do matters, and I'm stuck in a family where fixing a stupid sink is the most important thing I can do around here!"

"What about talking to your kids once in a while?"

"I try talking to them, but they don't think I exist. And if they do, then they don't *want* me to exist! And you! All you do is stand around and nag me, following my every move, watching my every step. You're nothing but a *nagging wife* who bothers me with stupid doctor appointments and more bills to pay than I ever know what to do with!"

This was the sword that pierced Rosalynn's heart. Robbie had used her illness to bite her in an argument.

Rosalynn looked like she had just received news of the death of a loved one. She turned herself around and faced away from Robbie, burying her face in her pillow and soaking it with tears.

Feeling helpless Robbie felt he needed to prove his worth once again. He longed for Reveloin more than ever, but he had just enough sense in that moment to know that getting in the box would cause damage he would be unable to repair.

CHAPTER 32

The irony was not lost on Robbie that Rosalynn's doctor called the morning after he had used her cancer as a tool against her. They were urged to come in and see him as soon as possible. An appointment was set for later that day. The drive to the clinic was excruciatingly silent. It was as if the whole idea of the check-up was a constant reminder of the last words Robbie had said to Rosalynn.

In truth his conscience had been pricking him all night, and he barely got any sleep.

When they got to the clinic they checked in and sat two chairs away from each other in the waiting room.

Robbie was about to lean over the chairs to attempt some sort of small talk but Dr. Allan invited them to join him in his office. He sat down behind his desk and explained, "I looked over the results of the tests from last week and while your blood sugar and heart level are fine, there seems to be a blockage which is just a bit concerning to me."

"How concerning?" asked Rosalynn, reaching for Robbie's hand, transcending any and all disputes that stood between them.

"Concerning enough that we're going to have to keep you overnight so we can better monitor you."

Robbie's heart sank. "Is that all the information we can have now? In the meantime you're just going to monitor her?"

"It's okay Robbie," said Rosalynn in a calm voice as if she wasn't the least bit concerned. "I'm sure he'll be able to tell us more information tomorrow. Right?"

Dr. Allan nodded his head. "You'll know everything I know. But nothing can be determined unless we run these tests overnight."

"I'll stay with you tonight," Robbie told Rosalynn as the nurse wheeled her into a room.

"You don't have to do that. I'll be all right. What you should do is edit some more books so we can pay for this hospital bill," she half joked.

Robbie wouldn't hear of leaving her in the hospital all by herself, despite their current dispute. So he told her he would take care of things at home, pick the kids up from school, and bring his computer for work, along with toiletries for the both of them. These things he would do gladly.

At home Robbie gathered up the things he had promised, and that she had requested, and finished up some chores around the house that he wouldn't want Rosalynn to come home to. His dad wasn't home and the kids didn't need to be picked up from school for another hour.

Once everything was gathered he headed downstairs. He circled the couch just so he could see his beloved box. There it sat, waiting for him, taunting him, loving him. But for the first time since he discovered it, Robbie was just too exhausted to get in. "Maybe some other time," he told the box. "Not now."

Robbie was just about to leave with the bags in his hands just as his dad walked in the door. Robbie nodded at his dad and told him he was going out to pick the kids up from school and he'd be back with them soon. He didn't bother saying anything about Rosalynn – he didn't know why he stayed mum about it, he just did. But before he could squeeze past his dad and out the door, Harvey uncharacteristically addressed the elephant in the room.

"I admire you for telling the truth last night and sticking it to the ol' man, as they say."

Robbie didn't bother telling him that that term didn't apply here. Instead he said, "Sure. There's too much unresolved stuff between us and there's no way we can work together, you know?"

"Why are your bags packed?" asked Harvey. "Where are you going?"

"Rosalynn's in the hospital. They're just doing some tests on her overnight. It's no big deal. I'm staying with her."

Robbie moved toward the door when his dad said, "Are you having an affair with your cell phone? Every night you're hanging out downstairs with your phone like you're waiting for someone to call."

Robbie hung his head, disconsolate. "No, Dad. I'm sitting in a box if you must know." He didn't care if anyone knew anymore. It's not like they would reach the conclusion that he was visiting a fantasy world whenever he sat in the box.

"You need to cut it out, whatever you're doing. That dame, or phone or whatever, is getting in the way of your family. You're marriage is awful. I've hardly seen you talk to your wife."

Robbie scoffed. "What would you know of a good marriage, Dad? Like you and Mom were a good example!"

"What do you know? Your mom was hardly around when you were alive. It was just me who raised you and you didn't give me much to work with!"

"Anything would have been good, Dad."

"Then why are you acting the same way to *your* kids if I was so terrible? Jeremy's always locked in his room just like you were at his age and you're letting him, just like I did with you."

"I don't want to talk about this," said Robbie.

Harvey sighed and said, "I know I didn't teach you much even when your mom was alive. But I had always hoped that you'd learned at least a little something from us while you could. I've made a lot of mistakes in my marriage and I'm sure you have too, but the important thing is that you still get through them all. I don't care if your kids rebel and run out on you, I don't care if you lose all your money and you end up on the street, just as long as you end up on the street *together*. I pulled a lot of crap with your mother, but I *never* walked out on her."

"You were let off easy because she died."

"No. I still think about her. I still miss her. I wish we had more time together. Her dying only proved that had I left her when I wanted, it would have been the biggest mistake of my life. But you and your issues that you've got with someone else or your work or whatever... you've got to deal with it if you're at all serious about staying with Rosalynn. The world's out to tear you apart. Are you going to let it?"

Robbie was silent as he let it all sink in. Then he said, "What's the cane for? Did you get hurt in the fire?"

Harvey laughed. "I've had this old thing since the last time we saw each other. Remember? We had a big blow out when you flew out to visit – one of your friends was getting hitched or something. We yelled at each other and you stormed out of the house..."

"I remember, Dad."

"When you got in the cab I figured that would be the last time I'd see you and I didn't want it to be that way. So I chased after you down the street and I fell and broke my hip."

Robbie was speechless. He had no idea. He hadn't seen his father come chasing after him.

"I told Rosalynn the night I got here, but she swore she wouldn't tell you. It's good to know she can be relied on. Now, whenever you come around to apologizing to me for the crap you pulled last night, you're off the hook. I forgive you so don't bring it up anymore."

"Thanks. But I'm still mad at you for being such a terrible father."

"That's fine. But just don't take it out on your family."

"I don't even know if I can forgive you."

"Let me know when you do. We'll move forward then. I found an apartment a few blocks down. That's where I've been today; that's why I borrowed your car. I hope you don't mind. I can move in whenever, so I'll be out of your hair soon. Maybe sometime you can come by and you can tell me what exactly is wrong with my diner idea."

"Sure, Dad."

Harvey patted Robbie on the back and headed toward the kitchen.

Despite that awkward confrontation, Robbie was still shaken up by the doctor's news, which was still fresh on his mind. For all he knew, tomorrow would be the day they give Rosalynn a set amount of time to live. How long would she have? A month? A year? With this thought Robbie was constricted by guilt over the way he had spoken to her. But even more so, the way he had been neglecting her for so long. And all she wanted was to show him love but he constantly refused it. And for what? A box. A stupid child's game – a fantasy world that didn't even exist! It's true; ever since he brought that box home he had become more and more distant, not just from Rosalynn but from the kids as well. He had been a huge disappointment to his family. And to think Rosalynn had never used his behavior against him, though she would have been justified by doing so. Even when he was at his worst she practiced nothing but grace, love, and warmth toward him, calling him out only on the rarest occasions.

At any rate his dad was right. The box was ruining his relationship with Rosalynn and the kids. He knew there was only one thing to do. He had to get rid of it.

It was the one thing standing between him and his wife, and his chances of ever becoming the father he once dreamed of being.

But then, there was so much unfinished business in Reveloin. He still hadn't found the castle on the ocean, and...

No! Life inside the box wasn't real. Even if it were, nothing about it or from it would aid him in being a better man here, in the real world. The point was, it wouldn't be fair to Rosalynn or the kids if he kept the box around because there was no way he could resist the temptation of going back every time. Forcing himself to ignore the pain, he walked the box out the door and stuffed it in the recycling barrel. It would be collected first thing in the morning.

Part III: Intruders

CHAPTER 33

Robbie felt a weight lifted when the dreadful task of discarding the box was over with. He finished the remaining chores around the house then picked the kids up from school. It was excruciating explaining to them that their mom was in the hospital and he didn't exactly know why.

They didn't take the news well, but that was also because they didn't want to be stuck with Robbie, considering his brash behavior the night before.

"I'm sorry about last night," he said. "Your mom and I talked it over and we decided that I've just been overly stressed about work and stuff."

"What stuff?" Taylor asked sternly.

"That's... you don't need to worry about that right now," stammered Robbie. "Grandpa and I talked too. We smoothed some things over and he'll drop by later. He found an apartment, so pretend you want to see it when he brings it up."

At the hospital hugs were exchanged and questions were asked. Robbie was taken aback when Taylor apologized to Rosalynn for trying to sneak out of the house the other night.

"Where were you going?" asked Rosalynn gently.

"I know you won't believe me, but a group of us were going over to Jen's to study for a math test we had the next day."

Rosalynn considered this for a moment, and just before Robbie accused his daughter of lying, she graciously said, "I believe you. Thank you for telling me."

That was it? Robbie wrecked the car because she wouldn't confess to *that?* And Rosalynn *believed* her? However, he knew Rosalynn's intuition could always be trusted, especially when it came to the kids.

Apparently Taylor had no interest in confiding in him. He could have chosen to sulk, but he reminded himself that the real problem was waiting to be picked up by the side of the road and taken to be recycled.

The Lake family spent the late afternoon hours playing cards with a deck Robbie purchased from the gift shop. Harvey arrived later with Chinese food. Little, if nothing, was said about the night before.

The evening drew to a close with everyone watching TV, except for Taylor who was working on her homework. When everyone grew sleepy Harvey took the kids home and Robbie and Rosalynn were left alone. He pulled a chair up by her bedside and settled down into it with a felt blanket. Once he saw that Rosalynn was sleeping peacefully Robbie himself drifted off to sleep.

He awoke at ten past seven with a twinge of guilt, feeling like he had done something very wrong. The feeling reminded him of when he was trying to quit smoking and he would dream that he had lit up when he really didn't, but still the guilt was just as bad as though he really had. His neck was stiff as a board from sleeping upright all night in a chair. The felt blanket was a far cry from keeping him warm.

The nurse walked in and nodded good morning to Robbie and proceeded to take Rosalynn's blood pressure. This roused Rosalynn and the nurse explained that she would be going home that day. She added that the doctor would be coming in to see her in just a couple of hours. Rosalynn nodded her appreciation and when the nurse left, Robbie got up and kissed her. "I think everything's going to be just fine," he told her.

"So do I. Thanks for staying with me all night."

"I'd have been lonely without you," said Robbie. "Dad is taking the kids to school, so don't worry about them."

At 11:15 Dr. Allen knocked and entered the room and informed them that the test results were in. He sat down on a chair and came right out with it.

"The cancer has spread significantly over the last few months. We can administer treatments to slow the process down, but even with treatments I can't promise more than twelve to fourteen weeks."

"To live?" asked Robbie.

Dr. Allen nodded sympathetically. "I'm very sorry."

A torrent of emotions flooded through Robbie. He wanted desperately to point an accusing finger at someone, anyone. And at the same time he felt like it was his own fault. He wanted to comfort his wife but he himself needed comfort as well.

On the way home from the hospital neither Robbie nor Rosalynn knew what to say, though they were thinking the same thoughts: should we go ahead with treatments? What should we tell the kids? and so on. But when words failed them Robbie reached for his wife's hand and squeezed it tight. Just as he did so, Rosalynn instantly exploded into tears. He pulled the car into the very next driveway, which led into the parking lot of a Safeway. He parked sloppily and pulled his wife up to him and held her. Between sobs Rosalynn just barely managed to say:

"I'm going to miss you guys so much."

Robbie's heart very painfully broke.

CHAPTER 34

As they pulled into their driveway, a very uneasy feeling settled upon them both. Something had happened. Rosalynn's car was parked in its usual spot and birds chirped gaily in the trees on the front lawn. But somehow these quaint particularities seemed misleading. There was a sense of dread that hung over the house that seemed to forbid them to enter. By the look in her eyes Robbie knew Rosalynn felt it too.

"Stay here," he told her. He got out of the car and jogged to the front door. He hesitated before he unlocked it and stepped in. The house was musty and dark. Furniture was upturned and family photos and treasures lay in heaps. Glass carpeted the floor.

Robbie rushed through the house quickly, trying to make sense of the madness.

He called out for his kids over and over. "Jeremy? Taylor?" They should have been home with Harvey.

His heart was pounding furiously in his chest. "Is anyone home?" Robbie called out desperately.

Thick clouds drifted in front of the sun. It was too dark to still be early afternoon. Robbie threw a light switch on as he ran up the staircase.

Both Jeremy and Taylor's rooms had been destroyed.

As Robbie was about to head back down the hallway he heard a noise coming from the master bedroom. It sounded like something had fallen – or was thrown.

He rushed into the bedroom, not at all surprised by its state of disarray.

And there it was. Unmolested and in perfect shape, sitting as if on display on top of his bed was the box.

Robbie cocked his head in confusion. This wasn't possible! He had just thrown it out yesterday.

This time the thud came from Taylor's room followed by her door slamming shut. Whoever was in the house *wanted* Robbie to find him. Though every fiber of his being screamed out against it, he strode down the hallway, pushed her door open, and stepped inside.

The next thing he knew he was flung back into the hallway and that same force grabbed him tightly by the neck.

Robbie was quickly losing oxygen. Somewhere in his brain within the millions of jumbled thoughts he recognized who was attacking him. But placing him was a different matter. He knew this person as if from a dream. The last thought he had just before nausea swept in and overtook his mind was:

Ames?

Rosalynn had been waiting in the car for almost three minutes. Something was dreadfully wrong. The fact that both of them had felt the same feeling of dread scared her. What had happened in the house? Did Harvey have a heart attack and now Robbie was trying to resuscitate him? Was one of the kids hurt? Rosalynn could hardly wait any longer. She would give Robbie two more minutes then she was coming in after him.

"Get... in... the... box."

"Not on your life!" Robbie sneered.

"It's not *my* life we're concerned with, Robbie... or yours." Ames pulled away from Robbie's face and strolled over to the window overlooking the front yard and driveway. "It's your family's lives you should be worried about. Get back in the box and I'll let them live."

"Where are my kids?!" Robbie yelled. The man lunged at Robbie and wrapped him in a headlock, pressing his scaly hand up against his mouth.

"Don't yell, Robbie. Your wife is sitting in the car in the driveway. She'll be up any minute. Don't think I won't snap her neck when she walks through the door."

Rosalynn couldn't stand the wait. What was happening in there? Where were the kids? Logic told her that Robbie would poke his head out the front door and wave her in any minute. But when that didn't happen and the two minutes had passed she got out of the car and walked into the house. It wasn't until she reached the door that she remembered that her cell phone was turned off. She reached into her purse and powered it on. When she saw the destruction in the house, fear nearly overtook her.

She called out, "Robbie?"

"Listen closely," came the scratchy voice in Robbie's ear. "You agree to get back in the box, got it? If not, I'll kill your wife right here in front of you. Agree to get back in it by sunrise tomorrow." Ames paused momentarily, then continued. "I'm sorry, did I hear you think you're going to promise to get in the box and then run away after I leave?"

Robbie was stunned. Ames could read his thoughts.

"Robbie! Jeremy? Taylor? Dad?" Rosalynn was in the kitchen now. Robbie could hear the panic in her voice.

Ames spoke quickly in a hushed voice. "That's fine and well, Robbie. But remember this. In the thick of night, when you're both asleep in this bed – or any other bed in the world – when you least expect it, I'll come back. If you run, I'll find you. I always know where you are. I'll find you both and I'll kill your wife slowly and painfully and you'll watch every bone in her body break, and hear every helpless pathetic moan she tries to make. She'll be just begging you to help her. But you won't be able to. I'll have others from the box holding you down.

"Remember this. Wherever you go, I'll follow you," he tapped Robbie's forehead with a bony finger, "in here. If you take a plane, I'll know exactly where you're headed because I'll see the very same ticket you're looking at.

"Do you agree to get back in the box?"

"Robbie? Kids?" Rosalynn's voice was growing to near hysterics. She was upstairs now.

Don't come in here, honey, Robbie begged, locking his eyes on the bedroom door. He knew calling out to her would be destructive to both of them.

With his head held tightly against his foe's chest, Robbie was barely able to nod once. He had no choice. He had to get back in.

"If you fail to get back in by sunrise tomorrow, I'll hurt your kids very badly." With that, Ames gave Robbie's head a shove. Then he picked up the box, flipped it upside down on top of himself and as if it were a hula-hoop it slid down his body but he did not come out through the top. Then the box lay motionless with the opening facedown on the floor.

At that moment Rosalynn entered the bedroom holding up her phone. "I got a message from your dad," she proclaimed, her face ashen from the disaster in the house.

“Where are the kids?”

“They’re fine. They’re with him right now.”

As they rummaged through the mess Rosalynn explained that Harvey said Jeremy wasn’t sleeping well because he kept hearing noises in their room. Harvey checked but there was nothing there. Jeremy woke him up four more times and then even Taylor got scared, so they packed their sleeping bags and stayed at his apartment. Apparently he picked up a rental car the day before so they took that. That’s why Rosalynn’s car was still in the driveway.

“Did he call the cops?” asked Robbie.

“I guess he didn’t have a reason to; the house was fine when they left,” Rosalynn answered. “I’ll call them right now.”

“No,” said Robbie before he could stop himself.

Rosalynn shot him a glance.

“Call my dad first. I’ll call the cops on my phone,” Robbie corrected.

“Robbie, what happened here?” Rosalynn said, fear swelling up in her voice. “Who would want to break in to our house?”

He hugged her and told her everything would be all right.

Soon the police were at the house and the procedural questions were asked.

Later, Harvey arrived with the kids who were clearly shaken up.

“Are they going to catch him, Dad?” asked Jeremy.

“I’m sure they’ll catch this guy,” said Robbie patting his son on the back. “These policemen are really good.”

“But will he be back before they do?” asked Taylor.

“No one returns to the crime scene more than once,” said Rosalynn. “So no, he won’t be back.”

Robbie didn’t have the heart to correct her. He wondered if they would be so lucky next time.

CHAPTER 35

If you're being called out by another world, then that world clearly has mastery over you. You need to do everything you can to cut strings from that place if you ever want to come back here undisturbed.

That's what Ames had said when Robbie first met him in Reveloin. Robbie knew that Ames primarily wanted him on the island to free them from the reign of ghosts. But he never thought Ames would go so far as to cut off Robbie's freedom to discard the box – or that he even had the ability to. How was he supposed to be the father and husband he wanted to be if he was going to be forced into the box time and again? He couldn't continue to live this double life. There was only one person in the world he could talk to who might have some answers.

"Steve," said Robbie, approaching him in the lobby of CipherMill. "I need your help."

"Of course you do," said Steve looking smug. "I knew you'd be back to talk about that box of yours." He draped his arm around Robbie's shoulders and pulled him around behind his desk and dropped his voice to almost a whisper. "So tell me, what kind of world is it? Mine's outer space. I get to tour the universe and command th' galaxy's largest ship."

"Can we…?" Robbie motioned toward the door to his office.

"Oh sure," said Steve, leading him inside and closing the door behind them. The office was just as messy as before and the smell just as nauseating. Steve hopped up on his desk and Robbie took a seat in a chair and said, "You have a… box, too?" Robbie felt foolish talking about this with someone else, as if confessing some great sin.

"Sure I've got a box."

"How long ago…?"

"Eight years and still strong, my friend."

Robbie couldn't believe this. He had so many questions to ask but he didn't know where to start. So he opened his mouth and let his brain do the talking. "How does this work? Have you ever been visited by people in your box? Is it all real or just subconscious?"

"Slow down, man. I've got questions for you too."

"Shoot."

"What kind of world do you go to? I figure if you go to space we can probably find each other." Unlikely.

"It's a jungle island. And the people are normal human beings. They're good people, but they're under the rule of the undead or… ghosts. But they're not really dead, or undead. They're just… monsters… ghosts."

"That's cool. Bet you don't get aliens like I do."

"No, I don't. Steve, why us? Why is it only us who can go to these worlds?"

"Who says it's only us? Just two minutes ago you didn't know *I* had my own box. Besides, how many grown men do you know that would willingly sit in a cardboard box?"

"True enough. So how does it work?" asked Robbie.

"You probably know as much as I do. But if I get hurt up there in that ship or on a planet, I sure feel it when I wake up back here."

"I know what you mean," Robbie said rubbing a scar he'd received on his shoulder from a low branch cutting him during the last visit.

"Well, that there tells me it's all pretty real. So can we die in our private worlds? Yes, I think so. You simply just won't wake up in your box and you'll stink up to high heaven when they find your corpse and carry you away to the mortuary."

Knowing Steve could go on like this forever Robbie got right down to it. "Do they come through your box?"

"They got to you, huh? If they feel you've abandoned their world, then yeah, they'll come after you."

"But why? How?"

"Think about it. Every time you get in that box you're giving them life. *You're* their life. These people live inside of you, like in your head, so they know what you're thinking all the time. If you start thinking about not getting back in the box, they'll know it and they'll come after you. And if you still don't get back in the box they'll just start taking things away from you until you have nothing here left to live for. Basically, man, you're stuck. Unless you want your life to fall apart you need to just keep going back."

"He said he would go after my family."

Steve nodded knowingly.

"What about you? Have you stopped going back?"

"Me? No way! I'm their slave here. I've always got to go back. I've learned my lesson. But once I'm there, I run the game; I'm in charge. The only thing certain about life inside the box is that you're completely in control. It's your world. But here, they'll control you and manipulate you any way they can to get you back so you can start running things again. They need their leader."

"If they live in my imagination, then how can they physically come here? It doesn't make sense."

"You just answered your own question," said Steve. "It *doesn't* make sense. You or me going there doesn't make sense either. Somehow, we just *can*. But they use that box as a portal just like we do."

"Then how did you get rid of the problem? What's the secret?"

"Who says I got rid of it? They still haunt me after eight years. And it never gets easier. When they first started showing up they threatened to kill my wife. I thought they was bluffing but then they come by one night, and quiet as a bug tie her up, stuff her mouth, and left her in the middle of the street like one of those chicks tied up and left on a railroad track like in some of those gringo shows.

"You think I would have taken them seriously after that. But instead I got so tired of being ordered around that I drove the box to the junkyard. But on my way there they crawled out of the box and started attacking me behind the wheel and nearly drove me off the road. I agreed to take the box back home and that was it. They were happy and went back inside. So of course I was just bluffing. I was just testing them. But they came back that night and actually forced me back in the box by dragging me in by my Marley locks – I was a big Bob Marley fan. Of course they were my friends in space and I didn't know any different when I was there. Seems I can't remember anything about my real life when I'm there, so of course I don't remember them being so mean to me."

"And since then?"

"I left my family. I had to. I couldn't support them no more. I was about to get fired from my job so I saved them the trouble and quit. How can you support a family if you're fighting for your life all the time, you know? I had to keep them away from my problems. Anyway, that's why I work here now. I figure a security guard has flexible hours and access to big empty warehouses all night long without worrying if anybody will walk in on me while I'm in the box. Plus, this seemed like an easy enough job where I can make just enough to pay rent, groceries, and whiskey. And I'm not above getting in while I'm on the clock. That's how I knew you had found your box by the way. I watched you that night."

"So you knew all along? That's why you lied to me about the box being shipped off?"

Steve nodded his head. "Just watching your back. They wouldn't have bugged you if you had only shown up to their world that one time. But you kept feeding them the more you went back. You kept giving them power; control over you. You know what I'm saying?"

"I don't think I know a thing about what you're saying, but yeah I get it," said Robbie, exhausted and angry with himself. "You're saying there's nothing I can do to get rid of it?"

Steve looked surprised. "Why would you want to?"

Robbie raised his eyebrows at Steve as if to ask if he was serious.

"Do you know why you kept going back to begin with?" asked Steve.

"To escape life I guess," answered Robbie. "Things were getting tense."

"That, sure. That's why you left. But why did you *go*?"

Robbie thought about Sarcadui but was too embarrassed to mention her. He couldn't think of any other reason beyond that.

"Because you wanted *adventure*. You wanted to test yourself, put yourself to the limit. You got to test yourself as a man, you know? Is it safe in your box world?"

"Not at all," said Robbie.

Steve laughed as if having just revealed a great revelation and lightly backhanded Robbie on the stomach. "You go to have yourself a time! Your life ain't exciting here one bit. Man, let me tell you, after eight years of going back into space, I've been made king. I'm the king of the universe, baby! It's great. I bet you feel a lot more important in your jungle island than you do at home."

"They say I'm their creator."

"You're a god," Steve reflected lustily. "That's better than king. But before you get too cocky, remember you're only god of that tiny little island. I'm king of the universe."

"That may sound nice and all," Robbie rebuked, "but it's not real. None of it is."

"Who's to say it's not real? It feels real to me. I even came back here with a broken leg. It was crushed by the control panel that fell off when I crashed the ship. Doctor checked it out and everything. He's got the X-rays to prove it. No one needs to tell me that my box world ain't real."

Now Robbie saw what was happening. Steve was stuck at the same conclusion he had been wrestling with. If it hadn't been for the cancer scare with Rosalynn, he might not have been able to throw out the box. Otherwise he would have just given up on life like Steve had.

"So why do you bother coming back here at all?" Robbie asked.

"I've got to eat, don't I? Once, I got in the box away everyone and any distractions. I turned off the phone and closed the blinds and all that. I was in the box for three whole days. The deliveryman had some package to deliver, so he knocked on the door of my apartment. I woke up with the driest throat you ever felt. I hadn't drunk anything for three days. And when I got out of the box to get a glass of water I could barely make it to the sink because I was so weak from hunger, and my joints were all stiff, you know? My body was still needing its nourishment here. So, I learned not to ever do *that* again. The way I see it, I've got to come back here at least once a day to take care of myself."

"What did you do before this?"

Steve smiled slyly and said, "I was a professor."

"You were?"

"I graduated with a master's and taught astronomy at the University, and I even wrote for an astronomy magazine for eighteen years. That all went down the hole when I found the box."

"And yet it's all worth it?" Robbie asked, astonished.

"Yes sir! Why *write* about the stars when you can actually visit them!"

"But your family, your career, everything you'd worked for?" Robbie was starting to feel like he was talking to a mirror. He was beginning to realize that if he didn't do something about this, then he would end up just like Steve: careless, apathetic, and alone.

At home Robbie pitched in with the house cleaning. Rosalynn and Harvey had been at it all day and a significant turnaround had been made to the house.

"The police confirmed the oddest things today," said Rosalynn.

"Yeah? What's that?" Robbie asked as he swept up the tile floor.

"There aren't any fingerprints around the house but ours. But weirder still is that there's no sign or indication as to *how* the culprit broke in. It's as if a hurricane just formed in the house, did its damage, then died out. Besides that, nothing is missing."

Robbie wasn't convinced that he should say anything to anyone about the box. Why stir up suspicion when it could be avoided? At least *he* knew who broke in. It was just the *how* that puzzled him. The last time he had seen the box he had discarded it. If Ames came from the box, then how did it get inside the house? It made no sense to Robbie no matter how he turned it around in his mind.

He also couldn't shake all the things Steve had told him earlier. How much was his own life on track with Steve's? Could Steve even be trusted as a reliable source? Sure, he may be missing a few marbles but he'd had Robbie's best interest at heart from the beginning. He had even tried getting rid of the box to save Robbie from it.

So if everything Steve said was true, that meant he'd have to get back in the box to avoid further encounters from Ames. He couldn't risk his family's safety. But he also couldn't sacrifice everything in his life to keep going back to the box, he just couldn't. He didn't want to end up like Steve, alone and disillusioned.

It seemed no matter what he chose he would lose. There had to be a loophole somewhere, a way to beat the system.

Robbie concluded that his only other option was to wait for Ames, or someone, to come through the box then confront him face to face.

CHAPTER 36

In order for his plan to succeed, he would have to refrain from getting in the box to provoke Ames to come back through. But, he'd have to keep the box with him at all times so as to catch him when he did come.

That night he kept the box by his side of the bed but he stayed awake with a book. He didn't want anyone coming through the box, sneaking through the house and finding his kids. But this proved harder than he thought. The book, though it was his favorite Steinbeck novel, eventually lulled him to sleep.

One quick image of Ames jolted him awake an hour later. He instantly panicked, thinking that he had missed his opportunity to catch his enemy. The lamp on his nightstand was still on and Rosalynn had draped her arm around his waist holding herself close to him. He glanced at the box and it still sat where he had left it. Still, he couldn't go back to sleep until he checked on the kids.

He crawled out of bed careful not to disturb Rosalynn. He stealthily opened the bedroom door and tiptoed down the hall toward the kids' rooms. He felt a strange sense of fear creeping up his spine. He fought the urge to flip on a light.

What was that? Did he just hear a noise coming from Jeremy's room? His knees shook. He couldn't decide whether to exercise caution or action. He reached for the door handle, turned it, and pushed the door slightly open.

Inside it was dark with the exception of a lava lamp and the light from the clock radio. The Beatles were playing from an iPod plugged into some speakers. Jeremy was in bed, peacefully asleep and breathing steadily. Robbie gently let out his breath. He closed the door and headed further down the hall to Taylor's room.

There, he found the same thing. She was asleep in her bed with some music playing from somewhere in the room. Some boy band, no doubt.

Robbie returned to his bed, glad that there hadn't been any disturbances while he was asleep. But he was still not convinced that Ames wasn't about to come, and he needed to be ready for him when he did. So he grabbed the book off his nightstand and continued reading from where he left off.

But his comprehension was failing. All he could think about was life inside the box. He wanted to be back on that island. He wanted to find the castle on the sea and fulfill his promise. He tried to fight these feelings at first. He remembered how Steve had turned out, being a slave to his box. He reminded himself that he needed to wait for Ames to come back through the box so he could confront him, telling him that he would not be controlled. But Sarcadui, and Hail…

His heart raced. His pulse quickened. His breathing became choppy. All of this happened because he knew that with each passing moment he was getting closer and closer to convincing himself it was time to get back in the box and reunite with Sarcadui. Maybe then, once closure has been established, he would be able to resist going back. Plus, why not confront Ames on the island? Why did he have to wait for him to come back, uninvited, to his home? So *what* if he couldn't remember anything about his life here while he was in the box; he would *make* himself remember. Forgetting was not an option. His objective by getting inside the box would be twofold: establish closure with Sarcadui and confront Ames.

Giving into the temptation, he placed one foot inside the box and was about to get out of bed to sit in it when Rosalynn's voice stopped him.

"Where are you going?"

Not answering, Robbie lay back down in bed and allowed Rosalynn to hold him in a tight cuddle.

"I'm scared," she said as she drifted back to sleep.

Me too, thought Robbie.

CHAPTER 37

Three days had passed and there was still no visit from Ames. Robbie struggled through the nights fighting off the temptation to go back, determined to ride his plan through. Who knows, maybe Ames wasn't going to come back and now he could go on with his life. He had been carrying the box around with him, keeping it in his car whenever he went anywhere, placing it in the closet when he was at home. Each uneventful day lowered his anxiety to near-carelessness.

He continued to struggle with the urge to go back to Reveloin. But the longer he was away from it, it seemed, the easier the pressure got. Though he went through minor withdrawals, he was able to manage his way through them when he reminded himself why he was not giving in.

On this particular weekend afternoon Rosalynn and the kids were out catching a movie, and Robbie, being home alone with the box, decided he was going to throw caution to the wind and do away with it once and for all. It took a tremendous amount of effort to refrain from getting in the box just one last time.

He dragged the box out to the backyard. In the other hand he held a lighter. He turned the box upside down and hesitated before touching the flame to the box. When he came around to realizing it was now or never he brought the flame to the box and suddenly everything turned into slow motion.

He heard something directly behind him. Heavy breathing. He turned and saw that a ghost, from Reveloin, towering behind him. Instinctively Robbie cast the lighter in the ghost's direction, but it only swapped at Robbie's hand and the lighter went flying against the house. He panicked.

He darted toward the sliding glass door and bolted through the house. He didn't have to turn around to know that the ghost was right on his trail, swiping at him, hissing, clicking its tongue. Stumbling up the stairs Robbie grabbed Jeremy's wooden baseball bat and began swatting at it, which had little effect on the ghost.

He dove into his son's bedroom and slammed the door shut behind him, locking the door. He was about to slide the bed up against the door when he realized the door would snap against the ghost's thunderous pounding.

He needed to hide.

He ran to the closet and closed the door, holding the handle down as he did so, so it wouldn't betray him. It was dark, but he knew he could access the attic from inside. He just had to be as quiet as he could be climbing up the shelves and pray that they didn't collapse under his weight.

Whomp! The bedroom door swung open. The ghost was inside.

Robbie quickly climbed the shelves, and finally found the loose board that covered the attic's opening. He lifted it and slid it across the beams. He was about to pull himself up when a noise from inside the attic froze him in his place. It was a sort of scurrying, like claws scampering across the wood. But it wasn't the sound of a little mouse skittering away, this noise sounded *heavier*. He saw the ghost's shadow through the crack underneath the closet door. He had no choice. He heaved himself up as quickly and quietly as possible and covered the opening just as the ghost swung the closet door open.

The attic was hot and sweat formed immediately. He was careful not to make any noises as he crawled across the two-by-fours that held him above the drywall.

The clawing sounds made Robbie freeze in his place. There was more than one of whatever it was because he could hear it from in front and behind. And then at least one of them hissed. Robbie recognized the hiss.

It was an eoraptor. Maybe two or three.

How had all of these vile things come out of the box? And when? Robbie hadn't been too careful about where he stored it lately. The ghost, the dinosaurs, they must have been waiting for him.

It dawned on him, then, that if more than one person could come out of the box, then it was perfectly reasonable that Ames had had help getting the box inside the house while he was at the hospital with Rosalynn. All that needed to occur was that either he or a ghost came up from the box while it was by the road, slide it through a crack in the window, or some other opening, and once it was inside, someone would have come through the box and let Ames or the ghost in the house.

The tapping claws came nearer and he could see the silhouette of the little dinosaur sneaking closer toward him. His mind rushed back to the agouti. He scooted back a foot or two, but he heard another dinosaur hissing behind him. It was all over. He couldn't possibly outrun these carnivores balancing on the two-by-fours while ducking below the beams. Plus, where would he go? The only way was through the attic door and that would just lead him directly to the ghost.

The lizard in front of him hopped forward, sticking its neck out toward him, baring its sharp teeth. Suddenly the wood beneath it shook and wobbled, knocking the agitated lizard to its side. The ghost had punched through the attic. The dinosaur lunged at the ghost's beefy hand and bit it hard. It went sailing across the attic when the ghost shook it off. Then the other dinosaur lunged at the ghost but it only fell through the hole in the floor. Robbie wasn't certain, but by the sound of it, he was sure the ghost stepped on the lizard's head, crushing its skull.

He quickly scurried across the sturdy wood and hid behind some boxes. He listened as the ghost heaved itself up and started dragging itself across the attic straight toward him. He was out of options. Ahead of him were a wall and another dinosaur, almost nose-to-nose with him, peering hungrily into his eyes. Up close, even in the dark, Robbie could get a sense of what the hard scaly flesh must feel like to the touch, and he trembled at the exact sharpness of its teeth that looped around the outside of its mouth like a picket fence.

Robbie had to act or it would bite his face. He grabbed a heavy box from behind him and whipped the dinosaur with it, knocking it down. This no doubt caught the ghost's attention and it hurried toward Robbie, dragging itself across the floorboards with its muscular arms. But before it got too close, the weight of the drywall gave in under it and the ghost fell through the ceiling. Robbie took the opportunity to push another large box over the edge and let it fall directly on the stunned ghost. He began to jump out himself but the dinosaur he had knocked down grabbed his pant leg and began pulling on it. He jumped down, regardless of this setback, landing right on the box, which stunned the ghost even more. The dinosaur was separated from his leg but quickly set its sights on the ghost and began attacking its face. These creatures were hungry for anything.

They had landed in the master bathroom. The other dinosaur that had fallen through earlier entered just as Robbie was leaving and was about to jump on him, but Robbie pointed to the ghost and the dinosaur attacked it alongside its comrade.

He made a beeline down the stairs and back out the sliding glass door, but as soon as he bent down to pick the box up, another ghost appeared from inside of it as though it were poking its head out from a sewage drain. The ghost pulled itself out just enough to yank on Robbie's arm, and bashed his head in on the hard concrete floor.

"Robbie? Robbie?"

It was Rosalynn's voice.

When he finally opened his eyes he saw that she was kneeling over him, near tears.

The first thing he realized was the intense pain in his head. He felt like his brain was pounding itself against his skull, trying to get out. For several seconds he was lost somewhere between time and space where neither of them played an accurate role in his perception. He reached toward Rosalynn wanting to touch her. As he stroked her face she blushed, thankful that he was okay. The two were silent as Robbie racked his brain.

He looked around and saw that he was in the backyard. What had happened that had caused him to be lying on his back on the concrete? Why was his cheekbone throbbing with pain? What had he been doing in the backyard to begin—

Then it hit him. Rosalynn and the kids going to the movie, everything with the box, the struggle not to get back in, the lighter, then the terrifying hunt in the house. The ghosts were here!

As Rosalynn asked what happened, Robbie began looking around frantically for the box. It wasn't anywhere to be seen. He struggled to his feet and said, "Where's the box?"

"I don't know Robbie." Rosalynn spoke slowly, as though he was still fragile.

Panic began to set in. Ames had said he'd hurt the kids if he didn't get back in the box. The box was Ames's and the ghosts' doorway to this world. "Where are the kids?"

"They're in the house. Jeremy's room is a mess. We thought you were gone, but I saw you from the kitchen window and just now came running out," said Rosalynn.

"Get them. Now," demanded Robbie, letting the fear show on his face.

Rosalynn, irritated and needing answers said, "Rob, tell me what happened. Was the robber here?"

"You can say that," answered Robbie as they both entered the house. Rosalynn flipped out and started screaming, "Kids! Jeremy! Taylor!"

Jeremy and Taylor came downstairs asking questions about the destruction upstairs.

Robbie hugged them both and said, "How was the movie? Was it good? Hey, we're going to go for a little overnight trip. I need you to go pack your bags."

"We're going to Hawaii now?" asked Jeremy.

"No," corrected Robbie.

"You don't think he'll come back, do you?" asked Rosalynn.

"Who will come back?" asked Taylor looking alarmed.

"No one, sweetheart," said Robbie.

"Dad, who punched you?" asked Jeremy, more amused than alarmed. Robbie's cheekbone was swelling up.

"No one. But right now you guys need to get out of here."

"Where are we going?" asked Taylor, shaken by Robbie's strange behavior.

"To Grandpa's. Go throw some stuff together. Now!"

When they had obeyed, Robbie searched the backyard for any sign of the box or the ghosts. Did they get back in the box? Was Ames here yet? Did he miss his opportunity to confront him? Worse yet, what if the ghosts were still in the house?

Just as these thoughts swarmed his already spinning mind, a loud shriek came from upstairs. It was Taylor. Robbie dashed back inside and met Taylor halfway up the stairs. She was brushing herself off frantically, near tears.

"What is it?" asked Robbie.

"Bugs! My bathroom is filled with bugs!" Just then, an extra long centipede crawled out of her hair and across Taylor's face. She screamed and threw it across the wall, then she screamed again, brushing past Robbie. He took another step up to get Jeremy and his foot stepped on something that made a hard crunch. He didn't have to look to know that he had just smeared another centipede into the carpet. Who knew if the dinosaurs were still upstairs?

"Jeremy, Rosalynn! We've got to go now."

"What happened?" asked Rosalynn as she met Robbie at the stairs. "What's wrong with Taylor?"

Robbie ignored her and called for Jeremy to forget packing and to get back downstairs.

"Robbie you're scaring me," insisted Rosalynn. "What's happening to our house?"

Jeremy came down with his backpack full of comic books. Taylor, while brushing herself off frantically, was complaining that she didn't get to pack anything. "That's okay," said Robbie hurriedly. "You've got bugs in your hairbrush. Do you really want to take that with you? You guys need to go to Grandpa's and I'll let you know when you can come back."

"What about you?" asked Rosalynn. "You're not coming? Aren't you even going to call the cops?"

"Just let me handle this, okay?" said Robbie looking at Rosalynn intently in the face. "Please. I need you to trust me on this."

"He's probably running from the cops himself," said Jeremy. "What'd you do, Dad?"

Cute.

"Not now Jeremy," said Rosalynn as she scooted the kids out the front door and grabbed the keys. "Get in the car." Once settled, she turned to Robbie, who was standing outside her car window and said, "Honey, I don't know what's going on, but please be careful. I love you."

He kissed her and said, "I love you too. Drive safe, I'll call you."

He watched as she fastened her seatbelt and started the car. As she did this he remembered something Ames had said. Something about how he lives inside his mind. That any information he knew, Ames knew too because he could hear his thoughts.

Robbie blurted through the driver's side window, "Drive anywhere. Don't go to Grandpa's. Go anywhere where I wouldn't know about."

"This is getting weird, Robbie…"

"Just do it. Don't go anywhere where I would go. Stay at a hotel or something – one we've never stayed at."

"Awesome! We're going on vacation," came Jeremy's voice from the backseat.

Rosalynn and Robbie looked at each other as if they couldn't believe their son was actually showing an interest in something outside of a comic book or game console. If only it was a moment worth savoring.

"Shut up, Jeremy," said Taylor from the passenger seat, enhancing the sweetness. "This is serious. Dad's turned into an even bigger lunatic than he already was."

"Just don't tell me where you're going. Even if I call," concluded Robbie. "I love you guys."

Rosalynn pulled out of the driveway and Robbie watched as they disappeared down the road. He replayed the last few moments in his head and hoped he had told them everything that needed to be said.

But something didn't quite rest well with him. It was what he had seen in the car that he should have done something about. Rosalynn was in the driver's seat and Taylor in the passenger seat. He had noticed his long-lost sunglasses were hanging in the visor. They all had their seatbelts buckled. But there was something else that gnawed at his conscience. Robbie worried the inside of his cheek. It was while he was looking at Jeremy in the backseat. Something struck him as odd; out of place.

Then it dawned on him: He didn't notice it because he wasn't looking for it, and he was preoccupied with a host of other worries, but he had seen the box in the car. It was sitting in the backseat next to Jeremy.

CHAPTER 38

It was too late for Robbie to go chasing them down the street on foot; it had taken too long for the realization to reach his brain. He ran inside the house, grabbed his phone and speed-dialed Rosalynn's number. He jumped when he heard a familiar show tune play suddenly from the kitchen. It was Rosalynn's phone. She left it! He couldn't blame her. He couldn't have kicked her out any faster.

Wait, Taylor had to have her phone! She always did. He scrolled through his list of contacts but he didn't have her listed. What kind of father didn't have his own daughter's phone number?

Putting the matter aside, he retrieved Taylor's number from Rosalynn's phone and dialed it on his own device. Voicemail.

"Tay, it's Dad. Call me when you get this." He'd never known her to have her phone off unless she was grounded.

Robbie relaxed a bit. Either Rosalynn will come back home to get her phone or Taylor would return his call. It's going to be okay, he told himself.

But try as he might, he didn't believe it.

Rosalynn was angry with herself for forgetting her phone. "Do you have your cell?" she asked Taylor.

"Yeah. But the battery's dying," she answered.

"Keep it off for now. We're going to need to use it later to call Dad."

"Mom, why is Dad acting like a crazy face?" asked Jeremy.

Rosalynn suppressed a smirk. "He's just scared that the robber will be back. He doesn't want us there if he comes back."

"Is that who punched him?" Jeremy asked. "I think he got in a fight with the robber in my room. My closet was all messed up."

"There's a hole in the bathroom ceiling," added Taylor.

"I don't know how Dad hurt himself, or what went on in there. We're just going to do what he says and stay away from the house for a while."

"We're not going to move, are we?" asked Taylor.

Rosalynn shook her head. "I don't know, Taylor, to be honest. At this point I hope we do. It could be good for all of us."

"So where are we going?" Taylor asked, after about a mile of silence.

"How about Bullwinkle's?" suggested Jeremy.

"No," said Rosalynn. "We're just going to drop by Grandpa's. Besides, I haven't seen his new place yet."

Taylor protested, "But Dad said not to go there."

"What difference does it make where we go? He got us out of the house, didn't he?"

"I just don't think that's a very good idea. Dad did say..."

"I don't care what Dad said," interrupted Rosalynn. Then, catching herself said, "Besides, what do you care what Dad says? You haven't obeyed a thing he's said since you were ten."

Jeremy laughed from the backseat.

Taylor ignored him. Then she said, "Look. All I'm saying is that Dad looked really worried. I've never seen him look like that before. And obviously someone was at the house. I just think we should do what he says. I have a weird feeling, you know?"

Rosalynn took her daughter's words to heart and for once didn't see any ulterior motive behind her words. She was scared, and she was right. She shouldn't go where Robbie had specifically told them not to go.

She drove past the street where she would have turned to go to Harvey's.

"Thanks Mom," Taylor said, again to Rosalynn's surprise.

"Where are we going then?" asked Jeremy. "I'm getting hungry."

"We'll get some Mexican food as soon as we figure out what we're doing, hon," said Rosalynn.

"I hate Mexican food," said Taylor.

Rosalynn rolled her eyes. "We'll stop at the orchard and let you pick a bushel of organic apples."

"Very funny Mom," said Taylor with resentment.

"Hey, guys?" said Jeremy.

"So are we going to a hotel or something?" asked Taylor.

"Yes. We're going to that little inn on the coast," said Rosalynn.

"Guys?" said Jeremy again.

"You mean the one Dad promised to take you for your anniversary last year?"

Rosalynn smiled. "Yes."

"Guys," said Jeremy, louder. "There's something moving in this box back here."

"Eew!" yelled Taylor. "Is it another one of those snaky bug-things? I'm sick of finding those things everywhere."

"Not a bug. Actually, it keeps shaking like there's something big in it. But it's open and nothing's in it."

"It's probably just the bumps in the road, sweetheart," said Rosalynn. "We'll be there in about forty minutes, then we'll take care of it."

The more time that passed the more anxious Robbie grew. Why were they not calling him back? Why hadn't Rosalynn come back for her phone? Did the ghosts already come out of the box and cause them to crash? He shuddered when he remembered the stories Steve had told him.

Where could they have gone? Is it possible Rosalynn decided to go to his dad's apartment regardless of his warning? Maybe a friend's house? No, that wouldn't be like her to barge in on someone and expect to be entertained.

He couldn't remain stagnant any longer. He needed to do something, anything. He grabbed his and Rosalynn's phones and hopped in his car and began driving. At least if they called back he would already be on the road.

The Cottage on the Sound was a quaint little inn that overlooked the Puget Sound. The Jetta rolled across the rocks in the parking lot and parked in one of the many open spots. "You kids stay here. I'm going to go check in."

"No more than one night. I want to go home," said Taylor. "And I hate that my phone's dead because I can't talk to anybody."

"That reminds me. You should probably call Dad. I'll be back in a minute," said Rosalynn as she shut the door and headed for the front desk. The water was soothing. The pebbles crunched underneath her feet as she walked in her sandals toward the front door of the country-style cottage.

A bell jingled above her head as she stepped in and an elderly man came through a door behind the desk and took a seat on his stool. It smelled like fresh potpourri. No wonder Robbie never wanted to come. "Hello," he said kindly. "How can I be of service to you today?"

"I'd like to check me and my two kids in for the night if you have room," said Rosalynn.

"I've got room 8 available. My daughter just cleaned it this morning; you'll love your stay. Now, have you gotten a chance to look at any of the attractions—"

Suddenly Taylor burst through the door with the phone in her hand. "Mom, Dad says we need to come home now."

Rosalynn hung her head in frustration. "What?"

The innkeeper took off his glasses to rub them down with a silk cloth and interjected with a grandfatherly smile, "Go home to him, dear. I'm sure he's sorry for whatever he's done. The kids need him."

"At this point I'm doubting that," muttered Rosalynn. Then, turning back to Taylor asked, "Why does he want us to come back home?"

"He didn't say why. He just sounded really scared, like he did in the driveway. I told him where we are and he said he's on his way. Then my battery died."

"Then we don't need to leave. We'll take that room please," said Rosalynn turning back to the innkeeper.

"We do have another room for the kids if you'd like."

"Even better," said Rosalynn. Robbie needed this getaway more than anybody, so why pass up the opportunity? It wasn't Hawaii, but it would have to do until he found another job.

She gave him the credit card and he passed some papers over to Rosalynn to look over and sign. "Here you go, ma'am."

"Thank you," said Rosalynn taking a pen from its holder. "Taylor, go get Jeremy, will you?"

While Rosalynn was listening to the innkeeper's instructions and tour recommendations, and looking through some pamphlets he pushed her way, Taylor came back in the cottage and announced that Jeremy wasn't in the car.

CHAPTER 39

Guided by his GPS, Robbie pulled up to the Cottage on the Sound a half hour after his brief conversation with Taylor. The Jetta was parked in the empty lot and a police car was across the road. *We're going to be on the news*, Robbie thought, not in good humor.

He had called the inn from Rosalynn's phone and an older man allowed Rosalynn to talk to him. He was going to beg her to start driving his way when she told him that Jeremy was missing. She was too hysterical to say anything more. Though he had been warned, he couldn't believe this was actually happening.

A swelling pain rose in Robbie's chest as he jumped out of the car and ran toward the lodge, kicking pebbles up behind him. Passing the car, he saw that the backseat was empty. The box was gone.

Inside the lodge, he found Rosalynn, tear-stained, rushing toward him with open arms. "We still can't find him," she cried, as she hugged him tight.

Taylor sat in a chair against the wall looking dumbfounded.

The policeman briefed him on everything. The rangers and neighbors had been alerted about the missing child.

Robbie took Rosalynn aside and asked her, "Was the box with you on the way here?"

Rosalynn sniffed and said, "He mentioned something about the box next to him. Why? Why is this box suddenly a part of everything?"

Robbie, at that moment, finally felt he could have gone into all the bizarre details then and there, and insisted on her belief, but considering the company, he decided to wait. "I'm going to go look for him," he said.

The sheriff advised him against the idea, but Robbie shot past him and jumped back in the Accord, which he still hadn't taken to get fixed from his accident with Cruella de Vil. As he drove several miles along the coastline, there was no doubt in his mind that someone from the box had crawled out and taken Jeremy.

Ames had promised to hurt his kids if he tried anything funny. He should have known Ames would make good on his threat. What did he think, that he was going to conceive the idea of burning the box, find a lighter, walk it outside, and set it on fire before Ames could hear his thoughts? Robbie was angry with himself for attempting such a stupid stunt. How could he have been so careless?

He slammed on his brakes when he saw a woman just standing in the middle of the road. It was Sarcadui; her face was ashen and she was in a trance. She made no eye contact with Robbie. Instead, she pointed into the trees. He sloppily parked the car on the side of the road, got out, and walked down through the thickets along the water's edge. Walking through the wild terrain brought back a strong longing to return to Reveloin. He had a fleeting temptation to talk to Sarcadui, but his son was more important right now.

After a few minutes of walking Robbie spotted the box wedged against a tree just a few feet from the water. Had Ames planted it there for him to find on purpose? Was it a challenge? A trap? Surely Jeremy was around. Robbie called out his name. The only response was some rustling of trees and the lapping water on the shore. Was Ames watching him? Were there ghosts about?

A car drove past on the road above him. Robbie apprehensively walked toward the box, hoping to provoke something, anything. A centipede placidly crawled along the ground at Robbie's feet. He squashed it with his foot as he crept further still. He kept his eyes fixed solely on the box, just waiting for someone to pop out of it. He would be ready this time.

But that didn't happen. Instead, a voice came from the water saying, "You want to know where your son is?"

Robbie turned his head and saw Ames standing waist-deep in the green water. "Where is he?" he yelled running after him. But just as he reached the water's edge a figure emerged from beneath the water next to Ames. It was a ghost in all its muscular, haunting form. Horrified of the creature, Robbie stopped in his tracks.

"No more steps, Robbie. That's right," said Ames. "Just stay right where you are."

"It's not dark out – that ghost can't be alive. What have you done with Jeremy?" said Robbie, bordering on hysteria.

"Things don't work the same way here as they do back home," said Ames, ignoring the question. "Would I have been able to fight you like I did the other day if we were back on the island?"

He was right about that. Back on the island Ames was a crotchety old man who could barely keep up with them. Robbie hadn't even considered how overpowering the old man had been in his house. He shuddered when he wondered how rough he had been with his son. As soon as the thought plagued his mind, Ames smirked and added poison to it. "I told you I'd hurt your kids if you didn't get back in the box. And not only did you not get back in, but you tried to set it on fire." His voice was calm and cool, yet icy to hear.

"Why not just kill *me* then, if I offended you so badly?" Robbie asked, nearly sobbing over what might have happened to Jeremy.

"Oh, please. You know full well that if you die, we all die with you. I'm just here to remind you that we need you. You should feel special, really."

"I'm not getting back in the box."

"Determination. That's good that you have that. But be careful, because while determination can get you far, it can also hold you back. For instance, you're determined to not get in the box, but for what? Because you made up your mind and now you want to stick with it? You've never been able to stick with a decision in your entire life."

"Where's my son?" Robbie demanded.

"But you've got determination when you're in Reveloin. You're determined to get to that castle and take your throne. You're determined to prove yourself and be hailed as a god. That's good. You had that kind of determination when you first found the box. You were determined to keep coming back to Reveloin. And judging by your life here, I can't blame you. You kept going back to Reveloin because it gave you a rush. Look around. There's nothing for you here and you know it. You're how old and you haven't even adapted to your own world yet? How pathetic! On the island you're a fighter. You believe in things over there. But here, it just doesn't seem like you really care much about anything. Admit it, you've tried proving yourself here, but it always just gets thrown back in your face, doesn't it? You try to do something nice for Rosalynn, but somehow you screw it up. You try to console your daughter, but she continues to hate you just as before. You try to connect with Jeremy, but he just ignores you. You're failing here, and you know it."

"I'm not getting in that box," said Robbie, unmoving.

Ames calmly took a few steps toward Robbie holding the ghost back with his arm. "Yes you will. Because as I've said before, if you don't get in the box, it's not you I'll come after, it's your family. And I'll kill them. One after another after another until you have nothing left here to live for. That at least ought to make your decision much easier; you'll *want* to come live with us." By now Ames was right in Robbie's face. He could feel his hot breath sticking to his skin like flypaper. "Do I make myself clear? Besides, your wife will die soon, and you don't want to be stuck here to face your grief alone, do you?"

Drained, Robbie said, "If you want me to get back in the box, I will. I just want my son back. Unharmed."

Ames smiled. "Good. But that's not all I want from you."

"What else?"

Another smile. "Don't leave the box."

"Can't do that."

"Don't want to starve, huh? Die of thirst? Decompose without a friend to mourn you?"

"Exactly," Robbie nodded. He was thinking about what Steve had told him about not nourishing his body for a few days and how he would have starved to death if it weren't for the deliveryman knocking on the door.

"You don't need to worry about that. Because when you cross the sea and take your place on that throne you'll live in Reveloin forever."

"That's not possible. I'd die here."

"Sure. Your body will die in the box, but that's no problem. I hear that when you die your body ends up in a box anyway. Might as well be this one. But that's the thing. You won't ever have to be called back..." Ames looked around with contempt etched on his face, "...*here* again because you'll be dead. But you won't be missing much. In Reveloin, you won't only live, but you'll live as a god; you'll live with us forever!"

"What would make me possibly want to live where you are?" asked Robbie, unconvinced of Ames's vision.

"Hey, as soon as you sit on the throne, I'll be out of your hair and you'll never have to see me again. But Sarcadui won't have to leave..." Robbie's heart leapt at the mention of her name and Ames must have sensed it because his lips curled. Just like him, he milked the topic for all it was worth. "She's quite a wild heart isn't she? So young. So beautiful. I never thought anyone would be able to catch her heart, but you've come close. I wouldn't be surprised if you've won it already. And really, once you've got a girl's trust then she's all yours. You see, she's known me for a long time and she's got my trust. I've never lied to her. But you? You keep promising you'll always be back. But one day you're just not going to come back. So guess who's next in line to have her?"

"You're a filthy liar," snarled Robbie in disgust.

Ames looked offended. "Have I lied to you? How many times have I saved your life on the island? The day we met I told you to get rid of everything in this world so you wouldn't be called back. I told you I'd hurt your kids if you tried damaging the box, and I made good on that promise."

"Where is he?" Robbie roared.

"Anything else you want to call me out on? Huh? I didn't think so. So have I ever lied to you? Have I?"

"No." Robbie spat the word out like it was a hot coal sizzling in his mouth.

"I agree with you."

Robbie glowered at him, filling up with more hate than he'd ever felt in his life. But all he could say was, "Where is my son?"

Ames turned his head and nodded at the ghost standing in the water. The ghost reached in below the surface and pulled Jeremy up, lifeless, by the back of his shirt.

Robbie pushed Ames aside and wadded rapidly through the water, desperate to get to his son. He took him from the ghost's hand, who snarled at him, and held him and cried over his limp body saying his name over and over.

Robbie hadn't noticed his son's killer stride up to him or how long he had been hovering over them. But after what seemed to be an eternity of torment and sorrow, Ames reached down toward Jeremy's face, which Robbie had yet to have the heart to look at. He slapped Ames's hand away, but Ames grabbed Robbie's wrist with his other hand and proceeded to reach toward Jeremy.

He dug a piece of bark out of his mouth and let it drop onto the water where it floated toward Robbie and bumped him on the chest. Breathing bark. Like Hale had in the lake by the Walei Cave. Jeremy was breathing, just shallowly, eyes closed and body limp.

"You'll be needing that when we reach the ocean. I'll hold on to it for you. I said I'd hurt your kids. Not kill them. I don't lie."

Ames grabbed the bark in his hand and proceeded to walk back up the bank toward the box, the ghost in tow. Jeremy began coughing and twisting in Robbie's arms, long lashes fluttering. Suddenly he knew his son's resurrection was the most beautiful thing he'd ever seen. Everything was so surreal that he barely heard Ames's final warning before climbing into the box.

"I want you back in the box before sunrise tomorrow. If you break the rules, I'll kill them. Taylor will be first."

CHAPTER 40

According to Jeremy he had no recollection of who or what had knocked him out. All he knew was that he was sitting alone in the car facing forward when suddenly the lights went out.

Rosalynn was desperate for answers to questions like, who could have snuck in the car quietly enough before Jeremy knew someone was there; what was the motivation behind the attack; will this result in any long-term injuries; how will this affect Jeremy psychologically, etc.

The medics who arrived on the scene thought it would be a good idea to monitor Jeremy overnight.

Robbie declined a free night at the Cottage on the Sound and, along with Rosalynn and Taylor, took up residence with Jeremy in his hospital room.

To avoid questions or suspicion Robbie had hid the box a short distance away from the crime scene. If Ames wanted Robbie back in the box that badly, he would bring the box to Robbie himself.

Unable to sleep, Robbie paced the hallway outside of Jeremy's room. Before it was too late in the night, Taylor snuck out from behind the door and approached Robbie. "Hey, hon," he said, welcoming her. "Can't sleep?"

Taylor nodded her head. "What's going on? Why are these things happening?" she asked.

Even with Taylor accompanying him it was strange how quiet the hospital was in contrast to that day's chaos. "I wish I could tell you," said Robbie, pulling his daughter in for a hug. "But I can tell you everything will be alright eventually."

"It's not just the robbery or what happened to Jeremy. It's you."

Robbie gave her his undivided attention.

"You were really freaky today at home, telling us to leave for no reason."

"I had a good reason, Taylor."

Taylor shook her head. "You can't keep being like that. Things are really sucking right now and you're not helping."

"You came out here to lecture me? Really?"

"No. I'm sorry; I'm just mad, or scared. I don't know. Good night."

Taylor turned to go back in the room but before she reached the door Robbie asked, "Why didn't you tell me you were just going to Jen's house to study?"

Taylor shrugged. "It's not like it would have made a difference. You still would have grounded me."

"What about Derek? Are you two still…?"

"It's Dwayne, and yes. And the party he wants me to go to is tomorrow night."

"No."

"Fine. Good night." And she was back in the room leaving Robbie alone in the hallway once more.

He pitied her that she had no idea that her life was in his hands. As angry as she made him, he wanted so desperately not only to preserve it, but to restore it.

Robbie awoke with a sick feeling in his stomach while it was still dark out. He glanced at the clock hanging up on the wall in front of him and it read 5:55. Ames wanted him back in the box by sunrise. He looked around the room and was shocked when he saw that the box wasn't there. Ames hadn't delivered it like he thought he would. How stupid to think that he would have! Ames didn't care if he got in at a certain time or not. He would just kill his daughter and set another deadline, with Jeremy or Rosalynn on the line, until Robbie made good on his promise to return to Reveloin.

If you break the rules, Taylor will be first.

He glanced at Taylor, stretched out on the couch that an orderly had been kind enough to bring in at her request. With just twenty minutes left before sunrise he hoped the box would still be where he left it.

He left a note for Rosalynn saying, "I'll be back later today. Call Dad if you need anything. Head home if they discharge Jer, I'll see you there."

The inn was only about a twenty minute drive from the hospital. Still, Robbie broke the speed limit to get to the box before sunrise. If a cop pulled him over, he would just have to outrun him until he got in the box and then the cop would have to use discretion once Robbie was in a trance.

He was getting close to where he met Ames the day before. He had driven about four miles from the inn then pulled over. He glanced at his GPS. He was six miles from his previous destination. He had to trust that he hadn't passed it yet. The clock read 6:12. The sky was breaking color behind him. He sped up. *I'm on my way Ames*, he thought. *Don't come back here yet. I'm going to get in the box.*

The GPS informed him that he was now four miles from his previous destination.

6:13.

Robbie veered off the road and slammed the car to a sudden halt. He toppled out of the car in a rush. The sky was a shade of violet in the east and he was barely able to see a crimson outline peeking over the mountains. *Not yet Ames. Just give me one more minute.*

As he stumbled down the bank away from the road toward the water he willed himself to remember everything Ames had told him the day before. But mostly he tried engraining it into his head that once he reached the island he was not, under any circumstances, to trust Ames.

Speak of the devil. Robbie nearly bumped right into him as he stepped out from behind a tree. "I never break my promises, Robbie," he said with that nasty smirk on his face.

"The sun hasn't raised yet, Ames. I'm here now. Just take me to the box and I'll get in."

Ames furrowed his brow in mock protest. "But that would make me out to be a liar Robbie, someone you can't trust. I don't mind being against you, but I don't want to be someone you can't trust."

Ames was hinting at something, but Robbie just couldn't quite put his finger on it. He studied Ames's face to translate what he was saying. Then a twitch of his gaze gave it away. Ames's eyes glazed past Robbie. He turned and looked. At first he saw nothing. Then he realized what he was communicating.

The sun hadn't risen yet. It was still climbing the mountain ridge. If Ames was going to make good on his promise to kill Taylor if Robbie was not in the box by sunrise, then he had to be there himself to see it.

"I'm here now, let's go," said Robbie, starting to rush past him.

"You broke a rule," said Ames, unmoving.

"What rule?"

"You left the box here all night. You were hoping for someone to find it and discard it so you wouldn't have to deal with it yourself."

Robbie was perplexed by this outlandish observation. "That's not true! I didn't have any intention of the box being taken. I thought you'd bring it *to* me."

"A car could have spun out of control and smashed the box."

Robbie stared at him not believing his ears. "You *know* I didn't think that. You're making that up!"

"A wild animal could have chewed a hole in it," said Ames woodenly, staring straight ahead toward the sun.

Then Robbie understood. Ames was stalling him.

Ignoring Ames, Robbie continued on ahead, searching frantically for the box. Could Ames have hidden it? The sun was half over the mountains. He had only about three minutes left. He saw the tree that the box had been wedged against the day before, but no box. At least he was sure it was the same tree.

He panicked, not knowing if he was in the right place. At least he had enough sense to not try to reason with Ames.

"A fire could have started here last night and you know how that can destroy things," Ames was saying.

On a whim, Robbie happened to look up and there he saw the box resting securely atop a thicket of branches in a tree well over twenty feet up. He grabbed a rock and was about to throw it up at the box to knock it free but his arm was caught by Ames's grip. "Don't hurt the box, Robbie."

He was telling him to climb the tree.

Robbie had about two minutes to climb up, knock the box down, jump down, and get inside. He didn't hesitate. He jumped up and reached the highest branch he could.

The test was proving more difficult than he imagined. Hadn't he climbed up a vine to get away from the centipods when he met Rhoe? No, that was in Reveloin. He was different there, more cunning, stronger.

Here, he was just an average middle-aged man sporting love handles. He had no business – or stamina – for climbing trees.

"You remember how I told you how things are different in Reveloin from here? Here, you're as weak as a mouse, but if you were in Reveloin you'd have scaled that tree by now. Why in the world would you want to remain in a place that makes you weaker than you really are? Your limitations are unbearable!"

Finally Robbie got high enough to grab one of the hindering branches and shake it free from supporting the box. The box fell to the ground.

Robbie looked toward the east. The sun would clear the mountaintops in less than a minute. Robbie let go of the branch and fell ten feet to the ground, careful to avoid the box. His ankle gave out from under him and searing pain shot through his entire body making his head swim and his ears ring. Not to mention his head wound from the ghost knocking him out yesterday was irritated. He crawled toward the box in desperation, the ground tilting to and fro. He flipped the box right side up, but before crawling in, Ames walked up to him and said, "You're not going to leave me here, are you?"

"What?" Robbie asked, his mouth dry and his vision blurred.

"I can't get in *after* you. You'd be in my way. You don't want me stuck here with your daughter do you?"

"Please," Robbie gasped looking up at Ames towering over him. The dizziness was beginning to subside, but anxiety was quickly taking its place. He knew he could say nothing to persuade Ames to get in the box. It would have to be a choice made entirely on his part; a sheer act of grace. And he was certain Ames had none to offer. The sun was just seconds from clearing the mountains. Ames was going to just stand there and let Robbie watch the sunrise that would mark the last day of Taylor's life.

At the last minute Ames looked from the rising sun to Robbie and said, "I'll see you back there." He then stepped inside the box as though it were a hatch and disappeared inside. Robbie breathed a sigh of relief and crawled inside the box after him, careful not to aggravate his sprained ankle.

He had just missed the sun clearing over the mountaintops.

CHAPTER 41

... his left foot collapsed underneath him like a rag when he tried to stand up. He looked down at his new clothing. By this time he was used to reappearing from time lapses in different apparel and covering them up with his cloak that always laid on hand.

But what had happened to his foot? He didn't remember busting it. Had he been knocked out from behind and that's when it twisted? Where were Rhoe and Sarcadui? What about Ames? Robbie hated these time lapses that occurred for whatever reason. The sun cast bars of light through the trees onto the jungle floor. It seemed still, peaceful even. He thought about calling for help, but he didn't want to draw attention from unwanted stalkers.

He attempted to walk again and this time was able to limp forward toward the aroma of a campfire. He followed the scent until he found Rhoe and Sarcadui sitting around the small fire. Sarcadui was the first to spot him and she ran up to embrace him. "You've been gone for so long. We were beginning to wonder if you'd ever be back."

Rhoe respectfully bowed to him and said, "We're glad you're back, Sir."

They all resumed their places around the campfire and Robbie was glad to sit next to Sarcadui.

Rhoe had caught a couple eoraptors overnight with some vines and netting he collected in the jungle and that was their breakfast. The meat was as rubbery as Robbie expected and did not wash down his gullet easily. "Where's Ames?" he asked.

"We haven't seen him since we woke up. But we're sure he'll be back soon," said Sarcadui.

"Can you smell the ocean?" asked Rhoe, crunching down onto a crispy neck. "We're so close I've had to keep myself from going without you. We should be there in just a few hours."

"That's great," said Robbie, perking up at the news. "Let's find Ames so we can go."

A scoff came from behind them and they turned and saw Ames standing near the trees, half hidden in the shadows. "Don't get too excited, Robbie. I know we've seen some rough times, but the worst still lies ahead of us."

"Ames, there's no need—" started Rhoe.

"Yes great hunter, I do need to warn him. We all know *other* people..." here, he shot an accusing glance at Sarcadui. "...aren't capable of warning our prophesied one of looming dangers. Seems the two of you don't care to give your boy a fair chance at making it to the castle."

"What do you need to tell me, Ames?" Robbie asked.

Ames sat down next to the fire and grabbed part of a lizard. "You know the island is infested with ghosts at night. And it's not any easier during the day with the trenchers. But what you don't know is that the closer we get to the ocean the more in sync the island is in with the ghosts' will. During the day, when they're not out, they've got most of the island working for them. They've made pacts with the animals and creatures who are closest to the ocean in case anyone happens to make it this far. Even the trees will start standing in our way, if you want to believe that."

"If you don't believe it, then why are you telling me?" asked Robbie.

Ames shrugged. "I just want you to be prepared is all. But hey, congratulations are in order for all of us. No one's made it this far to the ocean."

"You don't know that," said Sarcadui.

"I don't?" asked Ames, arching an eyebrow. "Haven't you noticed the trees have been growing closer together? Kind of like forming a fence to keep us out? And what about yesterday when our fearless Rhoe got his foot snagged in a vine? He's not normally clumsy in the jungle. And haven't you noticed it's been getting rather easier to catch food? No one's been out here. Even the trenchers are scared to come this far. The jungle is against *any*one reaching the ocean, and right now it's being threatened by our presence, and it *will* fight us every step of the way. Trust me, *no* one's made it this far since the floods came."

Robbie, Rhoe, and Sarcadui looked at each other as if determining if there was any merit to Ames's words.

Ames sighed as if exhausted from talking of such mundane matters. Then, making his narrative more applicable he added, "But no matter. We're close, and that's what counts, right? At least now we're all on guard." Then he took another bite of his eoraptor and tossed the rest of the cooked lizard to the ground. "Let's keep moving."

They all stood up and Ames looked at Robbie and said, "I hope your foot's better."

Robbie had forgotten all about his sprained ankle, and in fact it did feel much better as if it had never suffered to begin with. He was about to ask Ames how he knew it had been hurt but he was already walking up ahead leading the way.

The four continued walking through the jungle but whether it was because of Ames's harrowing warning or just exhaustion they walked in deeper silence than they had before. Still, Robbie couldn't help but notice that Ames was right about the trees being much closer together. The further into the jungle they walked the more entwined the branches were with other trees, as though hugging one another.

An odious stench soon filled the air, forcing Robbie to cover his nose with a handful of his cloak. The more they walked the more pungent the smell became. Even Rhoe and Sarcadui were looking sick and had to cover their mouths and noses.

Soon there was foliage scattered all around. Broken tree branches and leaves lay desolate everywhere they looked. The trees were now broken off at the lower branches, and bark was ripped off of them. Some trees were even split right down the middle, and the sky was starting to expose itself more because of so many limbs having been ripped apart from above. It wasn't long before they had to climb over giant branches that had crashed to the ground as though they were up in the trees themselves.

As they continued, the smell grew nauseatingly worse. Robbie heard flies up ahead. It sounded like there were hundreds of them, but where were they? Robbie reached up high to hurdle a branch with a width larger than he had ever thought possible. He felt like a bug crawling around the forest. But before he had a chance to tackle it, Ames grabbed his arm and lead him around it, which turned out not to be a branch at all.

Following the group to the other side, Robbie saw that he was about to attempt to climb over a massive dinosaur's foot. There it laid, its stomach ripped open by some larger, more vicious beast. The flies were busy laying their eggs on the innards that lay spilt out of the carcass. All four of them could have comfortably fit in its open stomach, with room to spare. Its eyes were open but glazed over in a pasty film.

Robbie held his stomach tight as he turned around to vomit into a bush. "What could have done this?" he asked.

"Another dinosaur," said Rhoe. "Which means there's one still out there."

"Or the island did it," suggested Ames.

They all looked at him.

"There's no other broken trees around, are there? And besides, why would something achieve a kill like this and not eat it? But don't worry, I'm sure if you all want to see another one, you'll have your chance. After all, where there's one, there's bound to be others."

Ames continued to lead the group forward.

Robbie was growing claustrophobic as they continued through the ever-denser jungle, though he was glad to be away from the dinosaur corpse and able to breathe the fresh air once more. But it became darker as the jungle grew tighter around them, even though it was still late morning. A feeling of dread was coming over Robbie in torrents. If they were really getting close to the ocean then there was bound to be something to get in their way, supposing Ames's warning was accurate.

Soon the trees grew so close together that no one was able to squeeze in between their trunks. At one point they had to walk a long way to get around a cluster of trees that were too tight to crawl through. When Robbie suggested that they go through the tops of the trees like Rhoe had taught him when they were running from the centipods Ames rejected the idea on the grounds that he was still injured pretty badly from the panther and had a hard enough time walking, let alone climbing through trees. So on they walked.

Robbie was losing oxygen by the minute as the trees were closing in on all sides. Soon it didn't seem like it was as gradual as the distance they were making, but perhaps the trees were moving in closer on them by themselves. He shook his head free of the notion and pressed on.

No one talked as it seemed the fear of being closed in had captured everyone's minds. Not even Ames had the gall to say anything.

Then Robbie noticed something he hadn't before. The trees were creaking and groaning, like old rocking chairs moving back and forth, or more precisely, it sounded like timber was being bent past its endurance. The groaning became louder and soon Sarcadui broke the mortal silence.

"I'm stuck!" she cried.

Just when she said this, Robbie's shin was pinned by two tree trunks pressing together on him and he was suddenly face to face with a tree that wasn't there before. He couldn't see the others; the trees had moved in and separated them.

"I can't move either," came Rhoe's voice from somewhere to his left. "Robbie, are you with us?"

"Yeah, I'm stuck, though," he answered. "What do we do?"

"I'm thinking," said Rhoe. "Ames, what's going on?"

There was a pause.

"Ames?"

No answer.

The creaking noises in the trees stopped. At least Robbie wasn't crushed to death. And no bones had been broken that he could tell.

"Sarcadui, are you okay?" asked Robbie, wishing desperately to see her.

"I'm okay. I think they're holding us captive," she answered.

"That's exactly what they're doing," said Rhoe.

"Holding us captive for who, though?" asked Robbie.

"For me," came Ames's voice, not obstructed by pain or struggle. "I tried to get you to the ocean, but I'm sorry; I got caught."

"Caught by who?" asked Sarcadui. "What are you talking about?"

"Some trenchers found me. I can't keep running from them. It's time I comply."

"What do you mean?" asked Rhoe, wrath seething through his teeth.

"I'm one of them. And you're my prisoners for the Harvest tonight."

CHAPTER 42

Robbie's feet and wrists were tied together before the trees released their hold on him and when he could finally see Sarcadui and Rhoe, he saw that they were tied up in the same way. They were surrounded by five men. Three of them were dressed like ordinary islanders and two were wearing long trench coats. These were the trenchers Ames was in cahoots with.

"Lead the way, gentlemen," Ames instructed. "And make it fast, we don't want to lose this one," he said as he patted Robbie on the back.

The five trenchers lead the way, pulling Rhoe and Sarcadui by leather leashes that slipped around their necks. Ames led Robbie but kept his leash short so they could remain within speaking distance.

"I'm sorry it had to end this way," said Ames. "But you should know it's really because you didn't do what I said. If you'd have cut ties with the other world sooner we would have been out to sea by now and you'd be sitting on your throne and all would be well."

Robbie took a vow of silence, not wanting any association with this traitor.

"You kept taking so long to come back each time you left," continued Ames, "that tonight is the second Harvest since you've arrived. Now, it's a good thing Rhoe killed that panther that was after me, otherwise I would have had to comply then. That panther was after me because I was assigned to it and it was sent to kill me because I missed the last festival.

"Oh don't look at me like that. I'm not all that bad. I really wanted to get you to the ocean so you could complete the mission. I had to fight off a lot of people to throw them off your trail these last few weeks. But these trenchers... I had no idea they'd be back there in the jungle. They were sneaky. And so close to the ocean, too! They assumed I was taking you all prisoner so I had to play along if I didn't want to get killed. I just told them I had gotten lost, being a forgetful old man and all. It's survival of the strongest, and since I swore allegiance to the ghosts long before you came, I've got to keep up the act."

"It was you who gave away the underground shelter, wasn't it?" asked Robbie.

Ames looked at him knowingly.

"You kept the ghosts away from us that first night by alerting them of the shelter in Langly. That's why all those people died while Sarcadui and I were in the library, isn't it?"

"You're very good," said Ames. "Want to know another secret? Now, don't tell her or it'll really upset her. I was the one who led Sarcadui's parents into the jungle to collect food. I told them it would be all right. Don't give me that look. You think they'd be stupid enough to go on their own accord so late at night? It was them I presented to the ghosts to represent my conversion to the trencherhood."

Robbie was seething. But he had to stay calm. As Ames was talking, Robbie was formulating a plan in his mind. He gathered up all the knowledge he had learned about Reveloin and himself and decided something could surely work against Ames and thwart his entire scheme.

"But you've got to hand it to me," continued Ames. "I had it set up pretty good for myself. If I could have gotten you safely to your throne the ghosts would have been destroyed and everyone would have been happy. But seeing as that's no longer the case and we've been caught, all I have to do is turn you in to the ghosts, they kill you, the world goes dark forever, but I as your captor will receive a very large reward."

Acting impulsively on an idea, Robbie threw himself to the ground, half pulling Ames down along with him. "What are you doing?" asked Ames angrily. "Get up."

Hoping to buy time toward his next time lapse he said, "I twisted my foot; I can't walk."

"Well you better try. We need to be at the Pit by midnight."

The trenchers dragging Sarcadui and Rhoe stopped and looked back at the commotion, as the other three continued to press forward. "Is everything okay?" one of them asked.

"Everything's fine," Robbie called out.

Ames kicked him in the ribs and called out to the other trenchers, "I think this one may need to be carried."

The bigger of the two trenchers handed Rhoe's leash to his comrade, walked over to Robbie, and said, "I'll take care of this one." He then bent down and looked Robbie in the eyes and said, "It looks like you need some assistance to the festival." He picked a rock up from the ground and pelted Robbie on the back of the head.

Robbie woke up and everything was in a blur. He was lying flat on his back staring up at the trees. It felt like early afternoon. He heard voices ahead of him. He lifted his head just enough to see what was going on. Ames was standing idle holding onto Rhoe's and Sarcadui's leashes, still wrapped around their necks. Three of the five trenchers were walking further into the jungle not about to wait for the other two who were uncovering leaves and branches from a hole in the ground. Once it was uncovered, one of the trenchers lowered a branch down into it. After nothing happened for a long moment the other trencher began to yell ferociously into the hole for someone to take the branch. This being accomplished, the other trencher pulled up on a large branch. Out came a young woman on the other end, dusty and weeping. Ames cast a glance toward Robbie, but he quickly dropped his head back to feign unconsciousness. He held his breath, hoping Ames didn't see him awake. A moment passed and there seemed to be no alarm. Not daring to open his eyes again he heard one of the trenchers say a couple minutes later, "That's six. Tie the last one up and let's go."

Robbie understood what was going on. This was where these particular trenchers held their prisoners. They gathered three for each of them so they'd each meet the quota for that night's festival. Sarcadui, Rhoe, and he were Ames's prisoners.

As soon as all six were tied to their leashes, the caravan resumed its journey. Two of the prisoners were forced to drag Robbie's thin stretcher along the ground. But when a sharp rock jabbed into the wound Robbie had received just hours before, the pain sent a wild shock through him and he blacked out once again.

The most evident sound of all the noises that erupted around him when he came to was the blaring of a giant conch shell, loud enough to cause his ears to ring. Other sounds were of monstrous tumults of jubilee – howling, growling, snarling, shrieking. If Evil itself were to host a celebration in honor of all of its demons and evil-makers, this would be the pinnacle of celebrations.

As Robbie's eyes came back into focus he slowly began to take inventory of his horrid surroundings. The first thing he noticed was the faceless, blotchy-skinned ghosts everywhere. There were thousands of them of every shape and size strolling around. Many of them held on to leashes connected to other prisoners just like himself, who were tied up by hand and foot. There were many people walking about, trenchers accompanied by panthers, escorting prisoners mercilessly. The prisoners were of every age, from as young as children to elders who could barely walk. He spotted Rhoe and Sarcadui ahead of him, who were being kept separate from the six prisoners that were picked up earlier. Ames still held their leashes while the other two trenchers held on to their share of prisoners. He himself was being pulled on a jungle-made stretcher, and his back and rear end were sore from being dragged so pitilessly across the hard terrain over rocks and sticks and branches. It was in the thickest part of the night – midnight, and the conch horn continued to blow from somewhere nearby. It was loud enough to be heard throughout the whole island just like they had heard it before when they were on the roof of the cottage where they found Ames. Had it really been a month since then? More importantly, where were they all being taken?

When the throbbing in his head began to subside he was able to more coherently register what was happening around him. The light came from the full moon, which the ghosts didn't seem to mind. Some shielded their faces against it, but it was the only reason he was able to see anything at all. The prisoners were being led to a large row of sloppily built booths where they were being traded in for food or other goods. He and the other captors were in line for one of the booths, but while they were waiting, he still continued to fake being unconscious, occasionally peering out from beneath lowered eyelids. Once the prisoners were brought forth to the booths, their captors began to bargain with the ghosts behind the booths. It seemed the stronger and healthier the prisoner, the more goods they received. But this was not done at all in any orderly fashion. Often a violent fight would break out between the buyers and the sellers, and others would join in leaving their prisoners fair game for someone else to claim as their own, which would then cause another uncivil brawl.

Once the exchange was made the buyer would then escort the purchased prisoners into a large cage, which looked to be the size of a town block, made of bamboo and sturdy tree branches. The cage was filled with crying, weeping people, holding each other, speaking useless words of hope to one another. The mourning was nearly as loud as the tumult of the ghosts. Outside the cage the ghosts taunted and jeered at the helpless victims, occasionally trying unsuccessfully to break in to the cage and reap havoc before "officials" broke them away. The ghosts seemed to be famished with anticipation to handle the victims in their own demented ways. The trenchers just stood idly by watching the commotion with unsympathetic eyes that had certainly seen this horrible scene often.

Robbie then started trembling for his life. What was to become of him? What about Rhoe and Sarcadui? Then he heard a familiar yet unfriendly voice call out, "He's awake!" One of the trenchers had seen Robbie's eyes partly open and ratted him out. Robbie quickly closed his eyes before anyone else could notice, but a pair of footsteps made their way toward him and suddenly he was yanked up to his feet by a wad of his cloak. He stood, not seeing the point of pretending to be unconscious any longer.

One of the other trenchers in their group had pulled him up and Ames came striding toward him. "Glad to see you're up, Mr. Robbie."

He briefly made eye contact with Rhoe and Sarcadui but all hope and life had been drained from them. Not even seeing Robbie awake could instill a spirit of survival in them. To this, Robbie's heart sank into the depths.

Ames turned toward the front of the line and yelled, "Come on, I don't have all night! Let's keep this line moving!"

Robbie could tell Ames was anxious about selling Robbie before he vanished into a time lapse. He longed to disappear from this nightmare, but that wouldn't affect Rhoe's and Sarcadui's fate in the least. For their sake alone he hoped to remain.

Once their group had finally reached the booth, Ames and the two other trenchers began bartering with the buyer. The ghost who ran the booth, though it didn't speak, recognized their words and made head gestures according to its meanings. Ames finally pulled the ghost aside and whispered something in a small hole on the side of its head where its ear was supposed to be. As he did this, he continually gestured toward Robbie. Robbie was certain he was telling it he was the prophesied one but the ghost wasn't being very receptive. But as Ames was talking privately with the ghost, the other two trenchers on his team were beginning to pull Sarcadui and Rhoe over toward them along with their other prisoners.

"Hey!" cried Ames, glancing over at them. "Those are *my* prisoners, *I* caught them!"

"Sorry man," said the bigger one. "It looks like you've only got one. You failed to meet the quota."

Ames started to panic. "No! These two are mine! Rhoe, Sarcadui, tell them!"

But Sarcadui and Rhoe remained silent. The ghost glared at Ames as clearly as though it had eyes. Two others gathered near it and their lips turned up into a snarl, sensing trouble in the air.

"You traitors! Robbie, tell them! ...It doesn't matter. I've got the prophesied one. I've got the *only* one you really want."

"Right," laughed the other trenchers.

"In that case," said a man directly behind Robbie, putting his hands on Robbie's shoulders, "I'll claim him. Now it looks like *I've* captured the prophesied one."

Ames grew instantly fierce and lunged toward Robbie, but gathering ghosts caught Ames by the arms and legs and dragged him toward the cage and threw him in with all the other prisoners, kicking and screaming erratically. The prisoners, upon being handed a traitor, quickly went from despondence to fierce anger and they began to push him around, yelling and screaming at him. He was, after all, one of those who had forged an allegiance against them. Robbie almost felt sorry for him, but not quite.

But now his new captor was bartering for him. The two trenchers had received their pay for their prisoners, including Sarcadui and Rhoe, and walked off in a different direction. He watched as a ghost led his friends and the other prisoners to the massive cage. Then his new captor gave him a shove from behind and said, "Answer the question. Are you the prophesied one?"

Robbie just hung his head, refusing to answer.

"I didn't think so." His captor received his payment, laughing about the so-called "prophesied one" to the stranger behind him. While he did this, a ghost dragged Robbie away toward the cage. He was warmly received by Sarcadui and Rhoe, but others kept their faces down and had long ago given up hiding their tears.

"Sir," said Rhoe with much anticipation. "You need to listen to me. I've been here before."

"What?" asked Robbie. Sarcadui didn't seem as surprised. Instead, there was sympathy in her eyes.

"There's hope," continued Rhoe, dismissively. "You can get out of here too and we can all be saved..."

But suddenly a loud voice cried out above the ruckus from the booths:

"We've got him! We've got the prophesied one!"

Most eyes turned toward the claim, but some still went about their business. Rhoe tried to keep talking to Robbie but he ignored him, wanting to see what was going on. Through a crowd of ghosts and trenchers he could see a prisoner jerking away from his captor and yelling, "That's right! It's me! I am the one you seek!" Then he jumped up onto the wobbly booth and continued raving, "I am the one who will bring you all to ruin! Throw me into the Pit and I will touch the timber that will make me king over all! I am Robbie!" Then he broke into a manic laugh and the creatures and people all booed and hissed at him, shouting "Kill him! Kill him! Kill him! Kill him!"

Then without warning a ghost leapt up onto the table and, placing two monstrous hands on the man's face, ripped the skin from around his mouth, separating his lower jaw from the rest of his face with a deafening crack, leaving the jaw to dangle freely from the rest of his face. The body went limp but continued to stand, partially by the assistance of the ghost's hand still on the man's head. He was screaming, but the cries came out ghastly and inhuman. The ghost then took its free hand and shoved it down the open throat. The crowd screamed and hollered their approval. The prisoners, both jailed and in line, looked away in disgust, many plugging their ears, some breaking out into open sobs. Robbie looked on through his fingers as he shielded his eyes with his hand. The ghost's arm was nearly to its elbow as it shoved deeper into the open cavity that was the man's throat. Muffled cries could be heard from the dying man as his insides were being completely destroyed. Even from where he stood Robbie could hear the man's cervical vertebrae cracking and splitting, his liver gushing. His neck pulsated and was practically ripping on all sides because of the ghost's beefy arm shoving into it like a foot trying to fit into a small sock. Finally the ghost pulled its blood-soaked arm back out of the man's throat, letting the body fall to the ground like a rag doll, and held up the man's glossy heart. The ghost's arm was drenched in blood and chunks of membrane which splattered all over the nearing crowd, who seemed to enjoy gathering drops of the red and yellow gore on their faces. Two panthers dived in and began ripping into the man's body.

The cheers grew louder and louder and Robbie could hear some people yelling, "Liar! False alarm! Imposter!" He was grateful that he had not admitted to being the prophesied one when asked.

Then there was a fresh torrent of screaming and crying from within the cage, and a wave of people knocked Robbie off his feet. He was nearly trampled as everyone seemed to be moving away from the bars. Rhoe quickly helped Robbie to his feet and both they and Sarcadui moved with the terrified crowd toward the center of the cage. The cage doors were open on both ends and four ghosts came in and started grabbing people by their arms and pushing them toward the opening where other ghosts stood by with ropes to tie them up.

Rhoe was trying desperately to tell Robbie what he needed to say, but he was impossible to hear over the terrified screams. A small boy near Robbie's leg was crying desperately as his mother was torn from him. The woman screamed with every amount of terror she could involuntarily muster as she reached out for her boy. Robbie pushed him back behind his leg to keep him from being snatched.

The crowd grew more resistant as the ghosts continued to drag out random prisoners, even mercilessly pulling some out by their hair. Robbie checked to see that Sarcadui and Rhoe were still with him as he dodged the ghost's prying hands. He saw Sarcadui in the middle of the crowd desperately reaching out her hand toward the opening. Robbie looked to where she was reaching and to his horror he saw Rhoe being escorted by a ghost outside the jail bars. The first Harvest of the night was over and the cage doors closed and all the chosen prisoners, including Rhoe, were led down a slope toward the Pit.

CHAPTER 43

Robbie pushed his way through the now silent crowd to the far side of the cage. Sarcadui, dumbstruck, followed. Once there, he peered through the bars and saw before him a massive arena dug into the ground that likely had a radius of nearly half a mile. This was the Game Pit Sarcadui had told him about. All around the Pit were several wooden cranes that reached over the edge. Attached to these cranes were ropes that tied to giant birdcages that looked like they could each hold a dozen or so people. At the bottom of the Pit were handfuls of ghosts and panthers walking about. It was hard to tell in the darkness but the light from the moon seemed to suggest that these ghosts and panthers were insane; they were screaming themselves hoarse and the panthers were acting erratically, attacking each other, and jerking wildly. The Pit was nothing but a dry desert terrain with boulders here and there and some dead trees scattered throughout. But the thing that sent shivers up Robbie's spine was the countless blood stains everywhere, and torn rags that must have been clothing, and human bones strewn about.

Searching diligently for Rhoe, Robbie shifted his gaze toward the many prisoners who were being corralled around the cages. It was Sarcadui who spotted him and pointed him out. "There he is," she said in tears, pointing to the closest birdcage.

Robbie looked at the many faces of the prisoners and sure enough there was Rhoe. But instead of walking with his eyes downcast, or crying, or staring at the Pit ahead of him, like the other prisoners were doing, he was keeping his eyes fixed, deadlocked, on Robbie.

Others in the cage mourned for their stolen loved ones, calling out their names and reaching their hands out toward them, but the surrounding ghosts outside the cage nipped at their fingers and laughed, pounding the bars with their fists and heads while jumping jubilantly about.

Robbie watched as they marched Rhoe and several others into

the nearest birdcage that rested near the edge of the Pit. Others were marched to surrounding birdcages, made of bamboo sticks tied together with vines. Most of the people were weeping as they were locked up. Through all the drama and terror, Rhoe never took his eyes off Robbie. It took a few minutes before it dawned on him that Rhoe was going to try to communicate to Robbie what he hadn't been able to tell him before. Robbie nodded his head to assure Rhoe that he understood. Rhoe nodded back.

Once everyone was locked up, ghosts manned the cranes and began to wind the wheels that heaved the birdcages off the ground. The jibs swung over the Pit dangling the birdcages over the giant arena below. The cages were yanked mercilessly away from their resting places, causing the people inside to stumble and fall over one another. Legs fell through the bars in places, and others in the cages clung to the sides. Robbie watched as Rhoe stood resolutely keeping a brave face on. The birdcages all around the Pit now hung over the edge waiting to be dropped. Robbie feared for Rhoe's life and couldn't help but feel disgusted with himself for getting him into all this trouble. After all, he had just wanted to sit up in the trees and wait until life returned to normal. Sarcadui turned and covered her eyes with her hands, weeping for their lost friend.

A cloud drifted in front of the moon blocking its light from the arena and it suddenly became deathly dark. And silent. Only the crickets and birds could be heard singing their melancholy songs in the nearby trees. A few people began mourning once the shock of the sudden darkness wore off. And soon, more people joined in the cry for hopeless deliverance from the holding cage as well as from all the birdcages surrounding the Pit. The agonizing wailings of lament were enough to choke Robbie's throat. He thought about the mother, separated from her son, and what she must be thinking. He thought about all the lovers sitting in the cage with him, mourning the loss of their loved ones as their lives were just minutes away from entering into the void of eternal death. He had nearly forgotten about Sarcadui who was now squeezing his hand as tight as she could. There was no telling what caused him to think of it but he wondered what had become of Ames. Had the prisoners beat him to death? At any rate there would be no way of finding him now in this almost pitch darkness. Maybe he was awaiting his doom in the same manner as Rhoe.

What were they waiting for? Something wasn't right, and there was no reason why the ghosts should be so calm. So tame.

Minutes passed and nothing happened. After about ten minutes Robbie turned from the ghastly scene and sat down on the ground with his back to the cage. Sarcadui sat down next to him just as she had done in her underground home when they first met in Langly, and later when they sat next to each other in the library.

"Why didn't Rhoe say anything before about being in the Pit?" asked Robbie.

"He told me," said Sarcadui. "At some point when you were gone he told me he was my boyfriend when we were young."

"The one we read about in your book?"

Sarcadui nodded as she shivered from a cool breeze that swept past. Robbie wrapped his arm around her as she said, "I never knew what happened to him because I lost a lot of my memory when we were attacked by trenchers. I woke up hidden in a hollow tree, but he was gone. They had taken him to the Harvest. I don't remember what he looks like, I just know he existed. I don't believe Rhoe because no one can escape from the Pit. You see what it's like; it's impossible."

"Well if it was him, maybe he'll escape again and soon we can all be out of here," offered Robbie.

Sarcadui smiled and leaned her head on his shoulder. "Maybe," she said.

"Can you tell me about the ocean?" he asked.

"It's a beautiful place," started Sarcadui. Robbie could barely hear her above the constant wailing but he held on to every word his ears picked up on. "At the ocean there's life, and memories. Memories long ago forgotten..."

"What's going to happen to us?" asked Robbie after a long, somber pause.

Sarcadui just broke down and wrapped her arms around his neck and cried, trembling, her head pressed against his chest. Her tears were dampening his cloak.

Suddenly the moon was unveiled by the drifting cloud and the pale light seemed to cast a spell on the monsters as it sent them into a wild uproar twice as loud as before. With the violent bedlam, handfuls of ghosts climbed the cranes and scaled the jibs and began ripping and gnawing the ropes with their teeth and nails. Robbie watched Rhoe's encasement in particular as it swung impetuously about. His heart went out to Rhoe who continued to hold fast to his stalwart spirit while still maintaining eye contact with Robbie as he grasped the cage bars to keep from falling.

One cage from across the Pit gave way and crashed at the bottom on the rocks below. A horde of ghosts were upon the weakened survivors at once, ripping their bodies apart limb from limb. Only one victim managed to scramble away but she found herself trapped between the ledge and a crazed panther, which wasted no time in lunging for her throat. Another cage fell with two ghosts falling clumsily with it. Two others dropped at the same time. It quickly became clear to Robbie that the victims had absolutely zero chance of surviving once they were dropped inside the Pit. Friends and family members still trapped in the holding cage with Robbie screamed in horror as their loved ones dropped one by one into the hell-hold. Rhoe's cage was the last to fall.

CHAPTER 44

Knowing Rhoe's cage was going to fall made it no less heart-stopping for Robbie when it actually happened. He couldn't help a small cry of pain, and Sarcadui looked up just as the rope broke. She grabbed his hand and squeezed it so tight his knuckles were white. Being on the same side of the Pit, Rhoe's cage fell out of sight behind the ledge. Robbie and Sarcadui jumped up and strained on their tip-toes to catch a glimpse of their friend but it was useless. Robbie would have to wait until Rhoe ran away from the Pit's wall if he was going to see him again. But with the way the cages shattered on impact and taking into account the swiftness of the crazed ghosts and panthers, he had no reason to believe Rhoe would survive long enough to run very far.

Sarcadui turned away from the hell unfolding before them while Robbie felt inclined to watch for Rhoe as though his faithful gaze would cause his friend to appear against great odds. But when he thought of it, he couldn't imagine why he'd want Rhoe to survive for even a second amidst such a horrible circus of terror.

Nevertheless as he continued to keep a sharp eye out for Rhoe, Robbie couldn't help but notice some of the sickening torture and violence that ensued inside the Pit. Of the people who survived the crash, many were devoured within seconds of regaining their composure. Still, many more were left alone to run aimlessly about while their predators taunted them, daring them to move any which way. One ghost firmly hugged a wriggling old man to its body as it grinded its teeth against his bald head. Two panthers fought manically over a half-chewed leg of a crying young man. Blood was being spilt all over the arena as necks were broken, faces torn off, eyes dug out, and limbs being ripped apart.

To Robbie's outright horror it seemed like handfuls of people at a time were being beaten, mauled, and molested in every imaginable way. No one could possibly hope to survive this perverted form of execution. Not even Rhoe.

But before Robbie looked away for good, a figure dashing across the arena caught his eye. It caught the attention of the spectators as well because a huge uproar erupted from the watching crowd. The figure was indeed Rhoe. The killers in the arena took notice of his flight and suddenly he became their sole objective, save for the panthers, which were busy gorging themselves on human flesh.

What was it Rhoe was so anxious to get to? Was there indeed deliverance of some sort hidden in that blood-splattered hell-hold? Robbie watched as Rhoe leapt over boulders, scaled rocks, circled dead trees and came ever closer to the center of the arena. The blood-thirsty crowd was going crazy. The menacing monsters were nearly upon him, but he kept going. Finally he reached a place where two boulders hugged each other and between them protruded a white stick, about the length of a leg.

"Pay attention Robbie," came a scathingly familiar voice in his ear.

It was Ames.

Upon seeing his traitorous face Robbie instinctively shoved him back. Regaining his balance Ames repeated, "Pay attention to your friend out there! He's trying to show you something."

"Robbie, look!" said Sarcadui.

Robbie turned back toward the Pit just as Rhoe grabbed hold of the stick between the boulders, which caused his pursuers to stop in their tracks and the spectators erupted into an even more thunderous roar mixed with approval and disdain. He was sure bets were being made amongst the crowd.

Robbie looked at Rhoe who lay collapsed over one boulder clasping the stick as tightly as he could. He couldn't tell for certain, but it seemed to Robbie that Rhoe had found Robbie's eyes even from such a distance. What was going on? What was Rhoe trying to communicate? Why had his pursuers stopped advancing just as they had him in their grasp?

Suddenly Rhoe began to tremble. His body shook as though he were no longer in control of himself.

"What's happening?" Sarcadui asked, turning toward Ames who was pushing through the crowd to get closer to the bars.

"What Rhoe just did was incredibly stupid," Ames started as prisoners who were not presently mourning their loved ones inched closer to the bars to get a better view. "Having been to all of these games over the years I can tell you he just grabbed a leg of the throne brought from Robbie's castle."

Sarcadui buried her face in her hands and gave into a flood of tears. "Then that means?" asked Robbie.

"That he took on the curse," said Ames. "He's one of *them* now."

Robbie watched as Rhoe's transformation took affect over his body. He was somewhat glad for the distance as he couldn't see the details of the changes, but the spell was so drastic that his change in posture and shape clearly defined a reformation in reverse. Before the massive audience, Rhoe's posture took on a ghastly shape. His head strained and twisted as his physical elements struggled to take on a new identity. His nose started to disappear into pallid rotting flesh. And Robbie could see, most horrifically, the faraway look in Rhoe's eyes as though he were desperately lost in a trance. And then he snarled and arched backwards to let loose a devilish roar.

Rhoe was forever lost in the monstrous kingdom of darkness.

Sarcadui wept openly. Robbie was moved far beyond tears, possibly to complete numbness of spirit.

"What he did was stupid," said Ames. "But–"

Not thinking, Robbie turned and landed his fist in Ames's face, knocking him down to the ground with a loud crack. The gathering people parted, not willing to catch the trencher. Robbie heard a bone-shattering crunch in the blow and was convinced he had broken Ames's nose. This was proved right by the blood that streamed down Ames's face.

"You think I deserved that but I didn't," said Ames. "And no, I don't deserve more," he added when Robbie was about to make another strike at him. Sarcadui interfered by holding Robbie back, allowing Ames to continue. "Rhoe has just demonstrated that there's hope for us, but if you can't see that by now then clearly your friend's sacrifice was in vain."

"Then explain," Robbie seethed. "And fast."

"If that stick is part of the throne that brings the curse to all who touch it then you'd better get to that stick fast, oh prophesied one."

It was slowly starting to make sense to Robbie. That's why they killed the man who claimed to be the prophesied one earlier. If they suspected Robbie was the prophesied one, they would have killed him too. Giving people a chance to touch a piece of the throne adds to their numbers. The fastest and strongest people would join their ranks if they made it to the stick. But they could never risk the prophesied one to have a chance in the Pit, lest they be destroyed if he touched the leg of the throne.

Robbie then turned toward the massacre that had resumed and poor Rhoe was one of the ghosts now. He still resembled a human being, albeit a crazed homicidal one, with dripping skin, rotting like bruised fruit, and his bones were becoming stiffer, causing him to walk less human. Robbie guessed it would take hours before he became fully ghost-like.

It was Sarcadui who asked Ames, "How did Rhoe know about the stick?"

"Seems he's been down there before…" Ames suggested.

Robbie's chest tightened at this revelation and his heart went out to Sarcadui who broke down to near hysterics, protesting that Rhoe had been telling her the truth and that she should have believed him. All this time she had been near her true love and refused to believe it, and rejected him. He left this world with a broken heart, a heart he would never see to be mended.

Exasperated, Robbie's attention turned to Ames. It was *his* fault that they were all here; *his* treachery led them to this point. Because of Ames, Rhoe was doomed to spend the rest of eternity in the black world of ghostdom. But Rhoe had no choice. He *had* to show Robbie firsthand just what to go after when it was his turn in the Pit. Rhoe knew it would be above Ames to instruct him. He wanted so badly to hit Ames again but he thought better of it since he would soon be receiving his just punishment.

Soon the crowd seemed to be growing restless and began chanting something unintelligible in unison. In response to this, the cage doors were opened on both ends and a host of ghosts dutifully barged in and began choosing their next victims. The same screams and cries of terror ensued as before, only louder this time because now everyone knew full well what they were being chosen for and what was in store for them in the next several minutes.

A ghost grabbed Sarcadui's arm and pulled her through the crowd. Robbie punched the ghost's arm but it held fast and grabbed Robbie by the neck with its other arm. They were dragged outside the holding cage and awaited the rest of the unfortunates who would be led to a cage somewhere around the blood-soaked arena.

A line of new birdcages was rolled out next to the cranes around the Pit by trenchers. Robbie stayed close to Sarcadui hoping to be locked in the same cage as her, but to his fear they were separated as Robbie was led to the same crane Rhoe had been led to and Sarcadui was two cages over. Robbie stood on bars of the cage and held onto the side, keeping his eyes locked on Sarcadui for comfort. It wasn't until the door was locked that he heard Ames's panicky voice next to him.

"You've got to save me, Robbie-boy. I know you don't trust me anymore, but please… it wasn't supposed to end like this."

Robbie-boy? Now where had Robbie heard that before?

Instinctively he turned and said, "Rico?"

Ames nodded, his eyes welling up. "Hello Robbie-boy."

CHAPTER 45

Was this a trick? Was this some desperate ploy to form an alliance before the time of death? Robbie barely noticed one of the ghosts climbing up to the top of the cage to hitch the rope on.

"I couldn't tell you before," said Ames, "because I was afraid you wouldn't believe me." He wobbled over to Robbie and placed a clear rubbery object in his hand. "You're going to need this later. Don't lose it."

"It would have been easier to believe you before I knew you were a traitor," snapped Robbie, shoving the object in his pocket, not caring what it was.

"It had just been so long since you'd seen me… I wasn't even sure myself if you were the Robbie I used to play games with. You didn't remember anything! You never came back like you promised! We waited years for you to return! You took so long!" Ames said these things with his voice growing fiercer by the second.

The cage lurched off the ground, knocking Ames into one of Robbie's arms and the crowd roared in horror-filled excitement. The terrified prisoners held on tightly to the bars as the cage swung over the opening of the Pit. Robbie had no time to compute this new revelation about Ames, but he did know one thing for sure: he needed to get that stick before any harm could come to Sarcadui.

Upon hearing his old nickname and seeing his childhood friend behind Ames's eyes, many parts of his memory came back to him a few pieces at a time. His adventures with Rico, Lahni, and Ewin: hunting dinosaurs, catching fairies in the night, playing cowboys… Suddenly a fresh bout of energy erupted through Robbie. This was *his* jungle, *he* created this world, and he wasn't going to stand for it being controlled by demons any longer.

He turned to his cellmates and said, "We don't all have to die tonight. We can get out of here alive if you all listen to me."

One young man scoffed and said, “A fool’s hope. Give it up; we’re as good as dead.”

“Watch your mouth,” said Ames. “That’s King Robbie you’re talking to.”

The young man rolled his eyes and continued peering through the bars at his imminent doom below.

“I’ll help,” said a meek woman, approaching Robbie. “What do you command of me, my lord?” Three others reached out and pledged their allegiance to Robbie. His mind was racing; he didn’t have a plan.

While the cages were all suspended over the Pit, everyone waited in dreadful anticipation for the drop, but it never came. Instead the cages were all being lowered to the bottom at a steady pace.

“Why are they being lowered?” Robbie asked Ames. “Why not drop us like they did the others?”

“Sometimes they just like to mix things up. This gives the ghosts and panthers more time to gather ’round us.”

At any rate Robbie had one main concern: the cage was locked, so how were they expected to get out? Even though the ghosts were turning the handles of the cranes in quite a fervor, they were dropping at a slow rate. Seeing that this bought a small bit of time, he was beginning to be filled with hope of attaining the leg of the throne. Then he began kicking a cage bar with all his might.

“What are you doing?” asked the reluctant young man who had written Robbie off, as everyone held on tightly for balance.

“I’m breaking out,” said Robbie, kicking harder, this time causing one of the wooden bars to crack. “We’re going to be ready when we land.”

The others quickly caught on and soon the whole cage was swinging furiously around as everyone was breaking off whatever weapons from the hard timber they could. With a renewed sense of hope and fury Robbie and his cellmates bounded out of the cage even before it struck ground.

The ghosts did not seem to be taken aback at this change of play since it was clear they really were more demented than the ghosts Robbie had encountered before; they were completely oblivious to any sense of reality taking place around them. Compared to the ghosts up above, these monsters didn’t seem to have the ability to walk straight or hold their heads up as they stumbled around in any general direction. Yet once they found a target they liked they shot at it with full force. But these ghosts also didn't look like the others Robbie had encountered. Their skin was still pale and blotchy, but in most places it just hung off their bodies like torn rags revealing large open wounds all over. The panthers were the same way. They were just as big as the others, but patches of fur were missing from all over their bodies, and they acted in a more animalistic behavior than their counterparts, unable to keep still for the benefit of pouncing or stalking. Instead, they often gyrated quite erratically as though attacking some invisible prey that was taunting them. These were the sick rejects from the dark kingdom and this Pit was their leper's valley.

Bracing himself for the gut-wrenching terror of the cannibalistic ghosts, he was heartened to see people actually fighting them off with their broken bamboo sticks. Even the reluctant young man was defending his life.

Robbie fled through the arena as fast as he could go, beating off ghosts and panthers with the two sturdy poles that he had chosen. The adrenaline rushed through him so furiously that he felt like he could fly.

As he ran he noticed there were other cages still suspended in the air. People had taken their cue from Robbie and were breaking down their jail bars and making them into weapons. Some people even broke out at the top and began climbing the rope back toward the jib that hung over the edge of the Pit.

When he was just within reach of the leg of the throne a ghost leapt out from behind a boulder and tackled Robbie to the ground. Its strength was nearly too much for him to take, so the struggle was intense. The ghost bit Robbie's hand and pain mixed with utter rage sent Robbie into a fury. He threw the ghost back, clambering toward the stick on his hands and knees, but the ghost grabbed his leg. Robbie turned to shove a rock into the ghost's face, but stopped short when he saw it was Rhoe. His nose was breaking off, and his teeth were growing sharper and larger, but his eyes hadn't dissolved yet. Robbie detected Rhoe somewhere in those fading brown eyes, but it wasn't the same Rhoe he had grown to love. This Rhoe was somehow lost and delirious. Rhoe was struggling as he seemed to hold on to what small amount of humanity he had left. But a vicious rage was quickly subduing him.

From all around them ghosts and panthers were closing in. Robbie had no choice but to do to his friend what must be done in order to reach that coveted stick. He grasped a rock in his hand, pausing. Then a cry emerged from his throat when he cracked the rock into Rhoe's progressively softening skull. Robbie detected his friend's utter pain buried somewhere in those ghastly eyes, but he was still deteriorating into something that Robbie had despised ever since arriving on the island.

But impale him with the rock he did. And that at least stunned the shell of Rhoe enough to cause its growing fingers to lose a grip on Robbie's leg. Thus being freed, Robbie effortlessly lunged toward the stick and grabbed hold of it. The moment he did this, a silence resounded throughout the arena. Still, Robbie squeezed his face tightly, bracing himself for the full weight of his pursuers to crush him beneath their savage attack. But instead of that happening, Robbie heard his name called from across the arena. It was Sarcadui's voice. Robbie opened his eyes and slowly stood up with the stick in his hand. His hand throbbed from squeezing it so tightly. But what he saw when he stood up stunned him.

The ghosts, every single one of them, stood motionless as statues, frozen in time. Several of them were mid-air with their arms stretched out toward Robbie with open mouths.

The panthers that had been in pursuit of Robbie danced around wildly, completely shell shocked by what had just happened around them, rendering them temporarily insignificant as threats.

"Don't drop that stick!" yelled Sarcadui.

She was right. Grabbing the leg of the throne didn't destroy the ghosts, but it did impair them. It stood to reason that they would remain immobile as long as he held onto the stick.

When the sick panthers regained what little sense they had back, they directed their attention back to Robbie who struck the stick at their skulls, knocking them unconscious one at a time. Robbie's strength was returning to him.

Others around the arena were still being chased and attacked by panthers. Robbie looked on one of them and saw that it was Ames, pinned up against the wall of the Pit as a panther crouched down before him. He averted his gaze as he heard the panther lunge at him with a crazed growl and Ames's unmistakable screams slowly faded away forever.

He ran up to Sarcadui, who met him with two cage bars in her hands, and said, "Now what?"

"I don't know," she responded. "We have to get you to your throne as quickly as possible."

Without delay Robbie yelled up toward the unfrozen spectators, being the trenchers, who were growing restless for answers.

"Everybody, I am the prophesied one!" he announced, his voiced echoing all around the arena. I'm holding a piece of my throne in my hand. We need your help to get me out of here and to the ocean!"

Robbie half expected a rebuttal, but to his surprise a rope was lowered. He, Sarcadui, and other able survivors rushed toward it and they were helped up to the Pit's ledge. Halfway up Robbie noticed a sliver of a staircase out of the corner of his eye. He looked and saw jagged rocks chiseled into uneven steps that led from the bottom of the Pit to the top. He reckoned that's how Rhoe had escaped when he was there last.

At the top they were greeted by wary trenchers. One stepped toward Robbie and said, "You say you're the king? You caused the ghosts to freeze?"

Robbie nodded. "I need to get to the ocean as fast as possible. Will you help?"

Before the trencher answered, another one stepped forward and said, "If you take the throne, then what's going to happen to us?"

With no time to negotiate, Robbie said decidedly, "If you help me, you'll be pardoned for your treachery. But any sign of offense henceforth will be punishable by pain of death. Now, is anyone here against me?"

The gathering trenchers looked at each other and shook their heads.

"I didn't think so."

One trencher stepped humbly forward and said with a slight bow, "I would hate for the curse not to be lifted when you sit on the throne. I've worked in other regions of Reveloin and I can tell you that there are three more Game Pits besides this one. You'll find the other three legs in those Pits if you haven't already."

"We'll never get to all of them before you disappear again," said Sarcadui, discreetly.

Robbie nodded his agreement. The time was too short; there was no telling when he'd disappear again. "You," he said, addressing the man who had just delivered the bad news. "I take it you know the island well?"

The trencher nodded, saying, "I know the men well too."

"Good. Send out three groups of twelve of the best journeymen you can find. Send them out to gather the three legs and bring them to me on the northwest coast. That's where I'll be. If I'm not there, wait for me."

The man dutifully began his task yelling for volunteers and rejecting those who didn't meet his criteria.

"The rest of you, burn any ghost you see while they're still immobile, kill the panthers, and free the prisoners." Robbie ordered. "No prisoner will come against you if they see you carrying out the first two orders. Be faithful, I am here now and the curse will be broken!" With these words he grabbed Sarcadui's arm and led her back toward the jungle.

Once they were clear of all the trenchers Sarcadui asked, "They know the island really well. Shouldn't we have some of them lead the way?"

"There's no way we're making it to the ocean before I disappear again. When that happens I won't be here to touch this stick and the ghosts will come back to life and the trenchers will rejoin them – they're traitors, they're always going to look out for themselves, just like Ames. I don't want you stuck with a bunch of trenchers when I'm gone. Instead, when I disappear, I want you to wrap the stick up, be careful not to touch it, and hide until I return."

"But last time you were gone for almost a month," Sarcadui reminded him with panic in her voice.

"But I returned, didn't I?"

The two ran through the jungle as though they were being chased. They both knew Robbie had to cover as much ground as possible while he was on the island. They ran for several miles before Sarcadui needed to slow down. It was clear Robbie was stronger now, as he felt he could run all the way to the ocean and back. But he needed to remain with Sarcadui so she could take the stick when he disappeared.

The sun rose behind them as they walked. The warm rays had never felt so comforting. It was not lost on Robbie that it wasn't long ago when Sarcadui and he trekked together through the jungle as they did now. But so much had changed since then. Now Robbie was the leader, and Sarcadui had nothing to say about the beauty of the island. They each had no idea what was in store for them when they first walked together, but for the chance to be with Sarcadui, Robbie wouldn't trade it for anything – except for a chance to bring Rhoe back.

"Had you ever suspected Ames?" asked Robbie.

Sarcadui shook her head. "No. He was always like an uncle to me. My parents' deaths devastated him. When they died, he changed completely, even insisting that we call him Ames instead of Rico. He made me swear once never to use that name again."

Robbie didn't have the heart to tell her the truth about her parents and how it was Rico who had actually killed them.

"It was even Ames who raised the idea of the underground shelter. He even—" Sarcadui stopped as the truth hit her full force. Robbie had figured it out before she did. Ames hadn't created a shelter for all those people. It was a holding cell. That's where Ames pulled his quota each month if he couldn't find anyone else on the island. That explained the high rate of missing persons from Langly.

"Didn't you ever notice he was gone during the games?" asked Robbie.

"There were so many of us in Langly, I just never thought to take notice," said Sarcadui.

The two soberly walked on and just as Robbie was happily thinking that this was looking to be an uneventful walk, Sarcadui said:

"Run. Now."

CHAPTER 46

"What?" asked Robbie.

"Run!" repeated Sarcadui, grabbing Robbie's arm.

A loud crash from directly behind them nearly made Robbie jump out of his skin. He looked and saw that a dinosaur had stormed through the trees and was chasing them. It towered as high as the treetops themselves. Sarcadui pushed Robbie forward and they both took off at full speed to keep ahead of the approaching monster.

"Split up," yelled Sarcadui.

There was no time to discuss plans for meeting up later or how they would find each other. Sarcadui simply went one way and Robbie went the other. The dinosaur chased Sarcadui. Robbie, disheartened, listened as the heavy footsteps and the crashing thickets faded in the other direction.

He slowed down to a stop and rested his hands on his knees, giving his rapidly beating heart a moment to recover from the shock of the moment. But he couldn't rest long because a strange sound caught his attention. It was the sound of weeping. A child was crying somewhere nearby!

Robbie wanted to chase after Sarcadui but it would be wrong not to investigate the crying child. He called out quietly at first, "Hello?"

After a couple of tries the crying stopped.

"I'm not going to hurt you. I'm here to help," said Robbie, trying to detect where the sound was coming from. Suddenly, as he was sneaking around the trees, he had a vague remembrance of the exact place he was in. He really had been there before… playing hide-and-go-seek as a boy. He snooped around as though he were a boy again. Then he remembered there was a hole in the ground somewhere. When he walked across some branches he heard sniffling underneath his feet. Curiously, he bent down and removed the branches. Upon unveiling the hole in the ground he thought he saw Ewin, Sarcadui's mother, looking up at him, but he cleared his head and was overjoyed to see that it was none other than Hail, who, upon seeing Robbie, quickly dried her eyes and ran her arm across her wet nose as if she weren't crying.

Before he could call out her name, she put a finger to her lips. "Come down here," she instructed.

Reluctantly he crawled into the hole and joined her.

"You might want to cover the top," she said. He did so, careful not to let go of the stick and instructing Hail not to touch it under any circumstances.

"What are we hiding from?" he asked. He was tired of pits.

"Didn't you see the other one?" asked Hail.

"The other what? Dinosaur? Yeah, it almost trampled me and now it's chasing Sarcadui. Wait, there's another one out there?"

"They're eoraptors. They travel in groups."

"*That* was not an eoraptor that I saw," insisted Robbie.

"They come in all sizes."

"That's no surprise," commented Robbie dully, remembering the centipedes both big and small.

There was a rustle of branches just above them. Hail put a finger to her lips again and pointed upward. Robbie looked and at first thought it had just grown really dark outside, but through the leaves and branches he saw that he was looking up at the underside of a dinosaur. It had stopped walking, each foot planted on opposite sides of the hole. Its belly towered above them as it swayed its head to and fro as though it were sniffing the air. It wasn't as tall as the one that chased Sarcadui; this one was only about twice as tall as Robbie himself.

He and Hail held their breath as they waited for it to move forward. When it finally did, Robbie pulled himself up to peer over the edge of the hole. Upon seeing the dinosaur being naïve to their presence he told Hail that he had to go find Sarcadui. "You stay here and don't make a sound," he instructed her.

She protested at first but thought better of it.

Robbie, quiet as a mouse, crawled up out of the hole while clinging tightly to the stick. The dinosaur was still in sight but its back was to him. He thought it would lead him to the other dinosaur, which would then lead him to Sarcadui. He quickly covered the hole back up as Hail watched him from below. Then he scurried behind the nearest tree. He peered around it at the dinosaur, which was still standing in the same upright position. Its head was held high as if trying to detect something that had caught its attention. Robbie hoped it wasn't him it was detecting.

The dinosaur took a few steps forward and Robbie tip-toed up to the next nearest tree and hid behind it. When he peered around the trunk this time, the dinosaur was no longer where it had been. Robbie's heart stopped.

Was it on his trail?

He listened carefully for any sign of movement, but this dinosaur was good; it knew when to go into stealth mode and how to use it. After a few terrifying minutes it became clear to Robbie that the dinosaur had moved on and was up ahead by now. Robbie now had to find Sarcadui on his own.

He crept along through the jungle, his heart still racing, looking all about him for any sign of danger. Not knowing it, he looked everywhere but straight ahead and when he finally did – and not a moment too soon – he saw the back of the dinosaur, with its tail slowly swaying back and forth. It was not yet aware of Robbie, even though he was just feet away from it. Robbie eyed a nearby tree to hide behind but when he took a step in that direction a twig snapped under his foot and he froze, biting his lip so hard blood gushed out.

The dinosaur jerked up with a hiss and instantly its head swung back toward Robbie and peered right at him, its teeth-filled mouth just inches away from his face.

The hunt was on.

But another sound from back where they had just been stole the attention of both Robbie and the dinosaur. It was Hail and she was screaming at the top of her lungs. Robbie turned and looked, and to his horror saw that another dinosaur, the same size as this one, was furiously digging into the hole, wildly snapping its jaws, trying to get Hail.

Without a moment's thought, Robbie punched the dinosaur in the nose with his fist, stunning it momentarily. He ran toward the other dinosaur yelling, "No!" The creature looked up from the hole and set its sights on Robbie, leveling its head with its spine and beginning to sprint toward him. The dinosaur behind Robbie was now running after him as well and he was caught in the middle.

Upon instinct the only thing Robbie could think to do was drop flat on the ground, remembering his confrontation with the centipods. This was a lucky move since both dinosaurs had leapt from the ground just as he did this and collided into one another directly above him. He barrel-rolled out of the way and scampered toward the hole, leaving the two dinosaurs to bite and scratch at each other as they wrestled on the ground.

He reached the hole and Hail shot her arms up toward him. It wasn't until he reached down for her that he realized the stick was no longer in his hands. When he glanced up he saw that it lay right where he had ducked out of reach from the dinosaurs and now it was being trampled underneath their massive feet. Not able to do anything about it, he pulled Hail up out of the hole but just as she was free, both dinosaurs shot a menacing glare toward them, instantly forgetting about their opponent. Robbie and Hail slowly started to back away as the monsters hitched their bodies off the ground with their hind legs toward them, lowering slavering jaws and keeping their hungry eyes locked on Hail and Robbie.

Both dinosaurs, a team now, crept toward Hail and himself, their heads crouched down to eye level. They were several yards away but Robbie knew as soon as one of them pounced it would be all over and he and Hail wouldn't know what hit them. But suddenly the dinosaur on the left began twitching and its body gave into light convulsions. The other one ignored its partner and continued snaking its way toward its victims. But that one too began twitching and started gnawing at its deadly claws. With a screech, they were whinnying like dying animals. One of them threw itself on the ground with a thud, spinning its massive body around with its hind legs, kicking up dirt.

Robbie knew exactly what was going on and it was not good. Without wasting another moment he grabbed Hail's arm and pulled her past the sickly dinosaurs and he scoured the ground for the leg of the throne. He found it half buried in the brush confirming his suspicion – the dinosaurs had stepped on it and now they were cursed just like the ghosts.

The dinosaurs took no notice of Robbie and Hail sneaking away as they continued to shriek, writhe, and squirm in agony on the ground, their skin becoming paler by the second.

With the stick in one hand and Hail's trembling hand in the other, they jogged through the jungle trying to get as far away from the demented dinosaurs as possible. But their hopes were crushed when they heard a rumbling in the trees behind them growing closer. The hunt was back on. Shouldn't they be frozen by now if he was holding the stick? What was happening?

"Run!" yelled Robbie as he pushed her forward.

As they ran as fast as they could, Robbie looked over his shoulder and confirmed that the dinosaurs were indeed, back in full motion. They were faster and much bigger than they had been just a moment before. Their skin was paler and their teeth had already grown too big for their heads, longer and sharper. The sounds they emitted were terrifying, like a cat might sound like if it were thrown into a pot of boiling water.

Robbie faced forward again. He kept waiting for those enormous teeth to sink into his skull and lift him off his feet, or even worse, for Hail's hand to be snatched from his, only to see her thrown into the air like a piece of meat.

But the more they ran, the further away the threat seemed to be. Surely they weren't faster than the demonic dinosaurs, were they? Robbie stole another glance over his shoulder and, to his surprise, they were gone! He slowed down, cautiously at first, not believing his luck quite yet.

"Where did they go?" asked Hail, sounding as timid as he felt.

Robbie shook his head with realizing wonder. Upon touching the stick they had become ghosts, and as such, they couldn't remain alive – or present – on the island as long as the sun was out. So touching the stick made no difference; they didn't need to freeze. Since it was daylight, they just disappeared with all the other ghosts. He explained this to Hail who seemed to just barely understand, or at least humored Robbie with nods of slight comprehension.

Robbie couldn't believe that he hadn't been called into another time lapse yet. He feared that one would be upon him soon. With that reminder he quickly set his priorities in order. He reminded Hail not to ever touch the stick, "or you'll become as crazed as those dinosaurs. So don't touch it even if I disappear. Keep it wrapped up. Now, the first thing we need to do is find Sarcadui. Then as soon as we find her we have to get to the ocean."

"But we're already there," said Hail. "Can't you hear it? It's just as Sarcadui described it."

Robbie listened closely and he could just detect the welcoming sound of the ocean surf like thousands of jewels dancing on the shore.

They ran ahead several more yards and Robbie's heart pounded hard in his chest as he cleared a thick wall of branches out of the way.

Robbie looked, and there stretched out for infinity before them was the ocean.

CHAPTER 47

Robbie couldn't believe his eyes. Lying directly below the pure blue sky was the ocean, as flat and clear as could possibly be imagined. It was like a lake on a windless morning, only he couldn't see the other end and either side stretched out of his line of sight just like an ocean should. The water lapped up against the jungle terrain. But the jungle never ended. Instead, it descended into the water as trees broke the surface for nearly half a mile, their height growing smaller the farther out they went. Of course, he remembered that it wasn't really an ocean at all, but rather a flood that hadn't yet resided.

Robbie then heard his name being called from elsewhere, from beyond the island.

"Robbie."

He couldn't put a name or face to the voice, but still he knew that somewhere inside he recognized it. However, he didn't want to go to it, but he knew he was about to.

"Robbie."

"No," said Robbie, trying to will himself to stay.

"Are you leaving?" asked Hail in a dream-like way. She was beginning to fade away.

"Robbie."

"I don't want to leave. I'm almost there," said Robbie, his own voice sounding otherworldly as though it were coming from somewhere around them.

"Robbie."

"But I made it, I'm here now!"

"You're where now?" asked Rosalynn, who was sitting down next to the box by the Puget Sound. She was stroking the hair on his forehead. This aggravated Robbie. He didn't want to be woken. He was supposed to find Sarcadui, then cross the sea to find his castle and break the curse. "What are you doing here?" he asked.

"When you weren't at the hospital I knew where you might have gone," answered Rosalynn.

"You know me well," said Robbie, knowing he should have been happier to see his wife than he really was.

"Can I ask you something?" said Rosalynn.

"Sure," said Robbie getting out of the box, feeling silly for the first time since being awake.

"Where do you..." She hesitated for a moment. Then, "Where do you go when you're in that box?"

Robbie stuttered, not knowing how to answer. "I, uh..."

Rosalynn sighed as though this was exactly what she had expected Robbie to say. Then she said, "I see you in this box Robbie. All the time, I see you sitting in it as if you're someplace else. And I don't know if you're just dreaming or into some kind of weird magic or whatever, but the thing that hurts me most is that you *choose* to separate yourself from the family by spending all your time in this box."

"Rosalynn, I–"

But Rosalynn held up a hand to stop him. "For some stupid, ridiculous reason I feel like all of our troubles, everything that's been going wrong, is somehow connected to you and this box. Try as I might I just can't seem to place any pieces of the puzzle together. But with what I do know, the only thing I can tell you is this: If your life is so terrible that you absolutely must take any means of escape available to you, I can understand that... we'll work through it. My only question is why can't you just take me with you?"

Robbie shook his head. "I'm sorry. I can't." The truth was, he didn't know if he could.

Rosalynn lowered her head and let out a breath as though she had said her piece and received the final verdict and it was not favorable toward her. "Your dad took the kids home from the hospital."

"Maybe we should get home too then," said Robbie. "You can follow me." He carried the box with him to his car, despite the fact that Rosalynn was watching him. What did it matter? She now knew what it meant to him; there was no hiding it now. Apparently she knew all along.

As he followed her home on the winding coastal road he thought about how Rosalynn's knowing about the box would change things. How long had she known? How many times did she wake up in the night and find him in a trance in the box? Heck, how many times had she tried to wake him?

Suddenly Rosalynn's car began to swerve back and forth. After three long and confusing seconds of this, her car pulled over to the side of the road. Robbie parked behind her, got out, and ran up to Rosalynn's window. There he found his wife clutching the steering wheel with one hand and her chest with the other. She was gasping for air.

"I can't breathe," she managed.

After pulling the Accord up, Robbie helped her into the passenger seat, buckled her in, locked the Jetta then got back in his car and sped away toward the hospital. Rosalynn's breathing became more and more labored. Robbie knew it was the cancer unleashing its wrath.

Robbie, trying to keep his emotions under control, pulled the car up to the E.R. drop-off zone, yelling out the window for any paramedic to come to their aid. Two young men in hospital scrubs ran up to Rosalynn's side of the car, one pushing a gurney. They immediately got her out of the vehicle and strapped her to the bed. One asked Robbie questions about Rosalynn's medical history and Robbie rambled off any information he thought would be pertinent for the moment. He kept telling them she had cancer.

"Go park your car, Mr. Lake," said one of the medics. "The orderlies will tell you exactly where she'll be when you get back."

Their calm demeanor helped Robbie to get some sort of grip. He did as he was told and in less than five minutes he was at Rosalynn's bedside. She was already beginning to breathe a bit clearer. Already they had an IV in her arm and she was being monitored by an EKG. He pulled out his cell phone and called his dad to bring the kids.

Later, when they were settled into room 516 and the chaos of the doctors and nurses checking up on her subsided, Rosalynn, weak from exhaustion, turned to Robbie and said, "We're going to have to start paying rent to the hospital since we're here so much."

Robbie smiled at her attempt at the humor that only she could pull off at a time like this.

"I'm sorry this is going to end up costing us so much," she said.

"That's the least of my worries," said Robbie, dismissing her comment with a wave of his hand. "The kids should be here soon."

"What if this is it?" asked Rosalynn.

"What do you mean?" asked Robbie dumbly.

"You know what I'm talking about, Robbie. You've been avoiding this topic indefinitely. I'd like to know what your plans are for the kids for when after I'm… you know."

Robbie's eyes glistened over, but he gritted his teeth to keep the tears from coming. Try as he might he just couldn't look Rosalynn in the eyes lest he break down. In his mind, talking about it would only ensure the inevitable. But she was right; she had a right to know what his plans were for when she was gone.

"Well, for starters," he began, "I was thinking about enrolling Taylor into an all-girl school."

Rosalynn laughed. This was the most refreshing sound Robbie had heard in a long time. "What about you?" she asked. "Are you going to remarry?"

Robbie shrugged and said, "You're going to be hard to beat." This was not a topic Robbie cared to dwell on.

"You're biting your cheek," she said gently. "Are you ever going to wear your wedding ring for me again or are you keeping your finger vacant for the next one?"

Robbie felt his bare finger and was about to tell Rosalynn he honestly didn't know what happened to it when Harvey and Jeremy walked in. Rosalynn received them warmly as Robbie scooted away from her bedside to make room for them. He was relieved to be absolved from the topic at hand.

Jeremy gave his mom a hug and Harvey took her hand in his. "I thought you weren't due back for a few more weeks," he said jokingly.

Rosalynn grinned. "Where's Taylor?" she asked.

"She said she had plans to go somewhere and that you approved. Someone picked her up before you called," answered Harvey. "I would have called her, but I don't have her number."

Robbie flushed with anger. He knew exactly where she was. She was at that party he had forbade her to go to. He'd spend the night devising a punishment for her, but he wasn't about to tell Rosalynn any of this until she was better.

"I'm going to go down to the cafeteria. Does anyone want anything?" asked Robbie.

"A salad with no meat."

"Pizza."

"I'll come with you," said Harvey, "to see if they have some of that tomato soup."

"No Dad, I got it," Robbie protested.

After he had purchased the food and packed it up in two separate bags he returned upstairs to the room just as a doctor was leaving. "You must be Robbie," said the doctor whose nametag read David Durham, M.D.

"Yes," said Robbie. "Is everything okay? What did you find out?"

The doctor looked back at Robbie as if determining whether he were a straight shooter or not. "We did find some things out."

Harvey stepped out of the room and grabbed the bags from Robbie's hands and carried the food back inside the room. "Who ordered dinner?" he asked just as the door closed behind him.

The fact that the doctor didn't stop Harvey from leaving made Robbie's skin crawl.

The doctor delivered the news as simply and empathically as he could, but the only sentences Robbie comprehended was, "If there's any hope of her living through the night, then we're going to have to operate. On the bright side, this will give us the chance to remove the tumor if we find it."

It wasn't long after the doctor delivered the news before Rosalynn was being rolled into surgery. Good-byes were exchanged between Jeremy and Rosalynn and it was clear that even Harvey struggled to hold back the tears.

"Will you be here when I wake up?" Rosalynn asked when she and Robbie were alone for a moment.

Robbie's eyes were welling up as he struggled to nod his affirmation. He wondered if she would wake up.

"Tell Taylor I love her," said Rosalynn looking at Robbie from the pillow.

"You'll tell her yourself in just a few hours," Robbie insisted.

Rosalynn smiled. "Go easy on her, okay? Make the punishment swift and make it sting. But don't drag it out." How would he ever measure up to her stellar parenting?

"Are you all ready?" asked the doctor when he came in with all his assistants.

"I love you Robbie."

When he left the room, a tight feeling in his gut told him he would never see his wife again.

CHAPTER 48

Robbie couldn't wait in the waiting room for more than twenty minutes before he told his dad and son that he needed to take a drive. "Call me if they say anything."

"Shouldn't you be here if they do?" asked Harvey.

"Just call me, okay?"

In the car Robbie could barely see with the tears filling his eyes. There was no way Rosalynn was going to live and he didn't want to be there when the doctors told them. Jeremy had Harvey. He was a tough kid. But even if she did make it out alive, it wouldn't matter. It wouldn't change things. She would still only have a few weeks to live and Robbie would still be attached to the box and his nightmare world that would always control him. Maybe Steve was right. He needed to just spare his family of all of his problems and leave.

And Taylor... what was the point of managing a kid who didn't even have the decency to obey her father? He was absolutely livid about her going to that party, but if she wanted to go and be like that, then fine! As she herself said so often, it's *her* life.

The Accord hit a pothole in the road, but Robbie drove on. He turned on the radio to listen to something, anything, to get his mind off of everything. Oldies played through the speakers and they had a soothing effect on him taking him back to a childhood he often told himself was blissful. During a break, the weatherman announced a high chance of severe thunderstorms.

He didn't know where he was driving. He just needed to *go*.

After about a half hour of driving he pulled the car off the road and sped through the open terrain. When he pushed the car as far as it would go, he got out and began storming off into the evergreens. Then he stopped. He remembered the box was in the back of the car. He popped open the trunk and pulled the box out. He stormed through the forest, this time with the box in his hands.

It was growing colder and darker by the minute as leaves kicked up all around him. It was growing late in the evening and thick storm clouds were gathering overhead. He feared that panthers or ghosts would jump out at him.

After walking for a couple of minutes he glanced around and saw that there was no sign of civilization anywhere. Someone would find his car, certainly, but they would likely deem it as just a broken down vehicle waiting to be towed.

Shivering from the wind he stepped inside the box and took one last look around. If he didn't die of starvation, then he would certainly die of pneumonia in this weather. But at least he would be in a better place, lord over all. That certainly beat this life of feeble existence and heartache. As soon as he returned to Reveloin he would cross the sea, find the castle, and sit on the throne. Easy enough.

With that, he kneeled and sat his butt down, and closed his eyes for the last time inside the box.

"Robbie!" it was Sarcadui sitting right next to him.

"Hey," said Robbie. "How long was I gone? How did you escape from that dinosaur?"

It was dark out as he and Sarcadui sat back-to-back on the edge of the water. Above the sound of the lapping water Robbie could hear thousands of screams coming from deep inside the jungle. Without another word Sarcadui forced the stick in his hands. He looked down at it and saw that it was wrapped with layers of giant leaves. He unwrapped it and as soon as his hands touched the white leg of the throne the jungle became silent, the only sounds he heard were the gentle wind and the water licking the ground.

"The ghosts know you're here so they've been reaping havoc all night. I don't know if the trenchers were able to get the other three legs."

"We'll just have to wait and see, I guess. At least the ghosts can't move now."

Sarcadui nodded. "You've been gone all night. It wasn't a good time for you to disappear on us. But nothing ever comes easy when *you're* involved."

Robbie grinned. "And the dinosaur?"

"I was able to give it the slip. I'm sorry I couldn't find you earlier."

"What about Hail? Where is she?"

"Hail? You found her?" asked Sarcadui standing up.

"Yeah. Didn't you see her? Who's been guarding the stick?" asked Robbie, growing alarmed.

"I found it right here where you're sitting. It's a good thing I did, too. But Hail was nowhere near it. I also found this breathing bark, I figured it was yours too."

Robbie took the rubbery bark in his other hand and put it in his pocket.

They contemplated what might have happened and began searching around the area for any sign of Hail. After doing this for several moments they gave up and sat back down on the ground, their backs up against a tree.

"I hope she's okay," said Sarcadui. "I'd never forgive myself if anything happened to her. I promised her parents before they died that I'd watch after her always."

"I'm sure she's fine," said Robbie, doubting the validity of his words. "So now I guess we just sit here and wait for someone to show up with the other pieces from the throne?"

Sarcadui nodded. Maybe Hail will show up.

A couple of hours passed and suddenly branches rustled nearby causing them both to jump.

"Hello?" asked Robbie. "Who's there?"

"Ex-trenchers," came the response from the trees. "King?"

Robbie looked at Sarcadui then answered, "Yeah. It's me."

Two men stepped through the trees and one of them said, "Sorry we're late, my lord. But the ghosts have been after us all night. We lost four of our men, but as soon as the ghosts froze we knew you were back again. We brought you this." The man held a long stick out wrapped in many layers of thick netting. It was the exact same size as the one Robbie held in his hand.

Within the next couple of hours the next two groups arrived with their pieces from the throne and just as the sun was rising over the water Robbie, with two sticks under his arms and holding two with his hands was ready to finish his quest. "How do I cross?" he asked.

Two of the men looked at each other and smiled. "We gave up waiting a long time ago. We never thought this day would come. Forgive us for our unfaithfulness."

One man stepped forward whom Robbie almost didn't recognize. But his bulky frame was hard to forget. It was Remusathi, the guard he and Hail met just before entering into Langly. He stood before Robbie and bowed down to him, offering his deepest respect and approval. Then he stood back up and blew a deafening whistle through his fingers and suddenly, in the distance a whale's tail rose up high out of the water and slapped the surface with a thundering splash. Then the ground began to tremble and everyone stepped back, including Sarcadui and Robbie.

As the shaking grew more violent and the ground began to give way, a giant pole of some sort was being dragged from beneath the surface of the jungle. And soon, another one joined it right in its wake. It became apparent to Robbie that a boat was being pulled out of the ground and was making its way to the water to rest atop it. The poles were the foremasts of a great schooner. Robbie stared in disbelief as shards of rock and dirt fell from it into the water. It had three two and was made completely out of wood from the jungle trees. Robbie judged that it was thirty feet long.

"There is the vehicle that will guide you to your castle, my lord," said one man bowing down to him and the rest followed suit, including Sarcadui. "We were fortunate to have it built before they denied us access to the floodwaters. We buried it so the ghosts wouldn't find it and destroy it."

Robbie was too moved to say anything. Despite his happiness, however, a deep void filled his heart when he thought about Hail and Rhoe and even Ames. He wished they were there to see him off. He even thought about Sarcadui's parents whom he used to play with and wished they were there to witness this marvelous moment.

After ensuring he had the four sticks in his hand and the mouthpiece in his pocket, he began to wade out into the water to climb onto the schooner. He heard someone get in the water behind him and stopped when he saw Sarcadui following after him.

"You can't come with me, Sarcadui," said Robbie. "I'll come find you when this is all over. I promise."

Sarcadui said, "You can't go alone. I'm coming with you."

"I forbid it. Your job here is done." Seeing the hurt in her eyes moved Robbie to stroll toward her and take her hands in his. "Listen to me. I'll sit on my throne and make everything right again. I promise."

Sarcadui forced a smile and nodded her head. "Just come back to me."

"I always do."

"I'll be here waiting."

They hugged and Robbie turned back toward the awaiting vessel. As he continued walking toward the ladder that hung over the side of the ship, his foot kicked something that half floated away then sank back down. He looked into the water and saw one of his deepest fears realized. He had kicked Hail's lifeless hand in the water. Her body floated in the water and upon seeing her, Robbie let out a loud sob. Who had done this? Who had killed this small girl whom he loved so much?

"Robbie, watch out!" yelled Sarcadui from the shore.

As soon as she said this something broke out of the water for a split second and disappeared back under. He saw the rivulets of small waves on the surface churned up by the creature heading straight toward him. He immediately waded as fast as he could toward the rope ladder hanging off the boat. He chucked three of the sticks up over the edge and pulled himself up just as a giant fish snapped at his feet, bearing razor-sharp teeth all around its mouth. That's what must have pulled Hail into the water. It was using her as bait. He remembered Ames's words: *The jungle is against anyone reaching the ocean ... and it will fight us every step of the way.*

He was so furious he didn't even bother to wave goodbye to those on shore. Instead he wiped his eyes and took the helm and pointed the boat northwest. He would end this curse even if it cost him his life.

CHAPTER 49

After setting his course and unrolling the sails (which sent spades of dirt hailing down all over the deck), Robbie peered over the edge of the boat and looked down into the water, fascinated by what he saw beneath the crystal clear surface. The ocean was everything Sarcadui had claimed it was and more. The water did not grow murky or cover up anything below, even as it got deeper. It still just remained as clear as though looking through a window. Below the surface the jungle still continued. Trees stood perfectly alive and erect, boulders lay scattered about, and the jungle ground lay undisturbed and motionless at the base of the trees. This is what a bird must see when it flies over the jungle. Except instead of rabbits and squirrels scattering about, there were fish of all colors and sizes swimming in and out of the trees. Moss grew on the tree trunks, activating ocean life as though full-grown trees were a natural part of its existence. He had to steer clear of the trees that stood up above the water but he managed to handle the schooner fairly well.

Then the boat floated above what looked like a very large boulder that seemed to cover the entire jungle floor. For a while there was nothing but grayish white stone below. Robbie leaned over the edge and peered overboard at the grey mass stretched below him. Sure enough if he looked outward he could see a fin stretched lazily on the other side of the huge hump. Now he was floating just above the dorsal fin. Up ahead, bubbles spouted up in a fine column from the whale's blowhole.

Fearing that it might come up, Robbie wondered if he should go around it, trembling with fear over the majestic creature that lay just beneath him. But before he could change the direction of the boat he had already come to the whale's head and then it began to open its mouth. Robbie braced himself, but the only thing that happened was that dozens of ropes were released from the whale's bite and floated to the surface. Those were the ropes the whale pulled the boat out of the ground with. This thing was enormous!

As he sailed on, a strange sensation seemed to overtake Robbie as though he were losing grip of himself. He suddenly felt like he was being lifted from his body, as if the sweet moist air were intoxicating him. His senses all seemed to collide with one another as they all became one. As much as he could tell, it seemed that the sky was darkening and the clouds were morphing into more definite shapes. Voices began to filter in from the sky. Though they were otherworldly they seemed strangely familiar. Sarcadui's voice reverberated from somewhere in the back of his head: *"Memories. Memories long lost and forgotten..."*

He then began to recognize the voices and the pictures in the sky that began to appear. In the images Robbie himself was lying in a box, unmoved, unconscious. And while he slept away, a person, namely Ames, crept up to him and lifted Robbie's arm. He then proceeded to slip a wedding ring off Robbie's finger and put it in his pocket and sneak away. The images followed Ames as though it was a movie and Robbie watched as Ames snuck into the closet and closed the door.

So he was never restricted to just the box, thought Robbie, and his thought was audible through the clouds. Then he watched as Ames and Sarcadui were in Reveloin and Ames was saying, "...it'll get him to stay forever. You'll be doing a good thing."

Then the images projected Ames knocking a toaster off the counter and it slammed to the tile ground with a metallic thud. "Wake up, Robbie-boy," Ames cooed. Fast forward in time and Sarcadui was seen kneeling next to Robbie who was asleep in the box, calling for him saying, "Robbie? Are you there? Hello? It's Sarcadui. Call me back." As she was saying these things to him he knew somehow that he was in Reveloin defending himself against the centipedes. Ames stood next to her, holding Robbie's cell phone close to her lips. Her voice echoed from elsewhere in the room, and somehow Robbie knew it was coming through his answering machine in the kitchen. Then there was another woman vying for his attention from the box. He didn't quite recognize her, but his heart leapt when he saw her. She was beautiful. Sometimes he could hear her coughing from somewhere in the dark house while he slept in his box. She walked past him many times, sometimes calling to him, sometimes not. Who was that woman? And then a small boy came bounding into the room calling for Robbie but the woman told him, "Don't wake him up. He's, um... napping."

"In a box?" asked the boy.

"In a box?"

"That's where you end up when you're dead, anyway, isn't it? In a box?"

"How many grown men do you know who willingly get inside a box?"

"Why don't you take me with you … Where do you go when you get inside your box … Cut ties from that other world … Are you having an affair … You're really sucking right now … take me with you … in a box?"

Suddenly the boat jerked hard, knocking Robbie off his feet. It was dark now. He stood up to peer over the edge of the boat and what he saw petrified him to his soul. The ocean floor had sunk to a depth that was not visible to the eye, though the surface was still as transparent as before. And floating gently down into the abyss were the four sticks he had held onto so tightly. Had he knocked them overboard? No, someone had thrown them overboard. But who?

He turned around and saw a decaying ghost standing just feet away, with its arms reaching out toward him and its legs spread apart to keep balance on the rocking boat. Robbie instinctively kicked the ghost as hard as he could, but he fell back against the side in the process. He glanced back out into the water and what he saw horrified him more than his stowaway. Out of the depths, swimming upward toward the boat, with arms at their sides and kicking with their fluid legs like eels' tails came dozens and dozens of ghosts. Their skin had been rotted and decayed even worse than the ones in the Pit. Clearly they had been underwater for who knows how many years. They clawed at the schooner, eager to board, rocking and shaking it.

Robbie grabbed an oar that was lying idly by and started beating the ghosts off the boat after knocking the original one aside. Another one was halfway in, but Robbie gave it a good hard kick sending it back into the water. There was no way he would single-handedly be able to keep this many ghosts off the boat. It wasn't long before ghosts started coming on board and skulking toward him like bloodthirsty zombies.

He glanced out into the distance and saw an island resting on the horizon topped off by, evidently, a castle, almost beckoning him toward it. Robbie's heart skipped a beat as he was both filled with hope at being so near the castle and filled with terror at the ghosts who were climbing on board his boat in pairs.

Then, an epiphany came to him, which he immediately acted on. He threw off his heavy cloak and dove overboard into the pitch-black depths.

CHAPTER 50

Like the air, the water was lukewarm as he kicked his way down to the bottom of the ocean. When he ran out of breath he pulled the breathing bark Ames had given him out of his pocket and stuffed it in his mouth and instantly he was able to breathe again. It was rubbery and squishy, just as it looked, and when he chewed on it, air bubbles exploded from it, which shot down his throat into his lungs.

Even under the water Robbie was surrounded by the eerie cries and shrieks from the ghosts who continued to swim upward toward the boat. It was too dark now that they wouldn't be able to see him, and the darkness was a problem for him as well, as he had no way of collecting those four sticks. But at least he was out of harm's way for the moment with the ghosts distracted by the boat.

He swam, it seemed, for miles, down, down, down, further and further from the surface of the water. It was pitch black and Robbie was growing more terrified by the second, claustrophobia closing in around him. Just when he was beginning to think there was no ocean floor, his hands swept the ground, stirring up dirt that floated away. Exactly on plan he began to army crawl along the bottom in the direction he hoped was northwest, the direction he had seen the castle. There was no way he would be able to find those four sticks. He would have to go first to the castle and collect whatever supplies he could and return to the ocean with a light, or perhaps when the sun was shining. He would worry about that when the time came.

As he crawled, he breathed laboriously into the bark in his mouth, grateful that he remembered he had it with him. He was grateful that Ames had the decency to give it to him.

Robbie was so far below the surface that he felt like his skull was crushing against his brain. The weight of the water above him made it very difficult to crawl along the ocean floor and his body was wearing rather quickly.

As he continued to crawl, something caught his eye. At first he paid no attention to it, but the thought that something actually was there to be seen stopped him. He turned toward the direction he had seen it and there, in the ground was a light trying to penetrate from under the muck. He instantly crawled toward it and, with his heart beating furiously against his ribs, he began to dig into the dirt. He knew he needed to act fast before he caught the attention of any hunters. He didn't have to dig long before he realized water was being sucked down toward the light. Curious and hopeful, he dug some more until finally the ground below him gave way and he too was sucked into the ground and he was suddenly caught up in a strong torrent of glowing white water.

As he was being pulled through he lost his mouthpiece and panicked for lack of oxygen. His body was tossed and thrown every which way, and soon he feared a limb was going to rip off of his body.

A couple minutes of this and he was suddenly shot up into the air and he landed hard on his stomach on dry ground, able to breathe fresh air without the help of the breathing bark. He looked around and discovered that he was inside a large cavern made of brick. Water continued to gush out of the spring he had just come through. After careful thought, he realized he was inside the castle. He had broken into the trench that was dug by the ghosts to get back onto the island many years ago. And the light that caused Robbie to dig through the trench in the first place was coming from the throne that sat perched up a mound of steps directly before him, glowing as bright as the sun. Its back was carved into the wall behind it so it still stood erect even without the legs to support its underside. But the sound of hard clay clicking against each other on a hard stone floor caused him to look back down at the trench opening, and there lay the four legs of the throne.

He was about to walk over to pick them up when suddenly they began to glow themselves, and before his very eyes they ascended upward all on their own and gently glided through the air toward the legless throne. Robbie watched as all the legs connected themselves to their rightful places directly underneath the seat. And now at last the throne awaited Robbie to take his place. This was the moment he and all of Reveloin had been waiting for.

He slowly walked toward the throne, having to shield his eyes from its bright illumination. But before he reached the stairway that led up to it he realized his feet were kicking up water more water than before. He looked at the trench entrance and it was long submerged in a foot of water. Assuming it all came from the trench he then noticed the bricks themselves began to flow down the walls of the castle as if they were sweating. Water pelted his head and shoulders as the cathedral ceiling melted away and came pouring down on him. He continued to proceed toward the steps but the wall behind him completely gave way as if transformed into a wave of water and then the connecting walls and even the wall behind the throne turned into liquid and washed away into the growing flood around him.

By now Robbie was up to his chest in water, but the throne still stood tall with the aid of its legs. He waded toward it, and as he did the images appeared in the sky once more, and this time he could see Sarcadui and the ex-trenchers standing on the shore where he had sailed from, all pleading for Robbie to hurry and sit on the throne. All around them the trees were melting away, as each branch, each needle, fell from its place and morphed into drops of water midair. The entire island was itself turning into water and washing away.

Sarcadui and the other men struggled to stay afloat, calling out for help. Robbie waded faster, but his feet could no longer touch the ground and he had to swim. When finally he reached the steps he climbed up them on all fours and made his way to the throne. He placed his hand on the seat but it ripped off in his hand like a wet piece of cardboard. He reached up with his other hand but produced the same result. He was swallowing water by the mouthful, and the great chair was no longer sturdy enough for Robbie to hold onto. The last thing he saw of Reveloin was the throne, its light and its glory long faded away, splitting in half as if it were a crumbling block of cheese. And behind it, projected into the sky was Sarcadui's hand grasping for help and then disappearing underneath the water along with the rest of his beloved world forever.

CHAPTER 51

Robbie woke up with a start, soaked to the skin and shivering from the icy cold wind that plastered his wet clothes. His legs were outstretched before him, not bent to his chest like they always were when he awoke from his adventures. His rear was the wettest of all, as he realized he was sitting in a deep puddle of mud. It had clearly been raining for quite some time, and hard. Robbie could barely see three feet in front of him past the pelting rain. But he could see what was directly underneath him. The box lay muddied, soggy, and torn on all sides from top to bottom.

It had ripped apart in the rain and now lay completely destroyed, with Robbie inside it unaffected by its power; fully awake in the world where he belonged. He shook his head free of the lingering thoughts of Reveloin, and brought his mind to Rosalynn.

The first thing he did was get back to the car. How he ever found his way back, he would never know. He set his GPS to get him back to the hospital. But the note on the floorboards of the passenger seat reminded him of Taylor. No way she was going to throw her life away, at least not on his watch. He hadn't been there for his mother's death, and he wasn't going to let Taylor live with the same regret for the rest of her life. He snatched the paper from the floor and programmed his GPS to take him straight to the address that was sloppily scrawled on it. He reached the house in twenty-five minutes.

Cars were parked everywhere and the music could be heard for blocks. It reminded him, in an uneasy way, of his own party days. He pushed his way through dancers and drinkers and screamers, calling out Taylor's name. The kids were pretty unhappy to see him there – an old guy sloshing water everywhere and soaking the carpet. He was called all sorts of profanities, but for the most part the kids were too buzzed to notice him.

Finally he recognized the back of Dwayne's head in the kitchen hanging out with a bunch of his pals, rooting someone on who was attempting to choke back a gallon of beer. He spun Dwayne around by his shoulder and asked, "Where's Taylor?"

"She's out back," he responded, not much affected by Robbie's presence. "I think she's been trying to call you."

Robbie jogged through the large house to the backyard and found his daughter sitting by herself on a patio chair underneath an awning out of the rain. A couple was making out next to her, sharing the covering.

"Taylor?" he asked, stepping outside.

She wasn't glad to see him when she looked up, like he had hoped. "Oh great. I thought Mom would come get me, but suddenly you care now?"

"I've always cared, Taylor. Get in the car, your mom's in the hospital."

"What! What for?"

"We'll talk on the way."

In the car Robbie asked why she had been trying to reach them. "The party was lame. Dwayne just wanted to goof off. I knew I'd get in trouble for going, but no one wanted to drive me home, so I had no choice. Why's Mom in the hospital?"

"They're operating on her. It doesn't look good."

The wipers labored against the rain on the windshield as the car bounced along the road.

"Why are you wet?" Taylor asked.

"I was going through a life change. Things are better now."

"So if we ever want to get you back, we just need to pretend that one of us is dying?"

Robbie couldn't keep the smile back even if he tried.

When they entered the hospital Robbie was still soaking wet. Orderlies gave him disdainful looks as he trailed in puddles of water on the floor and his shoes squeaked loud enough to wake people up from comas.

They found the waiting room, but Jeremy and Harvey weren't there. Robbie didn't have his phone with him. He walked over to the receptionist's desk and asked about Rosalynn Lake. The receptionist gave him the room number she was in.

Robbie suggested Taylor join him, but she insisted on hanging back.

The room was dark. Rosalynn was asleep as evidenced by her steady breathing. Robbie quietly pulled a chair up next to her and sat down. Upon taking her hands in his he was relieved to see his wedding ring back in its place. He sat a moment as he reflected on the last several weeks of his life, but mostly how poorly he had treated Rosalynn and the kids. To think that she would take these last memories of Robbie to the grave disturbed him beyond reason.

A nurse walked in to check Rosalynn's blood pressure and Robbie took the occasion to inquire about her status.

"Were you not here when the doctor spoke with her earlier?"

Robbie shook his head no.

"I take it you're her husband?" she asked.

Robbie nodded.

"They didn't find the tumor, Mr. Lake. I'm afraid her condition still stands. I'm sorry."

Robbie's eyes never left Rosalynn's face as the despicable news was being delivered.

"One of our chaplains is available if you need someone to pray with or just talk to."

Robbie shook his head and politely dismissed the young woman, who closed the door on her way out.

With privacy now granted to him, Robbie's emotions unleashed and flowed out of him like an overflowing well. He tried to keep his sobbing quiet so as not to wake Rosalynn, but a part of him wanted her to wake up so he would have someone to share his burden with. But how selfish! How often was he around for Rosalynn to share her burdens with? He wasn't even there with her when the doctor threw the verdict in her face after her surgery.

In the midst of such overwhelming sorrow, not only was Robbie unable to control the surging quantity of his emotions, but he couldn't keep track of the wide array they covered. Amongst being angry and sad, he was greedy and insensitive and disappointed at not being sad enough and hurt by being too sad and he felt guilty for noticing an itch on his ankle and scratching it instead of feeling more sympathetic for his dying wife. Oh, how complicated and mundane are the thoughts of the heart.

After a few moments of grieving, Rosalynn stirred and Robbie quickly dried his eyes with the back of his hands.

"Robbie?" asked Rosalynn with her eyes still closed and tightening her hands around his when he placed them back down on her stomach. When Robbie affirmed his identity Rosalynn smiled that sweet joyful smile of hers which caused a lump to rise in his throat. “I’m glad you’re here,” she said as she softly stroked his hands.

She could have rebuked him for not being there earlier when she was awake, but instead she maintained her true character to the very end by expressing her gratitude for Robbie’s presence. It was just like her to forget his faults. But now he wanted to talk about them! He wanted to nit-pick his failures, and endure a lecture.

“I have something I need to confess to you,” said Robbie. Then after taking a deep breath, he said, “I’ve been having an affair on you.”

Rosalynn opened her eyes.

“I haven’t been with any woman or anything like that, but it’s just as bad. I’ve been giving all of myself to something that wasn’t you.”

And so Robbie gave way to a rant of apologies and confessions about not being there and lying as often as he did and living a secret life apart from her. But in the end she seemed to not hear a word of it, yet she was still sympathetic and expressed her forgiveness toward him. Robbie was vaguely aware that Rosalynn must have known she was heaping lumps of burning coal onto his lap.

“So,” started Rosalynn after letting Robbie regain himself. “What are you doing for the next three to five weeks?”

Robbie laughed and answered, “Actually, I’ve thought about it. I’ll have to talk to your doctor, but I think I have an idea. How would you like to take one more excursion to Ventura?”

“Mmm,” Rosalynn started dreamily as she smiled. “That’s where we met. I’ve always wanted to go back there. I love the beach.”

“We can see your family. We’ll take the kids with us. What do you say?”

“Dr. Allen will never approve,” Rosalynn protested.

“Let me talk to him. I’ll see what I can do,” assured Robbie.

CHAPTER 52

Rosalynn was asleep when Robbie awoke. He was delirious from having maintained such an odd sleep schedule for the last few weeks, but he was determined to carry out his task. He dragged himself out of bed leaving Rosalynn to hug one of the pillows. He knew he had just two more hours before she woke up. Robbie had a lot to accomplish in that time. He disappeared downstairs into the study and sat down.

The weather was gorgeous for a wedding. Sarcadui was dressed in a beautiful white gown decorated modestly with beaded necklaces and ribbons and bows in her hair. The ocean spray felt like silk on his skin as he admired the lovely bride.

People from all over the country gathered together in celebration of the wedding. Many of the guests cried with sheer joy when they saw each other because for many, their last remembrances of each other were of terror and sadness. But the curse was now lifted and there was not a single ghost left in the country. And all were back to themselves as though the curse never happened. Even the waters had receded back to the coasts. Everyone was now free to live their lives in harmony and peace.

But of all the beaming faces on the beach that day, no one's face glowed more than the groom who was about to take his wife.

Sarcadui blushed as Rhoe, dressed in a sparkling white tunic and breeches, took both of her hands in his and they exchanged vows before everyone they loved. Lahni and Ewin, nearing midlife now, wiped away their tears as their daughter gave herself to her bridegroom.

The minister conducted the wedding marvelously and he enthusiastically pronounced them husband and wife at the end of the ceremony. When the newlyweds kissed, Hail lifted the lid off of a box and out flew hundreds of fairies into the air, flowing around the gushing bride, dazzling everybody, marking a pinnacle in the glorious occasion. When she was done with her job Hail raced back down the aisle to be the first one in line for the cake which Rico had spent all that week laboring over.

Steve, seeing that his work was done, bid adieu to his friends. He had completed his mission and sat on the throne, freeing Reveloin of any curse forever, so that its inhabitants could live safely and freely forever.

“What are you doing?” asked Jeremy standing at the doorway to the study.

Robbie turned away from his computer and facing Jeremy said, “I just finished my book.”

“Cool,” beamed Jeremy. “The one about Steve the adventurer?”

Robbie nodded his head.

“When can I read it?”

“When we get back from boogie boarding,” said Robbie. “Go get your mom and sister.”

Robbie laughed as he listened to Jeremy’s excited yells ring through the two-story condo. “We’re going back to the beach! Everyone get up!”

“Tell them about the book!” Robbie called out.

“Oh yeah. Dad finished his book! It’s real good! Let’s go swimming!”

It wasn’t Hawaii, but they were at least several thousand miles closer, and it was the same water, and Ventura gave an honest effort to give the look and feel of the islands.

Rosalynn and Taylor popped into the study. “You finished it?” asked Rosalynn.

“I’m sending it to Don right now to have him edit it,” Robbie said, attaching his manuscript to an email. If these last minor changes met Kurt’s expectations, then CipherMill would have it on the bookshelves and as an ebook within four months.

Before closing out of his email he glanced at a message his dad sent him. It said that he’d be flying out there in about a week to start looking for properties to open his diner. What better place than Southern California to open up a snazzy new mechanic shop that served burgers and milkshakes?

Rosalynn gave Robbie a congratulatory kiss. “I’ll print a copy up for you to read,” he told her.

“Thank you for sharing your adventures with me,” said Rosalynn.

Next was a hug from Taylor, which he mostly initiated himself. He knew that in time she would desire his company once again, as long as he stayed around to prove himself worthy of her affection. And someday she'll be married with kids of her own and maybe, just maybe, he'll be able to offer her marriage advice the way his dad had for that one brief moment in the doorway months ago.

Though Rosalynn's health was slowly and surely deteriorating, Robbie was convinced beyond a shadow of a doubt that relocating the family south next to his in-laws played a huge part in allowing her to stick it out the past four months she'd managed to hold on to, and even now the doctors were stunned at her ability to persevere this long.

Of course she wouldn't be swimming with the family, but she loved watching them from the sand with a soda in one hand and the multi-colored journal in the other hand which Robbie filled with more affectionate notes than he ever had before because he never knew which one would be her last.

About the Author

Andrew Toy lives with his wife and dachshunds in Louisville, KY. If he's not reading a book, he's writing one, always on the hunt for the next best idea. See more of his writing and upcoming books on his popular blog adoptingjames.wordpress.com.

Also from BlackWyrm...

DARK HALO

by Christopher Kokoski

A winged stranger appears during a violent lightning storm, chasing Landon Paddock out into the maddening night with his estranged 15-year old daughter.

As layer after layer of reality is dissolved by a series of violent encounters, the only way to survive might be for Landon to band together with the family he destroyed to make one last stand against a sinister army of unthinkable magnitude.
[Supernatural Horror, ages 14+]

VINE

an urban legend

by Michael Williams

An amateur theatre director's sensational production starring an eccentric fly-by-night cast and crew draws the attention of ancient and powerful forces. Vine weds Greek tragedy and urban legend with dangerous intoxication, as the drama rushes to its dark and inevitable conclusion.
[Modern Mythic Fiction, ages 14+]

Remnants of Life: Legends of Darkness

by Georgia L. Jones

Samantha Garrett lives and dies a good life in the human world. She awakens a new creature, Samoda, a vampire-like warrior in the army of Nuem. She is forced to realize that she has become a part of a world that humans believe to be only "Legends of Darkness." Samoda finds her new life is entwined with the age old story of greed, love, betrayal, and vengeance. [Urban Fantasy, ages 14+]

The Eyes of Sandala

by Cathy Benedetto

Over seven feet tall and as strong as three men, the dark-skinned Shala share a life-long bond with wild felines. The fierce fighters are blessed with telepathic powers and eyes that radiate a kaleidoscope of colors.

The Shala dwell inside the crater of an extinct volcano. But when invaders appear, they must obey the prophecy and rise to defend the land.
[Epic Fantasy, ages 14+]

IMMORTAL BETRAYAL

by Paul Lewis

Darien, viking and explorer, braves the treacherous seas to discover new lands. That changes when he falls in love. But his world is shattered when he learns she has already been promised her to another. Darien's loyalty is put to the test as he battles vampires and werewolves. Darien must choose between the woman he loves and his very soul.
[Tragic Horror, ages 14+]

Burning the Middle Ground

by L. Andrew Cooper

This dark fantasy about small-town America transforms fears about the country's direction into a haunting tale of religious conspiracy and supernatural mind control. Burning the Middle Ground has as much appeal for dedicated fans of fantasy and horror as for mainstream readers looking for an exciting ride.
[Spiritual Horror, ages 14+]

www.ingramcontent.com/pod-product-compliance
Lightning Source LLC
LaVergne TN
LVHW050616100826
845148LV00011B/1617

* 9 7 8 1 6 1 3 1 8 1 3 7 9 *